THE LAST
KINGDOM

≋

ALSO BY BERNARD CORNWELL

The Sharpe Novels (in chronological order)

SHARPE'S TIGER★
Richard Sharpe and the Siege of Seringapatam,
1799

SHARPE'S TRIUMPH★
Richard Sharpe and the Battle of Assaye,
September 1803

SHARPE'S FORTRESS★
Richard Sharpe and the Siege of Gawilghur,
December 1803

SHARPE'S TRAFALGAR★
Richard Sharpe and the Battle of Trafalgar,
21 October 1805

SHARPE'S PREY★
Richard Sharpe and the Expedition to
Copenhagen, 1807

SHARPE'S RIFLES
Richard Sharpe and the French Invasion of
Galicia, January 1809

SHARPE'S HAVOC★
Richard Sharpe and the Campaign in Northern
Portugal, Spring 1809

SHARPE'S EAGLE
Richard Sharpe and the Talavera Campaign,
July 1809

SHARPE'S GOLD
Richard Sharpe and the Destruction of Almeida,
August 1810

SHARPE'S ESCAPE*
Richard Sharpe and the Bussaco Campaign, 1810

SHARPE'S BATTLE*
Richard Sharpe and the Battle of Fuentes de
Onoro, May 1811

SHARPE'S COMPANY
Richard Sharpe and the Siege of Badajoz, January
to April 1812

SHARPE'S SWORD
Richard Sharpe and the Salamanca Campaign,
June and July 1812

SHARPE'S ENEMY
Richard Sharpe and the Defense of Portugal,
Christmas 1812

SHARPE'S HONOUR
Richard Sharpe and the Vitoria Campaign,
February to June 1813

SHARPE'S REGIMENT
Richard Sharpe and the Invasion of France, June to
November 1813

SHARPE'S SIEGE
Richard Sharpe and the Winter Campaign, 1814

SHARPE'S REVENGE
Richard Sharpe and the Peace of 1814

SHARPE'S WATERLOO
Richard Sharpe and the Waterloo Campaign,
15 June to 18 June 1815

SHARPE'S DEVIL★
Richard Sharpe and the Emperor, 1820–21

The Grail Quest Series

THE ARCHER'S TALE
VAGABOND
HERETIC

The Nathaniel Starbuck Chronicles

REBEL
COPPERHEAD
BATTLE FLAG
THE BLOODY GROUND

The Warlord Chronicles

THE WINTER KING
THE ENEMY OF GOD
EXCALIBUR

Other Novels

REDCOAT
A CROWNING MERCY
STORMCHILD
SCOUNDREL
GALLOWS THIEF
STONEHENGE, 2000 B.C.: A NOVEL

★ Published by HarperCollins Publishers

THE LAST KINGDOM

A NOVEL

Bernard Cornwell

HarperLargePrint
An Imprint of HarperCollins*Publishers*

HarperCollins books may be purchased for educational, business, or sales promotional use. For information, please write: Special Markets Department, HarperCollins Publishers Inc., 10 East 53rd Street, New York, NY 10022.

Originally published in Great Britain in 2004 by HarperCollins Publishers.

FIRST HARPER LARGE PRINT EDITION

Designed by Nancy Singer Olaguera

Printed on acid-free paper

Library of Congress Cataloging-in-Publication Data
Cornwell, Bernard.
The last kingdom: a novel / Bernard Cornwell—1st. ed.
p. cm.
ISBN 0-06-075933-X (Large Print)
ISBN 0-06-053051-0 (Hardcover)
1. Great Britain—History—Alfred, 871–899—Fiction.
2. Vikings—Fiction. I. Title
PR6053.O75L37 2005
823'.914—dc22
2004054236

05 06 07 08 09 BVG/RRD 10 9 8 7 6 5 4 3 2 1

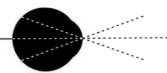

This Large Print Book carries the
Seal of Approval of N.A.V.H.

THE LAST KINGDOM

is for Judy, with love.

Wyrd bið ful āræd.

PLACE-NAMES

The spelling of place-names in Anglo-Saxon England was an uncertain business, with no consistency and no agreement even about the name itself. Thus London was variously rendered as Lundonia, Lundenberg, Lundenne, Lundene, Lundenwic, Lundenceaster, and Lundres. Doubtless some readers will prefer other versions of the names listed below, but I have usually employed whatever spelling is cited in the **Oxford Dictionary of English Place-Names** for the years nearest or contained within Alfred's reign, A.D. 871–899 , but even that solution is not foolproof. Hayling Island, in 956, was written as both Heilincigae and Hæglingaiggæ. Nor have I been consistent myself; I have preferred the modern England to Englaland and, instead of Norðhymbralond, have used Northumbria to avoid the suggestion that the boundaries of the ancient kingdom coincide with those of the modern county. So this list, like the spellings themselves, is capricious.

Æbbanduna	Abingdon, Berkshire
Æsc's Hill	Ashdown, Berkshire
Baðum (pronounced Bathum)	Bath, Avon
Basengas	Basing, Hampshire
Beamfleot	Benfleet, Essex
Beardastopol	Barnstable, Devon
Bebbanburg	Bamburgh Castle, Northumberland
Berewic	Berwick on Tweed, Northumberland
Berrocscire	Berkshire
Blaland	North Africa
Cantucton	Cannington, Somerset
Cetreht	Catterick, Yorkshire
Cippanhamm	Chippenham, Wiltshire
Cirrenceastre	Cirencester, Gloucestershire
Cridianton	Crediton, Devon
Cynuit	Cynuit Hillfort, near Cannington, Somerset
Contwaraburg	Canterbury, Kent
Cornwalum	Cornwall
Dalriada	Western Scotland
Deoraby	Derby, Derbyshire
Defnascir	Devonshire

Dic	Diss, Norfolk
Dunholm	Durham, County Durham
Eoferwic	York (also the Danish Jorvic, pronounced Yorvik)
Exanceaster	Exeter, Devon
Fromtun	Frampton-upon-Severn, Gloucestershire
Gegnesburh	Gainsborough, Lincolnshire
The Gewæsc	The Wash
Gleawecestre	Gloucester, Gloucestershire
Grantaceaster	Cambridge, Cambridgeshire
Gyruum	Jarrow, County Durham
Hamanfunta	Havant, Hampshire
Hamptonscir	Hampshire
Hamtun	Southampton, Hampshire
Haithabu	Hedeby, trading town in southern Denmark
Heilincigae	Hayling Island, Hampshire
Hreapandune	Repton, Derbyshire
Kenet	River Kennet
Ledecestre	Leicester
Lindisfarena	Lindisfarne (Holy Island), Northumberland
Lundene	London
Mereton	Marten, Wiltshire
Meslach	Matlock, Derbyshire
Pedredan	River Parrett
The Poole	Poole Harbour, Dorset
Pictland	Eastern Scotland
Readingum	Reading, Berkshire

Sæfern	River Severn
Scireburnan	Sherborne, Dorset
Snotengaham	Nottingham, Nottinghamshire
Streonshall	Strensall, Yorkshire
Sumorsæte	Somerset
Suth Seaxa	Sussex (South Saxons)
Synningthwait	Swinithwaite, Yorkshire
Temes	River Thames
Thornsæta	Dorset
Tine	River Tine
Trente	River Trente
Tuede	River Tweed
Twyfyrde	Tiverton, Devon
Uisc	River Exe
Werham	Wareham, Dorset
With	Isle of Wight
Wiire	River Wear
Wiltun	Wilton, Wiltshire
Wiltunscir	Wiltshire
Winburnan	Wimborne Minster, Dorset
Wintanceaster	Winchester, Hampshire

PROLOGUE

Northumbria, A.D. 866–867

My name is Uhtred. I am the son of Uhtred, who was the son of Uhtred and his father was also called Uhtred. My father's clerk, a priest called Beocca, spelt it Utred. I do not know if that was how my father would have written it, for he could neither read nor write, but I can do both and sometimes I take the old parchments from their wooden chest and I see the name spelled Uhtred or Utred or Ughtred or Ootred. I look at those parchments, which are deeds saying that Uhtred, son of Uhtred, is the lawful and sole owner of the lands that are carefully marked by stones and by dykes, by oaks and by ash, by marsh and by sea, and I dream of those lands, wave-beaten and wild beneath the wind-driven sky. I dream, and know that one day I will take back the land from those who stole it from me.

I am an ealdorman, though I call myself Earl Uhtred, which is the same thing, and the fading parchments are proof of what I own. The law says I own that land, and the law, we are told, is what makes us men under God instead of beasts in the ditch. But the law does not help me take back my land. The law wants compromise. The law thinks money will compensate for loss. The law, above all, fears the blood feud. But I am Uhtred, son of Uhtred, and this is the tale of a blood feud. It is a tale of how I will take from my enemy what the law says is mine. And it is the tale of a woman and of her father, a king.

He was my king and all that I have I owe to him. The food that I eat, the hall where I live, and the swords of my men, all came from Alfred, my king, who hated me.

This story begins long before I met Alfred. It begins when I was ten years old and first saw the Danes. It was the year 866 and I was not called Uhtred then, but Osbert, for I was my father's second son and it was the eldest who took the name Uhtred. My brother was seventeen then, tall and well built, with our family's fair hair and my father's morose face.

The day I first saw the Danes we were riding along the seashore with hawks on our wrists. There was my father, my father's brother, my brother, myself, and a dozen retainers. It was autumn. The sea cliffs were thick with the last growth of summer, there were seals on the rocks, and a host of seabirds wheeling and shrieking, too many to let the hawks off their leashes. We rode till we came to the crisscrossing shallows that rippled between our land and Lindisfarena, the Holy Island, and I remember staring across the water at the broken walls of the abbey. The Danes had plundered it, but that had been many years before I was born, and though the monks were living there again the monastery had never regained its former glory.

I also remember that day as beautiful and perhaps it was. Perhaps it rained, but I do not think so. The sun shone, the seas were low, the breakers gentle, and the world happy. The hawk's claws gripped my wrist through the leather sleeve, her hooded head twitching because she could hear the cries of the white birds. We had left the fortress in the forenoon, riding north, and though we carried hawks we did not ride to hunt, but rather so my father could make up his mind.

We ruled this land. My father, Ealdorman Uhtred, was lord of everything south of the Tuede and north of the Tine, but we did have a king in Northumbria and his name, like mine, was Osbert. He lived to the south of us, rarely came north, and did not bother us, but now a man called Ælla wanted the throne and Ælla, who was an ealdorman from the hills west of

Eoferwic, had raised an army to challenge Osbert and had sent gifts to my father to encourage his support. My father, I realize now, held the fate of the rebellion in his grip. I wanted him to support Osbert, for no other reason than the rightful king shared my name and foolishly, at ten years old, I believed any man called Osbert must be noble, good, and brave. In truth Osbert was a dribbling fool, but he was the king, and my father was reluctant to abandon him. But Osbert had sent no gifts and had shown no respect, while Ælla had, and so my father worried. At a moment's notice we could lead a hundred and fifty men to war, all well armed, and given a month we could swell that force to over four hundred foemen, so whichever man we supported would be the king and grateful to us.

Or so we thought.

And then I saw them.

Three ships.

In my memory they slid from a bank of sea mist, and perhaps they did, but memory is a faulty thing and my other images of that day are of a clear, cloudless sky, so perhaps there was no mist, but it seems to me that one moment the sea was empty and the next there were three ships coming from the south.

Beautiful things. They appeared to rest weightless on the ocean, and when their oars dug into the waves they skimmed the water. Their prows and sterns curled high and were tipped with gilded beasts, serpents, and dragons, and it seemed to me that on that far-off summer's day the three boats danced on the water, propelled by the rise and fall of the silver wings of their oar banks. The sun flashed off the wet blades, splinters of light, then the oars dipped, were tugged, and the beast-headed boats surged, and I stared entranced.

"The devil's turds," my father growled. He was not a very good Christian, but he was frightened enough at that moment to make the sign of the cross.

"And may the devil swallow them," my uncle said. His name was Ælfric and he was a slender man; sly, dark, and secretive.

The three boats had been rowing northward, their square sails furled on their long yards, but when we turned back south to canter homeward on the sand so that our horses' manes tossed like windblown spray and the hooded hawks mewed in alarm, the ships turned with us. Where the cliff had collapsed to leave a ramp of broken turf we rode inland, the horses heaving up the slope, and from there we galloped along the coastal path to our fortress.

To Bebbanburg. Bebba had been a queen in our land many years before, and she had given her name to my home, which is the dearest place in all the world. The fort stands on a high rock that curls out to sea. The waves beat on its eastern shore and break white on the rock's northern point, and a shallow sea lake ripples along the western side between the fortress and the land. To reach Bebbanburg you must take the causeway to the south, a low strip of rock and sand that is guarded by a great wooden tower, the Low Gate, which is built on top of an earthen wall. We thundered through the tower's arch, our horses white with sweat, and rode past the granaries, the smithy, the mews, and the stables, all wooden buildings well thatched with rye straw, and so up the inner path to the High Gate, which protected the peak of the rock that was surrounded by a wooden rampart encircling my father's hall. There we dismounted, letting slaves take our horses and hawks, and ran to the eastern rampart from where we gazed out to sea.

The three ships were now close to the islands where the puffins live and the seal-folk dance in winter. We watched them, and my stepmother, alarmed by the sound of hooves, came from the hall to join us on the rampart. "The devil has opened his bowels," my father greeted her.

"God and his saints preserve us," Gytha said, crossing herself. I had never known my real mother, who had been my father's second wife and, like his first, had died in childbirth, so both my brother and I, who were really half brothers, had no mother, but I thought of Gytha as my mother and, on the whole, she was kind to me, kinder indeed than my father, who did not much like children. Gytha wanted me to be a priest, saying that my elder brother would inherit the land and become a warrior to protect it so I must find another life path. She had given my father two sons and a daughter, but none had lived beyond a year.

The three ships were coming closer now. It seemed they had come to inspect Bebbanburg, which did not worry us for the fortress was reckoned impregnable, and so the Danes could stare all they wanted. The nearest ship had twin banks of twelve oars each and, as the ship coasted a hundred paces offshore, a man leaped from the ship's side and ran down the nearer bank of oars, stepping from one shaft to the next like a dancer, and he did it wearing a mail shirt and holding a sword. We all prayed he would fall, but of course he did not. He had long fair hair, very long, and when he had pranced the full length of the oar bank he turned and ran the shafts again.

"She was trading at the mouth of the Tine a week ago," Ælfric, my father's brother, said.

"You know that?"

"I saw her," Ælfric said, "I recognize that prow. See how there's a light-colored strake on the bend?" He spat. "She didn't have a dragon's head then."

"They take the beast heads off when they trade," my father said. "What were they buying?"

"Exchanging pelts for salt and dried fish. Said they were merchants from Haithabu."

"They're merchants looking for a fight now," my father said, and the Danes on the three ships were indeed challenging us by clashing their spears and swords against their painted shields, but there was little they could do against Bebbanburg and nothing we could do to hurt them, though my father ordered his wolf banner raised. The flag showed a snarling wolf's head and it was his standard in battle, but there was no wind and so the banner hung limp and its defiance was lost on the pagans who, after a while, became bored with taunting us, settled to their thwarts, and rowed off to the south.

"We must pray," my stepmother said. Gytha was much younger than my father. She was a small, plump woman with a mass of fair hair and a great reverence for Saint Cuthbert whom she worshipped because he had worked miracles. In the church beside the hall she kept an ivory comb that was said to have been Cuthbert's beard comb, and perhaps it was.

"We must act," my father snarled. He turned away from the battlements. "You," he said to my elder brother, Uhtred. "Take a dozen men, ride south. Watch the pagans, but nothing more, you understand? If they land their ships on my ground I want to know where."

"Yes, Father."

"But don't fight them," my father ordered. "Just watch the bastards and be back here by nightfall."

Six other men were sent to rouse the country. Every free man owed military duty and so my father was assembling his army, and by the morrow's dusk he expected to have close to two hundred men, some armed with axes, spears, or reaping hooks, while his retainers, those men who lived with us in Bebbanburg, would be equipped with well-made swords and hefty shields. "If the Danes are outnumbered," my father told me that night, "they won't fight. They're like dogs, the Danes. Cowards at heart, but they're given courage by being in a pack." It was dark and my brother had not returned, but no one was unduly anxious about that. Uhtred was capable, if sometimes reckless, and doubtless he would arrive in the small hours and so my father had ordered a beacon lit in the iron becket on top of the High Gate to guide him home.

We reckoned we were safe in Bebbanburg for it had never fallen to an enemy's assault, yet my father and uncle were still worried that the Danes had returned to Northumbria. "They're looking for food," my father said. "The hungry bastards want to land, steal some cattle, then sail away."

I remembered my uncle's words, how the ships had been at the mouth of the Tine trading furs for dried fish, so how could they be hungry? But I said nothing. I was ten years old and what did I know of Danes?

I did know that they were savages, pagans and terrible. I knew that for two generations before I was born their ships had raided our coasts. I knew that Father Beocca, my father's clerk and our mass priest, prayed every Sunday to spare us from the fury of the Northmen, but that fury had passed me by. No Danes had come to our land since I had been born, but my father had fought them often enough and that night, as we waited for my brother to return, he spoke of his old enemy. They came, he said, from northern lands where ice and mist prevailed, they worshipped the old gods, the same ones we had worshipped before the light of Christ came to bless us, and when they had first come to Northumbria, he told me, fiery dragons had whipped across the northern sky, great bolts of lightning had scarred the hills, and the sea had been churned by whirlwinds.

"They are sent by God," Gytha said timidly, "to punish us."

"Punish us for what?" my father demanded savagely.

"For our sins," Gytha said, making the sign of the cross.

"Our sins be damned," my father snarled. "They come here because they're hungry." He was irritated by my stepmother's piety, and he refused to give up his wolf's head banner that proclaimed our family's descent from Woden, the ancient Saxon god of battles. The wolf, Ealdwulf the smith had told me, was one of Woden's three favored beasts, the others being the eagle and the raven. My mother wanted our banner to show the cross, but my father was proud of his ancestors, though he rarely talked about Woden. Even at ten years old I understood that a good Christian should not boast of being spawned by a pagan god, but I also liked the idea of being a god's descendant and Ealdwulf often told me tales of Woden, how he had rewarded our people by giving us the land we called England, and how he had once thrown a war spear clear around the moon, and how his shield could darken the midsummer sky, and how he could reap all the corn in the world with one stroke of his great sword. I liked those tales. They were better than my stepmother's stories of Cuthbert's miracles. Christians, it seemed to me, were forever weeping and I did not think Woden's worshippers cried much.

We waited in the hall. It was, indeed it still is, a great wooden hall, strongly thatched and stout beamed, with a harp on a dais and a stone hearth in the center of the floor. It took a dozen slaves a day to keep that great fire going, dragging the wood along the causeway and up through the gates, and at summer's end we would make a log pile bigger than the church just as a winter store.

At the edges of the hall were timber platforms, filled with rammed earth and layered with woolen rugs, and it was on those platforms that we lived, up above the drafts. The hounds stayed on the bracken-strewn floor below, where lesser men could eat at the year's four great feasts.

There was no feast that night, just bread and cheese and ale, and my father waited for my brother and wondered aloud if the Danes were restless again. "They usually come for food and plunder," he told me, "but in some places they've stayed and taken land."

"You think they want our land?" I asked.

"They'll take any land," he said irritably. He was always irritated by my questions, but that night he was worried and so he talked on. "Their own land is stone and ice, and they have giants threatening them."

I wanted him to tell me more about the giants, but he brooded instead. "Our ancestors," he went on after a while, "took this land. They took it and made it and held it. We do not give up what our ancestors gave us. They came across the sea and they fought here, and they built here and they're buried here. This is our land, mixed with our blood, strengthened with our bone. Ours." He was angry, but he was often angry. He glowered at me, as if wondering whether I was strong enough to hold this land of Northumbria that our ancestors had won with sword and spear and blood and slaughter.

We slept after a while, or at least I slept. I think my father paced the ramparts, but by dawn he was back in the hall and it was then I was woken by the horn at the High Gate and I stumbled off the platform and out into the morning's first light. There was dew on the grass, a sea eagle circling overhead, and my father's hounds streaming from the hall door in answer to the horn's call. I saw my father running down to the Low Gate and I followed him until I could wriggle my way through the men who were crowding onto the earthen rampart to stare along the causeway.

Horsemen were coming from the south. There were a dozen of them, their horses' hooves sparkling with the dew. My brother's horse was in the lead. It was a brindled stallion, wild-eyed and with a curious gait. It threw its forelegs out as it cantered and no one could mistake that horse, but it was not Uhtred who rode it. The man astride the saddle had long, long hair the color of pale gold, hair that tossed like the horses' tails as he rode. He wore mail, had a flapping scabbard at his side and an ax slung across one shoulder, and I was certain he was the same man who had danced the oar shafts the previous day. His companions were in leather or wool and as they neared the fortress the long-haired man signaled that they should curb their horses as he rode ahead alone. He came within bowshot, though none of us on the rampart put an arrow on the string, then he pulled the horse to a stop and looked up at the gate. He stared all along the line of men, a mocking expression on his face, then he bowed, threw something on the path, and wheeled the horse away. He kicked his heels and the horse sped back and his ragged men joined him to gallop south.

What he had thrown onto the path was my brother's severed head. It was brought to my father who stared at it a long time, but betrayed no feelings. He did not cry, he did not grimace, he did not scowl, he just looked at his eldest son's head and then he looked at me. "From this day on," he said, "your name is Uhtred."

Which is how I was named.

Father Beocca insisted that I should be baptized again, or else heaven would not know who I was when I arrived with the name Uhtred. I protested, but Gytha wanted it and my father cared more for her contentment than for mine, and so a barrel was carried into the church and half filled with seawater and Father Beocca stood me in the barrel and ladled water over my hair. "Receive your servant Uhtred," he intoned, "into the holy company of the saints and into the ranks of the most bright angels." I hope the saints and angels are warmer than I was that day, and after the baptism was done Gytha wept for me, though why I did not know. She might have done better to weep for my brother.

We found out what had happened to him. The three Danish ships had put into the mouth of the river Alne where there was a small settlement of fishermen and their families. Those folk had prudently fled inland, though a handful stayed and watched the river mouth from woods on higher ground and they said my brother had come at nightfall and seen the Vikings torching the houses. They were called Vikings when they were raiders, but Danes or pagans when they were traders, and these men had been burning and plundering so were reckoned to be Vikings. There had seemed very few of them in the settlement, most were on their ships, and my brother decided to ride down to the cottages and kill those few, but of course it was a trap. The Danes had seen his horsemen coming and had hidden a ship's crew north of the village, and those forty men closed behind my brother's party and killed them all. My father claimed his eldest son's death must have been quick, which was a consolation to him, but of course it was not a quick death for he lived long enough for the Danes to discover who he was, or else why would they have brought his head back to Bebbanburg? The fishermen said they tried to warn my brother, but I doubt they did. Men say such things so that they are not blamed for disaster, but whether my brother was warned or not, he still died and the Danes took thirteen fine swords, thirteen good horses, a coat of mail, a helmet, and my old name.

But that was not the end of it. A fleeting visit by three ships was no great event, but a week after my brother's death we heard that a great Danish fleet had rowed up the rivers to capture Eoferwic. They had won that victory on All Saints Day, which made Gytha weep for it suggested God had abandoned us, but there was also good news for it seemed that my old namesake, King Osbert, had made an alliance with his rival, the would-be King Ælla, and they had agreed to put aside their rivalry, join forces, and take Eoferwic back. That sounds simple, but of course it took time. Messengers rode, advisers confused, priests prayed, and it was not till Christmas that Osbert and Ælla sealed their peace with oaths, and then they summoned my father's men, but of course we could not march in winter. The Danes were in Eoferwic and we left them there until the early spring when news came that the Northumbrian army would gather outside the city and, to my joy, my father decreed that I would ride south with him.

"He's too young," Gytha protested.

"He is almost eleven," my father said, "and he must learn to fight."

"He would be better served by continuing his lessons," she said.

"A dead reader is no use to Bebbanburg," my father said, "and Uhtred is now the heir so he must learn to fight."

That night he made Beocca show me the parchments kept in the church, the parchments that said we owned the land. Beocca had been teaching me to read for two years, but I was a bad pupil and, to Beocca's despair, I could make neither head nor tail of the writings. Beocca sighed, then told me what was in them. "They describe the land," he said, "the land your father owns, and they say the land is his by God's law and by our own law." And one day, it seemed, the lands would be mine for that night my father dictated a new will in which he said that if he died then Bebbanburg would belong to his son Uhtred, and I would be ealdorman, and all the folk between the rivers Tuede and the Tine would swear allegiance to me. "We were kings here once," he told me, "and our land was called Bernicia." He pressed his seal into the red wax, leaving the impression of a wolf's head.

"We should be kings again," Ælfric, my uncle, said.

"It doesn't matter what they call us," my father said curtly, "so long as they obey us," and then he made Ælfric swear on the comb of Saint Cuthbert that he would respect the new will and acknowledge me as Uhtred of Bebbanburg. Ælfric did so swear. "But it won't happen," my father said. "We shall slaughter these Danes like sheep in a fold, and we shall ride back here with plunder and honor."

"Pray God," Ælfric said.

Ælfric and thirty men would stay at Bebbanburg to guard the fortress and protect the women. He gave me gifts that night; a leather coat that would protect against a sword cut and, best of all, a helmet around which Ealdwulf the smith had fashioned a band of gilt bronze. "So they will know you are a prince," Ælfric said.

"He's not a prince," my father said, "but an ealdorman's heir." Yet he was pleased with his brother's gifts to me and added two of his own, a short sword and a horse. The sword was an old blade, cut down, with a leather scabbard lined with fleece. It had a chunky hilt, was clumsy, yet that night I slept with the blade under my blanket.

And next morning, as my stepmother wept on the ramparts of the High Gate, and under a blue, clean sky, we rode to war. Two hundred and fifty men went south, following our banner of the wolf's head.

That was in the year 867, and it was the first time I ever went to war.

And I have never ceased.

"You will not fight in the shield wall," my father said.

"No, Father."

"Only men can stand in the shield wall," he said, "but you will watch, you will learn, and you will discover that the most dangerous stroke is not the sword or ax that you can see, but the one you cannot see, the blade that comes beneath the shields to bite your ankles."

He grudgingly gave me much other advice as we followed the long road south. Of the two hundred and fifty men who went to Eoferwic from Bebbanburg, one hundred and twenty were on horseback. Those were my father's household men or else the wealthier farmers, the ones who could afford some kind of armor and had shields and swords. Most of the men were not wealthy, but they were sworn to my father's cause, and they marched with sickles, spears, reaping hooks, fish gaffs, and axes. Some carried hunting bows, and all had been ordered to bring a week's food, which was mostly hard bread, harder cheese, and smoked fish. Many were accompanied by women. My father had ordered that no women were to march south, but he did not send them back, reckoning that the women would follow anyway, and that men fought better when their wives or lovers were watching, and he was confident that those women would see the levy of Northumbria give the Danes a terrible slaughter. He claimed we were the hardest men of England, much harder than the soft Mercians. "Your mother was a Mercian," he added, but said nothing more. He never talked of her. I knew they had been married less than a year, that she had died giving birth to me, and that she was an ealdorman's daughter, but as far as my father was concerned she might never have existed. He claimed to despise the Mercians, but not as much as he scorned the coddled West Saxons. "They don't know hardship in Wessex," he maintained, but he reserved his severest judgment for the East Anglians. "They live in marshes," he once told me, "and live like frogs." We Northumbrians had always hated the East Anglians for long ago they had defeated us in battle, killing Ethelfrith, our king and husband to the Bebba after whom our fortress was named. I was to discover later that the East Anglians had given horses and winter shelter to the Danes who had captured Eoferwic so my father was right to despise them. They were treacherous frogs.

Father Beocca rode south with us. My father did not much like the priest, but did not want to go to war without a man of God to say prayers. Beocca, in turn, was devoted to my father who had freed him from slavery and provided him with his education. My father could have worshipped the devil and Beocca, I think, would have turned a blind eye. He was young, clean shaven, and extraordinarily ugly, with a fearful squint, a flattened nose, unruly red hair, and a palsied left hand. He was also very clever, though I did not appreciate it then, resenting that he gave me lessons. The poor man had tried so hard to teach me letters, but I mocked his efforts, preferring to get a beating from my father to concentrating on the alphabet.

We followed the Roman road, crossing their great wall at the Tine, and still going south. The Romans, my father said, had been giants who built wondrous things, but they had gone back to Rome and the giants had died and now the only Romans left were priests, but the giants' roads were still there and, as we went south, more men joined us until a horde marched on the moors either side of the stony road's broken surface. The men slept in the open, though my father and his chief retainers would bed for the night in abbeys or barns.

We also straggled. Even at ten years old I noticed how we straggled. Men had brought liquor with them, or else they stole mead or ale from the villages we passed, and they frequently got drunk and simply collapsed at the roadside and no one seemed to care. "They'll catch up," my father said carelessly.

"It's not good," Father Beocca told me.

"What's not good?"

"There should be more discipline. I have read the Roman wars and know there must be discipline."

"They'll catch up," I said, echoing my father.

That night we were joined by men from the place called Cetreht where, long ago, we had defeated the Welsh in a great battle. The newcomers sang of the battle, chanting how we had fed the ravens with the foreigners' blood, and the words cheered my father who told me we were near Eoferwic and that next day we might expect to join Osbert and Ælla, and how the day after that we would feed the ravens again. We were sitting by a fire, one of hundreds of fires that stretched across the fields. South of us, far off across a flat land, I could see the sky glowing from the light of still more fires and knew they showed where the rest of Northumbria's army gathered.

"The raven is Woden's creature, isn't it?" I asked nervously.

My father looked at me sourly. "Who told you that?"

I shrugged, said nothing.

"Ealdwulf?" He guessed, knowing that Bebbanburg's blacksmith, who had stayed at the fortress with Ælfric, was a secret pagan.

"I just heard it," I said, hoping I would get away with the evasion without being hit, "and I know we are descended from Woden."

"We are," my father acknowledged, "but we have a new God now." He stared balefully across the encampment where men were drinking. "Do you know who wins battles, boy?"

"We do, Father."

"The side that is least drunk," he said, and then, after a pause, "but it helps to be drunk."

"Why?"

"Because a shield wall is an awful place." He gazed into the fire. "I have been in six shield walls," he went on, "and prayed every time it would be the last. Your brother, now, he was a man who might have loved the shield wall. He had courage." He fell silent, thinking, then scowled. "The man who brought his head. I want his head. I want to spit into his dead eyes, then put his skull on a pole above the Low Gate."

"You will have it," I said.

He sneered at that. "What do you know?" he asked. "I brought you, boy, because you must see battle. Because our men must see that you are

here. But you will not fight. You're like a young
dog who watches the old dogs kill the boar, but
doesn't bite. Watch and learn, watch and learn
and maybe one day you'll be useful. But for now
you're nothing but a pup." He dismissed me with
a wave.

Next day the Roman road ran across a flat
land, crossing dykes and ditches, until at last we
came to where the combined armies of Osbert
and Ælla had made their shelters. Beyond them,
and just visible through the scattered trees, was
Eoferwic, and that was where the Danes were.

Eoferwic was, and still is, the chief city of
northern England. It possesses a great abbey, an
archbishop, a fortress, high walls, and a vast market. It stands beside the River Ouse, and boasts a
bridge, but ships can reach Eoferwic from the
distant sea, and that was how the Danes had
come. They must have known that Northumbria
was weakened by civil war, that Osbert, the rightful king, had marched westward to meet the
forces of the pretender Ælla, and in the absence
of the king they had taken the city. It would not
have been difficult for them to have discovered
Osbert's absence. The trouble between Osbert
and Ælla had been brewing for weeks, and Eoferwic was filled with traders, many from across the

sea, who would have known of the two men's bitter rivalry. One thing I learned about the Danes was that they knew how to spy. The monks who write the chronicles tell us that they came from nowhere, their dragon-prowed ships suddenly appearing from a blue vacancy, but it was rarely like that. The Viking crews might attack unexpectedly, but the big fleets, the war fleets, went where they knew there was already trouble. They found an existing wound and filled it like maggots.

My father took me close to the city, he and a score of his men, all of us mounted and all wearing mail or leather. We could see the enemy on the walls. Some of the wall was built of stone—that was the Roman work—but much of the city was protected by an earth wall, topped by a high wooden palisade, and to the east of the city part of that palisade was missing. It seemed to have been burned for we could see charred wood on top of the earthen wall where fresh stakes had been driven to hold the new palisade that would replace the burned fence.

Beyond the new stakes was a jumble of thatched roofs, the wooden bell towers of three churches, and, on the river, the masts of the Danish fleet. Our scouts claimed there were thirty four ships, which was said to mean the Danes had an army of around a thousand men. Our own army was larger, nearer to fifteen hundred, though it was difficult to count. No one seemed to be in charge. The two leaders, Osbert and Ælla, camped apart and, though they had officially made peace, they refused to speak to each other, communicating instead through messengers. My father, the third most important man in the army, could talk to both, but he was not able to persuade Osbert and Ælla to meet, let alone agree on a plan of campaign. Osbert wished to besiege the city and starve the Danes out, while Ælla urged an immediate attack. The rampart was broken, he said, and an assault would drive deep into the tangle of streets where the Danes could be hunted down and killed. I do not know which course my father preferred, for he never said, but in the end the decision was taken away from us.

Our army could not wait. We had brought some food, but that was soon exhausted, and men were going ever farther afield to find more, and some of those men did not return. They just slipped home. Other men grumbled that their farms needed work and if they did not return home they would face a hungry year. A meeting was called of every important man and they spent all day arguing. Osbert attended the meeting, which meant Ælla did not, though one of his chief supporters was there and hinted that Osbert's reluctance to assault the city was caused by cowardice. Perhaps it was, for Osbert did not respond to the jibe, proposing instead that we dig our own forts outside the city. Three or four such forts, he said, would trap the Danes. Our best fighters could man the forts, and our other men could go home to look after their fields. Another man proposed building a new bridge across the river, a bridge that would trap the Danish fleet, and he argued the point tediously, though I think everyone knew that we did not have the time to make a bridge across such a wide river. "Besides," King Osbert said, "we want the Danes to take their ships away. Let them go back to the sea. Let them go and trouble someone else." A bishop pleaded for more time, saying that Ealdorman Egbert, who held land south of Eoferwic, had yet to arrive with his men.

"Nor is Ricsig here," a priest said, speaking of another great lord.

"He's sick," Osbert said.

"Sickness of courage," Ælla's spokesman sneered.

"Give them time," the bishop suggested. "With Egbert's and Ricsig's men we shall have enough troops to frighten the Danes with sheer numbers."

My father said nothing at the meeting, though it was plain many men wanted him to speak, and I was perplexed that he stayed silent, but that night Beocca explained why. "If he said we should attack," the priest said, "then men would assume he had sided with Ælla, while if he encouraged a siege, he would be seen to be on Osbert's side."

"Does it matter?"

Beocca looked at me across the campfire, or one of his eyes looked at me while the other wandered somewhere in the night. "When the Danes are beaten," he said, "then Osbert and Ælla's feud will start again. Your father wants none of it."

"But whichever side he supports," I said, "will win."

"But suppose they kill each other?" Beocca asked. "Who will be king then?"

I looked at him, understood, said nothing.

"And who will be king thereafter?" Beocca asked, and he pointed at me. "You. And a king should be able to read and write."

"A king," I answered scornfully, "can always hire men who can read and write."

Then, next morning, the decision to attack or besiege was made for us, because news came that more Danish ships had appeared at the mouth of the river Humber, and that could only mean the enemy would be reinforced within a few days, and so my father, who had stayed silent for so long, finally spoke. "We must attack," he told both Osbert and Ælla, "before the new boats come."

Ælla, of course, agreed enthusiastically, and even Osbert understood that the new ships meant that everything was changed. Besides, the Danes inside the city had been having problems with their new wall. We woke one morning to see a whole new stretch of palisade, the wood raw and bright, but a great wind blew that day and the new work collapsed, and that caused much merriment in our encampments. The Danes, men said, could not even build a wall. "But they can build ships," Father Beocca told me.

"So?"

"A man who can build a ship," the young priest said, "can usually build a wall. It is not so hard as ship-building."

"It fell down!"

"Perhaps it was meant to fall down," Beocca said, and, when I just stared at him, he explained. "Perhaps they want us to attack there?"

I do not know if he told my father of his suspicions, but if he did then I have no doubt my father dismissed them. He did not trust Beocca's opinions on war. The priest's usefulness was in encouraging God to smite the Danes and that was all and, to be fair, Beocca did pray mightily and long that God would give us the victory.

And the day after the wall collapsed we gave God his chance to fulfill Beocca's prayers.

We attacked.

I do not know if every man who assaulted Eoferwic was drunk, but they would have been had there been enough mead, ale, and birch wine to go around. The drinking had gone on much of the night and I woke to find men vomiting in the dawn. Those few who, like my father, possessed mail shirts pulled them on. Most were armored in leather, while some men had no protection other than their coats. Weapons were sharpened on whetstones. The priests walked round the camp scattering blessings, while men swore oaths of brotherhood and loyalty. Some banded together and promised to share their plunder equally, a few looked pale, and more than a handful sneaked away through the dykes that crossed the flat, damp landscape.

A score of men were ordered to stay at the camp and guard the women and horses, though Father Beocca and I were both ordered to mount. "You'll stay on horseback," my father told me, "and you'll stay with him," he added to the priest.

"Of course, my lord," Beocca said.

"If anything happens," my father was deliberately vague, "then ride to Bebbanburg, shut the gate, and wait there."

"God is on our side," Beocca said.

My father looked a great warrior, which indeed he was, though he claimed to be getting too old for fighting. His graying beard jutted over his mail coat, above which he had hung a crucifix carved from ox bone that had been a gift from Gytha. His sword belt was leather studded with silver, while his great sword, Bone-Breaker, was sheathed in leather banded with gilt-bronze strappings. His boots had iron plates on either side of the ankles, reminding me of his advice about the shield wall, while his helmet was polished so that it shone, and its face piece, with its eyeholes and snarling mouth, was inlaid with silver. His round shield was made of limewood, had a heavy iron boss, was covered in leather and painted with the wolf's head. Ealdorman Uhtred was going to war.

The horns summoned the army. There was little order in the array. There had been arguments about who should be on the right or left, but Beocca told me the argument had been settled when the bishop cast dice, and King Osbert was now on the right, Ælla on the left, and my father in the center, and those three chieftains' banners were advanced as the horns called. The men assembled under the banners. My father's household troops, his best warriors, were at the front, and behind them were the bands of the thegns. Thegns were important men, holders of great lands, some of them with their own fortresses, and they were the men who shared my father's platform in the feasting hall, and men who had to be watched in case their ambitions made them try to take his place, but now they loyally gathered behind him, and the ceorls, free men of the lowest rank, assembled with them. Men fought in family groups, or with friends. There were plenty of boys with the army, though I was the only one on horseback and the only one with a sword and helmet.

I could see a scatter of Danes behind the unbroken palisades either side of the gap where their wall had fallen down, but most of their army filled that gap, making a shield barrier on top of the earthen wall, and it was a high earthen wall, at least ten or twelve feet high, and steep, so it would be a hard climb into the face of the waiting killers, but I was confident we would win. I was ten years old, almost eleven.

The Danes were shouting at us, but we were too far away to hear their insults. Their shields, round like ours, were painted yellow, black, brown, and blue. Our men began beating weapons on their shields and that was a fearsome sound, the first time I ever heard an army making that war music; the clashing of ash spear shafts and iron sword blades on shield wood.

"It is a terrible thing," Beocca said to me. "War, it is an awful thing."

I said nothing. I thought it was glorious and wonderful.

"The shield wall is where men die," Beocca said, and he kissed the wooden cross that hung about his neck. "The gates of heaven and hell will be jostling with souls before this day is done," he went on gloomily.

"Aren't the dead carried to a feasting hall?" I asked.

He looked at me very strangely, then appeared shocked. "Where did you hear that?"

"At Bebbanburg," I said, sensible enough not to admit that it was Ealdwulf the smith who told me those tales as I watched him beating rods of iron into sword blades.

"That is what heathens believe," Beocca said sternly. "They believe dead warriors are carried to Woden's corpse-hall to feast until the world's ending, but it is a grievously wrong belief. It is an error! But the Danes are always in error. They bow down to idols, they deny the true god, they are wrong."

"But a man must die with a sword in his hand?" I insisted.

"I can see we must teach you a proper catechism when this is done," the priest said sternly.

I said nothing more. I was watching, trying to fix every detail of that day in my memory. The sky was summer blue, with just a few clouds off in the west, and the sunlight reflected from our army's spear points like glints of light flickering on the summer sea. Cowslips dotted the meadow where the army assembled, and a cuckoo called from the woods behind us where a crowd of our women were watching the army. There were swans on the river that was placid for there was little wind. The smoke from the cooking fires inside Eoferwic rose almost straight into the air, and that sight reminded me that there would be a feast in the city that night, a feast of roasted pork or whatever else we found in the enemy's stores. Some of our men, those in the foremost ranks, were darting forward to shout at the enemy, or else dare him to come and do private battle between the lines, one man on one man, but none of the Danes broke rank. They just stared, waited, their spears a hedge, their shields a wall, and then our horns blew again and the shouting and the shield-banging faded as our army lurched forward.

It went raggedly. Later, much later, I was to understand the reluctance of men to launch themselves against a shield wall, let alone a shield wall held at the top of a steep earthen bank, but on that day I was just impatient for our army to hurry forward and break the impudent Danes and Beocca had to restrain me, catching hold of my bridle to stop me riding into the rearmost ranks. "We shall wait until they break through," he said.

"I want to kill a Dane," I protested.

"Don't be stupid, Uhtred," Beocca said angrily. "You try and kill a Dane," he went on, "and your father will have no sons. You are his only child now, and it is your duty to live."

So I did my duty and I hung back, and I watched as, so slowly, our army found its courage and advanced toward the city. The river was on our left, the empty encampment behind our right, and the inviting gap in the city wall was to our front; there the Danes were waiting silently, their shields overlapping.

"The bravest will go first," Beocca said to me, "and your father will be one of them. They will make a wedge, what the Latin authors call a **porcinum capet.** You know what that means?"

"No." Nor did I care.

"A swine's head. Like the tusk of a boar. The bravest will go first and, if they break through, the others will follow."

Beocca was right. Three wedges formed in front of our lines, one each from the household troops of Osbert, Ælla, and my father. The men stood close together, their shields overlapping like the Danish shields, while the rearward ranks of each wedge held their shields high like a roof, and then, when they were ready, the men in the three wedges gave a great cheer and started forward. They did not run. I had expected them to run, but men cannot keep the wedge tight if they run. The wedge is war in slow time, slow enough for the men inside the wedge to wonder how strong the enemy is and to fear that the rest of the army will not follow, but they did. The three wedges had not gone more than twenty paces before the remaining mass of men moved forward.

"I want to be closer," I said.

"You will wait," Beocca said.

I could hear the shouts now, shouts of defiance and shouts to give a man courage, and then the archers on the city walls loosed their bows and I saw the glitter of the feathers as the arrows slashed down toward the wedges, and a moment later the throwing spears came, arching over the Danish line to fall on the upheld shields. Amazingly, at least to me, it seemed that none of our men was struck, though I could see their shields were stuck with arrows and spears like hedgehog spines, and still the three wedges advanced, and now our own bowmen were shooting at the Danes, and a handful of our men broke from the ranks behind the wedges to hurl their own spears at the enemy shield wall.

"Not long now," Beocca said nervously. He made the sign of the cross. He was praying silently and his crippled left hand was twitching.

I was watching my father's wedge, the central

wedge, the one just in front of the wolf's head banner, and I saw the closely touching shields vanish into the ditch that lay in front of the earthen wall and I knew my father was perilously close to death and I urged him to win, to kill, to give the name Uhtred of Bebbanburg even more renown, and then I saw the shield wedge emerge from the ditch and, like a monstrous beast, crawl up the face of the wall.

"The advantage they have," Beocca said in the patient voice he used for teaching, "is that the enemy's feet are easy targets when you come from below." I think he was trying to reassure himself, but I believed him anyway, and it must have been true for my father's formation, first up the wall, did not seem to be checked when they met the enemy's shield wall. I could see nothing now except the flash of blades rising and falling, and I could hear that sound, the real music of battle, the chop of iron on wood, iron on iron, yet the wedge was still moving. Like a boar's razor-sharp tusk it had pierced the Danish shield wall and was moving forward, and though the Danes wrapped around the wedge, it seemed our men were winning for they pressed forward across the earthen bank, and the soldiers behind must have sensed that Ealdorman Uhtred had brought them victory for they suddenly cheered and surged to help the beleaguered wedge.

"God be praised," Beocca said, for the Danes were fleeing. One moment they had formed a thick shield wall, bristling with weapons, and now they were vanishing into the city and our army, with the relief of men whose lives have been spared, charged after them.

"Slowly, now," Beocca said, walking his horse forward and leading mine by the bridle.

The Danes had gone. Instead the earthen wall was black with our men who were scrambling through the gap in the city's ramparts, then down the bank's farther side into the streets and alleyways beyond. The three flags, my father's wolf head, Ælla's war ax, and Osbert's cross, were inside Eoferwic. I could hear men cheering and I kicked my horse, forcing her out of Beocca's grasp. "Come back!" he shouted, but though he followed me he did not try to drag me away. We had won, God had given us victory, and I wanted to be close enough to smell the slaughter.

Neither of us could get into the city because the gap in the palisade was choked with our men, but I kicked the horse again and she forced her way into the press. Some men protested at what I was doing. Then they saw the gilt-bronze circle on my helmet and knew I was nobly born and so they tried to help me through, while Beocca, stranded at the back of the crowd, shouted that I should not get too far ahead of him. "Catch up!" I called back to him.

Then he shouted again, but this time his voice was frantic, terrified, and I turned to see Danes streaming across the field where our army had advanced. It was a horde of Danes who must have sallied from the city's northern gate to cut off our retreat, and they must have known we would retreat, because it seemed they could build walls after all, and had built them across the streets inside the city, then feigned flight from the ramparts to draw us into their killing ground and now they sprang the trap. Some of the Danes who came from the city were mounted, most were on foot, and Beocca panicked. I do not blame him. The Danes like killing Christian priests and Beocca must have seen death, did not desire martyrdom, and so he turned his horse and kicked it hard and it galloped away beside the river and the Danes, not caring about the fate of one man where so many were trapped, let him go.

It is a truth that in most armies the timid men

and those with the feeblest weapons are at the back. The brave go to the front, the weak seek the rear, so if you can get to the back of an enemy army you will have a massacre.

I am an old man now and it has been my fate to see panic flicker through many armies. That panic is worse than the terror of sheep penned in a cleft and being assaulted by wolves, more frantic than the writhing of salmon caught in a net and dragged to the air. The sound of it must tear the heavens apart, but to the Danes, that day, it was the sweet sound of victory and to us it was death.

I tried to escape. God knows I panicked, too. I had seen Beocca racing away beside the riverside willows and I managed to turn the mare, but then one of our own men snatched at me, presumably wanting my horse, and I had the wit to draw my short sword and hack blindly at him as I kicked back my heels, but all I achieved was to ride out of the panicked mass into the path of the Danes, and all around me men were screaming and the Danish axes and swords were chopping and swinging. The grim work, the blood feast, the song of the blade, they call it, and perhaps I was saved for a moment because I was the only one in our army who was on horseback and a score of the Danes were also mounted and perhaps they mistook me for one of their own, but then one of those Danes called to me in a language I did not speak and I looked at him and saw his long hair, unhelmeted, his long fair hair and his silver-colored mail and the wide grin on his wild face and I recognized him as the man who had killed my brother and, like the fool I was, I screamed at him. A standard bearer was just behind the long-haired Dane, flaunting an eagle's wing on a long pole. Tears were blurring my sight, and perhaps the battle madness came onto me because, despite my panic, I rode at the long-haired Dane and struck at him with my small sword, and his sword parried mine, and my feeble blade bent like a herring's spine. It just bent and he drew back his own sword for the killing stroke, saw my pathetic bent blade, and began to laugh. I was pissing myself, he was laughing, and I beat at him again with the useless sword and still he laughed, and then he leaned over, plucked the weapon from my hand, and threw it away. He picked me up then. I was screaming and hitting at him, but he thought it all so very funny, and he draped me belly down on the saddle in front of him and then he spurred into the chaos to continue the killing.

And that was how I met Ragnar, Ragnar the Fearless, my brother's killer, and the man whose head was supposed to grace a pole on Bebbanburg's ramparts, Earl Ragnar.

PART ONE

A Pagan Childhood

ONE

The Danes were clever that day. They had made new walls inside the city, invited our men into the streets, trapped them between the new walls, surrounded them, and killed them. They did not kill all the Northumbrian army, for even the fiercest warriors tire of slaughter and, besides, the Danes made much money from slavery. Most of the slaves taken in England were sold to farmers in the wild northern isles, or to Ireland, or sent back across the sea to the Danish lands, but some, I learned, were taken to the big slave markets in Frankia and a few were shipped south to a place where there was no winter and where men with faces the color of scorched wood would pay good money for men and even better money for young women.

But they killed enough of us. They killed Ælla

and they killed Osbert and they killed my father. Ælla and my father were fortunate, for they died in battle, swords in their hands, but Osbert was captured and he was tortured that night as the Danes feasted in a city stinking of blood. Some of the victors guarded the walls, others celebrated in the captured houses, but most gathered in the hall of Northumbria's defeated king where Ragnar took me. I did not know why he took me there, I half expected to be killed or, at best, sold into slavery, but Ragnar made me sit with his men and put a roasted goose leg, half a loaf of bread, and a pot of ale in front of me, then cuffed me cheerfully round the head.

The other Danes ignored me at first. They were too busy getting drunk and cheering the fights that broke out once they were drunk, but the loudest cheers came when the captured Osbert was forced to fight against a young warrior who had extraordinary skill with a sword. He danced around the king, then chopped off his left hand before slitting his belly with a sweeping cut and, because Osbert was a heavy man, his guts spilled out like eels slithering from a ruptured sack. Some of the Danes were weak with laughter after that. The king took a long time to die, and while he cried for relief, the Danes crucified a captured priest who had fought against them in the battle. They were intrigued and repelled by our religion, and they were angry when the priest's hands pulled free of the nails and some claimed it was impossible to kill a man that way, and they argued that point drunkenly, then tried to nail the priest to the hall's timber walls a second time until, bored with it, one of their warriors slammed a spear into the priest's chest, crushing his ribs and mangling his heart.

A handful of them turned on me once the priest was dead and, because I had worn a helmet with a gilt-bronze circlet, they thought I must be a king's son and they put me in a robe and a man climbed onto the table to piss on me, and just then a huge voice bellowed at them to stop and Ragnar bullied his way through the crowd. He snatched the robe from me and harangued the men, telling them I knew not what, but whatever he said made them stop and Ragnar then put an arm around my shoulders and took me to a dais at the side of the hall and gestured I should climb up to it. An old man was eating alone there. He was blind, both eyes milky white, and had a deep-lined face framed by gray hair as long as Ragnar's. He heard me clamber up and asked a question, and Ragnar answered and then walked away.

"You must be hungry, boy," the old man said in English.

I did not answer. I was terrified of his blind eyes.

"Have you vanished?" he asked. "Did the dwarves pluck you down to the underearth?"

"I'm hungry," I admitted.

"So you are there after all," he said, "and there's pork here, and bread, and cheese, and ale. Tell me your name."

I almost said Osbert, then remembered I was Uhtred. "Uhtred," I said.

"An ugly name," the old man said, "but my son said I was to look after you, so I will, but you must look after me too. You could cut me some pork?"

"Your son?" I asked.

"Earl Ragnar," he said, "sometimes called Ragnar the Fearless. Who were they killing in here?"

"The king," I said, "and a priest."

"Which king?"

"Osbert."

"Did he die well?"

"No."

"Then he shouldn't have been king."

"Are you a king?" I asked.

He laughed. "I am Ravn," he said, "and once I was an earl and a warrior, but now I am blind so I am no use to anyone. They should beat me over the head with a cudgel and send me on my way to the netherworld." I said nothing to that because I did not know what to say. "But I try to be useful," Ravn went on, his hands groping for bread. "I speak your language and the language of the Britons and the tongue of the Wends and the speech of the Frisians and that of the Franks. Language is now my trade, boy, because I have become a skald."

"A skald?"

"A scop, you would call me. A poet, a weaver of dreams, a man who makes glory from nothing and dazzles you with its making. And my job now is to tell this day's tale in such a way that men will never forget our great deeds."

"But if you cannot see," I asked, "how can you tell what happened?"

Ravn laughed at that. "Have you heard of Odin? Then you should know that Odin sacrificed one of his own eyes so that he could obtain the gift of poetry. So perhaps I am twice as good a skald as Odin, eh?"

"I am descended from Woden," I said.

"Are you?" He seemed impressed, or perhaps he just wanted to be kind. "So who are you, Uhtred, descendant of the great Odin?"

"I am the Ealdorman of Bebbanburg," I said, and that reminded me I was fatherless and my defiance crumpled and, to my shame, I began to cry. Ravn ignored me as he listened to the drunken shouts and the songs and the shrieks of the girls who had been captured in our camp and who now provided the warriors with the reward for their victory, and watching their antics took my mind off my sorrow because, in truth, I had never seen such things before, though, God be thanked, I took plenty of such rewards myself in times to come.

"Bebbanburg?" Ravn said. "I was there before you were born. It was twenty years ago."

"At Bebbanburg?"

"Not in the fortress," he admitted, "it was far too strong. But I was to the north of it, on the island where the monks pray. I killed six men there. Not monks, men. Warriors." He smiled to himself, remembering. "Now tell me, Ealdorman

Uhtred of Bebbanburg," he went on, "what is happening."

So I became his eyes and I told him of the men dancing, and the men stripping the women of their clothes, and what they then did to the women, but Ravn had no interest in that. "What," he wanted to know, "are Ivar and Ubba doing?"

"Ivar and Ubba?"

"They will be on the high platform. Ubba is the shorter and looks like a barrel with a beard, and Ivar is so skinny that he is called Ivar the Boneless. He is so thin that you could press his feet together and shoot him from a bowstring."

I learned later that Ivar and Ubba were the two oldest of three brothers and the joint leaders of this Danish army. Ubba was asleep, his black-haired head cushioned by his arms that, in turn, were resting on the remnants of his meal, but Ivar the Boneless was awake. He had sunken eyes, a face like a skull, yellow hair drawn back to the nape of his neck, and an expression of sullen malevolence. His arms were thick with the golden rings Danes like to wear to prove their prowess in battle, while a gold chain was coiled around his neck. Two men were talking to him. One, standing just behind Ivar, seemed to whis-

per into his ear, while the other, a worried-
looking man, sat between the two brothers. I described all this to Ravn, who wanted to know
what the worried man sitting between Ivar and
Ubba looked like.

"No arm rings," I said, "a gold circlet round
his neck. Brown hair, long beard, quite old."

"Everyone looks old to the young," Ravn said.
"That must be King Egbert."

"King Egbert?" I had never heard of such a
person.

"He was Ealdorman Egbert," Ravn explained,
"but he made his peace with us in the winter and
we have rewarded him by making him king here
in Northumbria. He is king, but we are the lords
of the land." He chuckled, and young as I was I
understood the treachery involved. Ealdorman
Egbert held estates to the south of our kingdom
and was what my father had been in the north, a
great power, and the Danes had suborned him,
kept him from the fight, and now he would be
called king, yet it was plain that he would be a
king on a short leash. "If you are to live," Ravn
said to me, "then it would be wise to pay your respects to Egbert."

"Live?" I blurted out the word. I had somehow
thought that having survived the battle then of

course I would live. I was a child, someone else's responsibility, but Ravn's words hammered home my reality. I should never have confessed my rank, I thought. Better to be a living slave than a dead ealdorman.

"I think you'll live," Ravn said. "Ragnar likes you and Ragnar gets what he wants. He says you attacked him?"

"I did, yes."

"He would have enjoyed that. A boy who attacks Earl Ragnar? That must be some boy, eh? Too good a boy to waste on death he says, but then my son always had a regrettably sentimental side. I would have chopped your head off, but here you are, alive, and I think it would be wise if you were to bow to Egbert."

Now, I think, looking back so far into my past, I have probably changed that night's events. There was a feast, Ivar and Ubba were there, Egbert was trying to look like a king, Ravn was kind to me, but I am sure I was more confused and far more frightened than I have made it sound. Yet in other ways my memories of the feast are very precise. Watch and learn, my father had told me, and Ravn made me watch, and I did learn. I learned about treachery, especially when Ragnar, summoned by Ravn, took me by the collar and led me to the high dais where, after a surly gesture of permission from Ivar, I was allowed to approach the table. "Lord King," I squeaked, then knelt so that a surprised Egbert had to lean forward to see me. "I am Uhtred of Bebbanburg," I had been coached by Ravn in what I should say, "and I seek your lordly protection."

That produced silence, except for the mutter of the interpreter talking to Ivar. Then Ubba awoke, looked startled for a few heartbeats as if he was not sure where he was, then he stared at me and I felt my flesh shrivel for I had never seen a face so malevolent. He had dark eyes and they were full of hate and I wanted the earth to swallow me. He said nothing, just gazed at me and touched a hammer-shaped amulet hanging at his neck. Ubba had his brother's thin face, but instead of fair hair drawn back against the skull, he had bushy black hair and a thick beard that was dotted with scraps of food. Then he yawned and it was like staring into a beast's maw. The interpreter spoke to Ivar who said something, and the interpreter, in turn, talked to Egbert who tried to look stern. "Your father," he said, "chose to fight us."

"And is dead," I answered, tears in my eyes, and I wanted to say something more, but nothing would come, and instead I just sniveled like an infant and I could feel Ubba's scorn like the heat of a fire. I cuffed angrily at my nose.

"We shall decide your fate," Egbert said loftily, and I was dismissed.

I went back to Ravn who insisted I tell him what had happened, and he smiled when I described Ubba's malevolent silence. "He's a frightening man," Ravn agreed. "To my certain knowledge he's killed sixteen men in single combat, and dozens more in battle, but only when the auguries are good. Otherwise he won't fight."

"The auguries?"

"Ubba is a very superstitious young man," Ravn said, "but also a dangerous one. If I give you one piece of advice, young Uhtred, it is never, never, to fight Ubba. Even Ragnar would fear to do that and my son fears little."

"And Ivar?" I asked. "Would your son fight Ivar?"

"The boneless one?" Ravn considered the question. "He too is frightening, for he has no pity, but he does possess sense. Besides, Ragnar serves Ivar if he serves anyone, and they're friends, so they would not fight. But Ubba? Only the gods tell him what to do, and you should beware of men who take their orders from the gods.

Cut me some of the crackling, boy. I particularly like pork crackling."

I cannot remember now how long I was in Eoferwic. I was put to work, that I do remember. My fine clothes were stripped from me and given to some Danish boy, and in their place I was given a flea-ridden shift of tattered wool that I belted with a piece of rope. I cooked Ravn's meals for a few days. Then the other Danish ships arrived and proved to hold mostly women and children, the families of the victorious army, and it was then I understood that these Danes had come to stay in Northumbria. Ravn's wife arrived, a big woman called Gudrun with a laugh that could have felled an ox, and she chivvied me away from the cooking fire that she now tended with Ragnar's wife, who was called Sigrid and whose hair reached to her waist and was the color of sunlight reflecting off gold. She and Ragnar had two sons and a daughter. Sigrid had given birth to eight children, but only those three had lived. Rorik, his second son, was a year younger than me and on the very first day I met him he picked a fight, coming at me in a whirl of fists and feet, but I put him on his back and was throttling the breath out of him when Ragnar picked us both up, crashed our heads together, and told us to be friends. Ragnar's eldest son, also called Ragnar, was eighteen, already a man, and I did not meet him then for he was in Ireland where he was learning to fight and to kill so he could become an earl like his father. In time I did meet Ragnar the Younger who was very similar to his father: always cheerful, boisterously happy, enthusiastic about whatever needed to be done, and friendly to anyone who paid him respect.

Like all the other children I had work to keep me busy. There was always firewood and water to be fetched, and I spent two days helping to burn the green muck from the hull of a beached ship, and I enjoyed that even though I got into a dozen fights with Danish boys, all of them bigger than me, and I lived with black eyes, bruised knuckles, sprained wrists, and loosened teeth. My worst enemy was a boy called Sven who was two years older than me and very big for his age with a round, vacant face, a slack jaw, and a vicious temper. He was the son of one of Ragnar's shipmasters, a man called Kjartan. Ragnar owned three ships, he commanded one, Kjartan the second, and a tall, weather-hardened man named Egil steered the third. Kjartan and Egil were also warriors, of course, and as shipmasters they led their crews into battle and so were reckoned important men, their arms heavy with rings, and Kjartan's son Sven took an instant dislike to me. He called me English scum, a goat turd and dog breath, and because he was older and bigger he could beat me fairly easily, but I was also making friends and, luckily for me, Sven disliked Rorik almost as much as he hated me, and the two of us could just thrash him together and after a while Sven avoided me unless he was sure I was alone. So apart from Sven it was a good summer. I never had quite enough to eat, I was never clean, Ragnar made us laugh, and I was rarely unhappy.

Ragnar was often absent for much of the Danish army spent that summer riding the length and breadth of Northumbria to quell the last shreds of resistance, but I heard little news, and no news of Bebbanburg. It seemed the Danes were winning, for every few days another English thegn would come to Eoferwic and kneel to Egbert, who now lived in the palace of Northumbria's king, though it was a palace that had been stripped of anything useful by the victors. The gap in the city wall had been repaired in a day, the same day that a score of us dug a great hole in the field where our army had fled in panic. We filled the hole with the rotting corpses of the

Northumbrian dead. I knew some of them. I suppose my father was among them, but I did not see him. Nor, looking back, did I miss him. He had always been a morose man, expecting the worst, and not fond of children.

The worst job I was given was painting shields. We first had to boil down some cattle hides to make size, a thick glue, that we stirred into a powder we had made from crushing copper ore with big stone pestles, and the result was a viscous blue paste that had to be smeared on the newly made shields. For days afterward I had blue hands and arms, but our shields were hung on a ship and looked splendid. Every Danish ship had a strake running down each side from which the shields could hang, overlapping as though they were being held in the shield wall, and these shields were for Ubba's craft, the same ship I had burned and scraped clean. Ubba, it seemed, planned to leave, and wanted his ship to be beautiful. She had a beast on her prow, a prow that curved like a swan's breast from the waterline, then jutted forward. The beast, half dragon and half worm, was the topmost part, and the whole beast head could be lifted off its stem and stowed in the bilge. "We lift the beast heads off," Ragnar explained to me, "so they don't frighten the spirits." I had learned some of the Danish language by then.

"The spirits?"

Ragnar sighed at my ignorance. "Every land has its spirits," he said, "its own little gods, and when we approach our own lands we take off the beast heads so that the spirits aren't scared away. How many fights have you had today?"

"None."

"They're getting frightened of you. What's that thing around your neck?"

I showed him. It was a crude iron hammer, a miniature hammer the size of a man's thumb, and the sight of it made him laugh and cuff me around the head. "We'll make a Dane of you yet," he said, plainly pleased. The hammer was the sign of Thor, who was a Danish god almost as important as Odin, as they called Woden, and sometimes I wondered if Thor was the more important god, but no one seemed to know or even care very much. There were no priests among the Danes, which I liked, because priests were forever telling us not to do things or trying to teach us to read or demanding that we pray, and life without them was much more pleasant. The Danes, indeed, seemed very casual about their gods, yet almost every one wore Thor's hammer.

I had torn mine from the neck of a boy who had fought me, and I have it to this day.

The stern of Ubba's ship, which curved and reared as high as the prow, was decorated with a carved eagle's head, while at her masthead was a wind vane in the shape of a dragon. The shields were hung on her flanks, though I later learned they were only displayed there for decoration and that once the ship was under way the shields were stored inboard. Just underneath the shields were the oar holes, each rimmed with leather, fifteen holes on each side. The holes could be stopped with wooden plugs when the ship was under sail so that the craft could lean with the wind and not be swamped. I helped scrub the whole boat clean, but before we scrubbed her she was sunk in the river, just to drown the rats and discourage the fleas, and then we boys scraped every inch of wood and hammered wax-soaked wool into every seam, and at last the ship was ready and that was the day my uncle Ælfric arrived in Eoferwic.

The first I knew of Ælfric's coming was when Ragnar brought me my own helmet, the one with the gilt-bronze circlet, and a tunic edged with red embroidery, and a pair of shoes. It felt strange to walk in shoes again. "Tidy your hair, boy," he said, then remembered he had the helmet that he pushed onto my tousled head. "Don't tidy your hair," he said, grinning.

"Where are we going?" I asked him.

"To hear a lot of words, boy. To waste our time. You look like a Frankish whore in that robe."

"That bad?"

"That's good, lad! They have great whores in Frankia: plump, pretty, and cheap. Come on." He led me from the river. The city was busy, the shops full, the streets crowded with pack mules. A herd of small, dark-fleeced sheep was being driven to slaughter, and they were the only obstruction that did not part to make way for Ragnar whose reputation ensured respect, but that reputation was not grim for I saw how the Danes grinned when he greeted them. He might be called Jarl Ragnar, Earl Ragnar, but he was hugely popular, a jester and fighter who blew through fear as though it were a cobweb. He took me to the palace, which was only a large house, part built by the Romans in stone and part made more recently in wood and thatch. It was in the Roman part, in a vast room with stone pillars and lime-washed walls, that my uncle waited and with him was Father Beocca and a dozen warriors, all of whom I knew, and all of whom had stayed to defend Bebbanburg while my father rode to war.

Beocca's crossed eyes widened when he saw me. I must have looked very different for I was long haired, sun darkened, skinny, taller, and wilder. Then there was the hammer amulet about my neck, which he saw for he pointed to his own crucifix, then at my hammer and looked very disapproving. Ælfric and his men scowled at me as though I had let them down, but no one spoke, partly because Ivar's own guards, all of them tall men, and all of them in mail and helmets and armed with long-shafted war axes, stood across the head of the room where a simple chair, which now counted as Northumbria's throne, stood on a wooden platform.

King Egbert arrived, and with him was Ivar the Boneless and a dozen men, including Ravn who, I had learned, was a counselor to Ivar and his brother. With Ravn was a tall man, white haired and with a long white beard. He was wearing long robes embroidered with crosses and winged angels and I later discovered this was Wulfhere, the Archbishop of Eoferwic who, like Egbert, had given his allegiance to the Danes. The king sat, looking uncomfortable, and then the discussion began.

They were not there just to discuss me. They talked about which Northumbrian lords were to be trusted, which were to be attacked, what lands were to be granted to Ivar and Ubba, what tribute the Northumbrians must pay, how many horses were to be brought to Eoferwic, how much food was to be given to the army, which ealdormen were to yield hostages, and I sat, bored, until my name was mentioned. I perked up then and heard my uncle propose that I should be ransomed. That was the gist of it, but nothing is ever simple when a score of men decide to argue. For a long time they wrangled over my price, the Danes demanding an impossible payment of three hundred pieces of silver, and Ælfric not wanting to budge from a grudging offer of fifty. I said nothing, but just sat on the broken Roman tiles at the edge of the hall and listened. Three hundred became two hundred and seventy-five, fifty became sixty, and so it went on, the numbers edging closer, but still wide apart, and then Ravn, who had been silent, spoke for the first time. "The earl Uhtred," he said in Danish, and that was the first time I heard myself described as an earl, which was a Danish rank, "has given his allegiance to King Egbert. In that he has an advantage over you, Ælfric."

The words were translated and I saw Ælfric's anger when he was given no title. But nor did he have a title, except the one he had granted to himself, and I learned about that when he spoke softly to Beocca who then spoke up for him. "The ealdorman Ælfric," the young priest said, "does not believe that a child's oath is of any significance."

Had I made an oath? I could not remember doing so, though I had asked for Egbert's protection, and I was young enough to confuse the two things. Still, it did not much matter. What mattered was that my uncle had usurped Bebbanburg. He was calling himself ealdorman. I stared at him, shocked, and he looked back at me with pure loathing in his face.

"It is our belief," Ravn said, his blind eyes looking at the roof of the hall that was missing some tiles so that a light rain was spitting through the rafters, "that we would be better served by having our own sworn earl in Bebbanburg, loyal to us, than endure a man whose loyalty we do not know."

Ælfric could feel the wind changing and he did the obvious thing. He walked to the dais, knelt to Egbert, kissed the king's outstretched hand, and, as a reward, received a blessing from the archbishop. "I will offer a hundred pieces of silver," Ælfric said, his allegiance given.

"Two hundred," Ravn said, "and a force of thirty Danes to garrison Bebbanburg."

"With my allegiance given," Ælfric said angrily, "you will have no need of Danes in Bebbanburg."

So Bebbanburg had not fallen and I doubted it could fall. There was no stronger fortress in all Northumbria, and perhaps in all England.

Egbert had not spoken at all, nor did he, but nor had Ivar and it was plain that the tall, thin, ghost-faced Dane was bored with the whole proceedings for he jerked his head at Ragnar who left my side and went to talk privately with his lord. The rest of us waited awkwardly. Ivar and Ragnar were friends, an unlikely friendship for they were very different men, Ivar all savage silence and grim threat, and Ragnar open and loud, yet Ragnar's eldest son served Ivar and was even now, at eighteen years old, entrusted with the leadership of some of the Danes left in Ireland who were holding on to Ivar's lands in that island. It was not unusual for eldest sons to serve another lord, Ragnar had two earl's sons in his ships' crews, and both might one day expect to inherit wealth and position if they learned how to fight. So Ragnar and Ivar now talked and Ælfric shuffled his feet and kept looking at me, Beocca prayed, and King Egbert, having nothing else to do, just tried to look regal.

Ivar finally spoke. "The boy is not for sale," he announced.

"Ransom," Ravn corrected him gently.

Ælfric looked furious. "I came here . . ." he began, but Ivar interrupted him.

"The boy is not for ransom," he snarled, then turned and walked from the big chamber. Egbert looked awkward, half rose from his throne, sat again, and Ragnar came and stood beside me.

"You're mine," he said softly, "I just bought you."

"Bought me?"

"My sword's weight in silver," he said.

"Why?"

"Perhaps I want to sacrifice you to Odin?" he suggested, then tousled my hair. "We like you, boy," he said, "we like you enough to keep you. And besides, your uncle didn't offer enough silver. For five hundred pieces? I'd have sold you for that." He laughed.

Beocca hurried across the room. "Are you well?" he asked me.

"I'm well," I said.

"That thing you're wearing," he said, meaning Thor's hammer, and he reached as though to pull it from its thong.

"Touch the boy, priest," Ragnar said harshly, "and I'll straighten your crooked eyes before opening you from your gutless belly to your skinny throat."

Beocca, of course, could not understand what the Dane had said, but he could not mistake the tone and his hand stopped an inch from the hammer. He looked nervous. He lowered his voice so only I could hear him. "Your uncle will kill you," he whispered.

"Kill me?"

"He wants to be ealdorman. That's why he wished to ransom you. So he could kill you."

"But," I began to protest.

"Shh," Beocca said. He was curious about my blue hands, but did not ask what had caused them. "I know you are the ealdorman," he said instead, "and we will meet again." He smiled at me, glanced warily at Ragnar, and backed away.

Ælfric left. I learned later that he had been given safe passage to and from Eoferwic, which promise had been kept, but after that meeting he retreated to Bebbanburg and stayed there. Ostensibly he was loyal to Egbert, which meant he accepted the overlordship of the Danes, but they had not yet learned to trust him. That, Ragnar explained to me, was why he had kept me alive. "I like Bebbanburg," he told me. "I want it."

"It's mine," I said stubbornly.

"And you're mine," he said, "which means Bebbanburg is mine. You're mine, Uhtred, because I just bought you, so I can do whatever I like with you. I can cook you, if I want, except there's not enough meat on you to feed a weasel. Now, take off that whore's tunic, give me the shoes and helmet, and go back to work."

So I was a slave again, and happy. Sometimes, when I tell folk my story, they ask why I did not run away from the pagans, why I did not escape southward into the lands where the Danes did not yet rule, but it never occurred to me to try. I was happy, I was alive, I was with Ragnar, and it was enough.

More Danes arrived before winter. Thirty-six ships came, each with its contingent of warriors, and the ships were pulled onto the riverbank for the winter while the crews, laden with shields and weapons, marched to wherever they would spend the next few months. The Danes were casting a net over eastern Northumbria, a light one, but still a net of scattered garrisons. Yet they could not have stayed if we had not let them, but those ealdormen and thegns who had not died at Eoferwic had bent the knee and so we were a Danish kingdom now, despite the leashed Egbert on his pathetic throne. It was only in the west, in the wilder parts of Northumbria, that no Danes ruled, but nor were there any strong forces in those wild parts to challenge them.

Ragnar took land west of Eoferwic, up in the hills. His wife and family joined him there, and Ravn and Gudrun came, plus all Ragnar's ships' crews who took over homesteads in the nearby valleys. Our first job was to make Ragnar's house larger. It had belonged to an English thegn who had died at Eoferwic, but it was no grand hall, merely a low wooden building thatched with rye straw and bracken on which grass grew so thickly that, from a distance, the house looked like a long hummock. We built a new part, not for us, but for the few cattle, sheep, and goats who would survive the winter and give birth in the new year. The rest were slaughtered. Ragnar and the men did most of the killing, but as the last few beasts came to the pen, he handed an ax to Rorik, his younger son. "One clean, quick stroke," he ordered, and Rorik tried, but he was not strong enough and his aim was not true and the animal bellowed and bled and it took six men to restrain it while Ragnar did the job properly. The skinners moved on to the carcass and Ragnar held the ax to me. "See if you can do better."

A cow was pushed toward me, a man lifted her tail, she obediently lowered her head, and I swung the ax, remembering exactly where Ragnar had hit each time, and the heavy blade swung true, straight into the spine just behind the skull and she went down with a crash. "We'll make a Danish warrior of you yet," Ragnar said, pleased.

The work lessened after the cattle slaughter. The English who still lived in the valley brought Ragnar their tribute of carcasses and grain, just as they would have delivered the supplies to their English lord. It was impossible to read from their faces what they thought of Ragnar and his Danes, but they gave no trouble, and Ragnar took care not to disturb their lives. The local priest was allowed to live and give services in his church that was a wooden shed decorated with a cross, and Ragnar sat in judgment on disputes, but always made certain he was advised by an Englishman who was knowledgeable in the local customs. "You can't live somewhere," he told me, "if the people don't want you to be there. They can kill our cattle or poison our streams, and we would never know who did it. You either slaughter them all or learn to live with them."

The sky grew paler and the wind colder. Dead leaves blew in drifts. Our main work now was to feed the surviving cattle and to keep the log pile high. A dozen of us would go up into the woods and I became proficient with an ax, learning how to bring a tree down with an economy of strokes. We would harness an ox to the bigger trunks to drag them down to the shieling, and the best trees were put aside for building, while the others were split and chopped for burning. There was also time for play and so we children made our own hall high up in the woods, a hall of unsplit logs with a thatch of bracken and a badger's skull nailed to the gable in imitation of the boar's skull that crowned Ragnar's home, and in our pretend hall Rorik and I fought over who would be king, though Thyra, his sister, who was eight years old, was always the lady of the house. She would spin wool there, because if she did not spin enough thread by winter's end she would be punished, and she would watch while we boys fought our mock battles with toy wooden swords. Most of the boys were servants' sons, or slave children, and they always insisted I was the English chief while Rorik was the Danish leader, and my war-band only received the smallest, weakest boys and so we nearly always lost, and Thyra, who had her mother's pale gold hair, would watch and spin, ever spinning, the distaff in her left hand while her right teased the thread out of the sheared fleece.

Every woman had to spin and weave. Ragnar reckoned it took five women or a dozen girls a whole winter to spin enough thread to make a new sail for a boat, and boats were always need-ing new sails, and so the women worked every hour the gods sent. They also cooked, boiled wal-nut shells to dye the new thread, picked mush-rooms, tanned the skins of the slaughtered cattle, collected the moss we used for wiping our arses, rolled beeswax into candles, malted the barley, and placated the gods. There were so many gods and goddesses, and some were peculiar to our own house and those the women celebrated in their own rites, while others, like Odin and Thor, were mighty and ubiquitous, but they were rarely treated in the same way that the Christians wor-shipped their god. A man would appeal to Thor, or to Loki, or to Odin, or to Vikr, or to any of the other great beings who lived in Asgard, which seemed to be the heaven of the gods, but the

Danes did not gather in a church as we had gathered every Sunday and every saint's day in Bebbanburg, and just as there were no priests among the Danes, nor were there any relics or sacred books. I missed none of it.

I wish I had missed Sven, but his father, Kjartan, had a home in the next valley and it did not take long for Sven to discover our hall in the woods and, as the first winter frosts crisped the dead leaves and the berries shone on hawthorn and holly, we found our games turning savage. We no longer split into two sides, because we now had to fight off Sven's boys who would come stalking us, but for a time no great damage was done. It was a game, after all, just a game, but one Sven won repeatedly. He stole the badger's skull from our gable, which we replaced with a fox's head, and Thyra shouted at Sven's boys, skulking in the woods, that she had smeared the fox skull with poison, and we thought that very clever of her, but next morning we found our pretend hall burned to the ground.

"A hall-burning," Rorik said bitterly.

"Hall-burning?"

"It happens at home," Rorik explained. "You go to an enemy's hall and burn it to the ground. But there's one thing about a hall-burning. You have to make sure everyone dies. If there are any survivors then they'll take revenge, so you attack at night, surround the hall, and kill everyone who tries to escape the flames."

But Sven had no hall. There was his father's house, of course, and for a day we plotted revenge on that, discussing how we would burn it down and spear the family as they ran out, but it was only boastful boy talk and of course nothing came of it. Instead we built ourselves a new hall, higher in the woods. It was not as fanciful as the old, not nearly so weather-tight, really nothing more than a crude shelter of branches and bracken, but we nailed a stoat's skull to its makeshift gable and assured ourselves that we still had our kingdom in the hills.

But nothing short of total victory would satisfy Sven and, a few days later, when our chores were done, just Rorik, Thyra, and I went up to our new hall. Thyra spun while Rorik and I argued over where the best swords were made, he saying it was Denmark and I claiming the prize for England, neither of us old enough or sensible enough to know that the best blades come from Frankia, and after a while we got tired of arguing and picked up our sharpened ash poles that served as play spears and decided to look for the wild boar that sometimes trampled through the wood at nightfall. We would not have dared try to kill a boar, they were much too big, but we pretended we were great hunters, and just as we two great hunters were readying to go into the woods, Sven attacked. Just him and two of his followers, but Sven, instead of carrying a wooden sword, swung a real blade, long as a man's arm, the steel glittering in the winter light, and he ran at us, bellowing like a madman. Rorik and I, seeing the fury in his eyes, ran away. He followed us, crashing through the wood like the wild boar we had wanted to stalk, and it was only because we were much faster that we got away from that wicked blade, and then a moment later we heard Thyra scream.

We crept back, cautious of the sword that Sven must have taken from his father's house and, when we reached our pathetic hut, found that Thyra was gone. Her distaff was on the floor and her wool was all speckled with dead leaves and pieces of twig.

Sven had always been clumsy in his strength and he had left a trail through the woods that was easy enough to follow and after a while we heard voices. We kept following, crossing the ridgetop where beeches grew, then down into our enemy's valley, and Sven did not have the sense to post a rear guard who would have seen us. Instead, reveling in his victory, he had gone to the clearing that must have been his refuge in the wood because there was a stone hearth in the center and I remember wondering why we had never built a similar hearth for ourselves. He had tied Thyra to a tree and stripped the tunic from her upper body. There was nothing to see there, she was just a small girl, only eight years old and thus four or five years from being marriageable, but she was pretty and that was why Sven had half stripped her. I could see that Sven's two companions were unhappy. Thyra, after all, was Earl Ragnar's daughter and what had started as a game was now dangerous, but Sven had to show off. He had to prove he had no fear. He had no idea Rorik and I were crouched in the undergrowth, and I do not suppose he would have cared if he had known.

He had dropped the sword by the hearth and now he planted himself in front of Thyra and took down his breeches. "Touch it," he ordered her.

One of his companions said something I could not hear.

"She won't tell anyone," Sven said confidently, "and we won't hurt her." He looked back to Thyra. "I won't hurt you if you touch it!"

It was then that I broke cover. I was not being brave. Sven's companions had lost their appetite for the game, Sven himself had his breeches round his ankles, and his sword was lying loose in the clearing's center and I snatched it up and ran at him. He somehow kept his feet as he turned. "I'll touch it," I shouted, and I swung the long blade at his prick, but the sword was heavy, I had not used a man's blade before, and instead of hitting where I had aimed I sliced it down his bare thigh, opening the skin, and I swung it back, using all my strength, and the blade chopped into his waist where his clothes took most of the force. He fell over, shouting, and his two friends dragged me away as Rorik went to untie his sister.

That was all that happened. Sven was bleeding, but he managed to pull up his breeches and his friends helped him away and Rorik and I took Thyra back to the homestead where Ravn heard Thyra's sobs and our excited voices and demanded silence. "Uhtred," the old man said sternly, "you will wait by the pigsties. Rorik, you will tell me what happened."

I waited outside as Rorik told what had happened, then Rorik was sent out and I was summoned indoors to recount the afternoon's escapade. Thyra was now in her mother's arms, and her mother and grandmother were furious. "You tell the same tale as Rorik," Ravn said when I had finished.

"Because it's the truth," I said.

"So it would seem."

"He raped her!" Sigrid insisted.

"No," Ravn said firmly, "thanks to Uhtred, he did not."

That was the story Ragnar heard when he returned from hunting, and as it made me a hero I did not argue against its essential untruth, which was that Sven would not have raped Thyra for he would not have dared. His foolishness knew few limits, but limits there were, and committing rape on the daughter of Earl Ragnar, his father's warlord, was beyond even Sven's stupidity. Yet he had made an enemy and, next day, Ragnar led six men to Kjartan's house in the neighboring valley. Rorik and I were given horses and told to accompany the men, and I confess I was frightened. I felt I was responsible. I had, after all, started the games in the high woods, but Ragnar did not see it that way. "You haven't offended me. Sven has." He spoke darkly, his usual cheer-fulness gone. "You did well, Uhtred. You behaved like a Dane." There was no higher praise he could have given me, and I sensed he was disappointed that I had charged Sven instead of Rorik, but I was older and much stronger than Ragnar's younger son so it should have been me who fought.

We rode through the cold woods and I was cu-rious because two of Ragnar's men carried long branches of hazel that were too spindly to use as weapons, but what they were for I did not like to ask because I was nervous.

Kjartan's homestead was in a fold of the hills beside a stream that ran through pastures where he kept sheep, goats, and cattle, though most had been killed now, and the few remaining animals were cropping the last of the year's grass. It was a sunny day, though cold. Dogs barked as we ap-proached, but Kjartan and his men snarled at them and beat them back to the yard beside the house where he had planted an ash tree that did not look as though it would survive the coming winter, and then, accompanied by four men, none of them armed, he walked toward the ap-proaching horsemen. Ragnar and his six men were armed to the hilt with shields, swords, and war axes, and their broad chests were clad in mail, while Ragnar was wearing my father's helmet that he had purchased after the fighting at Eoferwic. It was a splendid helmet, its crown and face piece decorated with silver, and I thought it looked better on Ragnar than it had on my father.

Kjartan the shipmaster was a big man, taller than Ragnar, with a flat, wide face like his son's and small, suspicious eyes and a huge beard. He glanced at the hazel branches and must have recognized their meaning for he instinctively touched the hammer charm hanging on a silver chain about his neck. Ragnar curbed his horse and, in a gesture that showed his utter contempt, he tossed down the sword that I had carried back from the clearing where Sven had tied Thyra. By rights the sword belonged to Ragnar now, and it was a valuable weapon with silver wire wrapped around its hilt, but he tossed the blade at Kjartan's feet as though it were nothing more than a hay knife. "Your son left that on my land," he said, "and I would have words with him."

"My son is a good boy," Kjartan said stoutly, "and in time he will serve at your oars and fight in your shield wall."

"He has offended me."

"He meant no harm, lord."

"He has offended me," Ragnar repeated harshly. "He looked on my daughter's nakedness and showed her his own."

"And he was punished for it," Kjartan said, giving me a malevolent glance. "Blood was shed."

Ragnar made an abrupt gesture and the hazel branches were dropped to the ground. That was evidently Ragnar's answer, which made no sense to me, but Kjartan understood, as did Rorik who leaned over and whispered to me, "That means he must fight for Sven now."

"Fight for him?"

"They mark a square on the ground with the branches and they fight inside the square."

Yet no one moved to arrange the hazel branches into a square. Instead Kjartan walked back to his house and summoned Sven who came limping from under the low lintel, his right leg bandaged. He looked sullen and terrified, and no wonder, for Ragnar and his horsemen were in their war glory, shining warriors, sword Danes.

"Say what you have to say," Kjartan said to his son.

Sven looked up at Ragnar. "I am sorry," he mumbled.

"I can't hear you," Ragnar snarled.

"I am sorry, lord," Sven said, shaking with fear.

"Sorry for what?" Ragnar demanded.

"For what I did."

"And what did you do?"

Sven found no answer, or none that he cared to make, and instead he shuffled his feet and looked down at the ground. Cloud shadows raced across the far moor, and two ravens beat up to the head of the valley.

"You laid hands on my daughter," Ragnar said, "and you tied her to a tree, and you stripped her naked."

"Half naked," Sven muttered, and for his pains took a thump on the head from his father.

"A game," Kjartan appealed to Ragnar, "just a game, lord."

"No boy plays such games with my daughter," Ragnar said. I had rarely seen him angry, but he was angry now, grim and hard, no trace of the bighearted man who could make a hall echo with laughter. He dismounted and drew his sword, his battle blade called Heart-Breaker, and he held the tip toward Kjartan. "Well?" he asked. "Do you dispute my right?"

"No, lord," Kjartan said, "but he is a good

boy, strong and a hard worker, and he will serve you well."

"And he has seen things he should not see," Ragnar said, and he tossed Heart-Breaker into the air so that her long blade turned in the sun and he caught her by the hilt as she dropped, but now he was holding her backward, as if she were a dagger rather than a sword. "Uhtred!" Ragnar called, making me jump. "He says she was only half naked. Is that true?"

"Yes, lord."

"Then only half a punishment," Ragnar said, and he drove the sword forward, hilt first, straight into Sven's face. The hilts of our swords are heavy, sometimes decorated with precious things, but however pretty they appear, the hilts are still brutal lumps of metal, and Heart-Breaker's hilt, banded with silver, crushed Sven's right eye. Crushed it to jelly, blinding it instantly, and Ragnar spat at him then slid his blade back into its fleece-lined scabbard.

Sven was crouching, whimpering, his hands clasped over his ruined eye.

"It is over," Ragnar said to Kjartan.

Kjartan hesitated. He was angry, shamed, and unhappy, but he could not win a trial of strength with Earl Ragnar and so, at last, he nodded. "It is over," he agreed.

"And you no longer serve me," Ragnar said coldly.

We rode home.

The hard winter came, the brooks froze, snow drifted to fill the streambeds, and the world was cold, silent, and white. Wolves came to the edge of the woods and the midday sun was pale, as though its strength had been leeched away by the north wind.

Ragnar rewarded me with a silver arm ring, the first I ever received, while Kjartan was sent away with his family. He would no longer command one of Ragnar's ships and he would no longer receive a share of Ragnar's generosity, for now he was a man without a lord and he went to Eoferwic where he joined the garrison holding the town. It was not a prestigious job, any Dane with ambition would rather serve a lord like Ragnar who could make him rich, while the men guarding Eoferwic were denied any chance of plunder. Their task was to watch across the flat fields outside the city and to make certain that King Egbert fomented no trouble, but I was relieved that Sven was gone, and absurdly pleased with my arm ring. The Danes loved arm rings. The more a man possessed, the more he was regarded, for the rings came from success. Ragnar had rings of silver and rings of gold, rings carved as dragons and rings inlaid with glittering stones. When he moved you could hear the rings clinking. The rings could be used as money if there were no coins. I remember watching a Dane take off an arm ring and hack it to shreds with an ax, then offer a merchant scraps of the ring until the scales showed he had paid sufficient silver. That was down in the bigger valley, in a large village where most of Ragnar's younger men had settled and where traders brought goods from Eoferwic. The incoming Danes had found a small English settlement in the valley, but they needed more space for new houses and to make it they had burned down a grove of hazels, and that was what Ragnar called the place, Synningthwait, which meant the place cleared by fire. Doubtless the village had an English name, but it was already being forgotten.

"We're in England to stay now," Ragnar told me as we went home one day after buying supplies in Synningthwait. The road was a track pounded in the snow and our horses picked a careful path between the drifts through which the black twigs of the hedge tops just showed. I was leading the two pack horses laden with their precious bags of salt and asking Ragnar my usual questions; where swallows went in winter, why elves gave us hiccups, and why Ivar was called the Boneless. "Because he's so thin, of course," Ragnar said, "so that he looks as if you could roll him up like a cloak."

"Why doesn't Ubba have a nickname?"

"He does. He's called Ubba the Horrible." He laughed, because he had made the nickname up, and I laughed because I was happy. Ragnar liked my company and, with my long fair hair, men mistook me for his son and I liked that. Rorik should have been with us, but he was sick that day, and the women were plucking herbs and chanting spells. "He's often sick," Ragnar said, "not like Ragnar"; he meant his eldest son who helped hold on to Ivar's lands in Ireland. "Ragnar's built like an ox," he went on, "never gets sick! He's like you, Uhtred." He smiled, thinking of his eldest son, whom he missed. "He'll take land and thrive. But Rorik? Perhaps I shall have to give him this land. He can't go back to Denmark."

"Why not?"

"Denmark is bad land," Ragnar explained. "It's either flat and sandy and you can't grow a fart on that sort of field, or across the water it's great steep hills with little patches of meadow where you work like a dog and starve."

"Across the water?" I asked, and he explained that the Danes came from a country that was divided into two parts, and the two parts were surrounded by countless islands, and that the nearer part, from where he came, was very flat and very sandy, and that the other part, which lay to the east across a great sound of water, was where the mountains were. "And there are Svear there, too," he went on.

"Svear?"

"A tribe. Like us. They worship Thor and Odin, but they speak differently." He shrugged. "We get along with the Svear, and with the Norse." The Svear, the Norse, and the Danes were the Northmen, the men who went on Viking expeditions, but it was the Danes who had come to take my land, though I did not say that to Ragnar. I had learned to hide my soul, or perhaps I was confused. Northumbrian or Dane? Which was I? What did I want to be?

"Suppose," I asked, "that the rest of the English do not want us to stay here." I used the word **us** deliberately.

He laughed at that. "The English can want what they like! But you saw what happened at Yorvik." That was how the Danes pronounced Eoferwic. For some reason they found that name difficult, so they said Yorvik instead. "Who was the bravest English fighter at Yorvik?" Ragnar asked. "You! A child! You charged me with that little saxe! It was a gutting knife, not a sword, and you tried to kill me! I almost died laughing." He leaned over and cuffed me affectionately. "Of course the English don't want us here," he went on, "but what can they do? Next year we'll take Mercia, then East Anglia, and finally Wessex."

"My father always said Wessex was the strongest kingdom," I said. My father had said nothing of the sort. Indeed he despised the men of Wessex because he thought them effete and overpious, but I was trying to provoke Ragnar.

I failed. "It's the richest kingdom," he said, "but that doesn't make it strong. Men make a kingdom strong, not gold." He grinned at me. "We're the Danes. We don't lose, we win, and Wessex will fall."

"It will?"

"It has a new weak king," he said dismissively, "and if he dies, then his son is a mere child, so perhaps they'd put the new king's brother on the throne instead. We'd like that."

"Why?"

"Because the brother is another weakling. He's called Alfred."

Alfred. That was the first time I ever heard of Alfred of Wessex. I thought nothing of it at the time. Why should I have?

"Alfred," Ragnar continued scathingly. "All he cares about is rutting girls, which is good! Don't tell Sigrid I said that, but there's nothing wrong with unsheathing the sword when you can, but Alfred spends half his time rutting and the other half praying to his god to forgive him for rutting. How can a god disapprove of a good hump?"

"How do you know about Alfred?" I asked.

"Spies, Uhtred, spies. Traders, mostly. They talk to folk in Wessex, so we know all about King Æthelred and his brother Alfred. And Alfred's sick as a stoat half the time." He paused, perhaps thinking of his younger son who was ill. "It's a weak house," he went on, "and the West Saxons should get rid of them and put a real man on the throne, except they won't, and when Wessex falls there will be no more England."

"Perhaps they'll find their strong king," I said.

"No," Ragnar said firmly. "In Denmark," he went on, "our kings are the hard men, and if their sons are soft, then a man from another family becomes king, but in England they believe the throne passes through a woman's legs. So a feeble creature like Alfred could become king just because his father was a king."

"You have a king in Denmark?"

"A dozen. I could call myself king if I fancied, except Ivar and Ubba might not like it, and no man offends them lightly."

I rode in silence, listening to the horses' hooves crunching and squeaking in the snow. I was thinking of Ragnar's dream, the dream of no more England, of her land given to the Danes. "What happens to me?" I finally blurted out.

"You?" He sounded surprised that I had asked. "What happens to you, Uhtred, is what you make happen. You will grow, you will learn the sword, you will learn the way of the shield wall, you will learn the oar, you will learn to give honor to the gods, and then you will use what you have learned to make your life good or bad."

"I want Bebbanburg," I said.

"Then you must take it. Perhaps I will help you, but not yet. Before that we go south, and before we go south we must persuade Odin to look on us with favor."

I still did not understand the Danish way of religion. They took it much less seriously than we English, but the women prayed often enough and once in a while a man would kill a good beast, dedicate it to the gods, and mount its bloody head above his door to show that there would be a feast in Thor or Odin's honor in his house, but the feast, though it was an act of worship, was always the same as any other drunken feast.

I remember the Yule feast best because that was the week Weland came. He arrived on the coldest day of the winter when the snow was heaped in drifts, and he came on foot with a sword by his side, a bow on his shoulder, and rags on his back and he knelt respectfully outside Ragnar's house. Sigrid made him come inside and she fed him and gave him ale, but when he had eaten he insisted on going back into the snow and waiting for Ragnar who was up in the hills, hunting.

Weland was a snakelike man, that was my very first thought on seeing him. He reminded me of my uncle Ælfric, slender, sly, and secretive, and I disliked him on sight and I felt a flicker of fear as I watched him prostrate himself in the snow when Ragnar returned. "My name is Weland," he said, "and I am in need of a lord."

"You are not a youth," Ragnar said, "so why do you not have a lord?"

"He died, lord, when his ship sank."

"Who was he?"

"Snorri, lord."

"Which Snorri?"

"Son of Eric, son of Grimm, from Birka."

"And you did not drown?" Ragnar asked as he dismounted and gave me the reins of his horse.

"I was ashore, lord. I was sick."

"Your family? Your home?"

"I am son of Godfred, lord, from Haithabu."

"Haithabu!" Ragnar said sourly. "A trader?"

"I am a warrior, lord."

"So why come to me?"

Weland shrugged. "Men say you are a good lord, a ring-giver, but if you turn me down, lord, I shall try other men."

"And you can use that sword, Weland God-fredson?"

"As a woman can use her tongue, lord."

"You're that good, eh?" Ragnar asked, as ever unable to resist a jest. He gave Weland permission to stay, sending him to Synningthwait to find shelter, and afterward, when I said I did not like Weland, Ragnar just shrugged and said the stranger needed kindness. We were sitting in the house, half choking from the smoke that writhed about the rafters. "There is nothing worse, Uhtred," Ragnar said, "than for a man to have no lord. No ring-giver," he added, touching his own arm rings.

"I don't trust him," Sigrid put in from the fire where she was making bannocks on a stone. Rorik, recovering from his sickness, was helping her, while Thyra, as ever, was spinning. "I think he's an outlaw," Sigrid said.

"He probably is," Ragnar allowed, "but my ship doesn't care if its oars are pulled by outlaws." He reached for a bannock and had his hand slapped away by Sigrid who said the cakes were for Yule.

The Yule feast was the biggest celebration of the year, a whole week of food and ale and mead and fights and laughter and drunken men vomiting in the snow. Ragnar's men gathered at Synningthwait and there were horse races, wrestling matches, competitions in throwing spears, axes, and rocks, and, my favorite, the tug-of-war where two teams of men or boys tried to pull the other into a cold stream. I saw Weland watching me as I wrestled with a boy a year older than me. Weland already looked more prosperous. His rags were gone and he wore a cloak of fox fur. I got drunk that Yule for the first time, helplessly drunk so that my legs would not work, and I lay moaning with a throbbing head and Ragnar roared with laughter and made me drink more mead until I threw up. Ragnar, of course, won the drinking competition, and Ravn recited a long poem about some ancient hero who killed a monster and then the monster's mother who was even more fearsome than her son, but I was too drunk to remember much of it.

And after the Yule feast I discovered something new about the Danes and their gods, for Ragnar had ordered a great pit dug in the woods above his house, and Rorik and I helped make the pit in a clearing. We axed through tree roots, shoveled out earth, and still Ragnar wanted it deeper, and he was only satisfied when he could stand in the base of the pit and not see across its lip. A ramp led down into the hole, beside which was a great heap of excavated soil.

The next night all Ragnar's men, but no women, walked to the pit in the darkness. We boys carried pitch-soaked torches that flamed under the trees, casting flickering shadows that melted into the surrounding darkness. The men were all dressed and armed as though they were going to war.

Blind Ravn waited at the pit, standing at the far side from the ramp, and he chanted a great epic in praise of Odin. On and on it went, the words as hard and rhythmic as a drum beat, describing how the great god had made the world from the corpse of the giant Ymir, and how he had hurled the sun and moon into the sky, and how his spear, Gungnir, was the mightiest weapon in creation, forged by dwarves in the world's deeps, and on the poem went and the men gathered around the pit seemed to sway to the poem's pulse, sometimes repeating a phrase, and I confess I was almost as bored as when Beocca used to drone on in his stammering Latin, and I stared out into the woods, watching the shadows, wondering what things moved in the dark and thinking of the sceadugengan.

I often thought of the sceadugengan, the shadow-walkers. Ealdwulf, Bebbanburg's blacksmith, had first told me of them. He had warned me not to tell Beocca of the stories, and I never did, and Ealdwulf told me how, before Christ came to England, back when we English had worshipped Odin and the other gods, it had been well known that there were shadow-walkers who moved silent and half-seen across the land, mysterious creatures who could change their shapes. One moment they were wolves, then they were men, or perhaps eagles, and they were neither alive nor dead, but things from the shadow world, night beasts, and I stared into the dark trees and I wanted there to be sceadugengan out there in the dark, something that would be my secret, something that would frighten the Danes, something to give Bebbanburg back to me, something as powerful as the magic that brought the Danes victory.

It was a child's dream, of course. When you are young and powerless you dream of possessing mystical strength, and once you are grown and strong you condemn lesser folk to that same dream, but as a child I wanted the power of the sceadugengan. I remember my excitement that night at the notion of harnessing the power of the shadow-walkers before a whinny brought my attention back to the pit and I saw that the men at the ramp had divided, and that a strange procession was coming from the dark. There was a stallion, a ram, a dog, a goose, a bull, and a boar, each animal led by one of Ragnar's warriors, and at the back was an English prisoner, a man condemned for moving a field marker, and he, like the beasts, had a rope about his neck.

I knew the stallion. It was Ragnar's finest, a great black horse called Flame-Stepper, a horse Ragnar loved. Yet Flame-Stepper, like all the other beasts, was to be given to Odin that night. Ragnar did it. Stripped to his waist, his scarred chest broad in the flamelight, he used a war ax to kill the beasts one by one, and Flame-Stepper was the last animal to die and the great horse's eyes were white as it was forced down the ramp. It struggled, terrified by the stench of blood that had splashed the sides of the pit, and Ragnar went to the horse and there were tears on his face as he kissed Flame-Stepper's muzzle, and then he killed him, one blow between the eyes, straight and true, so that the stallion fell, hooves thrashing, but dead within a heartbeat. The man died last, and that was not so distressing as the horse's death, and then Ragnar stood in the mess of blood-matted fur and raised his gore-smothered ax to the sky. "Odin!" he shouted.

"Odin!" Every man echoed the shout, and they held their swords or spears or axes toward the steaming pit. "Odin!" they shouted again, and I saw Weland the snake staring at me across the firelit slaughter hole.

All the corpses were taken from the pit and hung from tree branches. Their blood had been given to the creatures beneath the earth and now their flesh was given to the gods above, and then we filled in the pit, we danced on it to stamp down the earth, and the jars of ale and skins of mead were handed around and we drank beneath the hanging corpses. Odin, the terrible god, had been summoned because Ragnar and his people were going to war.

I thought of the blades held over the pit of blood, I thought of the god stirring in his corpse hall to send a blessing on these men, and I knew that all England would fall unless it found a magic as strong as the sorcery of these strong men. I was only ten years old, but on that night I knew what I would become.

I would join the sceadugengan. I would be a shadow-walker.

TWO

Springtime, the year 868, I was eleven years old and the **Wind-Viper** was afloat.

She was afloat, but not at sea. The **Wind-Viper** was Ragnar's ship, a lovely thing with a hull of oak, a carved serpent's head at the prow, an eagle's head at the stern, and a triangular wind vane made of bronze on which a raven was painted black. The wind vane was mounted at her masthead, though the mast was now lowered and being supported by two timber crutches so that it ran like a rafter down the center of the long ship. Ragnar's men were rowing and their painted shields lined the ship's sides. They chanted as they rowed, pounding out the tale of how mighty Thor had fished for the dread Midgard Serpent that lies coiled about the roots of the world, and how the serpent had taken the hook baited with an ox's head, and how the giant Hymir, terrified of the vast snake, had cut the line. It is a good tale and its rhythms took us up the river Trente, which is a tributary of the Humber and flows from deep inside Mercia. We were going south, against the current, but the journey was easy, the ride placid, the sun warm, and the river's margins thick with flowers. Some men rode horses, keeping pace with us on the eastern bank, while behind us was a fleet of beast-prowed ships. This was the army of Ivar the Boneless and Ubba the Horrible, a host of Northmen, sword Danes, going to war.

All eastern Northumbria belonged to them, western Northumbria offered grudging allegiance, and now they planned to take Mercia, which was the kingdom at England's heartland. The Mercian territory stretched south to the river Temse where the lands of Wessex began, west to the mountainous country where the Welsh tribes lived, and east to the farms and marshes of East Anglia. Mercia, though not as wealthy as Wessex, was much richer than Northumbria, and the river Trente ran into the kingdom's heart and the **Wind-Viper** was the tip of a Danish spear aimed at that heart.

The river was not deep, but Ragnar boasted

that the **Wind-Viper** could float on a puddle, and that was almost true. From a distance she looked long, lean, and knifelike, but when you were aboard you could see how the midships flared outward so that she sat on the water like a shallow bowl rather than cut through it like a blade, and even with her belly laden with forty or fifty men, their weapons, shields, food, and ale, she needed very little depth. Once in a while her long keel would scrape on gravel, but by keeping to the outside of the river's sweeping bends we were able to stay in sufficient water. That was why the mast had been lowered, so that, on the outside of the river's curves, we could slide under the overhanging trees without becoming entangled.

Rorik and I sat in the prow with his grandfather, Ravn, and our job was to tell the old man everything we could see, which was very little other than flowers, trees, reeds, waterfowl, and the signs of trout rising to mayfly. Swallows had come from their winter sleep and swooped across the river while martins pecked at the banks to collect mud for their nests. Warblers were loud, pigeons clattered through new leaves, and the hawks slid still and menacing across the scattered clouds. Swans watched us pass and once in a while we would see otter cubs playing beneath the pale-leaved willows and there would be a flurry of water as they fled from our coming. Sometimes we passed a riverside settlement of thatch and timber, but the folks and their live-stock had already run away.

"Mercia is frightened of us," Ravn said. He lifted his white, blind eyes to the oncoming air, "and they are right to be frightened. We are warriors."

"They have warriors, too," I said.

Ravn laughed. "I think only one man in three is a warrior, and sometimes not even that many, but in our army, Uhtred, every man is a fighter. If you do not want to be a warrior you stay home in Denmark. You till the soil, herd sheep, fish the sea, but you do not take to the ships and become a fighter. But here in England? Every man is forced to the fight, yet only one in three or maybe only one in four has the belly for it. The rest are farmers who just want to run. We are wolves fighting sheep."

Watch and learn, my father had said, and I was learning. What else can a boy with an unbroken voice do? One in three men are warriors, remember the shadow-walkers, beware the cut beneath the shield, a river can be an army's road to a kingdom's heart, watch and learn.

"And they have a weak king," Ravn went on. "Burghred, he's called, and he has no guts for a fight. He will fight, of course, because we shall force him, and he will call on his friends in Wessex to help him, but in his weak heart he knows he cannot win."

"How do you know?" Rorik asked.

Ravn smiled. "All winter, boy, our traders have been in Mercia. Selling pelts, selling amber, buying iron ore, buying malt, and they talk and they listen and they come back and they tell us what they heard."

Kill the traders, I thought.

Why did I think that way? I liked Ragnar. I liked him much more than I had liked my father. I should, by rights, be dead, yet Ragnar had saved me and Ragnar spoiled me and he treated me like a son, and he called me a Dane, and I liked the Danes, yet even at that time I knew I was not a Dane. I was Uhtred of Bebbanburg and I clung to the memory of the fortress by the sea, of the birds crying over the breakers, of the puffins whirring across the whitecaps, of the seals on the rocks, of the white water shattering on the cliffs. I remembered the folk of that land, the men who had called my father "lord," but talked to him of cousins they held in common. It was the gossip of neighbors, the comfort of knowing every family within a half day's ride, and that was, and is, Bebbanburg to me: home. Ragnar would have given me the fortress if it could be taken, but then it would belong to the Danes and I would be nothing more than their hired man, ealdorman at their pleasure, no better than King Edgar who was no king but a pampered dog on a short rope, and what the Dane gives, the Dane can take away, and I would hold Bebbanburg by my own effort.

Did I know all that at eleven? Some, I think. It lay in my heart, unformed, unspoken, but hard as a stone. It would be covered over in time, half forgotten and often contradicted, but it was always there. Destiny is all, Ravn liked to tell me, destiny is everything. He would even say it in English, **"Wyrd bið ful āræd."**

"What are you thinking?" Rorik asked me.

"That it would be nice to swim," I said.

The oars dipped and the **Wind-Viper** glided on into Mercia.

Next day a small force waited in our path. The Mercians had blocked the river with felled trees, which did not quite bar the way but would certainly make it hard for our oarsmen to make progress through the small gap between the tangling branches. There were about a hundred Mercians and they had a score of bowmen and spear-throwers waiting by the blockage, ready to pick off our rowers, while the rest of their men were formed into a shield wall on the eastern bank. Ragnar laughed when he saw them. That was something else I learned, the joy with which the Danes faced battle. Ragnar was whooping with joy as he leaned on the steering oar and ran the ship into the bank, and the ships behind were also grounding themselves while the horsemen who had been keeping pace with us dismounted for battle.

I watched from the **Wind-Viper**'s prow as the ships' crews hurried ashore and pulled on leather or mail. What did those Mercians see? They saw young men with wild hair, wild beards, and hungry faces, men who embraced battle like a lover. If the Danes could not fight an enemy they fought among themselves. Most had nothing but monstrous pride, battle scars, and well-sharpened weapons, and with those things they would take whatever they wanted, and that Mercian shield wall did not even stay to contest the fight, but once they saw they would be outnumbered they ran away to the mocking howls of Ragnar's men who then stripped off their mail and leather and used their axes and the **Wind-Viper**'s hide-twisted ropes to clear away the fallen trees. It took a few hours to unblock the river, but then we were moving again. That night the ships clustered together on the riverbank, fires were lit ashore, men were posted as sentries, and every sleeping warrior kept his weapons beside him, but no one troubled us and at dawn we moved on, soon coming to a town with thick earthen walls and a high palisade. This, Ragnar assumed, was the place the Mercians had failed to defend, but there seemed to be no sign of any soldiers on the wall so he ran the boat ashore again and led his crew toward the town.

The earth walls and timber palisade were both in good condition, and Ragnar marveled that the town's garrison had chosen to march downriver to fight us, rather than stay behind their well-tended defenses. The Mercian soldiers were plainly gone now, probably fled south, for the gates were open and a dozen townsfolk were kneeling outside the wooden arch and holding out supplicant hands for mercy. Three of the terrified people were monks, their tonsured heads bowed. "I hate monks," Ragnar said cheerfully. His sword, Heart-Breaker, was in his hand and he swept her naked blade in a hissing arc.

"Why?" I asked.

"Monks are like ants," he said, "wriggling about in black, being useless. I hate them. You'll speak for me, Uhtred. Ask them what place this is?"

I asked and learned that the town was called Gegnesburh.

"Tell them," Ragnar instructed me, "that my name is Earl Ragnar, I am called the Fearless, and that I eat children when I'm not given food and silver."

I duly told them. The kneeling men looked up at Ragnar who had unbound his hair, which, had they known, was always a sign that he was in a mood for killing. His grinning men made a line behind him, a line heavy with axes, swords, spears, shields, and war hammers.

"What food there is," I translated a gray-bearded man's answer, "is yours. But he says there is not much food."

Ragnar smiled at that, stepped forward, and, still smiling, swung Heart-Breaker so that her blade half severed the man's head. I jumped back, not in alarm, but because I did not want my tunic spattered with his blood. "One less mouth to feed," Ragnar said cheerfully. "Now ask the others how much food there is."

The gray-bearded man was now red bearded and he was choking and twitching as he died. His struggles slowly ended and then he just lay, dying, his eyes gazing reprovingly into mine. None of his companions tried to help him; they were too frightened. "How much food do you have?" I demanded.

"There is food, lord," one of the monks said.

"How much?" I demanded again.

"Enough."

"He says there's enough," I told Ragnar.

"A sword," Ragnar said, "is a great tool for discovering the truth. What about the monk's church? How much silver does it have?"

The monk gabbled that we could look for ourselves, that we could take whatever we found, that it was all ours, anything we found was ours, all was ours. I translated these panicked statements and Ragnar again smiled. "He's not telling the truth, is he?"

"Isn't he?" I asked.

"He wants me to look because he knows I

won't find, and that means they've hidden their treasure or had it taken away. Ask him if they've hidden their silver."

I did and the monk reddened. "We are a poor church," he said, "with little treasure," and he stared wide-eyed as I translated his answer. Then he tried to get up and run as Ragnar stepped forward, but he tripped over his robe and Heart-Breaker pierced his spine so that he jerked like a landed fish as he died.

There was silver, of course, and it was buried. Another of the monks told us so, and Ragnar sighed as he cleaned his sword on the dead monk's robe. "They're such fools," he said plaintively. "They'd live if they answered truthfully the first time."

"But suppose there wasn't any treasure?" I asked him.

"Then they'd tell the truth and die," Ragnar said, and found that funny. "But what's the point of a monk except to hoard treasure for us Danes? They're ants who hoard silver. Find the ants' nest, dig, and a man's rich." He stepped over his victims. At first I was shocked by the ease with which he would kill a defenseless man, but Ragnar had no respect for folk who cringed and lied. He appreciated an enemy who fought, who showed spirit, but men who were weakly sly like the ones he killed at Gegnesburh's gate were beneath his contempt, no better than animals.

We emptied Gegnesburh of food, then made the monks dig up their treasure. It was not much: two silver mass cups, three silver plates, a bronze crucifix with a silver Christ, a bone carving of angels climbing a ladder, and a bag of silver pennies. Ragnar distributed the coins among his men, then hacked the silver plates and cups to pieces with an ax and shared out the scraps. He had no use for the bone carving so shattered it with his sword. "A weird religion," he said. "They worship just one god?"

"One god," I said, "but he's divided into three."

He liked that. "A clever trick," he said, "but not useful. This triple god has a mother, doesn't he?"

"Mary," I said, following him as he explored the monastery in search of more plunder.

"I wonder if her baby came out in three bits," he said. "So what's this god's name?"

"Don't know." I knew he had a name because Beocca had told me, but I could not remember it. "The three together are the trinity," I went on, "but that's not god's name. Usually they just call him god."

"Like giving a dog the name dog," Ragnar declared, then laughed. "So who's Jesus?"

"One of the three."

"The one who died, yes? And he came back to life?"

"Yes," I said, suddenly fearful that the Christian god was watching me, readying a dreadful punishment for my sins.

"Gods can do that," Ragnar said airily. "They die, come back to life. They're gods." He looked at me, sensing my fear, and ruffled my hair. "Don't you worry, Uhtred, the Christian god doesn't have power here."

"He doesn't?"

"Of course not!" He was searching a shed at the back of the monastery and found a decent sickle that he tucked into his belt. "Gods fight each other! Everyone knows that. Look at our gods! The Aesir and Vanir fought like cats before they made friends." The Aesir and the Vanir were the two families of Danish gods who now shared Asgard, though at one time they had been the bitterest of enemies. "Gods fight," Ragnar went on earnestly, "and some win, some lose. The Christian god is losing. Otherwise why would we be here? Why would we be winning? The gods reward us if we give them respect, but the Christian god doesn't help his people, does he? They weep rivers of tears for him, they pray to him, they give him their silver, and we come along and slaughter them! Their god is pathetic. If he had any real power then we wouldn't be here, would we?"

It seemed an unassailable logic to me. What was the point of worshipping a god if he did not help you? And it was incontrovertible that the worshippers of Odin and Thor were winning, and I surreptitiously touched the hammer of Thor hanging from my neck as we returned to the **Wind-Viper.** We left Gegnesburh ravaged, its folk weeping and its storehouses emptied, and we rowed on down the wide river, the belly of our boat piled with grain, bread, salted meat, and smoked fish. Later, much later, I learned that Ælswith, King Alfred's wife, had come from Gegnesburh. Her father, the man who had failed to fight us, was ealdorman there and she had grown up in the town and always lamented that, after she had left, the Danes had sacked the place. God, she always declared, would have his revenge on the pagans who had ravaged her hometown, and it seemed wise not to tell her that I had been one of the ravagers.

We ended the voyage at a town called Snotengaham, which means the Home of Snot's people, and it was a much greater place than Gegnes-burh, but its garrison had fled and those people who remained welcomed the Danes with piles of food and heaps of silver. There would have been time for a horseman to reach Snotengaham with news of Gegnesburh's dead, and the Danes were always happy for such messengers to spread fear of their coming, and so the larger town, with its walls, fell without a fight.

Some ships' crews were ordered to man the walls, while others raided the countryside. The first thing they sought was more horses, and when the war bands were mounted they ranged farther afield, stealing, burning, and harrowing the land. "We shall stay here," Ragnar told me.

"All summer?"

"Till the world ends, Uhtred. This is Danish land now." At winter's end Ivar and Ubba had sent three ships back to the Danish homeland to encourage more settlers, and those new ships began arriving in ones and twos, bringing men, women, and children. The newcomers were allowed to take whatever houses they wished, except for those few that belonged to the Mercian leaders who had bent the knee to Ivar and Ubba. One of those was the bishop, a young man called Æthelbrid, who preached to his congregations that God had sent the Danes. He never said why God had done this, and perhaps he did not know, but the sermons meant that his wife and children lived and his house was safe and his church was allowed to retain one silver mass cup, though Ivar insisted that the bishop's twin sons be held as hostages in case the Christian god changed his mind about the Danes.

Ragnar, like the other Danish leaders, constantly rode out into the country to bring back food and he liked me to go with him, for I could translate for him, and as the days passed we heard more and more stories of a great Mercian army gathering to the south, at Ledecestre, which Ragnar said was the greatest fortress in Mercia. It had been made by the Romans, who built better than any man could build now, and Burghred, Mercia's king, was assembling his forces there, and that was why Ragnar was so intent on gathering food. "They'll besiege us," he said, "but we'll win and then Ledecestre will be ours and so will Mercia." He spoke very calmly, as though there could be no possibility of defeat.

Rorik stayed in the town while I rode with his father. That was because Rorik was sick again, struck by cramping pains in his belly so severe that he was sometimes reduced to helpless tears.

He vomited in the night, was pale, and the only relief came from a brew of herbs made for him by an old woman who was a servant of the bishop. Ragnar worried about Rorik, yet he was pleased that his son and I were such good friends. Rorik did not question his father's fondness for me, nor was he jealous. In time, he knew, Ragnar planned to take me back to Bebbanburg and I would be given my patrimony and he assumed I would stay his friend and so Bebbanburg would become a Danish stronghold. I would be Earl Uhtred and Rorik and his older brother would hold other strongholds, and Ragnar would be a great lord, supported by his sons and by Bebbanburg, and we would all be Danes, and Odin would smile on us, and so the world would go on until the final conflagration when the great gods fought the monsters and the army of the dead would march from Valhalla and the underworld give up its beasts and fire would consume the great tree of life, Yggdrasil. In other words everything would stay the same until it was all no more. That was what Rorik thought, and doubtless Ragnar thought so, too. Destiny, Ravn said, is everything.

News came in the high summer that the Mercian army was marching at last and that King Æthelred of Wessex was bringing his army to support Burghred, and so we were to be faced by two of the three remaining English kingdoms. We stopped our raids into the countryside and readied Snotengaham for the inevitable siege. The palisade on the earth wall was strengthened and the ditch outside the wall was deepened. The ships were drawn up on the town's riverbank far from the walls so they could not be reduced to ash by fire arrows shot from outside the defenses, and the thatch of the buildings closest to the wall was pulled off the houses so that they could not be set ablaze.

Ivar and Ubba had decided to endure a siege because they reckoned we were strong enough to hold what we had taken, but that if we took more territory then the Danish forces would be stretched thin and could be defeated piece by piece. It was better, they reckoned, to let the enemy come and break himself on Snotengaham's defenses.

That enemy came as the poppies bloomed. The Mercian scouts arrived first, small groups of horsemen who circled the town warily, and at midday Burghred's foot soldiers appeared, band after band of men with spears, axes, swords, sickles, and hay knives. They camped well away from the walls, using branches and turf to make a township of crude shelters that sprang up across the low hills and meadows. Snotengaham lay on the north bank of the Trente, which meant the river was between the town and the rest of Mercia, but the enemy army came from the west, having crossed the Trente somewhere to the south of the town. A few of their men stayed on the southern bank to make sure our ships did not cross the river to land men for foraging expeditions, and the presence of those men meant that the enemy surrounded us, but they made no attempt to attack us. The Mercians were waiting for the West Saxons to come and in that first week the only excitement occurred when a handful of Burghred's archers crept toward the town and loosed a few arrows at us and the missiles whacked into the palisade and stuck there, perches for birds, and that was the extent of their belligerence. After that they fortified their camp, surrounding it with a barricade of felled trees and thorn bushes. "They're frightened that we'll make a sally and kill them all," Ragnar said, "so they're going to sit there and try to starve us out."

"Will they?" I asked.

"They couldn't starve a mouse in a pot," Ragnar said cheerfully. He had hung his shield on the outer side of the palisade, one of over twelve hundred bright-painted shields that were displayed there. We did not have twelve hundred men, but nearly all the Danes possessed more than one shield and they hung them all on the wall to make the enemy think our garrison equaled the number of shields. The great lords among the Danes hung their banners on the wall, Ubba's raven flag and Ragnar's eagle wing among them. The raven banner was a triangle of white cloth, fringed with white tassels, showing a black raven with spread wings, while Ragnar's standard was a real eagle's wing, nailed to a pole, and it was becoming so tattered that Ragnar had offered a golden arm ring to any man who could replace it. "If they want us out of here," he went on, "then they'd best make an assault, and they'd best do it in the next three weeks before their men go home and cut their harvest."

But the Mercians, instead of attacking, tried to pray us out of Snotengaham. A dozen priests, all robed and carrying cross-tipped poles, and followed by a score of monks carrying sacred banners on cross-staffs, came out from behind their barricades and paraded just beyond bowshot. The flags showed saints. One of the priests scattered holy water, and the whole group stopped every few yards to pronounce curses on us. That was the day the West Saxon forces arrived to support Burghred whose wife was sister to Alfred and to King Æthelred of Wessex, and that was the first day I ever saw the dragon standard of Wessex. It was a huge banner of heavy green cloth on which a white dragon breathed fire, and the standard-bearer galloped to catch up with the priests and the dragon streamed behind him. "Your turn will come," Ragnar said quietly, talking to the rippling dragon.

"When?"

"The gods only know," Ragnar said, still watching the standard. "This year we should finish off Mercia, then we'll go to East Anglia, and after that, Wessex. To take all the land and treasure in England, Uhtred? Three years? Four? We need more ships though." He meant we needed more ships' crews, more shield Danes, more swords.

"Why not go north?" I asked him.

"To Dalriada and Pictland?" he laughed. "There's nothing up there, Uhtred, except bare rocks, bare fields, and bare arses. The land there is no better than at home." He nodded out toward the enemy encampment. "But this is good land. Rich and deep. You can raise children here. You can grow strong here." He fell silent as a group of horsemen appeared from the enemy camp and followed the rider who carried the dragon standard. Even from a long way off it was possible to see that these were great men for they rode splendid horses and had mail coats glinting beneath their dark red cloaks. "The King of Wessex?" Ragnar guessed.

"Æthelred?"

"It's probably him. We shall find out now."

"Find out what?"

"What these West Saxons are made of. The Mercians won't attack us, so let's see if Æthelred's men are any better. Dawn, Uhtred, that's when they should come. Straight at us, ladders against the wall, lose some men, but let the rest slaughter us." He laughed. "That's what I'd do, but that lot?" He spat in derision.

Ivar and Ubba must have thought the same thing, for they sent two men to spy on the Mercian and West Saxon forces to see if there was any sign that ladders were being made. The two men went out at night and were supposed to skirt the besiegers' encampment and find a place to watch the enemy from outside their fortifications, but somehow they were both seen and caught. The two men were brought to the fields in front of the wall and made to kneel there with their hands tied behind their backs. A tall Englishman stood behind them with a drawn sword and I watched as he poked one of the Danes in the back, as the Dane lifted his head and then as the sword swung. The second Dane died in the same way, and the two bodies were left for the ravens to eat. "Bastards," Ragnar said.

Ivar and Ubba had also watched the executions. I rarely saw the brothers. Ubba stayed in his house much of the time while Ivar, so thin and wraithlike, was more evident, pacing the walls every dawn and dusk, scowling at the enemy and saying little, though now he spoke urgently to Ragnar, gesturing south to the green fields beyond the river. He never seemed to speak without a snarl, but Ragnar was not offended. "He's angry," he told me afterward, "because he needs to know if they plan to assault us. Now he wants some of my men to spy on their camp, but after that?" He nodded at the two headless bodies in the field. "Maybe I'd better go myself."

"They'll be watching for more spies," I said, not wanting Ragnar to end up headless before the walls.

"A leader leads," Ragnar said, "and you can't

ask men to risk death if you're not willing to risk
it yourself."

"Let me go," I said.

He laughed at that. "What kind of leader sends
a boy to do a man's job, eh?"

"I'm English," I said, "and they won't suspect
an English boy."

Ragnar smiled at me. "If you're English," he
said, "then how could we trust you to tell us the
truth of what you see?"

I clutched Thor's hammer. "I will tell the
truth," I said, "I swear it. And I'm a Dane now!
You've told me that! You say I'm a Dane!"

Ragnar began to take me seriously. He knelt to
look into my face. "Are you really a Dane?" he
asked.

"I'm a Dane," I said, and at that moment I
meant it. At other times I was sure I was a
Northumbrian, a secret sceadugengan hidden
among the Danes, and in truth I was confused. I
loved Ragnar as a father, was fond of Ravn, wrestled and raced and played with Rorik when he
was well enough, and all of them treated me as
one of them. I was just from another tribe. There
were three main tribes among the Northmen—
the Danes, the Norse, and the Svear—but

Ragnar said there were others, like the Getes, and he was not sure where the Northmen ended and the others began, but suddenly he was worried about me. "I'm a Dane," I repeated forcibly, "and who better than me to spy on them? I speak their language!"

"You're a boy," Ragnar said, and I thought he was refusing to let me go, but instead he was getting used to the idea. "No one will suspect a boy," he went on. He still stared at me, then stood and glanced again at the two bodies where ravens were pecking at the severed heads. "Are you sure, Uhtred?"

"I'm sure."

"I'll ask the brothers," he said, and he did, and Ivar and Ubba must have agreed for they let me go. It was after dark when the gate was opened and I slipped out. Now, I thought, I am a shadow-walker at last, though in truth the journey needed no supernatural skills for there was a slew of camp fires in the Mercian and West Saxon lines to light the way. Ragnar had advised me to skirt the big encampment and see if there was an easy way in at the back, but instead I walked straight toward the nearest fires that lay behind the felled trees that served as the English protective wall, and beyond that black tangle I could see the dark shapes of sentries outlined by the camp fires. I was nervous. For months I had been treasuring the idea of the sceadugengan, and here I was, out in the dark, and not far away there were headless bodies and my imagination invented a similar fate for myself. Why? One small part of me knew I could walk into the camp and say who I was, then demand to be taken to Burghred or to Æthelred, yet I had spoken the truth to Ragnar. I would go back, and I would tell the truth. I had promised that, and to a boy promises are solemn things, buttressed by the dread of divine revenge. I would choose my own tribe in time, but that time had not yet come, and so I crept across the field feeling very small and vulnerable, my heart thumping against my ribs, and my soul consumed by the importance of what I did.

And halfway to the Mercian camp I felt the hairs on the back of my neck prickle. I had the sensation I was being followed and I twisted, listened, and stared, and saw nothing but the black shapes that shudder in the night, but like a hare I sprinted to one side, dropped suddenly, and listened again, and this time I was sure I heard a footfall in the grass. I waited, watched, saw nothing, and crept on until I reached the Mercian barricade and I waited again there, but heard nothing more behind me and decided I had been imagining things. I had also been worrying that I would not be able to pass the Mercian obstacles, but in the end it was simple enough because a big felled tree left plenty of space for a boy to wriggle through its branches, and I did it slowly, making no noise, then ran on into the camp and was almost immediately challenged by a sentry. "Who are you?" The man snarled and I could see the firelight reflecting from a glittering spear head that was being run toward me.

"Osbert," I said, using my old name.

"A boy?" The man checked, surprised.

"Needed a piss."

"Hell, boy, what's wrong with pissing outside your shelter?"

"My master doesn't like it."

"Who's your master?" The spear had been lifted and the man was peering at me in the small light from the fires.

"Beocca," I said. It was the first name that came to my head.

"The priest?"

That surprised me, and I hesitated, but then nodded and that satisfied the man. "Best get back to him then," he said.

"I'm lost."

"Shouldn't come all this way to piss on my sentry post then, should you?" he said, then pointed. "It's that way, boy."

So I walked openly through the camp, past the fires and past the small shelters where men snored. A couple of dogs barked at me. Horses whinnied. Somewhere a flute sounded and a woman sang softly. Sparks flew up from the dying fires.

The sentry had pointed me toward the West Saxon lines. I knew that because the dragon banner was hung outside a great tent that was lit by a larger fire, and I moved toward that tent for lack of anywhere else to go. I was looking for ladders, but saw none. A child cried in a shelter, a woman moaned, and some men sang near a fire. One of the singers saw me, shouted a challenge, and then realized I was just a boy and waved me away. I was close to the big fire now, the one that lit the front of the bannered tent, and I skirted it, going toward the darkness behind the tent that was lit from within by candles or lanterns. Two men stood guard at the tent's front and voices murmured from inside, but no one noticed me as I slipped through the shadows, still looking for ladders. Ragnar had said the ladders would be stored together, either at the heart of the camp or close to its edge, but I saw none. Instead I heard sobbing.

I had reached the back of the big tent and was hiding beside a great stack of firewood and, judging by the stink, was close to a latrine. I crouched and saw a man kneeling in the open space between the woodpile and the big tent and it was that man who was sobbing. He was also praying and sometimes beating his chest with his fists. I was astonished, even alarmed by what he did, but I lay on my belly like a snake and wriggled in the shadows to get closer to see what else he might do.

He groaned as if in pain, raised his hands to the sky, then bent forward as if worshipping the earth. "Spare me, God," I heard him say, "spare me. I am a sinner." He vomited then, though he did not sound drunk, and after he had spewed up he moaned. I sensed he was a young man. Then a flap of the tent lifted and a wash of candlelight spilled across the grass. I froze, still as a log, and saw that it was indeed a young man who was so miserable, and then also saw, to my astonishment, that the person who had lifted the tent flap was Father Beocca. I had thought it a coincidence that there should be two priests with that name, but it was no coincidence at all. It was indeed red-haired, cross-eyed Beocca and he was here, in Mercia.

"My lord," Beocca said, dropping the flap and casting darkness over the young man.

"I am a sinner, father," the man said. He had stopped sobbing, perhaps because he did not want Beocca to see such evidence of weakness, but his voice was full of sadness. "I am a grievous sinner."

"We are all sinners, my lord."

"A grievous sinner," the young man repeated, ignoring Beocca's solace. "And I am married!"

"Salvation lies in remorse, my lord."

"Then, God knows, I should be redeemed for my remorse would fill the sky." He lifted his head to stare at the stars. "The flesh, father," he groaned, "the flesh."

Beocca walked toward me, stopped, and turned. He was almost close enough for me to touch, but he had no idea I was there. "God sends temptation to test us, my lord," he said quietly.

"He sends women to test us," the young man said harshly, "and we fail, and then he sends the Danes to punish us for our failure."

"His way is hard," Beocca said, "and no one has ever doubted it."

The young man, still kneeling, bowed his head. "I should never have married, father. I should have joined the church. Gone to a monastery."

"And God would have found a great servant in you, my lord, but he had other plans for you. If your brother dies . . ."

"Pray God he does not! What sort of king would I be?"

"God's king, my lord."

So that, I thought, was Alfred. That was the very first time I ever saw him or heard his voice and he never knew. I lay in the grass, listening, as Beocca consoled the prince for yielding to temptation. It seemed Alfred had humped a servant girl and, immediately afterward, had been overcome by physical pain and what he called spiritual torment.

"What you must do, my lord," Beocca said, "is bring the girl into your service."

"No!" Alfred protested.

A harp began to play in the tent and both men checked to listen, then Beocca crouched by the unhappy prince and put a hand on his shoulder. "Bring the girl into your service," Beocca repeated, "and resist her. Lay that tribute before God, let him see your strength, and he will reward you. Thank God for tempting you, lord, and praise him when you resist the temptation."

"God will kill me," Alfred said bitterly. "I swore I wouldn't do it again. Not after Osferth." Osferth? The name meant nothing to me. Later, much later, I discovered Osferth was Alfred's bastard son, whelped on another servant girl. "I prayed to be spared the temptation," Alfred went on, "and to be afflicted with pain as a reminder, and as a distraction, and God in his mercy made me sick, but still I yielded. I am the most miserable of sinners."

"We are all sinners," Beocca said, his good hand still on Alfred's shoulder, "and we are all fallen short of the glory of God."

"None has fallen as far as me," Alfred moaned.

"God sees your remorse," Beocca said, "and he will lift you up. Welcome the temptation, lord," he went on urgently, "welcome it, resist it, and give thanks to God when you succeed. And God will reward you, lord, he will reward you."

"By removing the Danes?" Alfred asked bitterly.

"He will, my lord, he will."

"But not by waiting," Alfred said, and now there was a sudden hardness in his voice that made Beocca draw away from him. Alfred stood, towering over the priest. "We should attack them!"

"Burghred knows his business," Beocca said soothingly, "and so does your brother. The pagans will starve, my lord, if that is God's will."

So I had my answer, and it was that the English were not planning an assault, but rather hoped to starve Snotengaham into surrender. I dared not carry that answer straight back to the town, not while Beocca and Alfred were so close to me, and so I stayed and listened as Beocca prayed with the prince and then, when Alfred was calm, the two moved back to the tent and went inside.

And I went back. It took a long time, but no one saw me. I was a true sceadugengan that night, moving among the shadows like a specter, climbing the hill to the town until I could run the last hundred paces and I called Ragnar's name and the gate creaked open and I was back in Snotengaham.

Ragnar took me to see Ubba when the sun rose and, to my surprise, Weland was there, Weland the snake, and he gave me a sour look, though not so sour as the scowl on Ubba's dark face. "So what did you do?" he growled.

"I saw no ladders . . ." I began.

"What did you do?" Ubba snarled, and so I told my tale from the beginning, how I had crossed the fields and had thought I was being followed, and had dodged like a hare, then gone through the barricade and spoken to the sentry. Ubba stopped me there and looked at Weland. "Well?"

Weland nodded. "I saw him through the barricade, lord, heard him speak to a man."

So Weland had followed me? I looked at Ragnar, who shrugged. "My lord Ubba wanted a second man to go," he explained, "and Weland offered."

Weland gave me a smile, the kind of smile the devil might give a bishop entering hell. "I could not get through the barrier, lord," he told Ubba.

"But you saw the boy go through?"

"And heard him speak to the sentry, lord, though what he said I could not tell."

"Did you see ladders?" Ubba asked Weland.

"No, lord, but I only skirted the fence."

Ubba stared at Weland, making him uncomfortable, then transferred his dark eyes to me and made me uncomfortable. "So you got through the barrier," he said. "So what did you see?" I told him how I had found the large tent, and of the conversation I had overheard, how Alfred had wept because he had sinned, and how he had wanted to attack the town and how the priest had said that God would starve the Danes if that was his will, and Ubba believed me because he reckoned a boy could not make up the story of the servant girl and the prince.

Besides, I was amused, and it showed. Alfred, I thought, was a pious weakling, a weeping penitent, a pathetic nothing, and even Ubba smiled as I described the sobbing prince and the earnest priest. "So," Ubba asked me, "no ladders?"

"I saw none, lord."

He stared at me with that fearsomely bearded face and then, to my astonishment, he took off one of his arm rings and tossed it to me. "You're right," he told Ragnar, "he is a Dane."

"He's a good boy," Ragnar said.

"Sometimes the mongrel you find in the field turns out to be useful," Ubba said, then beckoned to an old man who had been sitting on a stool in the room's corner.

The old man was called Storri and, like Ravn, he was a skald, but also a sorcerer and Ubba would do nothing without his advice, and now, without saying a word, Storri took a sheaf of thin white sticks, each the length of a man's hand, and he held them just above the floor, muttered a prayer to Odin, then let them go. They made a small clattering noise as they fell, and then Storri leaned forward to look at the pattern they made.

They were runesticks. Many Danes consulted the runesticks, but Storri's skill at reading the signs was famous, and Ubba was a man so riddled with superstition that he would do nothing unless he believed the gods were on his side. "Well?" he asked impatiently.

Storri ignored Ubba, instead he stared at the score of sticks, seeing if he could detect a rune letter or a significant pattern in their random scatter. He moved around the small pile, still peering, then nodded slowly. "It could not be better," he said.

"The boy told the truth?'

"The boy told the truth," Storri said, "but the sticks talk of today, not of last night, and they tell me all is well."

"Good." Ubba stood and took his sword from a peg on the wall. "No ladders," he said to Ragnar, "so no assault. We shall go."

They had been worried that the Mercians and West Saxons would launch an attack on the walls while they made a raid across the river. The southern bank was lightly garrisoned by the besiegers, holding little more than a cordon of men to deter forage parties crossing the Trente, but that afternoon Ubba led six ships across the river and attacked those Mercians, and the rune-sticks had not lied for no Danes died and they brought back horses, weapons, armor, and prisoners.

Twenty prisoners.

The Mercians had beheaded two of our men, so now Ubba killed twenty of theirs, and did it in their sight so they could see his revenge. The headless bodies were thrown into the ditch in front of the wall and the twenty heads were stuck on spears and mounted above the northern gate.

"In war," Ragnar told me, "be ruthless."

"Why did you send Weland to follow me?" I asked him, hurt.

"Because Ubba insisted on it," he said.

"Because you didn't trust me?"

"Because Ubba trusts no one except Storri," he said. "And I trust you, Uhtred."

The heads above Snotengaham's gate were pecked by birds till they were nothing but skulls with hanks of hair that stirred in the summer wind. The Mercians and the West Saxons still did not attack. The sun shone. The river rippled prettily past the town where the ships were drawn up on the bank.

Ravn, though he was blind, liked to come to the ramparts where he would demand that I describe all I could see. Nothing changes, I would say, the enemy are still behind their hedge of felled trees, there are clouds above the distant hills, a hawk hunts, the wind ripples the grass, the swifts are gathering in groups, nothing changes, and tell me about the runesticks, I begged him.

"The sticks!" he laughed.

"Do they work?"

He thought about it. "If you can read them, yes. I was good at reading the runes before I lost my eyes."

"So they do work," I said eagerly.

Ravn gestured toward the landscape he could not see. "Out there, Uhtred," he said, "there are a dozen signs from the gods, and if you know the signs then you know what the gods want. The runesticks give the same message, but I have noticed one thing." He paused and I had to prompt him, and he sighed as though he knew he should not say more. But he did. "The signs are best read by a clever man," he went on, "and Storri is clever. I dare say I am no fool."

I did not really understand what he was saying. "But Storri is always right?"

"Storri is cautious. He won't take risks, and Ubba, though he doesn't know it, likes that."

"But the sticks are messages from the gods?"

"The wind is a message from the gods," Ravn said, "as is the flight of a bird, the fall of a feather, the rise of a fish, the shape of a cloud, the cry of a vixen, all are messages, but in the end, Uhtred, the gods speak in only one place." He tapped my head. "There."

I still did not understand and was obscurely disappointed. "Could I read the sticks?"

"Of course," he said, "but it would be sensible to wait till you're older. What are you now?"

"Eleven," I said, tempted to say twelve.

"Maybe you'd best wait a year or two before reading the sticks. Wait till you're old enough to marry, four or five years from now?"

That seemed an unlikely proposition for I had no interest in marriage back then. I was not even interested in girls, though that would change soon enough.

"Thyra, perhaps?" Ravn suggested.

"Thyra!" I thought of Ragnar's daughter as a playmate, not as a wife. Indeed, the very idea of it made me laugh.

Ravn smiled at my amusement. "Tell me, Uhtred, why we let you live."

"I don't know."

"When Ragnar captured you," he said, "he thought you could be ransomed, but he decided to keep you. I thought he was a fool, but he was right."

"I'm glad," I said, meaning it.

"Because we need the English," Ravn went on. "We are few, the English are many, despite which we shall take their land, but we can only hold it with the help of Englishmen. A man cannot live in a home that is forever besieged. He needs peace to grow crops and raise cattle, and we need you. When men see that Earl Uhtred is on our side then they won't fight us. And you must marry a Danish girl so that when your children grow they will be both Dane and English and see no difference." He paused, contemplating that distant future, then chuckled. "Just make sure they're not Christians, Uhtred."

"They will worship Odin," I said, again meaning it.

"Christianity is a soft religion," Ravn said savagely, "a woman's creed. It doesn't ennoble men, it makes them into worms. I hear birds."

"Two ravens," I said, "flying north."

"A real message!" he said delightedly. "Huginn and Muminn are going to Odin."

Huginn and Muminn were the twin ravens that perched on the god's shoulders where they whispered into his ear. They did for Odin what I did for Ravn, they watched and told him what they saw. He sent them to fly all over the world and to bring back news, and the news they carried back that day was that the smoke from the Mercian encampment was less thick. Fewer fires were lit at night. Men were leaving that army.

"Harvesttime," Ravn said in disgust.

"Does that matter?"

"They call their army the fyrd," he explained, forgetting for a moment that I was English, "and every able man is supposed to serve in the fyrd, but when the harvest ripens they fear hunger in the winter so they go home to cut their rye and barley."

"Which we then take?"

He laughed. "You're learning, Uhtred."

Yet the Mercians and West Saxons still hoped they could starve us and, though they were losing men every day, they did not give up until Ivar loaded a cart with food. He piled cheeses, smoked fish, newly baked bread, salted pork, and a vat of ale onto the cart and, at dawn, a dozen men dragged it toward the English camp. They stopped just out of bow shot and shouted to the enemy sentries that the food was a gift from Ivar the Boneless to King Burghred.

The next day a Mercian horseman rode toward the town carrying a leafy branch as a sign of truce. The English wanted to talk. "Which means," Ravn told me, "that we have won."

"It does?"

"When an enemy wants to talk," he said, "it means he does not want to fight. So we have won."

And he was right.

THREE

The next day we made a pavilion in the valley between the town and the English encampment,
stretching two ships' sails between timber poles,
the whole thing supported by seal-hide ropes
lashed to pegs, and there the English placed three
high-backed chairs for King Burghred, King
Æthelred, and Prince Alfred, and draped the
chairs with rich red cloths. Ivar and Ubba sat on
milking stools.

Both sides brought thirty or forty men to witness the discussions, which began with an agreement that all weapons were to be piled twenty
paces behind the two delegations. I helped carry
swords, axes, shields, and spears, then went back
to listen.

Beocca was there and he spotted me. He
smiled. I smiled back. He was standing just be-

hind the young man I took to be Alfred, for though I had heard him in the night I had not seen him clearly. He alone among the three English leaders was not crowned with a circlet of gold, though he did have a large, jeweled cloak brooch that Ivar eyed rapaciously. I saw, as Alfred took his seat, that the prince was thin, long legged, restless, pale, and tall. His face was long, his nose long, his beard short, his cheeks hollow, and his mouth pursed. His hair was a nondescript brown, his eyes worried, his brow creased, his hands fidgety, and his face frowning. He was only nineteen, I later learned, but he looked ten years older. His brother, King Æthelred, was much older, over thirty, and he was also long faced, but burlier and even more anxious-looking, while Burghred, King of Mercia, was a stubby man, heavy bearded, with a bulging belly and a balding pate.

Alfred said something to Beocca who produced a sheet of parchment and a quill, which he gave to the prince. Beocca then held a small vial of ink so that Alfred could dip the quill and write.

"What is he doing?" Ivar asked.

"He is making notes of our talks," the English interpreter answered.

"Notes?"

"So there is a record, of course."

"He has lost his memory?" Ivar asked, while Ubba produced a very small knife and began to clean his fingernails. Ragnar pretended to write on his hand, which amused the Danes.

"You are Ivar and Ubba?" Alfred asked through his interpreter.

"They are," our translator answered. Alfred's pen scratched, while his brother and brother-in-law, both kings, seemed content to allow the young prince to question the Danes.

"You are sons of Lothbrok?" Alfred continued.

"Indeed," the interpreter answered.

"And you have a brother? Halfdan?"

"Tell the bastard to shove his writing up his arse," Ivar snarled, "and to shove the quill up after it, and then the ink until he shits black feathers."

"My lord says we are not here to discuss family," the interpreter said suavely, "but to decide your fate."

"And to decide yours," Burghred spoke for the first time.

"Our fate?" Ivar retorted, making the Mercian king quail from the force of his skull gaze. "Our fate is to water the fields of Mercia with your blood, dung the soil with your flesh, pave it with your bones, and rid it of your filthy stink."

The discussion carried on like that for a long time, both sides threatening, neither yielding, but it had been the English who called for the meeting and the English who wanted to make peace and so the terms were slowly hammered out. It took two days, and most of us who were listening became bored and lay on the grass in the sunlight. Both sides ate in the field, and it was during one such meal that Beocca cautiously came across to the Danish side and greeted me warily. "You're getting tall, Uhtred," he said.

"It is good to see you, father," I answered dutifully. Ragnar was watching, but without any sign of worry on his face.

"You're still a prisoner, then?" Beocca asked.

"I am," I lied.

He looked at my two silver arm rings which, being too big for me, rattled at my wrist. "A privileged prisoner," he said wryly.

"They know I am an ealdorman," I said.

"Which you are, God knows, though your uncle denies it."

"I have heard nothing of him," I said truthfully.

Beocca shrugged. "He holds Bebbanburg. He married your father's wife and now she is pregnant."

"Gytha!" I was surprised. "Pregnant?"

"They want a son," Beocca said, "and if they have one . . ." He did not finish the thought, nor did he need to. I was the ealdorman, and Ælfric had usurped my place, yet I was still his heir and would be until he had a son. "The child must be born any day now," Beocca said, "but you need not worry." He smiled and leaned toward me so he could speak in a conspiratorial whisper. "I brought the parchments."

I looked at him with utter incomprehension. "You brought the parchments?"

"Your father's will! The land charters!" He was shocked that I did not immediately understand what he had done. "I have the proof that you are the ealdorman!"

"I am the ealdorman," I said, as if proof did not matter. "And always will be."

"Not if Ælfric has his way," Beocca said, "and if he has a son then he will want the boy to inherit."

"Gytha's children always die," I said.

"You must pray that every child lives," Beocca

said crossly, "but you are still the ealdorman. I owe that to your father, God rest his soul."

"So you abandoned my uncle?" I asked.

"Yes, I did!" he said eagerly, plainly proud that he had fled Bebbanburg. "I am English," he went on, his crossed eyes blinking in the sun, "so I came south, Uhtred, to find Englishmen willing to fight the pagans, Englishmen able to do God's will, and I found them in Wessex. They are good men, godly men, stalwart men!"

"Ælfric doesn't fight the Danes?" I asked. I knew he did not, but I wanted to hear it confirmed.

"Your uncle wants no trouble," Beocca said, "and so the pagans thrive in Northumbria and the light of our Lord Jesus Christ grows dimmer every day." He put his hands together as if in prayer, his palsied left hand quivering against his ink-stained right. "And it is not just Ælfric who succumbs. Ricsig of Dunholm gives them feasts, Egbert sits on their throne, and for that betrayal there must be weeping in heaven. It must be stopped, Uhtred, and I went to Wessex because the king is a godly man and knows it is only with God's help that we can defeat the pagans. I shall see if Wessex is willing to ransom you." That last sentence took me by surprise so that instead of looking pleased I looked puzzled, and Beocca frowned. "You didn't hear me?" he asked.

"You want to ransom me?"

"Of course! You are noble, Uhtred, and you must be rescued! Alfred can be generous about such things."

"I would like that," I said, knowing it was what I was supposed to say.

"You should meet Alfred," he said enthusiastically. "You'll enjoy that!"

I had no wish to meet Alfred, certainly not after listening to him whimper about a servant girl he had humped, but Beocca was insistent and so I went to Ragnar and asked his permission. Ragnar was amused. "Why does the squinty bastard want you to meet Alfred?" he asked, looking at Beocca.

"He wants me to be ransomed. He thinks Alfred might pay."

"Pay good money for you!" Ragnar laughed. "Go on," he said carelessly, "it never hurts to see the enemy close up."

Alfred was with his brother, some distance away, and Beocca talked to me as he led me toward the royal group. "Alfred is his brother's chief helper," he explained. "King Æthelred is a good man, but nervous. He has sons, of course, but both are very young . . ." His voice trailed away.

"So if he dies," I said, "the eldest son becomes king?"

"No, no!" Beocca sounded shocked. "Æthelwold's much too young. He's no older than you!"

"But he's the king's son," I insisted.

"When Alfred was a small boy," Beocca leaned down and lowered his voice, though not its intensity, "his father took him to Rome. To see the pope! And the pope, Uhtred, invested him as the future king!" He stared at me as if he had proved his point.

"But he's not the heir," I said, puzzled.

"The pope made him heir!" Beocca hissed at me. Later, much later, I met a priest who had been in the old king's entourage and he said Alfred had never been invested as the future king, but instead had been given some meaningless Roman honor, but Alfred, to his dying day, insisted the pope had conferred the succession on him, and so justified his usurpation of the throne that by rights should have gone to Æthelred's eldest son.

"But if Æthelwold grows up," I began.

"Then of course he might become king,"

Beocca interrupted me impatiently, "but if his father dies before Æthelwold grows up then Alfred will be king."

"Then Alfred will have to kill him," I said, "him and his brother."

Beocca gazed at me in shocked amazement. "Why do you say that?" he asked.

"He has to kill them," I said, "just like my uncle wanted to kill me."

"He did want to kill you. He probably still does!" Beocca made the sign of the cross. "But Alfred is not Ælfric! No, no. Alfred will treat his nephews with Christian mercy, of course he will, which is another reason he should become king. He is a good Christian, Uhtred, as I pray you are, and it is God's will that Alfred should become king. The pope proved that! And we have to obey God's will. It is only by obedience to God that we can hope to defeat the Danes."

"Only by obedience?" I asked. I thought swords might help.

"Only by obedience," Beocca said firmly, "and by faith. God will give us victory if we worship him with all our hearts, and if we mend our ways and give him the glory. And Alfred will do that! With him at our head the very hosts of heaven will come to our aid. Æthelwold can't do that. He's a lazy, arrogant, tiresome child." Beocca seized my hand and pulled me through the entourage of West Saxon and Mercian lords. "Now remember to kneel to him, boy, he is a prince." He led me to where Alfred was sitting and I duly knelt as Beocca introduced me. "This is the boy I spoke of, lord," he said. "He is the ealdorman Uhtred of Northumbria, a prisoner of the Danes since Eoferwic fell, but a good boy."

Alfred gave me an intense look that, to be honest, made me uncomfortable. I was to discover in time that he was a clever man, very clever, and thought twice as fast as most others, and he was also a serious man, so serious that he understood everything except jokes. Alfred took everything heavily, even a small boy, and his inspection of me was long and searching as if he tried to plumb the depths of my unfledged soul. "Are you a good boy?" he finally asked me.

"I try to be, lord," I said.

"Look at me," he ordered, for I had lowered my eyes. He smiled when I met his gaze. There was no sign of the sickness he had complained of when I eavesdropped on him and I wondered if, after all, he had been drunk that night. It would have explained his pathetic words, but now he was all earnestness. "How do you try to be good?" he asked.

"I try to resist temptation, lord," I said, remembering Beocca's words to him behind the tent.

"That's good," he said, "very good, and do you resist it?"

"Not always," I said, then hesitated, tempted to mischief, and then, as ever, yielded to temptation. "But I try, lord," I said earnestly, "and I tell myself I should thank God for tempting me and I praise him when he gives me the strength to resist the temptation."

Both Beocca and Alfred stared at me as if I had sprouted angel's wings. I was only repeating the nonsense I had heard Beocca advise Alfred in the dark, but they thought it revealed my great holiness, and I encouraged them by trying to look meek, innocent, and pious. "You are a sign from God, Uhtred," Alfred said fervently. "Do you say your prayers?"

"Every day, lord," I said, and did not add that those prayers were addressed to Odin.

"And what is that about your neck? A crucifix?" He had seen the leather thong and, when I did not answer, he leaned forward and plucked out Thor's hammer that had been hidden behind my shirt. "Dear God," he said, and made the sign of the cross. "And you wear those, too," he added, grimacing at my two arm rings that were cut with Danish rune letters. I must have looked a proper little heathen.

"They make me wear them, lord," I said, and felt his impulse to tear the pagan symbol off the thong, "and beat me if I don't," I added hastily.

"Do they beat you often?" he asked.

"All the time, lord," I lied.

He shook his head sadly, then let the hammer fall. "A graven image," he said, "must be a heavy burden for a small boy."

"I was hoping, lord," Beocca intervened, "that we could ransom him."

"Us?" Alfred asked. "Ransom him?"

"He is the true ealdorman of Bebbanburg," Beocca explained, "though his uncle has taken the title, but the uncle will not fight the Danes."

Alfred gazed at me, thinking, then frowned. "Can you read, Uhtred?" he asked.

"He has begun his lessons," Beocca answered for me. "I taught him, lord, though in all honesty he was ever a reluctant pupil. Not good with his letters, I fear. His thorns were prickly and his ashes spindly."

I said that Alfred did not understand jokes, but he loved that one, even though it was feeble as watered milk and stale as old cheese. But it was beloved of all who taught reading, and both Beocca and Alfred laughed as though the jest were fresh as dew at sunrise. The thorn, ð, and the ash, æ, were two letters of our alphabet. "His thorns are prickly," Alfred echoed, almost incoherent with laughter, "and his ashes spindly. His **b**'s don't buzz and his **i**'s—" He stopped, suddenly embarrassed. He had been about to say my **i**'s were crossed, then he remembered Beocca and he looked contrite. "My dear Beocca."

"No offense, my lord, no offense." Beocca was still happy, as happy as when he was immersed in some tedious text about how Saint Cuthbert baptized puffins or preached the gospel to the seals. He had tried to make me read that stuff, but I had never got beyond the shortest words.

"You are fortunate to have started your studies early," Alfred said to me, recovering his seriousness. "I was not given a chance to read until I was twelve years old!" His tone suggested I should be shocked and surprised by this news so I dutifully looked appalled. "That was grievously wrong of my father and stepmother," Alfred went on sternly. "They should have started me much earlier."

"Yet now you read as well as any scholar, my lord," Beocca said.

"I do try," Alfred said modestly, but he was plainly delighted with the compliment.

"And in Latin, too!" Beocca said. "And his Latin is much better than mine!"

"I think that's true," Alfred said, giving the priest a smile.

"And he writes a clear hand," Beocca told me, "such a clear, fine hand!"

"As must you," Alfred told me firmly, "to which end, young Uhtred, we shall indeed offer to ransom you, and if God helps us in that endeavor then you shall serve in my household and the first thing you will do is become a master of reading and writing. You'll like that!"

"I will, lord," I said, meaning it to sound as a question, though it came out as dull agreement.

"You will learn to read well," Alfred promised me, "and learn to pray well, and learn to be a good honest Christian, and when you are of age you can decide what to be!"

"I will want to serve you, lord," I lied, thinking that he was a pale, boring, priest-ridden weakling.

"That is commendable," he said, "and how will you serve me, do you think?"

"As a soldier, lord, to fight the Danes."

"If God wishes it," he said, evidently disappointed in my answer, "and God knows we shall need soldiers, though I pray daily that the Danes will come to a knowledge of Christ and so discover their sins and be led to end their wicked ways. Prayer is the answer," he said vehemently, "prayer and fasting and obedience, and if God answers our prayers, Uhtred, then we shall need no soldiers, but a kingdom always has need of good priests. I wanted that office for myself, but God disposed otherwise. There is no higher calling than the priestly service. I might be a prince, but in God's eyes I am a worm while Beocca is a jewel beyond price!"

"Yes, lord," I said, for want of anything else to say. Beocca tried to look modest.

Alfred leaned forward, hid Thor's hammer behind my shirt, then laid a hand on my head. "God's blessing on you, child," he said, "and may his face shine upon you and release you from your thralldom and bring you into the blessed light of freedom."

"Amen," I said.

They let me go then and I went back to Ragnar. "Hit me," I said.

"What?"

"Thump me round the head."

He glanced up and saw that Alfred was still watching me, so he cuffed me harder than I expected. I fell down, grinning. "So why did I just do that?" Ragnar asked.

"Because I said you were cruel to me," I said, "and beat me constantly." I knew that would amuse Ragnar and it did. He hit me again, just for luck. "So what did the bastards want?" he asked.

"They want to ransom me," I said, "so they can teach me to read and write, and then make me into a priest."

"A priest? Like the squinty little bastard with the red hair?"

"Just like him."

Ragnar laughed. "Maybe I should ransom you. It would be a punishment for telling lies about me."

"Please don't," I said fervently, and at that moment I wondered why I had ever wanted to go back to the English side. To exchange Ragnar's freedom for Alfred's earnest piety seemed a miserable fate to me. Besides, I was learning to despise the English. They would not fight, they prayed instead of sharpening their swords, and it was no wonder the Danes were taking their land.

Alfred did offer to ransom me, but balked at Ragnar's price that was ludicrously high, though not nearly so steep as the price Ivar and Ubba extracted from Burghred.

Mercia was to be swallowed. Burghred had no fire in his big belly, no desire to go on fighting the Danes who got stronger as he grew weaker. Perhaps he was fooled by all those shields on Snotengaham's walls, but he must have decided he could not beat the Danes and instead he surrendered. It was not just our forces in Snotengaham that persuaded him to do this. Other Danes were raiding across the Northumbrian border, ravaging Mercian lands, burning churches, slaughtering monks and nuns, and those horsemen were now close to Burghred's army and were forever harassing his forage parties, and so Burghred, weary of unending defeat, weakly agreed to every outrageous demand, and in return he was allowed to stay as King of Mercia, but that was all. The Danes were to take his fortresses and garrison them, and they were free to take Mercian estates as they wished, and

Burghred's fyrd was to fight for the Danes if they demanded it, and Burghred, moreover, was to pay a vast price in silver for this privilege of losing his kingdom while keeping his throne. Æthelred and Alfred, having no part to play in the discussions, and seeing that their ally had collapsed like a pricked bladder, left on the second day, riding south with what remained of their army, and thus Mercia fell.

First Northumbria, then Mercia. In just two years half of England was gone and the Danes were only just beginning.

We ravaged the land again. Bands of Danes rode into every part of Mercia and slaughtered whoever resisted, took whatever they wished, then garrisoned the principal fortresses before sending messages to Denmark for more ships to come: more ships, more men, more families, and more Danes to fill the great land that had fallen into their laps.

I had begun to think I would never fight for England because by the time I was old enough to fight there would be no England. So I decided I would be a Dane. Of course I was confused, but I did not spend much time worrying about my confusion. Instead, as I approached twelve years old, I began my proper education. I was made to stand for hours holding a sword and shield stretched out in front of me until my arms ached, I was taught the strokes of the blade, made to practice with throwing spears, and given a pig to slaughter with a war spear. I learned to fend with a shield, how to drop it to stop the lunge beneath the rim, and how to shove the heavy shield boss into an enemy's face to smash his nose and blind him with tears. I learned to pull an oar. I grew, put on muscle, began to speak in a man's voice, and was slapped by my first girl. I looked like a Dane. Strangers still mistook me for Ragnar's son for I had the same fair hair that I wore long and tied with a strip of leather at the nape of my neck, and Ragnar was pleased when that happened though he made it plain that I would not replace Ragnar the Younger or Rorik. "If Rorik lives," he said sadly, for Rorik was still sickly, "you will have to fight for your inheritance," and so I learned to fight and, that winter, to kill.

We returned to Northumbria. Ragnar liked it there and, though he could have taken better land in Mercia, he liked the northern hills and the deep vales and the dark hanging woods where, as the first frosts crisped the morning, he took me hunting. A score of men and twice as many dogs beat through the woods, trying to trap boar. I stayed with Ragnar, both of us armed with heavy boar spears. "A boar can kill you, Uhtred," he warned me. "He can rip you from the crotch to the neck unless you place the spear just right."

The spear, I knew, must be placed in the beast's chest or, if you were lucky, down its throat. I knew I could not kill a boar, but if one came, I would have to try. A full-grown boar can be twice the weight of a man and I did not have the strength to drive one back, but Ragnar was determined to give me first strike and he would be close behind to help. And so it happened. I have killed hundreds of boar since, but I will always remember that first beast, the small eyes, the sheer anger, the determination, the stench, the bristling hairs flecked with mud, and the sweet thud of the spear going deep into the chest, and I was hurled back as if I had been kicked by Odin's eight-legged horse, and Ragnar drove his own spear through the thick hide and the beast squealed and roared, legs scrabbling, and the pursuing dogs howled, and I found my feet, gritted my teeth, and put my weight on the spear and felt the boar's life pulsing up the ash shaft. Ragnar gave me a tusk from that carcass and I hung it next to Thor's hammer and in the days that followed I wanted to do nothing except hunt, though I was not allowed to pursue boar unless Ragnar was with me, but when Rorik was well enough he and I would take our bows into the woods to look for deer.

It was on one of those expeditions, high up at the edge of the woods, just beneath the moors that were dappled by melting snow, that the arrow almost took my life. Rorik and I were creeping through undergrowth and the arrow missed me by inches, sizzling past my head to thump into an ash tree. I turned, putting an arrow on my own string, but saw no one, then we heard feet racing away downhill through the trees and we followed, but whoever had shot the arrow ran too fast for us.

"An accident," Ragnar said. "He saw movement, thought you were a deer, and loosed. It happens." He looked at the arrow we had retrieved, but it had no marks of ownership. It was just a goose-fledged shaft of hornbeam tipped with an iron head. "An accident," he decreed.

Later that winter we moved back to Eoferwic and spent days repairing the boats. I learned to split oak trunks with wedge and mallet, cleaving out the long pale planks that patched the rotted hulls. Spring brought more ships, more men, and with them was Halfdan, youngest brother of Ivar and Ubba. He came ashore roaring with energy, a tall man with a big beard and scowling eyes. He embraced Ragnar, thumped me on the shoulder, punched Rorik in the head, swore he would kill every Christian in England, then went to see his brothers. The three of them planned the new war, which, they promised, would strip East Anglia of its treasures and, as the days warmed, we readied for it.

Half the army would march by land, while the other half, which included Ragnar's men, would go by sea and so I anticipated my first proper voyage, but before we left Kjartan came to see Ragnar, and trailing him was his son Sven, his missing eye a red hole in his angry face. Kjartan knelt to Ragnar and bowed his head. "I would come with you, lord," he said.

Kjartan had made a mistake by letting Sven follow him, for Ragnar, usually so generous, gave the boy a sour look. I call him a boy, but in truth Sven was almost a man now and promised to be a big one, broad in the chest, tall, and strong. "You would come with me," Ragnar echoed flatly.

"I beg you, lord," Kjartan said, and it must have taken a great effort to say those words, for

Kjartan was a proud man, but in Eoferwic he had found no plunder, earned no arm rings, and made no reputation for himself.

"My ships are full," Ragnar said coldly, and turned away. I saw the look of hatred on Kjartan's face.

"Why doesn't he sail with someone else?" I asked Ravn.

"Because everyone knows he offended Ragnar, so to give him a place at the oars is to risk my son's dislike." Ravn shrugged. "Kjartan should go back to Denmark. If a man loses his lord's trust then he has lost everything."

But Kjartan and his one-eyed son stayed in Eoferwic instead of going back to Denmark, and we sailed, first flowing with the current back down the Ouse and so into the Humber where we spent the night. Next morning we took the shields off the ships' sides, then waited till the tide lifted their hulls and we could row eastward into the first great seas.

I had been offshore at Bebbanburg, going with fishermen to cast nets about the Farne Islands, but this was a different sensation. The **Wind-Viper** rode those waves like a bird instead of thrashing through like a swimmer. We rowed out of the river, then took advantage of a northwest wind to hoist the great sail, and the oars were fiddled out of their holes, the holes were covered with wooden plugs, and the great sweeps stored inboard as the sail cracked, bellied, trapped the wind, and drove us southward. There were eighty-nine ships altogether, a fleet of dragon-headed killers, and they raced one another, calling insults whenever they traveled faster than some other boat. Ragnar leaned on the steering oar, his hair flying in the wind and a smile as broad as the ocean on his face. Seal-hide ropes creaked; the boat seemed to leap up the seas, seethe through their tops, and slide in flying spray down their faces. I was frightened at first, for the **Wind-Viper** bent to that wind, almost dropping her leeward side beneath the great green sea, but then I saw no fear on the other men's faces and I learned to enjoy the wild ride, whooping with delight when the bow smashed into a heavy sea and the green water flew like an arrow shower down the deck.

"I love this!" Ragnar called to me. "In Valhalla I hope to find a ship, a sea, and a wind!"

The shore was ever in sight, a low green line to our right, sometimes broken by dunes, but never by trees or hills, and as the sun sank we turned toward that land and Ragnar ordered the sail furled and the oars out.

We rowed into a water land, a place of marsh and reed, of bird cries and long-legged herons, of eel traps and ditches, of shallow channels and long meres, and I remembered my father saying the East Anglians were frogs. We were on the edge of their country now, at the place where Mercia ended and East Anglia began in a tangle of water, mud, and salt flats. "They call it the Gewæsc," Ragnar said.

"You've been here?"

"Three years ago," he said. "Good country to raid, Uhtred, but treacherous water. Too shallow."

The Gewæsc was very shallow and Weland was in the **Wind-Viper**'s bow, weighing the depth with a lump of iron tied to a rope. The oars only dipped if Weland said there was sufficient water and so we crept westward into the dying light followed by the rest of the fleet. The shadows were long now, the red sun slicing into the open jaws of the dragon, serpents and eagle heads on the ships' prows. The oars worked slowly, their blades dripping water as they swept forward for the next stroke, and our wake spread in long slow ripples touched red by dying sun fire.

We anchored that night and slept aboard the ships and in the dawn Ragnar made Rorik and me climb his mast. Ubba's ship was nearby and he, too, had men clambering up toward the painted wind vane at the masthead.

"What can you see?" Ragnar called up to us.

"Three men on horseback," Rorik answered, pointing south, "watching us."

"And a village," I added, also pointing south.

To the men on shore we were something from their darkest fears. All they could see was a thicket of masts and the savage carved beasts at the high prows and sterns of our ships. We were an army, brought here by our dragon boats, and they knew what would follow and, as I watched, the three horsemen turned and galloped south.

We went on. Ubba's ship led the way now, following a twisting shallow channel, and I could see Ubba's sorcerer, Storri, standing in the bows and I guessed he had cast the runes and predicted success. "Today," Ragnar told me wolfishly, "you will learn the Viking way."

To be a Viking was to be a raider, and Ragnar had not conducted a shipborne raid in many

years. He had become an invader instead, a set-
tler, but Ubba's fleet had come to ravage the
coastline and draw the East Anglian army toward
the sea while his brother, Ivar, led the land army
south from Mercia, and so that early summer I
learned the Viking ways. We took the ships to the
mainland where Ubba found a stretch of land
with a thin neck that could easily be defended
and, once our ships were safely drawn onto the
beach, we dug an earthwork across the neck as a
rampart. Then large parties of men disappeared
into the countryside, returning next morning
with captured horses, and the horses were used
to mount another warband that rode inland as
Ragnar led his men on foot along the tangled
shoreline.

We came to a village, I never did learn its
name, and we burned it to the ground. There was
no one there. We burned farmsteads and a
church and marched on, following a road that
angled away from the shore, and at dusk we saw
a larger village and we hid in a wood, lit no fires,
and attacked at dawn.

We came shrieking from the half-light. We were
a nightmare in the dawn: men in leather with iron
helmets, men with round painted shields, men
with axes, swords, and spears. The folk in that

place had no weapons and no armor, and perhaps they had not even known there were Danes in their countryside for they were not ready for us. They died. A few brave men tried to make a stand by their church, but Ragnar led a charge against them and they were slaughtered where they stood, and Ragnar pushed open the church door to find the small building filled with women and children. The priest was in front of the altar and he cursed Ragnar in Latin as the Dane stalked up the small nave, and the priest was still cursing when Ragnar disemboweled him.

We took a bronze crucifix, a dented silver plate, and some coins from the church. We found a dozen good cooking pots in the houses and some shears, sickles, and iron spits. We captured cattle, goats, sheep, oxen, eight horses, and sixteen young women. One woman screamed that she could not leave her child and I watched Weland spit the small boy on a spear, then thrust the bloodied corpse into the woman's arms. Ragnar sent her away, not because he pitied her, but because one person was always spared to carry news of the horror to other places. Folk must fear the Danes, Ragnar said, and then they would be ready to surrender. He gave me a piece of burning wood he had taken from a fire. "Burn the thatch, Uhtred," he ordered, so I went from house to house, putting fire to the reed thatch. I burned the church and then, just as I approached the last house, a man burst from the door with a three-pronged eel spear that he lunged at me. I twisted aside, avoiding his thrust by luck rather than judgment, and I hurled the burning wood at the man's face and the flames made him duck as I backed away, and Ragnar threw me a spear, a heavy war spear made for thrusting rather than throwing, and it skidded in the dust in front of me and I understood he was letting me fight as I plucked it up. He would not have let me die, for he had two of his bowmen standing ready with arrows on their strings, but he did not interfere as the man ran at me and lunged again.

I parried, knocking the rusted eel spear aside and stepping back again to give myself room. The man was twice my size and more than twice my weight. He was cursing me, calling me a devil's bastard, a worm of hell, and he rushed me again and I did what I had learned hunting the boar. I stepped to my left, waited till he leveled the spear, stepped back to the right, and thrust.

It was not a clean thrust, nor did I have the weight to hurl him back, but the spear point punctured his belly and then his weight pushed me back as he half snarled and half gasped, and I fell, and he fell on top of me, forced sideways because the spear was in his guts, and he tried to take a grip of my throat, but I wriggled out from beneath him, picked up his own eel spear, and rammed it at his throat. There were rivulets of blood on the earth, droplets spraying in the air, and he was jerking and choking, blood bubbling at his ripped throat, and I tried to pull the eel spear back, but the barbs on the points were caught in his gullet, so I ripped the war spear from his belly and tried to stop him jerking by thrusting it down hard into his chest, but it only glanced off his ribs. He was making a terrible noise, and I suppose I was in a panic, and I was unaware that Ragnar and his men were almost helpless with laughter as they watched me try to kill the East Anglian. I did, in the end, or else he just bled to death, but by then I had poked and stabbed and torn him until he looked as though a pack of wolves had set on him.

But I got a third arm ring, and there were grown warriors in Ragnar's band who only wore three. Rorik was jealous, but he was younger and his father consoled him that his time would come. "How does it feel?" Ragnar asked me.

"Good," I said, and God help me, it did.

It was then that I first saw Brida. She was my age, black haired, thin as a twig, with big dark eyes and a spirit as wild as a hawk in spring, and she was among the captured women and, as the Danes began dividing those captives among themselves, an older woman pushed the child forward as if giving her to the Vikings. Brida snatched up a piece of wood and turned on the woman and beat at her, driving her back, screaming that she was a sour-faced bitch, a dried up hank of gristle, and the older woman tripped and fell into a patch of nettles where Brida went on thrashing her. Ragnar was laughing, but eventually pulled the child away and, because he loved anyone with spirit, gave her to me. "Keep her safe," he said, "and burn that last house."

So I did.

And I learned another thing.

Start your killers young, before their consciences are grown. Start them young and they will be lethal.

We took our plunder back to the ships and that night, as I drank my ale, I thought of myself as a Dane. Not English, not anymore. I was a Dane and I had been given a perfect childhood, perfect, at least, to the ideas of a boy. I was raised among men, I was free, I ran wild, I was encumbered by no laws, I was troubled by no priests, I was encouraged to violence, and I was rarely alone.

And it was that, that I was rarely alone, which kept me alive.

Every raid brought more horses, and more horses meant more men could go farther afield and waste more places, steal more silver, and take more captives. We had scouts out now, watching for the approach of King Edmund's army. Edmund ruled East Anglia and unless he wished to collapse as feebly as Burghred of Mercia, he had to send men against us to preserve his kingdom, and so we watched the roads and waited.

Brida stayed close to me. Ragnar had taken a strong liking to her, probably because she treated him defiantly and because she alone did not weep when she was captured. She was an orphan and had been living in the house of her aunt, the woman whom she had beaten and whom she hated, and within days Brida was happier among the Danes than she had ever been among her own people. She was a slave now, a slave who was supposed to stay in the camp and cook, but one dawn as we went raiding she ran after us and hauled herself up behind my saddle and Ragnar was amused by that and let her come along.

We went far south that day, out of the flatlands where the marshes stretched, and into low wooded hills among which were fat farms and a fatter monastery. Brida laughed when Ragnar killed the abbot, and afterward, as the Danes collected their plunder, she took my hand and led me over a low rise to a farm that had already been plundered by Ragnar's men. The farm belonged to the monastery and Brida knew the place because her aunt had frequently gone to the monastery to pray. "She wanted children," Brida said, "and only had me." Then she pointed at the farm and watched for my reaction.

It was a Roman farm, she told me, though like me she had little idea who the Romans really were, only that they had once lived in England and then had gone. I had seen plenty of their buildings before—there were some in Eoferwic— but those other buildings had crumbled, then been patched with mud and reroofed with thatch, while this farm looked as though the Romans had only just left.

It was astonishing. The walls were of stone,

perfectly cut, square, and close-mortared, and the roof was of tile, patterned and tight-fitting, and inside the gate was a courtyard surrounded with a pillared walkway, and in the largest room was an amazing picture on the floor, made up of thousands of small colored stones, and I gaped at the leaping fish that were pulling a chariot in which a bearded man stood holding an eel spear like the one I had faced in Brida's village. Hares surrounded the picture, chasing one another through looping strands of leaves. There had been other pictures painted on the walls, but they had faded or else been discolored by water that had leaked through the old roof. "It was the abbot's house," Brida told me, and she took me into a small room where there was a cot beside which one of the abbot's servants lay dead in his own blood. "He brought me in here," she said.

"The abbot did?"

"And told me to take my clothes off."

"The abbot did?" I asked again.

"I ran away," she said in a very matter-of-fact tone, "and my aunt beat me. She said I should have pleased him and he'd have rewarded us."

We wandered through the house and I felt a wonder that we could no longer build like this.

We knew how to sink posts in the ground and make beams and rafters and roof them with thatch from rye or reed, but the posts rotted, the thatch moldered, and the houses sagged. In summer our houses were winter dark, and all year they were choked with smoke, and in winter they stank of cattle, yet this house was light and clean and I doubted any cow had ever dunged on the man in his fish-drawn chariot. It was an unsettling thought, that somehow we were sliding back into the smoky dark and that never again would man make something so perfect as this small building. "Were the Romans Christians?" I asked Brida.

"Don't know," she said. "Why?"

"Nothing," I said, but I had been thinking that the gods reward those they love and it would have been nice to know which gods had looked after the Romans. I hoped they had worshipped Odin, though these days, I knew, they were Christians because the pope lived in Rome and Beocca had taught me that the pope was the chief of all the Christians, and was a very holy man. His name, I remembered, was Nicholas. Brida could not have cared less about the gods of the Romans. Instead she knelt to explore a hole in the floor that seemed to lead only to a cellar so shallow that no person could ever get inside. "Maybe elves lived there?" I suggested.

"Elves live in the woods," she insisted. She decided the abbot might have hidden treasures in the space and borrowed my sword so she could widen the hole. It was not a real sword, merely a saxe, a very long knife, but Ragnar had given it to me and I wore it proudly.

"Don't break the blade," I told her, and she stuck her tongue out at me, then began prising the mortar at the hole's edge while I went back to the courtyard to look at the raised pond that was green and scummy now, but somehow I knew it had once been filled with clear water. A frog crawled onto the small stone island in the center and I again remembered my father's verdict on the East Anglians: mere frogs.

Weland came through the gate. He stopped just inside and licked his lips, tongue flickering, then half smiled. "Lost your saxe, Uhtred?"

"No," I said.

"Ragnar sent me," he said. "We're leaving."

I nodded, said nothing, but knew that Ragnar would have sounded a horn if we were truly ready to leave.

"So come on, boy," he said.

I nodded again, still said nothing.

His dark eyes glanced at the building's empty windows, then at the pool. "Is that a frog," he asked, "or a toad?"

"A frog."

"In Frankia," he said, "men say you can eat frogs." He walked toward the pool and I moved to stay on the far side from him, keeping the raised stone structure between us. "Have you eaten a frog, Uhtred?"

"No."

"Would you like to?"

"No."

He put a hand into a leather bag that hung from his sword belt, which was strapped over a torn mail coat. He had money now, two arm rings, proper boots, an iron helmet, a long sword, and the mail coat that needed mending, but was far better protection than the rags he had worn when he first came to Ragnar's house. "This coin if you catch a frog," he said, spinning a silver penny in the air.

"I don't want to catch a frog," I said sullenly.

"I do," he said, grinning, and he drew the sword, its blade hissing on the scabbard's wooden throat, and he stepped into the pool, the water not reaching the tops of his boots, and the frog leaped away, plopping into the green scum, and Weland was not looking at the frog, but at me, and I knew he was going to kill me, but for some reason I could not move. I was astonished, and yet I was not astonished. I had never liked him, never trusted him, and I understood that he had been sent to kill me and had only failed because I had always been in company until this moment when I had let Brida lead me away from Ragnar's band. So Weland had his chance now. He smiled at me, reached the center of the pool, came closer, raised the sword, and I found my feet at last and raced back into the pillared walkway. I did not want to go into the house, for Brida was there, and I knew he would kill her if he found her. He jumped out of the pond and chased me, and I raced down the walkway, around the corner, and he cut me off, and I dodged back, wanting to reach the gateway, but he knew that was what I wanted and he took care to keep between me and my escape. His boots left wet footprints on the Roman flagstones.

"What's the matter, Uhtred," he asked, "frightened of frogs?"

"What do you want?" I asked.

"Not so cocky now, eh, ealdorman?" He

stalked toward me, sword flashing from side to side. "Your uncle sends his regards and trusts you will burn in hell while he lives in Bebbanburg."

"You come from . . ." I began, but it was obvious Weland was serving Ælfric so I did not bother to finish the question, but instead edged backward.

"The reward for your death will be the weight of his newborn child in silver," Weland said, "and the child should be born by now. And he's impatient for your death, your uncle is. I almost managed to track you down that night outside Snotengaham, and almost hit you with an arrow last winter, but you ducked. Not this time, but it will be quick, boy. Your uncle said to make it quick, so kneel down, boy, just kneel." He swept the blade left and right, his wrist whippy so the sword hissed. "I haven't given her a name yet," he said. "Perhaps after this she'll be known as Orphan-Killer."

I feinted right, went left, but he was quick as a stoat and he blocked me, and I knew I was cornered, and he knew it, too, and smiled. "I'll make it quick," he said, "I promise."

Then the first roof tile hit his helmet. It could not have hurt much, but the unexpected blow jarred him backward and confused him, and the second tile hit his waist and the third smacked him on the shoulder, and Brida shouted from the roof, "Back through the house!" I ran, the lunging sword missing me by inches, and I twisted through the door, ran over the fish-drawn chariot, through a second door, another door, saw an open window and dove through, and Brida jumped down from the roof and together we ran for the nearby woods.

Weland followed me, but he abandoned the pursuit when we vanished in the trees. Instead he went south, on his own, fleeing what he knew Ragnar would do to him, and for some reason I was in tears by the time I found Ragnar again. Why did I cry? I do not know, unless it was the confirmation that Bebbanburg was gone, that my beloved refuge was occupied by an enemy, and an enemy who, by now, might have a son.

Brida received an arm ring, and Ragnar let it be known that if any man touched her he, Ragnar, would personally geld that man with a mallet and a plank-splitter. She rode home on Weland's horse.

And next day the enemy came.

Ravn had sailed with us, blind though he was, and I was required to be his eyes so I described how the East Anglian army was forming on a low ridge of dry land to the south of our camp. "How many banners?" he asked me.

"Twenty-three," I said, after a pause to count them.

"Showing?"

"Mostly crosses," I said, "and some saints."

"He's a very pious man, King Edmund," Ravn said. "He even tried to persuade me to become a Christian." He chuckled at the memory. We were sitting on the prow of one of the beached ships, Ravn in a chair, Brida and I at his feet, and the Mercian twins, Ceolnoth and Ceolberht, on his far side. They were the sons of Bishop Æthelbrid of Snotengaham and they were hostages even though their father had welcomed the Danish army, but as Ravn said, taking the bishop's sons hostage would keep the man honest. There were dozens of other such hostages from Mercia and Northumbria, all sons of prominent men, and all under sentence of death if their fathers caused trouble. There were other Englishmen in the army, serving as soldiers, and, if it were not for the language they spoke, they would have been indistinguishable from the Danes. Most of them were either outlaws or masterless men, but all were savage fighters, exactly the kind of men the

English needed to face their enemy, but now those men were fighting for the Danes against King Edmund. "And he's a fool," Ravn said scornfully.

"A fool?" I asked.

"He gave us shelter during the winter before we attacked Eoferwic," Ravn explained, "and we had to promise not to kill any of his churchmen." He laughed softly. "What a very silly condition. If their god was any use then we couldn't have killed them anyway."

"Why did he give you shelter?"

"Because it was easier than fighting us," Ravn said. He was using English because the other three children did not understand Danish, though Brida was learning quickly. She had a mind like a fox, quick and sly. Ravn smiled. "The silly King Edmund believed we would go away in the springtime and not come back, yet here we are."

"He shouldn't have done it," one of the twins put in. I could not tell them apart, but was annoyed by them for they were fierce Mercian patriots, despite their father's change of allegiance. They were ten years old and forever upbraiding me for loving the Danes.

"Of course he shouldn't have done it," Ravn agreed mildly.

"He should have attacked you!" Ceolnoth or Ceolberht said.

"He would have lost if he had," Ravn said. "We made a camp, protected it with walls, and stayed there. And he paid us money to make no trouble."

"I saw King Edmund once," Brida put in.

"Where was that, child?" Ravn asked.

"He came to the monastery to pray," she said, "and he farted when he knelt down."

"No doubt their god appreciated the tribute," Ravn said loftily, frowning because the twins were now making farting noises.

"Were the Romans Christians?" I asked him, remembering my curiosity at the Roman farm.

"Not always," Ravn said. "They had their own gods once, but they gave them up to become Christians and after that they knew nothing but defeat. Where are our men?"

"Still in the marsh," I said.

Ubba had hoped to stay in the camp and so force Edmund's army to attack along the narrow neck of land and die on our short earthen wall, but instead the English had remained south of the treacherous lowland and were inviting us to attack them. Ubba was tempted. He had made Storri cast the runesticks and rumor said that the result was uncertain, and that fed Ubba's caution. He was a fearsome fighter, but always wary when it came to picking a fight, but the rune-sticks had not predicted disaster and so he had taken the army out into the marsh where it now stood on whatever patches of drier land it could find, and from where two tracks led up to the low ridge. Ubba's banner, the famous raven on its three-sided cloth, was midway between the two paths, both of which were strongly guarded by East Anglian shield walls, and any attack up either path would mean that a few of our men would have to attack a lot of theirs, and Ubba must have been having second thoughts for he was hesitating. I described all that to Ravn.

"It doesn't do," he told me, "to lose men, even if we win."

"But if we kill lots of theirs?" I asked.

"They have more men, we have few. If we kill a thousand of theirs then they will have another thousand tomorrow, but if we lose a hundred men then we must wait for more ships to replace them."

"More ships are coming," Brida said.

"I doubt there will be any more this year," Ravn said.

"No," she insisted, "now," and she pointed

and I saw four ships nosing their way through the tangle of low islands and shallow creeks.

"Tell me," Ravn said urgently.

"Four ships," I said, "coming from the west."

"From the west? Not the east?"

"From the west," I insisted, which meant they were not coming from the sea, but from one of the four rivers that flowed into the Gewæsc.

"Prows?" Ravn demanded.

"No beasts on the prows," I said, "just plain wooden posts."

"Oars?"

"Ten a side, I think, maybe eleven. But there are far more men than rowers."

"English ships!" Ravn sounded amazed, for other than small fishing craft and some tubby cargo vessels the English had few ships, yet these four were warships, built long and sleek like the Danish ships, and they were creeping through the mazy waterways to attack Ubba's beached fleet. I could see smoke trickling from the foremost ship and knew they must have a brazier on board and so were planning to burn the Danish boats and thus trap Ubba.

But Ubba had also seen them, and already the Danish army was streaming back toward the camp. The leading English ship began to shoot fire arrows at the closest Danish boat and, though there was a guard on the boats, that guard was composed of the sick and the lame, and they were not strong enough to defend the ships against a seaborne attack. "Boys!" one of the guards bellowed.

"Go," Ravn told us, "go," and Brida, who considered herself as good as any boy, came with the twins and me. We jumped down to the beach and ran along the water's edge to where smoke was thickening above the beached Danish boat. Two English ships were shooting fire arrows now, while the last two attackers were trying to edge past their companions to reach more of our craft.

Our job was to extinguish the fire while the guards hurled spears at the English crews. I used a shield to scoop up sand that I dumped onto the fire. The English ships were close and I could see they were made of new raw wood. A spear thumped close to me and I picked it up and threw it back, though feebly because it clattered against an oar and fell into the sea. The twins were not trying to put out the fire and I hit one of them and threatened to hit him harder if they did not make an effort, but we were too late to save the first Danish ship, which was well ablaze, so we abandoned it and tried to rescue the next one, but a score of fire arrows slammed into the rowers' benches, another landed on the furled sail, and two of the boys were dead at the water's edge. The leading English ship turned to the beach then, its prow thick with men bristling with spears, axes, and swords. "Edmund!" they shouted. "Edmund!" The bow grated on the beach and the warriors jumped off to begin slaughtering the Danish ship guard. The big axes slammed down and blood spattered up the beach or was sluiced away by the tiny waves that washed the sand. I grabbed Brida's hand and pulled her away, splashing through a shallow creek where tiny silver fish scattered in alarm. "We have to save Ravn!" I told her.

She was laughing. Brida always enjoyed chaos.

Three of the English ships had beached themselves and their crews were ashore, finishing off the Danish guards. The last ship glided on the falling tide, shooting fire arrows, but then Ubba's men were back in the camp and they advanced on the English with a roar. Some men had stayed with the raven banner at the earthen wall to make sure King Edmund's forces could not swarm over the neck of land to take the camp, but the rest came screaming and vengeful. The Danes love their ships. A ship, they say, is like a woman or a sword, sharp and beautiful, worth dying for, and certainly worth fighting for, and the East Anglians, who had done so well, had now made a mistake for the tide was ebbing and they could not shove their boats off into the small waves. Some of the Danes protected their own unharmed boats by raining throwing axes, spears, and arrows at the crew of the single enemy boat afloat, while the rest attacked the Englishmen ashore.

That was a slaughter. That was Danish work. That was a fit fight for the skalds to celebrate. Blood was thick on the tideline, blood slurping with the rise and fall of the small waves, men screaming and falling, and all about them the smoke of the burning boats was whirling so that the hazed sun was red above a sand turned red, and in that smoke the rage of the Danes was terrible. It was then I first saw Ubba fight and marveled at him, for he was a bringer of death, a grim warrior, sword lover. He did not fight in a shield wall, but ran into his enemies, shield slamming one way as his war ax gave death in the other, and it seemed he was indestructible for at one moment he was surrounded by East Anglian fighters, but there was a scream of hate, a clash of blade on blade, and Ubba came out of the tangle of men, his blade red, blood in his beard, trampling his enemies into the blood-rich tide, and looking for more men to kill. Ragnar joined him, and Ragnar's men followed, harvesting an enemy beside the sea, screaming hate at men who had burned their ships, and when the screaming and killing were done we counted sixty-eight English bodies, and some we could not count for they had run into the sea and drowned there, dragged down by the weight of weapons and armor. The sole East Anglian ship to escape was a ship of the dying, its new wooden flanks running with blood. The victorious Danes danced over the corpses they had made, then made a heap of captured weapons. There were thirty Danish dead, and those men were burned on a half-burned ship, another six Danish craft had been destroyed, but Ubba captured the three beached English boats, which Ragnar declared to be pieces of shit. "It's astonishing they even floated," he said, kicking at a badly caulked strake.

Yet the East Anglians had done well, I thought. They had made mistakes, but they had hurt Danish pride by burning dragon ships, and if King Edmund had attacked the wall protecting the camp he might have turned the slaughter into a massacre of Danes, but King Edmund had not attacked. Instead, as his shipmen died beneath the smoke, he had marched away.

He thought he was facing the Danish army by the sea, only to learn that the real attack had come by land. He had just learned that Ivar the Boneless was invading his land.

And Ubba was enraged. The few English prisoners were sacrificed to Odin, their screams a call to the god that we needed his help. And next morning, leaving the burned boats like smoking black skeletons on the beach, we rowed the dragon fleet west.

FOUR

King Edmund of East Anglia is now remembered as a saint, as one of those blessed souls who live forever in the shadow of God. Or so the priests tell me. In heaven, they say, the saints occupy a privileged place, living on the high platform of God's great hall where they spend their time singing God's praises. Forever. Just singing. Beocca always told me that it would be an ecstatic existence, but to me it seems very dull. The Danes reckon their dead warriors are carried to Valhalla, the corpse hall of Odin, where they spend their days fighting and their nights feasting and swiving, and I dare not tell the priests that this seems a far better way to endure the afterlife than singing to the sound of golden harps. I once asked a bishop whether there were any women in heaven. "Of course there are, my lord," he answered, happy that I was taking an interest in doctrine. "Many of the most blessed saints are women."

"I mean women we can hump, bishop."

He said he would pray for me. Perhaps he did.

I do not know if King Edmund was a saint. He was a fool, that was for sure. He had given the Danes refuge before they attacked Eoferwic, and given them more than refuge. He had paid them coin, provided them with food, and supplied their army with horses, all on the two promises that they would leave East Anglia in the spring and that they would not harm a single churchman. They kept their promises, but now, two years later and much stronger, the Danes were back, and King Edmund had decided to fight them. He had seen what had happened to Mercia and Northumbria, and must have known his own kingdom would suffer the same fate, and so he gathered his fyrd and prayed to his god and marched to do battle. First he faced us by the sea, then, hearing that Ivar was marching around the edge of the great watery wastes west of the Gewæsc, he turned about to confront him. Ubba then led our fleet up the Gewæsc and we nosed into one of the rivers until the channel was so narrow our oars could not be used, and then men towed the boats, wading through waist-deep water until we could go no farther and there we left the ships under guard while the rest of us followed soggy paths through endless marshland until, at long last, we came to higher ground. No one knew where we were, only that if we went south we had to reach the road along which Edmund had marched to confront Ivar. Cut that road and we would trap him between our forces and Ivar's army.

Which is precisely what happened. Ivar fought him, shield wall against shield wall, and we knew none of it until the first East Anglian fugitives came streaming eastward to find another shield wall waiting for them. They scattered rather than fight us, we advanced, and from the few prisoners we took we discovered that Ivar had beaten them easily. That was confirmed next day when the first horsemen from Ivar's forces reached us.

King Edmund fled southward. East Anglia was a big country, he could easily have found refuge in a fortress, or else he could have gone to Wessex, but instead he put his faith in God and took shelter in a small monastery at Dic. The monastery was lost in the wetlands and perhaps he believed he would never be found there, or else, as I heard, one of the monks promised him that God would shroud the monastery in a perpetual fog in which the pagans would get lost, but the fog never came and the Danes arrived instead.

Ivar, Ubba, and their brother, Halfdan, rode to Dic, taking half their army, while the other half set about pacifying East Anglia, which meant raping, burning, and killing until the people submitted, which most did swiftly enough. East Anglia, in short, fell as easily as Mercia, and the only bad news for the Danes was that there had been unrest in Northumbria. Rumors spoke of some kind of revolt, Danes had been killed, and Ivar wanted that rising quenched, but he dared not leave East Anglia so soon after capturing it, so at Dic he made a proposal to King Edmund that would leave Edmund as king just as Burghred still ruled over Mercia.

The meeting was held in the monastery's church, which was a surprisingly large hall made of timber and thatch, but with great leather panels hanging on the walls. The panels were painted with gaudy scenes. One of the pictures showed naked folk tumbling down to hell where a massive serpent with a fanged mouth swallowed them up. "Corpse-Ripper," Ragnar said with a shudder.

"Corpse-Ripper?"

"A serpent that waits in Niflheim," he explained, touching his hammer amulet. Niflheim, I knew, was a kind of Norse hell, but unlike the Christian hell Niflheim was icy cold. "Corpse-Ripper feeds on the dead," Ragnar went on, "but he also gnaws at the tree of life. He wants to kill the whole world and bring time to an end." He touched his hammer again.

Another panel, behind the altar, showed Christ on the cross, and next to it was a third painted leather panel that fascinated Ivar. A man, naked but for a loincloth, had been tied to a stake and was being used as a target by archers. At least a score of arrows had punctured his white flesh, but he still had a saintly expression and a secret smile as though, despite his troubles, he was quite enjoying himself. "Who is that?" Ivar wanted to know.

"The blessed Saint Sebastian." King Edmund was seated in front of the altar, and his interpreter provided the answer. Ivar, skull eyes staring at the painting, wanted to know the whole story, and Edmund recounted how the blessed Saint Sebastian, a Roman soldier, had refused to renounce his faith and so the emperor had ordered him shot to death with arrows. "Yet he lived!" Edmund said eagerly. "He lived because God protected him and God be praised for that mercy."

"He lived?" Ivar asked suspiciously.

"So the emperor had him clubbed to death instead," the interpreter finished the tale.

"So he didn't live?"

"He went to heaven," King Edmund said, "so he lived."

Ubba intervened, wanting to have the concept of heaven explained to him, and Edmund eagerly sketched its delights, but Ubba spat in derision when he realized that the Christian heaven was Valhalla without any of the amusements. "And Christians want to go to heaven?" he asked in disbelief.

"Of course," the interpreter said.

Ubba sneered. He and his two brothers were attended by as many Danish warriors as could cram themselves into the church, while King Edmund had an entourage of two priests and six monks who all listened as Ivar proposed his settlement. King Edmund could live, he could rule in East Anglia, but the chief fortresses were to be garrisoned by Danes, and Danes were to be granted whatever land they required, except for royal land. Edmund would be expected to provide horses for the Danish army, coin and food for the Danish warriors, and his fyrd, what was left of it, would march under Danish orders. Edmund had no sons, but his chief men, those who lived, had sons who would become hostages to ensure that the East Anglians kept the terms Ivar proposed.

"And if I say no?" Edmund asked.

Ivar was amused by that. "We take the land anyway."

The king consulted his priests and monks. Edmund was a tall, spare man, bald as an egg though he was only about thirty years old. He had protruding eyes, a pursed mouth, and a perpetual frown. He was wearing a white tunic that made him look like a priest himself. "What of God's church?" he finally asked Ivar.

"What of it?"

"Your men have desecrated God's altars, slaughtered his servants, defiled his image, and stolen his tribute!" The king was angry now. One of his hands was clenched on the arm of his chair that was set in front of the altar, while the other hand was a fist that beat time with his accusations.

"Your god cannot look after himself?" Ubba enquired.

"Our god is a mighty god," Edmund declared, "the creator of the world, yet he also allows evil to exist to test us."

"Amen," one of the priests murmured as Ivar's interpreter translated the words.

"He brought you," the king spat, "pagans from the north! Jeremiah foretold this!"

"Jeremiah?" Ivar asked, quite lost now.

One of the monks had a book, the first I had seen in many years, and he unwrapped its leather cover, paged through the stiff leaves, and gave it to the king who reached into a pocket and took out a small ivory pointer that he used to indicate the words he wanted. **"Quia malum ego,"** he thundered, the pale pointer moving along the lines, **"adduco ab aquilone et contritionem magnam!"**

He stopped there, glaring at Ivar, and some of the Danes, impressed by the forcefulness of the king's words, even though none of them understood a single one of them, touched their hammer charms. The priests around Edmund looked reproachfully at us. A sparrow flew in through a high window and perched for a moment on an arm of the high wooden cross that stood on the altar.

Ivar's dread face showed no reaction to Jeremiah's words and it finally dawned on the East Anglian interpreter, who was one of the priests, that the king's impassioned reading had meant nothing to any of us. "For I will bring evil from the north," he translated, "and great destruction."

"It is in the book!" Edmund said fiercely, giving the volume back to the monk.

"You can keep your church," Ivar said carelessly.

"It is not enough!" Edmund said. He stood up to give his next words more force. "I will rule here," he went on, "and I will suffer your presence if I must, and I will provide you with horses, food, coin, and hostages, but only if you, and all of your men, submit to God. You must be baptized!"

That word was lost on the Danish interpreter, and on the king's, and finally Ubba looked to me for help. "You have to stand in a barrel of water," I said, remembering how Beocca had baptized me after my brother's death, "and they pour more water over you."

"They want to wash me?" Ubba asked, astonished.

I shrugged. "That's what they do, lord."

"You will become Christians!" Edmund said, then shot me an irritated look. "We can baptize in the river, boy. Barrels are not necessary."

"They want to wash you in the river," I explained to Ivar and Ubba, and the Danes laughed.

Ivar thought about it. Standing in a river for a few minutes was not such a bad thing, especially if it meant he could hurry back to quell whatever trouble afflicted Northumbria. "I can go on worshipping Odin once I'm washed?" he asked.

"Of course not!" Edmund said angrily. "There is only one god!"

"There are many gods," Ivar snapped back, "many! Everyone knows that."

"There is only one god, and you must serve him."

"But we're winning," Ivar explained patiently, almost as if he talked to a child, "which means our gods are beating your one god."

The king shuddered at this awful heresy. "Your gods are false gods," he said. "They are turds of the devil, they are evil things who will bring darkness to the world, while our god is great, he is all powerful, he is magnificent."

"Show me," Ivar said.

Those two words brought silence. The king, his priests, and his monks all stared at Ivar in evident puzzlement.

"Prove it," Ivar said, and his Danes murmured their support of the idea.

King Edmund blinked, evidently lost for inspiration, then had a sudden idea and pointed at the leather panel on which was painted Saint Sebastian's experience of being an archer's target. "Our god spared the blessed Saint Sebastian from death by arrows," Edmund said, "which is proof enough, is it not?"

"But the man still died," Ivar pointed out.

"Only because that was God's will."

Ivar thought about that. "So would your god protect you from my arrows?" He asked.

"If it is his will, yes."

"So let's try," Ivar proposed. "We shall shoot arrows at you, and if you survive then we'll all be washed."

Edmund stared at the Dane, wondering if he was serious, then looked nervous when he saw that Ivar was not joking. The king opened his mouth, found he had nothing to say, and closed it again, then one of his tonsured monks murmured to him and he must have been trying to persuade the king that God was suggesting this ordeal in order to extend his church, and that a miracle would result, and the Danes would become Christians and we would all be friends and end up singing together on the high platform in heaven. The king did not look entirely convinced by this argument, if that was indeed what the monk was proposing, but the Danes wanted to attempt the miracle now and it was no longer up to Edmund to accept or refuse the trial.

A dozen men shoved the monks and priests aside while more went outside to find bows and arrows. The king, trapped in his defense of God, was kneeling at the altar, praying as hard as any man has ever prayed. The Danes were grinning. I was enjoying it. I think I rather hoped to see a miracle, not because I was a Christian, but because I just wanted to see a miracle. Beocca had often told me about miracles, stressing that they were the real proof of Christianity's truths, but I had never seen one. No one had ever walked on the water at Bebbanburg and no lepers were healed there and no angels had filled our night skies with blazing glory, but now, perhaps, I would see the power of God that Beocca had forever preached to me. Brida just wanted to see Edmund dead.

"Are you ready?" Ivar demanded of the king.

Edmund looked at his priests and monks and I wondered if he was about to suggest that one of them should replace him in this test of God's power. Then he frowned and looked back to Ivar. "I will accept your proposal," he said.

"That we shoot arrows at you?"

"That I remain king here."

"But you want to wash me first."

"We can dispense with that," Edmund said.

"No," Ivar said. "You have claimed your god is all powerful, that he is the only god, so I want it proved. If you are right then all of us will be washed. Are we agreed?" This question was asked of the Danes, who roared their approval.

"Not me," Ravn said, "I won't be washed."

"We will all be washed!" Ivar snarled, and I realized he truly was interested in the outcome of the test, more interested, indeed, than he was in making a quick and convenient peace with Edmund. All men need the support of their god and Ivar was trying to discover whether he had, all these years, been worshipping at the wrong shrine. "Are you wearing armor?" he asked Edmund.

"No."

"Best to be sure," Ubba intervened and

glanced at the fatal painting. "Strip him," he ordered.

The king and the churchmen protested, but the Danes would not be denied and King Edmund was stripped stark naked. Brida enjoyed that. "He's puny," she said. Edmund, the butt of laughter now, did his best to look dignified. The priests and monks were on their knees, praying, while six archers took their stance a dozen paces from Edmund.

"We are going to find out," Ivar told us, stilling the laughter, "whether the English god is as powerful as our Danish gods. If he is, and if the king lives, then we shall become Christians, all of us!"

"Not me," Ravn said again, but quietly so that Ivar could not hear. "Tell me what happens, Uhtred."

It was soon told. Six arrows hit, the king screamed, blood spattered the altar, he fell down, he twitched like a gaffed salmon, and six more arrows thumped home. Edmund twitched some more, and the archers kept on shooting, though their aim was bad because they were half helpless with laughter, and they went on shooting until the king was as full of feathered shafts as a hedgehog has spikes. And he was quite dead by then. He was bloodied, his white skin red-laced, open-mouthed, and dead. His god had failed him miserably. Nowadays, of course, that story is never told; instead children learn how brave Saint Edmund stood up to the Danes, demanded their conversion, and was murdered. So now he is a martyr and a saint, warbling happily in heaven, but the truth is that he was a fool and talked himself into martyrdom.

The priests and monks wailed, so Ivar ordered them killed as well, then he decreed that Earl Godrim, one of his chiefs, would rule in East Anglia and that Halfdan would savage the country to quench the last sparks of resistance. Godrim and Halfdan would be given a third of the army to keep East Anglia quiet, while the rest of us would return to subdue the unrest in Northumbria.

So now East Anglia was gone.

And Wessex was the last kingdom of England.

We returned to Northumbria, half rowing and half sailing the **Wind-Viper** up the gentle coast, then rowing against the rivers' currents as we traveled up the Humber, then the Ouse, until Eoferwic's walls came into sight, and there we hauled the ship onto dry land so she would not rot through the winter. Ivar and Ubba returned with us, so that a whole fleet skimmed the river, oars dripping, beastless prows bearing branches of green oak to show we came home victorious. We brought home much treasure. The Danes set much store by treasure. Their men follow their leaders because they know they will be rewarded with silver, and in the taking of three of England's four kingdoms the Danes had amassed a fortune that was shared among the men and some, a few, decided to take their money back home to Denmark. Most stayed, for the richest kingdom remained undefeated and men reckoned they would all become as wealthy as gods once Wessex fell.

Ivar and Ubba had come to Eoferwic expecting trouble. They had their shields displayed on the flanks of their ships, but whatever unrest had disturbed Northumbria had not affected the city and King Egbert, who ruled at the pleasure of the Danes, sulkily denied there had been any rising at all. Archbishop Wulfhere said the same. "There is always banditry," he declared loftily, "and perhaps you heard rumors of it?"

"Or perhaps you are deaf," Ivar snarled, and Ivar was right to be suspicious for, once it was known that the army had returned, messengers came from Ealdorman Ricsig of Dunholm. Dunholm was a great fortress on a high crag that was almost surrounded by the river Wiire, and the crag and the river made Dunholm almost as strong as Bebbanburg. It was ruled by Ricsig who had never drawn his sword against the Danes. When we attacked Eoferwic and my father was killed, Ricsig had claimed to be sick and his men had stayed home, but now he sent servants to tell Ivar that a band of Danes had been slaughtered at Gyruum. That was the site of a famous monastery where a man called Bede wrote a history of the English church that Beocca had always praised to me, saying that when I learned to read properly I could give myself the treat of reading it. I have yet to do so, but I have been to Gyruum and seen where the book was written for Ragnar was asked to take his men there and discover what had happened.

It seemed six Danes, all of them masterless men, had gone to Gyruum and demanded to see the monastery's treasury and, when the monks claimed to be penniless, the six had started killing, but the monks had fought back and, as there were over a score of monks, and as they were helped by some men from the town, they succeeded in killing the six Danes who had then been spitted on posts and left to rot on the foreshore. Thus far, as Ragnar admitted, the fault lay with the Danes, but the monks, encouraged by this slaughter, had marched west up the river Tine, and attacked a Danish settlement where there were only a few men, those too old or too sick to travel south with the army, and there they had raped and killed at least a score of women and children, proclaiming that this was now a holy war. More men had joined the makeshift army, but Ealdorman Ricsig, fearing the revenge of the Danes, had sent his own troops to disperse them. He had captured a good number of the rebels, including a dozen monks, who were now held at his fortress above the river at Dunholm.

All this we heard from Ricsig's messengers, then from folk who had survived the massacre, and one of those was a girl the same age as Ragnar's daughter, and she said the monks had raped her one at a time, and afterward they had forcibly baptized her. She said there had been nuns present as well, women who had urged the men on and had taken part in the slaughter afterward. "Nests of vipers," Ragnar said. I had never seen him so angry, not even when Sven had exposed

himself to Thyra. We dug up some of the Danish
dead and all were naked and all were blood spattered. They had all been tortured.

A priest was found and made to tell us the
names of the chief monasteries and nunneries in
Northumbria. Gyruum was one, of course, and
just across the river was a large nunnery, while to
the south, where the Wiire met the sea, was a second monastery. The house at Streonshall was
close to Eoferwic, and that held many nuns,
while close to Bebbanburg, on the island that
Beocca had always told me was sacred, was the
monastery of Lindisfarena. There were many
others, but Ragnar was content with the chief
places, and he sent men to Ivar and Ubba suggesting that the nuns of Streonshall should be
dispersed, and any found to have joined the revolt should be killed. Then he set about Gyruum.
Every monk was killed, the buildings that were
not made of stone were burned, the treasures, for
they did indeed have silver and gold hidden beneath their church, were taken. I remember we
discovered a great pile of writings, sheet upon
sheet of parchments, all smothered in tight black
writing, and I have no idea what the writings
were, and now I never will, for they were all
burned, and once Gyruum was no more we went

south to the monastery at the mouth of the Wiire and we did the same there, and afterward crossed the Tine and obliterated the nunnery on the northern bank. The nuns there, led by their abbess, deliberately scarred their own faces. They knew we were coming and so, to deter rape, cut their cheeks and foreheads and so met us all bloody, screaming, and ugly. Why they did not run away I do not know, but instead they waited for us, cursed us, prayed for heaven's revenge on us, and died.

I never told Alfred that I took part in that famous harrowing of the northern houses. The tale is still told as evidence of Danish ferocity and untrustworthiness, indeed every English child is told the story of the nuns who cut their faces to the bone so that they would be too ugly to rape, though that did not work any more than King Edmund's prayers had saved him from arrows. I remember one Easter listening to a sermon about the nuns, and it was all I could do not to interrupt and say that it had not happened as the priest described. The priest claimed that the Danes had promised that no monk or nun would ever be hurt in Northumbria, and that was not true, and he claimed that there was no cause for the massacres, which was equally false, and then he told a marvelous tale how the nuns had prayed and God had placed an invisible curtain at the nunnery gate, and the Danes had pushed against the curtain and could not pierce it, and I was wondering why, if the nuns had this invisible shield, they had bothered to scar themselves, but they must have known how the story would end, because the Danes were supposed to have fetched a score of small children from the nearby village and threatened to cut their throats unless the curtain was lifted, which it was.

None of that happened. We arrived, they screamed, the young ones were raped, and then they died. But not all of them, despite the famous tales. At least two were pretty and not at all scarred, and both of them stayed with Ragnar's men and one of them gave birth to a child who grew up to become a famous Danish warrior. Still, priests have never been great men for the truth and I kept quiet, which was just as well. In truth we never killed everybody because Ravn drove it home to me that you always left one person alive to tell the tale so that news of the horror would spread.

Once the nunnery was burned we went to Dunholm where Ragnar thanked the ealdorman Ricsig, though Ricsig was plainly shocked by the revenge the Danes had taken. "Not every monk and nun took part in the slaughter," he pointed out reprovingly.

"They are all evil," Ragnar insisted.

"Their houses," Ricsig said, "are places of prayer and of contemplation, places of learning."

"Tell me," Ragnar demanded, "what use is prayer, contemplation, or learning? Does prayer grow rye? Does contemplation fill a fishing net? Does learning build a house or plow a field?"

Ricsig had no answer to those questions, nor indeed did the Bishop of Dunholm, a timid man who made no protest at the slaughter, not even when Ricsig meekly handed over his prisoners who were put to death in various imaginative ways. Ragnar had become convinced that the Christian monasteries and nunneries were sources of evil, places where sinister rites were performed to encourage folk to attack the Danes, and he saw no point in letting such places exist. The most famous monastery of all, though, was that at Lindisfarena, the house where Saint Cuthbert had lived, and the house that had first been sacked by the Danes two generations before. It had been that attack that had been portended by dragons in the sky and whirlwinds churning the sea and lightning storms savaging the hills, but I saw no such strange wonders as we marched north.

I was excited. We were going close to Bebbanburg and I wondered whether my uncle, the false ealdorman Ælfric, would dare come out of his fortress to protect the monks of Lindisfarena who had always looked to our family for their safety. We all rode horses, three ships' crews, over a hundred men, for it was late in the year and the Danes did not like taking their ships into hard weather. We skirted Bebbanburg, riding in the hills, catching occasional glimpses of the fortress's wooden walls between the trees. I stared at it, seeing the fretting sea beyond, dreaming.

We crossed the flat coastal fields and came to the sandy beach where a track led to Lindisfarena, but at high tide the track was flooded and we were forced to wait. We could see the monks watching us on the farther shore. "The rest of the bastards will be burying their treasures," Ragnar said.

"If they have any left," I said.

"They always have some left," Ragnar said grimly.

"When I was last here," Ravn put in, "we took a chest of gold! Pure gold!"

"A big chest?" Brida asked. She was mounted

behind Ravn, serving as his eyes this day. She came everywhere with us, spoke good Danish by now, and was regarded as bringing luck by the men who adored her.

"As big as your chest," Ravn said.

"Not much gold then," Brida said, disappointed.

"Gold and silver," Ravn reminisced, "and some walrus tusks. Where did they get those?"

The sea relented, the bickering waves slunk back down the long sands, and we rode through the shallows, past the withies that marked the track, and the monks ran off. Small flickers of smoke marked where farmsteads dotted the island and I had no doubt those folk were burying what few possessions they owned.

"Will any of these monks know you?" Ragnar asked me.

"Probably."

"Does that worry you?"

It did, but I said it did not, and I touched Thor's hammer and somewhere in my thoughts there was a tendril of worry that God, the Christian god, was watching me. Beocca always said that everything we did was watched and recorded, and I had to remind myself that the Christian god was failing and that Odin, Thor, and the other Danish gods were winning the war in heaven. Edmund's death had proved that and so I consoled myself that I was safe.

The monastery lay on the south of the island from where I could see Bebbanburg on its crag of rock. The monks lived in a scatter of small timber buildings, thatched with rye and moss, and built about a small stone church. The abbot, a man called Egfrith, came to meet us carrying a wooden cross. He spoke Danish, which was unusual, and he showed no fear. "You are most welcome to our small island," he greeted us enthusiastically, "and you should know that I have one of your countrymen in our sick chamber."

Ragnar rested his hands on the fleece-covered pommel of his saddle. "What is that to me?" he asked.

"It is an earnest of our peaceful intentions, lord," Egfrith said. He was elderly, gray haired, thin, and missing most of his teeth so that his words came out sibilant and distorted. "We are a humble house," he went on, "we tend the sick, we help the poor, and we serve God." He looked along the line of Danes, grim helmeted men with their shields hanging by their left knees, swords and axes and spears bristling. The sky was low that day, heavy and sullen, and a small rain was darkening the grass. Two monks came from the church carrying a wooden box that they placed behind Egfrith, then backed away. "That is all the treasure we have," Egfrith said, "and you are welcome to it."

Ragnar jerked his head at me and I dismounted, walked past the abbot, and opened the box to find it was half full of silver pennies, most of them clipped, and all of them dull because they were of bad quality. I shrugged at Ragnar as if to suggest they were poor reward.

"You are Uhtred!" Egfrith said. He had been staring at me.

"So?" I answered belligerently.

"I heard you were dead, lord," he said, "and I praise God you are not."

"You heard I was dead?"

"That a Dane killed you."

We had been talking in English and Ragnar wanted to know what had been said, so I translated. "Was the Dane called Weland?" Ragnar asked Egfrith.

"He is called that," Egfrith said.

"Is?"

"Weland is the man lying here recovering from his wounds, lord." Egfrith looked at me again as though he could not believe I was alive.

"His wounds?" Ragnar wanted to know.

"He was attacked, lord, by a man from the fortress. From Bebbanburg."

Ragnar, of course, wanted to hear the whole tale. It seemed Weland had made his way back to Bebbanburg where he claimed to have killed me, and so received his reward in silver coins, and he was escorted from the fortress by a half dozen men who included Ealdwulf, the blacksmith who had told me stories in his forge, and Ealdwulf had attacked Weland, hacking an ax down into his shoulder before the other men dragged him off. Weland had been brought here, while Ealdwulf, if he still lived, was back in Bebbanburg.

If Abbot Egfrith thought Weland was his safeguard, he had miscalculated. Ragnar scowled at him. "You gave Weland shelter even though you thought he had killed Uhtred?" he demanded.

"This is a house of God," Egfrith said, "so we give every man shelter."

"Including murderers?" Ragnar asked, and he reached behind his head and untied the leather lace that bound his hair. "So tell me, monk, how many of your men went south to help their comrades murder Danes?"

Egfrith hesitated, which was answer enough, and then Ragnar drew his sword and the abbot found his voice. "Some did, lord," he admitted. "I could not stop them."

"You could not stop them?" Ragnar asked, shaking his head so that his wet unbound hair fell around his face. "Yet you rule here?"

"I am the abbot, yes."

"Then you could stop them." Ragnar was looking angry now and I suspected he was remembering the bodies we had disinterred near Gyruum, the little Danish girls with blood still on their thighs. "Kill them," he told his men.

I took no part in that killing. I stood by the shore and listened to the birds cry and I watched Bebbanburg and heard the blades doing their work, and Brida came to stand beside me and she took my hand and stared south across the white-flecked gray to the great fortress on its crag. "Is that your house?" she asked.

"That is my house."

"He called you lord."

"I am a lord."

She leaned against me. "You think the Christian god is watching us."

"No," I said, wondering how she knew that I had been thinking about that very question.

"He was never our god," she said fiercely. "We worshipped Woden and Thor and Eostre and all the other gods and goddesses, and then the Christians came and we forgot our gods, and now the Danes have come to lead us back to them." She stopped abruptly.

"Did Ravn tell you that?"

"He told me some," she said, "but the rest I worked out. There's war between the gods, Uhtred, war between the Christian god and our gods, and when there is war in Asgard the gods make us fight for them on earth."

"And we're winning?" I asked.

Her answer was to point to the dead monks, scattered on the wet grass, their robes bloodied, and now that their killing was done Ragnar dragged Weland out of his sickbed. The man was plainly dying, for he was shivering and his wound stank, but he was conscious of what was happening to him. His reward for killing me had been a heavy bag of good silver coins that weighed as much as a newborn babe, and that we found beneath his bed and we added it to the monastery's small hoard to be divided among our men.

Weland himself lay on the bloodied grass, looking from me to Ragnar. "You want to kill him?" Ragnar asked me.

"Yes," I said, for no other response was expected. Then I remembered the beginning of my tale, the day when I had seen Ragnar oar-dancing just off this coast and how, next morning, Ragnar had brought my brother's head to Bebbanburg. "I want to cut off his head," I said.

Weland tried to speak, but could only manage a guttural groan. His eyes were on Ragnar's sword.

Ragnar offered the blade to me. "It's sharp enough," he said, "but you'll be surprised by how much force is needed. An ax would be better."

Weland looked at me now. His teeth chattered and he twitched. I hated him. I had disliked him from the first, but now I hated him, yet I was still oddly anxious about killing him even though he was already half dead. I have learned that it is one thing to kill in battle, to send a brave man's soul to the corpse hall of the gods, but quite another to take a helpless man's life, and he must have sensed my hesitation for he managed a pitiful plea for his life. "I will serve you," he said.

"Make the bastard suffer," Ragnar answered for me. "Send him to the corpse goddess, but let her know he's coming by making him suffer."

I do not think he suffered much. He was already so feeble that even my puny blows drove him to swift unconsciousness, but even so it took a long time to kill him. I hacked away. I have always been surprised by how much effort is needed to kill a man. The skalds make it sound easy, but it rarely is. We are stubborn creatures, we cling to life and are very hard to kill, but Weland's soul finally went to its fate as I chopped and sawed and stabbed and at last succeeded in severing his bloody head. His mouth was twisted into a rictus of agony, and that was some consolation.

Now I asked more favors of Ragnar, knowing he would give them to me. I took some of the poorer coins from the hoard, then went to one of the larger monastery buildings and found the writing place where the monks copied books. They used to paint beautiful letters on the books and, before my life was changed at Eoferwic, I used to go there with Beocca and sometimes the monks would let me daub scraps of parchment with their wonderful colors.

I wanted the colors now. They were in bowls, mostly as powder, a few mixed with gum, and I needed a piece of cloth, which I found in the church, a square of white linen that had been used to cover the sacraments. Back in the writing place I drew a wolf's head in charcoal on the white cloth and then I found some ink and began to fill in the outline. Brida helped me and she proved to be much better at making pictures than I was, and she gave the wolf a red eye and a red tongue, and flecked the black ink with white and blue that somehow suggested fur, and once the banner was made we tied it to the staff of the dead abbot's cross. Ragnar was rummaging through the monastery's small collection of sacred books, tearing off the jewel-studded metal plates that decorated their front covers, and once he had all the plates, and once my banner was made, we burned all the timber buildings.

The rain stopped as we left. We trotted across the causeway, turned south, and Ragnar, at my request, went down the coastal track until we reached the place where the road crossed the sands to Bebbanburg.

We stopped there and I untied my hair so that it hung loose. I gave the banner to Brida, who would ride Ravn's horse while the old man waited with his son. And then, a borrowed sword at my side, I rode home.

Brida came with me as standard-bearer and the two of us cantered along the track. The sea broke white to my right and slithered across the sands to my left. I could see men on the walls and up on the Low Gate, watching, and I kicked the horse, making it gallop, and Brida kept pace, her banner flying above, and I curbed the horse where the track turned north to the gate and now I could see my uncle. He was there, Ælfric the Treacherous, thin faced, dark haired, gazing at me from the Low Gate, and I stared up at him so he would know who I was, and then I threw Weland's severed head onto the ground where my brother's head had once been thrown. I followed it with the silver coins.

I threw thirty coins. The Judas price. I remembered that church tale. It was one of the few that I had liked.

There were archers on the wall, but none drew. They just watched. I gave my uncle the evil sign, the devil's horns made with the two outer fingers, and then I spat at him, turned, and trotted away. He knew I was alive now, knew I was his enemy, and knew I would kill him like a dog if ever I had the chance.

"Uhtred!" Brida called. She had been looking behind and I twisted in the saddle to see that one warrior had jumped over the wall, had fallen heavily, but was now running toward us. He was a big man, heavily bearded, and I thought I could never fight such a man, and then I saw the archers loose their arrows and they flecked the ground about the man who I now saw was Eald-wulf, the smith.

"Lord Uhtred!" Ealdwulf called. "Lord Uhtred!" I turned the horse and went to him, shielding him from the arrows with my horse's bulk, but none of the arrows came close and I suspect, looking back on that distant day, that the bowmen were deliberately missing. "You live, lord!" Ealdwulf beamed up at me.

"I live."

"Then I come with you," he said firmly.

"But your wife, your son?" I asked.

"My wife died, lord, last year, and my son was drowned while fishing."

"I am sorry," I said. An arrow skidded through the dune grass, but it was yards away.

"Woden gives, and Woden takes away," Eald-wulf said, "and he has given me back my lord." He saw Thor's hammer about my neck and, because he was a pagan, he smiled.

And I had my first follower. Ealdwulf the smith.

"He's a gloomy man, your uncle," Ealdwulf told me as we journeyed south, "miserable as shit, he is. Even his new son don't cheer him up."

"He has a son?"

"Ælfric the Younger, he's called, and he's a bonny wee thing. Healthy as you like. Gytha's sick though. She won't last long. And you, lord? You look well."

"I am well."

"You'd be twelve now?"

"Thirteen."

"A man, then. Is that your woman?" He nodded at Brida.

"My friend."

"No meat on her," Ealdwulf said, "so better as a friend." The smith was a big man, almost forty years old, with hands, forearms, and face black-scarred from countless small burns from his forge. He walked beside my horse, his pace apparently effortless despite his advanced years. "So tell me about these Danes," he said, casting a dubious look at Ragnar's warriors.

"They're led by Earl Ragnar," I said, "who is the man who killed my brother. He's a good man."

"He's the one who killed your brother?" Ealdwulf seemed shocked.

"Destiny is everything," I said, which might have been true but also avoided having to make a longer answer.

"You like him?"

"He's like a father to me. You'll like him."

"He's still a Dane, though, isn't he, lord? They might worship the right gods," Ealdwulf said grudgingly, "but I'd still like to see them gone."

"Why?"

"Why?" Ealdwulf seemed shocked that I had asked. "Because this isn't their land, lord, that's why. I want to walk without being afraid. I don't want to touch my forelock to a man just because he has a sword. There's one law for them and another for us."

"There's no law for them," I said.

"If a Dane kills a Northumbrian," Ealdwulf said indignantly, "what can a man do? There's no wergild, no reeve to see, no lord to seek justice."

That was true. Wergild was the blood price of a man's life, and every person had a wergild. A man's was more than a woman's, unless she was a great woman, and a warrior's was greater than a farmer's, but the price was always there, and a murderer could escape being put to death if the family of the murdered man would accept the wergild. The reeve was the man who enforced the law, reporting to his ealdorman, but that whole careful system of justice had vanished since the Danes had come. There was no law now except what the Danes said it was, and that was what they wanted it to be, and I knew that I reveled in that chaos, but then I was privileged. I was Ragnar's man, and Ragnar protected me, but without Ragnar I would be no better than an outlaw or a slave.

"Your uncle doesn't protest," Ealdwulf went on, "but Beocca did. You remember him? Red-haired priest with a shriveled hand and crossed eyes?"

"I met him last year," I said.

"You did? Where?"

"He was with Alfred of Wessex."

"Wessex!" Ealdwulf said, surprised. "Long way to go. But he was a good man, Beocca, despite being a priest. He ran off because he couldn't stand the Danes. Your uncle was furious. Said Beocca deserved to be killed."

Doubtless, I thought, because Beocca had taken the parchments that proved me to be the rightful ealdorman. "My uncle wanted me killed, too," I said, "and I never thanked you for attacking Weland."

"Your uncle was going to give me to the Danes for that," he said, "only no Dane complained, so he did nothing."

"You're with the Danes now," I said, "and you'd better get used to it."

Ealdwulf thought about that for a moment. "Why not go to Wessex?" he asked.

"Because the West Saxons want to turn me into a priest," I said, "and I want to be a warrior."

"Go to Mercia then," Ealdwulf suggested.

"That's ruled by the Danes."

"But your uncle lives there."

"My uncle?"

"Your mother's brother!" He was astonished that I did not know my own family. "He's Ealdorman Æthelwulf, if he still lives."

"My father never talked about my mother," I said.

"Because he loved her. She was a beauty, your mother, a piece of gold, and she died giving birth to you."

"Æthelwulf," I said.

"If he lives."

But why go to Æthelwulf when I had Ragnar? Æthelwulf was family, of course, but I had never met him and I doubted he even remembered my existence, and I had no desire to find him, and even less desire to learn my letters in Wessex, so I would stay with Ragnar. I said as much to Ealdwulf. "He's teaching me to fight," I said.

"Learn from the best, eh?" Ealdwulf said grudgingly. "That's how you become a good smith. Learn from the best."

Ealdwulf was a good smith and, despite himself, he came to like Ragnar for Ragnar was generous and he appreciated good workmanship. A smithy was added onto our home near Synningthwait and Ragnar paid good silver for a forge, an anvil, and the great hammers, tongs, and files that Ealdwulf needed. It was late winter before all was ready, and then ore was purchased from Eoferwic and our valley echoed to the clang of iron on iron, and even on the coldest days the smithy was warm and men gathered there to exchange stories or to tell riddles. Ealdwulf was a great man for riddles and I would translate for him as he baffled Ragnar's Danes. Most of his riddles were about men and women and what they did together and those were easy enough to guess, but I liked the complicated ones. My father and mother gave me up for dead, one riddle began, then a loyal kinswoman wrapped and protected me, and I killed all her children, but she still loved me and fed me until I rose above the dwelling houses of men and so left her. I could not guess that one, nor could any of the Danes, and Ealdwulf refused to give me the answer even when I begged him and it was only when I told the riddle to Brida that I learned the solution. "A cuckoo, of course," she said instantly. She was right, of course.

By spring the forge needed to be larger, and all that summer Ealdwulf made metal for swords, spears, axes, and spades. I asked him once if he minded working for the Danes and he just shrugged. "I worked for them in Bebbanburg," he said, "because your uncle does their bidding."

"But there are no Danes in Bebbanburg?"

"None," he admitted, "but they visit and are made welcome. Your uncle pays them tribute." He stopped suddenly, interrupted by a shout of what I thought was pure rage.

I ran out of the smithy to see Ragnar standing in front of the house while, approaching up the track, was a crowd of men led by a mounted warrior. And such a warrior. He had a mail coat, a fine helmet hanging from the saddle, a bright-painted shield, a long sword, and arms thick with rings. He was a young man with long fair hair and a thick gold beard, and he roared back at Ragnar like a rutting stag. Then Ragnar ran toward him and I half thought the young man would draw the sword and kick at his horse, but instead he dismounted and ran uphill and, when the two met, they embraced and thumped each other's backs and Ragnar, when he turned toward us, had a smile that would have lit the darkest crypt of hell. "My son!" he shouted up at me. "My son!"

It was Ragnar the Younger, come from Ireland with a ship's crew and, though he did not know me, he embraced me, lifting me off the ground, whirled his sister round, thumped Rorik, kissed his mother, shouted at the servants, scattered gifts of silver chain links, and petted the hounds. A feast was ordered, and that night he gave us his news, saying he now commanded his own ship, that he had come for a few months only, and that Ivar wanted him back in Ireland by the spring. He was so like his father, and I liked him immediately, and the house was always happy when Ragnar the Younger was there. Some of his men lodged with us, and that autumn they cut trees and added a proper hall to the house, a hall fit for an earl with big beams and a high gable on which a boar's skull was nailed.

"You were lucky," he told me one day. We were thatching the new roof, laying down the thick rye straw and combing it flat.

"Lucky?"

"That my father didn't kill you at Eoferwic."

"I was lucky," I agreed.

"But he was always a good judge of men," he said, passing me a pot of ale. He perched on the roof ridge and gazed across the valley. "He likes it here."

"It's a good place. What about Ireland?"

He grinned. "Bog and rock, Uhtred, and the skraelings are vicious." The skraelings were the natives. "But they fight well! And there's silver there, and the more they fight the more silver we get. Are you going to drink all that ale, or do I get some?"

I handed him back the pot and watched as the ale ran down his beard as he drained it. "I like Ireland well enough," he said when he had finished, "but I won't stay there. I'll come back here. Find land in Wessex. Raise a family. Get fat."

"Why don't you come back now?"

"Because Ivar wants me there, and Ivar's a good lord."

"He frightens me."

"A good lord should be frightening."

"Your father isn't."

"Not to you, but what about the men he kills? Would you want to face Earl Ragnar the Fearless in a shield wall?"

"No."

"So he is frightening," he said, grinning. "Go and take Wessex," he said, "and find the land that will make me fat."

We finished the thatch, and then I had to go up into the woods because Ealdwulf had an insatiable appetite for charcoal, which is the only substance that burns hot enough to melt iron. He had shown a dozen of Ragnar's men how to produce it, but Brida and I were his best workers and we spent much time among the trees. The charcoal heaps needed constant attention and, as each would burn for at least three days, Brida and I would often spend all night beside such a pile, watching for a telltale wisp of smoke coming from the bracken and turf covering the burn. Such smoke betrayed that the fire inside was too hot and we would have to scramble over the warm heap to stuff the crack with earth and so cool the fire deep inside the pile.

We burned alder when we could get it, for that was the wood Ealdwulf preferred, and the art of it was to char the alder logs, but not let them burst into flame. For every four logs we put into a pile we would get one back, while the rest vanished to leave the lightweight, deep black, dirty charcoal. It could take a week to make the pile.

The alder was carefully stacked in a shallow pit, and a hole was left in the stack's center which we filled with charcoal from the previous burn. Then we would put a layer of bracken over the whole thing, cover that with thick turves, and, when all was done, put fire down the central hole and, when we were sure the charcoal was alight, stuff the hole tight. Now the silent, dark fire had to be controlled. We would open gaps at the base of the pit to let a little air in, but if the wind changed then the air holes had to be stuffed and others made. It was tedious work, and Ealdwulf's appetite for charcoal seemed unlimited, but I enjoyed it. To be all night in the dark, beside the warm burn, was to be a sceadugengan, and besides, I was with Brida and we had become more than friends.

She lost her first baby up beside the charcoal burn. She had not even known she was pregnant, but one night she was assailed with cramps and spearlike pains, and I wanted to go and fetch Sigrid, but Brida would not let me. She told me she knew what was happening, but I was scared helpless by her agony and I shuddered in fear throughout the dark until, just before dawn, she gave birth to a tiny dead baby boy. We buried it with its afterbirth, and Brida stumbled back to the homestead where Sigrid was alarmed by her appearance and gave her a broth of leeks and sheep brains and made her stay home. Sigrid must have suspected what had happened for she was sharp with me for a few days and she told Ragnar it was time Brida was married. Brida was certainly of age, being thirteen, and there were a dozen young Danish warriors in Synningthwait who were in need of wives, but Ragnar declared that Brida brought his men luck and he wanted her to ride with us when we attacked Wessex.

"And when will that be?" Sigrid asked.

"Next year," Ragnar suggested, "or the year after. No longer."

"And then?"

"Then England is no more," Ragnar said. "It will all be ours." The last of the four kingdoms would have fallen and England would be Daneland and we would all be Danes or slaves or dead.

We celebrated the Yule feast and Ragnar the Younger won every competition in Synningthwait: he hurled rocks farther than anyone, wrestled men to the ground, and even drank his father into insensibility. Then followed the dark months, the long winter, and in spring, when the gales had subsided, Ragnar the Younger had to leave and we had a melancholy feast on the eve of his going. The next morning he led his men away from the hall, going down the track in a gray drizzle. Ragnar watched his son all the way down into the valley and when he turned back to his newly built hall he had tears in his eyes. "He's a good man," he told me.

"I liked him," I said truthfully, and I did, and many years later, when I met him again, I still liked him.

There was an empty feeling after Ragnar the Younger had left, but I remember that spring and summer fondly for it was in those long days that Ealdwulf made me a sword. "I hope it's better than my last one," I said ungraciously.

"Your last one?"

"The one I carried when we attacked Eoferwic," I said.

"That thing! That wasn't mine. Your father bought it in Berewic, and I told him it was crap, but it was only a short sword. Good for killing ducks, maybe, but not for fighting. What happened to it?"

"It bent," I said, remembering Ragnar laughing at the feeble weapon.

"Soft iron, boy, soft iron."

There were two sorts of iron, he told me, the

soft and the hard. The hard made the best cutting edge, but it was brittle and a sword made of such iron would snap at the first brutal stroke, while a sword made of the softer metal would bend as my short sword had done. "So what we do is use both," he told me, and I watched as he made seven iron rods. Three were of the hard iron, and he was not really sure how he made the iron hard, only that the glowing metal had to be laid in the burning charcoal, and if he got it just right then the cooled metal would be hard and un-bending. The other four rods were longer, much longer, and they were not exposed to the char-coal for the same time, and those four he twisted until each had been turned into a spiral. They were still straight rods, but tightly twisted until they were the same length as the hard iron rods. "Why do you do that?" I asked.

"You'll see," he said mysteriously, "you'll see."

He finished with seven rods, each as thick as my thumb. Three were of the hard metal, which Ragnar called steel, while the four softer rods were prettily twisted into their tight spirals. One of the hard rods was longer and slightly thicker than the others, and that one was the sword's spine and the extra length was the tang onto which the hilt would eventually be riveted. Ealdwulf began by hammering that rod flat so that it looked like a very thin and feeble sword, then he placed the four twisted rods either side of it, two to each side so that they sheathed it, and he welded the last two steel rods on the outside to become the sword's edges, and it looked grotesque then, a bundle of mismatched rods, but this was when the real work began, the work of heating and hammering, metal glowing red, the black dross twisting as it burned away from the iron, the hammer swinging, sparks flying in the dark forge, the hiss of burning metal plunged into water, the patience as the emerging blade was cooled in a trough of ash shavings. It took days, yet as the hammering and cooling and heating went on I saw how the four twisted rods of soft iron, which were now all melded into the harder steel, had been smoothed into wondrous patterns, repetitive curling patterns that made flat, smoky wisps in the blade. In some light you could not see the patterns, but in the dusk, or when, in winter, you breathed on the blade, they showed. Serpent breath, Brida called the patterns, and I decided to give the sword that name: Serpent-Breath. Ealdwulf finished the blade by hammering grooves that ran down the center of each side. He said they helped stop the sword being trapped in an enemy's flesh. "Blood channels," he grunted.

The boss of the hilt was of iron, as was the heavy crosspiece, and both were simple, undecorated, and big, and when all was done, I shaped two pieces of ash to make the handle. I wanted the sword decorated with silver or gilt bronze, but Ealdwulf refused. "It's a tool, lord," he said, "just a tool. Something to make your work easier, and no better than my hammer." He held the blade up so that it caught the sunlight. "And one day," he went on, leaning toward me, "you will kill Danes with her."

She was heavy, Serpent-Breath, too heavy for a thirteen-year-old, but I would grow into her. Her point tapered more than Ragnar liked, but that made her well balanced for it meant there was not much weight at the blade's outer end. Ragnar liked weight there, for it helped break down enemy shields, but I preferred Serpent-Breath's agility, given her by Ealdwulf's skill, and that skill meant she never bent nor cracked, not ever, for I still have her. The ash handles have been replaced, the edges have been nicked by enemy blades, and she is slimmer now because she has been sharpened so often, but she is still beautiful, and sometimes I breathe on her flanks and see the patterns emerge in the blade, the curls and wisps, the blue and silver appearing in the metal like magic, and I remember that spring and summer in the woods of Northumbria and I think of Brida staring at her reflection in the newly made blade.

And there is magic in Serpent-Breath. Ealdwulf had his own spells that he would not tell me, the spells of the smith, and Brida took the blade into the woods for a whole night and never told me what she did with it, and those were the spells of a woman, and when we made the sacrifice of the pit slaughter, and killed a man, a horse, a ram, a bull, and a drake, I asked Ragnar to use Serpent-Breath on the doomed man so that Odin would know she existed and would look well on her. Those are the spells of a pagan and a warrior.

And I think Odin did see her, for she has killed more men than I can ever remember.

It was late summer before Serpent-Breath was finished and then, before autumn brought its sea-churning storms, we went south. It was time to obliterate England, so we sailed toward Wessex.

FIVE

We gathered at Eoferwic where the pathetic King Egbert was forced to inspect the Danes and wish them well. He rode down the riverbank where the boats waited and where the ragged crews lined on the shore and gazed at him scornfully, knowing he was not a real king, and behind him rode Kjartan and Sven, now part of his Danish bodyguard, though I assumed their job was as much to keep Egbert a prisoner as to keep him alive. Sven, a man now, wore a scarf over his missing eye, and he and his father looked far more prosperous. Kjartan wore mail and had a huge war ax slung on his shoulder, while Sven had a long sword, a coat of fox pelts, and two arm rings. "They took part in the massacre at Streonshall," Ragnar told me. That was the large nunnery near Eoferwic, and it was evident that the men who had taken their revenge on the nuns had made good plunder.

Kjartan, a dozen rings on his arms, looked Ragnar in the eye. "I would still serve you," he said, though without the humility of the last time he had asked.

"I have a new shipmaster," Ragnar said, and said no more, and Kjartan and Sven rode on, though Sven gave me the evil sign with his left hand.

The new shipmaster was called Toki, a nickname for Thorbjorn, and he was a splendid sailor and a better warrior who told tales of rowing with the Svear into strange lands where no trees grew except birch and where winter covered the land for months. He claimed the folk there ate their own young, worshipped giants, and had a third eye at the back of their heads, and some of us believed his tales.

We rowed south on the last of the summer tides, hugging the coast as we always did and spending the nights ashore on East Anglia's barren coast. We were going toward the river Temes, which Ragnar said would take us deep inland to the northern boundary of Wessex.

Ragnar now commanded the fleet. Ivar the Boneless had returned to the lands he had conquered in Ireland, taking a gift of gold from Ragnar to his eldest son, while Ubba was ravaging Dalriada, the land north of Northumbria. "Small pickings up there," Ragnar said scornfully, but Ubba, like Ivar, had amassed so much treasure in his invasions of Northumbria, Mercia, and East Anglia that he was not minded to gather more from Wessex, though, as I shall tell you in its proper place, Ubba was to change his mind later and come south.

But for the moment Ivar and Ubba were absent and so the main assault on Wessex would be led by Halfdan, the third brother, who was marching his land army out of East Anglia and would meet us somewhere on the Temes, and Ragnar was not happy about the change of command. Halfdan, he muttered, was an impetuous fool, too hotheaded, but he cheered up when he remembered my tales of Alfred that confirmed that Wessex was led by men who put their hopes in the Christian god who had been shown to possess no power at all. We had Odin, we had Thor, we had our ships, we were warriors.

After four days we came to the Temes and rowed against its great current as the river slowly narrowed on us. On the first morning that we came to the river only the northern shore, which was East Anglian territory, was visible, but by midday the southern bank, which used to be the Kingdom of Kent and was now a part of Wessex, was a dim line on the horizon. By evening the banks were a half mile apart, but there was little to see for the river flowed through flat, dull marshland. We used the tide when we could, blistered our hands on the oars when we could not, and so pulled upstream until, for the very first time, I came to Lundene.

I thought Eoferwic was a city, but Eoferwic was a village compared to Lundene. It was a vast place, thick with smoke from cooking fires, and built where Mercia, East Anglia, and Wessex met. Burghred of Mercia was Lundene's lord, so it was Danish land now, and no one opposed us as we came to the astonishing bridge that stretched so far across the wide Temes.

Lundene. I came to love that place. Not as I love Bebbanburg, but there was a life to Lundene that I found nowhere else, because the city was like nowhere else. Alfred once told me that every wickedness under the sun was practiced there, and I am glad to say he was right. He prayed for the place, I reveled in it, and I can still remember gawking at the city's two hills as Ragnar's ship ghosted against the current to come close to the bridge. It was a gray day and a spiteful rain was pitting the river, yet to me the city seemed to glow with sorcerous light.

It was really two cities built on two hills. The first, to the east, was the old city that the Romans had made, and it was there that the bridge began its span across the wide river and over the marshes on the southern bank. That first city was a place of stone buildings and had a stone wall, a real wall, not earth and wood, but masonry, high and wide, skirted by a ditch. The ditch had filled with rubbish and the wall was broken in places and it had been patched with timber, but so had the city itself where huge Roman buildings were buttressed by thatched wooden shacks in which a few Mercians lived, though most were reluctant to make their homes in the old city. One of their kings had built himself a palace within the stone wall and a great church, its lower half of masonry and upper parts of wood, had been made atop the hill, but most of the folk, as if fearing the Roman ghosts, lived outside the walls, in a new city of wood and thatch that stretched out to the west.

The old city once had wharves and quays, but they had long rotted so that the waterfront east of the bridge was a treacherous place of rotted pilings and broken piers that stabbed the river like shattered teeth. The new city, like the old, was on the river's northern bank, but was built on a low hill to the west, a half mile upstream from the old, and had a shingle beach sloping up to the houses that ran along the riverside road. I have never seen a beach so foul, so stinking of carcasses and shit, so covered in rubbish, so stark with the slimy ribs of abandoned ships, and loud with squalling gulls, but that was where our boats had to go and that meant we first had to negotiate the bridge.

The gods alone know how the Romans had built such a thing. A man could walk from one side of Eoferwic to the other and he would still not have walked the length of Lundene's bridge, though in that year of 871 the bridge was broken and it was no longer possible to walk its full length. Two arches in the center had long fallen in, though the old Roman piers that had supported the missing roadway were still there and the river foamed treacherously as its water seethed past the broken piers. To make the bridge the Romans had sunk pilings into the Temes's bed, then into the tangle of fetid marshes on the southern bank, and the pilings were so close together that the water heaped up on their farther side, then fell through the gaps in a glistening rush. To reach the dirty beach by the new city we would have to shoot one of the two gaps, but neither was wide enough to let a ship through with its oars extended. "It will be interesting," Ragnar said drily.

"Can we do it?" I asked.

"They did it," he said, pointing at ships beached upstream of the bridge, "so we can." We had anchored, waiting for the rest of the fleet to catch up. "The Franks," Ragnar went on, "have been making bridges like this on all their rivers. You know why they do it?"

"To get across?" I guessed. It seemed an obvious answer.

"To stop us getting upriver," Ragnar said. "If I ruled Lundene I'd repair that bridge, so let's be grateful the English couldn't be bothered."

We shot the gap in the bridge by waiting for the heart of the rising tide. The tide flows strongest midway between high and low water, and halfway through the flood tide there was a surge of water coming upstream that diminished the flow of the current cascading between the piers. In that short time we might get seven or eight ships through the gap and it was done by rowing at full speed toward the gap and, at the very last minute, raising the oar blades so they would clear the rotted piers, and the momentum of the ship should then carry her through. Not every ship made it on the first try. I watched two slew back, thump against a pier with the crash of breaking blades, then drift back downstream with crews of cursing men, but **Wind-Viper** made it, almost coming to a stop just beyond the bridge, but we managed to get the frontmost oars in the water, hauled, and inch by inch we crept away from the sucking gap, then men from two ships anchored upstream managed to cast us lines and they hauled us away from the bridge until suddenly we were in slack water and could row her to the beach.

On the southern bank, beyond the dark marshes, where trees grew on low hills, horsemen watched us. They were West Saxons, and they would be counting ships to estimate the size of the Great Army. That was what Halfdan called it, the Great Army of the Danes come to take all of England, but so far we were anything but great. We would wait in Lundene to let more ships come and for more men to march down the long Roman roads from the north. Wessex could wait awhile as the Danes assembled.

And, as we waited, Brida, Rorik, and I explored Lundene. Rorik had been sick again, and Sigrid had been reluctant to let him travel with his father, but Rorik pleaded with his mother to let him go. Ragnar assured her that the sea voyage would mend all the boy's ills, and so he was here. He was pale, but not sickly, and he was as excited as I was to see the city. Ragnar made me leave my arm rings and Serpent-Breath behind for, he said, the city was full of thieves. We wandered the newer part first, going through malodorous alleys where the houses were full of men working leather, beating at bronze, or forging iron. Women sat at looms, a flock of sheep was being slaughtered in a yard, and there were shops selling pottery, salt, live eels, bread, cloth, weapons, any imaginable thing. Church bells set up a hideous clamor at every prayer time or whenever a corpse was carried for burial in the city's graveyards. Packs of dogs roamed the streets, red kites roosted everywhere, and smoke lay like a fog over the thatch that had all turned a dull black. I saw a wagon so loaded with thatching reed that the wagon itself was hidden by its heap of sagging reeds that scraped on the road and ripped and tore against the buildings either side of the street as two slaves goaded and whipped the bleeding oxen. Men shouted at the slaves that the load was too big, but they went on whipping, and then a fight broke out when the wagon tore down a great piece of rotted roof. There were beggars everywhere: blind children, women without legs, a man with a weeping ulcer on his cheek. There were folk speaking languages I had never heard, folk in strange costumes who had come across the sea, and in the old city, which we explored the next day, I saw two men with skin the color of chestnuts and Ravn told me later they came from Blaland, though he was not certain where that was. They wore thick robes, had curved swords, and were talking to a slave dealer whose premises were full of captured English folk who would be shipped to the mysterious Blaland. The dealer called to us. "You three belong to anyone?" He was only half joking.

"To Earl Ragnar," Brida said, "who would love to pay you a visit."

"Give his lordship my respects," the dealer said, then spat, and eyed us as we walked away.

The buildings of the old city were extraordinary. They were Roman work, high and stout, and even though their walls were broken and their roofs had fallen in they still astonished. Some were three or even four floors high and we chased one another up and down their abandoned stairways. Few English folk lived here, though many Danes were now occupying the houses as the army assembled. Brida said that sensible people would not live in a Roman town because of the ghosts that haunted the old buildings, and maybe she was right, though I had seen no ghosts in Eoferwic, but her mention of specters made us all nervous as we peered down a flight of steps into a dark, pillared cellar.

We stayed in Lundene for weeks and even when Halfdan's army reached us we did not move west. Mounted bands did ride out to forage, but the Great Army still gathered and some men grumbled we were waiting too long, that the West Saxons were being given precious time to ready themselves, but Halfdan insisted on lingering. The West Saxons sometimes rode close to the city, and twice there were fights between our horsemen and their horsemen, but after a while, as Yule approached, the West Saxons must have decided we would do nothing till winter's end and their patrols stopped coming close to the city.

"We're not waiting for spring," Ragnar told me, "but for deep winter."

"Why?"

"Because no army marches in winter," he said

wolfishly, "so the West Saxons will all be at home, sitting around their fires and praying to their feeble god. By spring, Uhtred, all England will be ours."

We all worked that early winter. I hauled firewood, and when I was not hauling logs from the wooded hills north of the city, I was learning the skills of the sword. Ragnar had asked Toki, his new shipmaster, to be my teacher and he was a good one. He watched me rehearse the basic cuts, then told me to forget them. "In a shield wall," he said, "it's savagery that wins. Skill helps, and cunning is good, but savagery wins. Get one of these." He held out a saxe with a thick blade, much thicker than my old saxe. I despised the saxe for it was much shorter than Serpent-Breath and far less beautiful, but Toki wore one beside his proper sword, and he persuaded me that in the shield wall the short, stout blade was better. "You've no room to swing or hack in a shield wall," he said, "but you can thrust, and a short blade uses less room in a crowded fight. Crouch and stab, bring it up into their groins." He made Brida hold a shield and pretend to be the enemy, and then, with me on his left, he cut at her from above and she instinctively raised the shield. "Stop!" he said, and she froze into stillness.

"See?" he told me, pointing at the raised shield. "Your partner makes the enemy raise their shield, then you can slice into their groin." He taught me a dozen other moves, and I practiced because I liked it and the more I practiced the more muscle I grew and the more skillful I became.

We usually practiced in the Roman arena. That is what Toki called it, the arena, though what the word meant neither he nor I had any idea, but it was, in a place of extraordinary things, astonishing. Imagine an open space as large as a field surrounded by a great circle of tiered stone where weeds now grew from the crumbling mortar. The Mercians, I later learned, had held their folkmoots here, but Toki said the Romans had used it for displays of fighting in which men died. Maybe that was another of his fantastic stories, but the arena was huge, unimaginably huge, a thing of mystery, the work of giants, dwarfing us, so big that all the Great Army could have collected inside and there would still have been room for two more armies just as big on the tiered seats.

Yule came, and the winter feast was held and the army vomited in the streets and still we did not march, but shortly afterward the leaders of the Great Army met in the palace next to the arena. Brida and I, as usual, were required to be Ravn's eyes and he, as usual, told us what we were seeing.

The meeting was held in the church of the palace, a Roman building with a roof shaped like a half barrel on which the moon and stars were painted, though the blue and golden paint was peeling and discolored now. A great fire had been lit in the center of the church and it was filling the high roof with swirling smoke. Halfdan presided from the altar, and around him were the chief earls. One was an ugly man with a blunt face, a big brown beard, and a finger missing from his left hand. "That is Bagseg," Ravn told us, "and he calls himself a king, though he's no better than anyone else." Bagseg, it seemed, had come from Denmark in the summer, bringing eighteen ships and nearly six hundred men. Next to him was a tall, gloomy man with white hair and a twitching face. "Earl Sidroc," Ravn told us, "and his son must be with him?"

"Thin man," Brida said, "with a dripping nose."

"Earl Sidroc the Younger. He's always sniffing. My son is there?"

"Yes," I said, "next to a very fat man who keeps whispering to him and grinning."

"Harald!" Ravn said. "I wondered if he would turn up. He's another king."

"Really?" Brida asked.

"Well, he calls himself king, and he certainly rules over a few muddy fields and a herd of smelly pigs."

All those men had come from Denmark, and there were others besides. Earl Fraena had brought men from Ireland, and Earl Osbern who had provided the garrison for Lundene while the army gathered, and together these kings and earls had assembled well over two thousand men.

Osbern and Sidroc proposed crossing the river and striking directly south. This, they argued, would cut Wessex in two and the eastern part, which used to be the kingdom of Kent, could then be taken quickly. "There has to be much treasure in Contwaraburg," Sidroc insisted. "It's the central shrine of their religion."

"And while we march on their shrine," Ragnar said, "they will come up behind us. Their power is not in the east, but in the west. Defeat the west and all Wessex falls. We can take Contwaraburg once we've beaten the west."

This was the argument. Either take the easy part of Wessex or else attack their major strongholds that lay to the west, and two merchants were asked to speak. Both men were Danes who had been trading in Readingum only two weeks before. Readingum lay a few miles upriver and was on the edge of Wessex, and they claimed to have heard that King Æthelred and his brother, Alfred, were gathering the shire forces from the west and the two merchants reckoned the enemy army would number at least three thousand.

"Of whom only three hundred will be proper fighting men," Halfdan interjected sarcastically, and was rewarded by the sound of men banging swords or spears against their shields. It was while this noise echoed under the church's barrel roof that a new group of warriors entered, led by a very tall and very burly man in a black tunic. He looked formidable, clean shaven, angry, and very rich for his black cloak had an enormous brooch of amber mounted in gold, his arms were heavy with golden rings, and he wore a golden hammer on a thick golden chain about his neck. The warriors made way for him, his arrival causing silence among the crowd nearest to him, and the silence spread as he walked up the church until the mood, which had been of celebration, suddenly seemed wary.

"Who is it?" Ravn whispered to me.

"Very tall," I said, "many arm rings."

"Gloomy," Brida put in, "dressed in black."

"Ah! The earl Guthrum," Ravn said.

"Guthrum?"

"Guthrum the Unlucky," Ravn said.

"With all those arm rings?"

"You could give Guthrum the world," Ravn said, "and he would still believe you had cheated him."

"He has a bone hanging in his hair," Brida said.

"You must ask him about that," Ravn said, evidently amused, but he would say no more about the bone, which was a human rib and tipped with gold.

I learned Guthrum the Unlucky was an earl from Denmark who had been wintering at Beamfleot, a place that lay a good distance east of Lundene on the northern side of the Temes estuary, and once he had greeted the men bunched about the altar, he announced that he had brought fourteen ships upriver. No one applauded. Guthrum, who had the saddest, sourest face I had ever seen, stared at the assembly like a man standing trial and expecting a dire verdict. "We had decided," Ragnar broke the uncomfortable silence, "to go west." No such decision had been made, but nor did anyone contradict Ragnar.

"Those ships that are already through the bridge," Ragnar went on, "will take their crews upstream and the rest of the army will march on foot or horseback."

"My ships must go upstream," Guthrum said.

"They are through the bridge?"

"They will still go upstream," Guthrum insisted, thus letting us know that his fleet was below the bridge.

"It would be better," Ragnar said, "if we went tomorrow." In the last few days the whole of the Great Army had assembled in Lundene, marching in from the settlements east and north where some had been quartered, and the longer we waited, the more of the precious food supply would be consumed.

"My ships go upstream," Guthrum said flatly.

"He's worried," Ravn whispered to me, "that he can't carry away the plunder on horseback. He wants his ships so he can fill them with treasure."

"Why let him come?" I asked. It was plain no one liked Earl Guthrum, and his arrival seemed as unwelcome as it was inconvenient, but Ravn just shrugged the question off. Guthrum, it seemed, was here, and if he was here he must take part. That still seems incomprehensible to me, just as I still did not understand why Ivar and Ubba were not joining the attack on Wessex. It was true that both men were rich and scarcely needed more riches, but for years they had talked of conquering the West Saxons and now both had simply turned away. Guthrum did not need land or wealth either, but he thought he did, so he came. That was the Danish way. Men served in a campaign if they wished, or else they stayed home, and there was no single authority among the Danes. Halfdan was the Great Army's ostensible leader, but he did not frighten men as his two older brothers did and so he could do nothing without the agreement of the other chieftains. An army, I learned in time, needs a head. It needs one man to lead it, but give an army two leaders and you halve its strength.

It took two days to get Guthrum's ships past the bridge. They were beautiful things, those ships, larger than most Danish boats, and each decorated at prow and stern with black-painted serpent heads. His men, and there were many of them, all wore black. Even their shields were painted black, and while I thought Guthrum to be one of the most miserable men I had ever seen, I had to confess his troops were impressive.

We might have lost two days, but we had gained the black warriors.

And what was there to fear? The Great Army had gathered, it was midwinter when no one fought so the enemy should not be expecting us, and that enemy was led by a king and a prince more interested in prayer than in fighting. All Wessex lay before us and common report said that Wessex was as rich a country as any in all the world, rivaling Frankia for its treasures, and inhabited by monks and nuns whose houses were stuffed with gold, spilling over with silver, and ripe for slaughter. We would all be rich.

So we went to war.

Ships on the winter Temes. Ships sliding past brittle reeds and leafless willows and bare alders. Wet oar blades shining in the pale sunlight. The prows of our ships bore their beasts to quell the spirits of the land we invaded, and it was good land with rich fields, though all were deserted. There was almost a celebratory air to that brief voyage, a celebration unspoiled by the presence of Guthrum's dark ships. Men oar-walked, the same feat I had watched Ragnar perform on that far-off day when his three ships had appeared off

Bebbanburg. I tried it myself and raised a huge cheer when I fell in. It looked easy to run along the oar bank, leaping from shaft to shaft, but a rower only had to twitch an oar to cause a man to slip and the river water was bitterly cold so that Ragnar made me strip off my wet clothes and wear his bearskin cloak until I was warm. Men sang, the ships forged against the current, the far hills to the north and south slowly closed on the river's banks and, as evening came, we saw the first horsemen on the southern skyline. Watching us.

We reached Readingum at dusk. Each of Ragnar's three ships was loaded with spades, many of them forged by Ealdwulf, and our first task was to start making a wall. As more ships came, more men helped, and by nightfall our camp was protected by a long, straggling earth wall that would have been hardly any obstacle to an attacking force for it was merely a low mound that was easy to cross, but no one did come and assault us, and no Wessex army appeared the next morning and so we were free to make the wall higher and more formidable.

Readingum was built where the river Kenet flows into the Temes, and so our wall was built between the two rivers. It enclosed the small town that had been abandoned by its inhabitants and provided shelter for most of the ships' crews. The land army was still out of sight for they had marched along the north bank of the Temes, in Mercian territory, and were seeking a ford, which they found further upstream, so that our wall was virtually finished by the time they marched in. At first we thought it was the West Saxon army coming, but it was Halfdan's men, marching out of enemy territory they had found deserted.

The wall was high now and, because there were deep woods to the south, we had cut trees to make a palisade along its whole length that was about eight hundred paces. In front of the wall we dug a ditch that flooded when we broke through the two rivers' banks, and across the ditch we were making four bridges guarded by wooden forts. This was our base. From here we could march deep into Wessex, and we needed to for, with so many men and now horses inside the wall, there was a risk of hunger unless we found supplies of grain, hay, and cattle. We had brought barrels of ale and a large amount of flour, salt meat, and dried fish in the ships, but it was astonishing how fast those great heaps diminished.

The poets, when they speak of war, talk of the shield wall, they talk of the spears and arrows flying, of the blade beating on the shield, of the heroes who fall and the spoils of the victors, but I was to discover that war was really about food. About feeding men and horses. About finding food. The army that eats wins. And, if you keep horses in a fortress, it is about shoveling dung. Just two days after the land army came to Readingum, we were short of food and the two Sidrocs, father and son, led a large force west into enemy territory to find stores of food for men and horses, and instead they found the fyrd of Berrocscire.

We learned later that the whole idea of attacking in winter was no surprise to the West Saxons after all. The Danes were good at spying, their merchants exploring the places the warriors would go, but the West Saxons had their own men in Lundene and they knew how many men we were, and when we would march, and they had assembled an army to meet us. They had also sought help from the men of southern Mercia, where Danish rule was lightest, and Berrocscire lay immediately north of the West Saxon border and the men of Berrocscire had crossed the river to help their neighbors and their fyrd was led by an ealdorman called Æthelwulf.

Was it my uncle? There were many men called

Æthelwulf, but how many were ealdormen in Mercia? I admit I felt strange when I heard the name, and I thought of the mother I had never met. In my mind she was the woman who was ever kind, ever gentle, ever loving, and I thought she must be watching me from somewhere, heaven or Asgard or wherever our souls go in the long darkness, and I knew she would hate that I was with the army that marched against her brother, and so that night I was in a black mood.

But so was the Great Army for my uncle, if Æthelwulf was indeed my uncle, had trounced the two earls. Their foraging party had walked into an ambush and the men of Berrocscire had killed twenty-one Danes and taken another eight prisoner. The Englishmen had lost a few men themselves, and yielded one prisoner, but they had gained the victory, and it made no difference that the Danes had been outnumbered. The Danes expected to win, and instead they had been chased home without the food we needed. They felt shamed and a shudder went through the army because they did not think mere Englishmen could beat them.

We were not starving yet, but the horses were desperately short of hay, which, anyway, was not the best food for them, but we had no oats and so forage parties simply cut whatever winter grass we could find beyond our growing wall and the day after Æthelwulf's victory Rorik, Brida, and I were in one of those groups, slashing at grass with long knives and stuffing sacks with the poor feed, when the army of Wessex came.

They must have been encouraged by Æthelwulf's victory, for now the whole enemy army attacked Readingum. The first I knew of it was the sound of screaming from farther west, then I saw horsemen galloping among our forage parties, hacking down with swords or skewering men with spears, and the three of us just ran, and I heard the hooves behind and snatched a look and saw a man riding at us with a spear and knew one of us must die and I took Brida's hand to drag her out of his path and just then an arrow shot from Readingum's wall slapped into the horseman's face and he twisted away, blood pouring from his cheek, and meanwhile panicking men were piling around the two central bridges and the West Saxon horsemen, seeing it, galloped toward them. The three of us half waded and half swam the ditch, and two men hauled us, wet, muddy, and shivering, up across the wall.

It was chaos outside now. The foragers crowding at the ditch's far side were being hacked down, and then the Wessex infantry appeared, band after band of them emerging from the far woods to fill the fields. I ran back to the house where Ragnar was lodging and found Serpent-Breath beneath the cloaks where I hid her, and I strapped her on and ran out to find Ragnar. He had gone north, to the bridge close beside the Temes, and Brida and I caught up with his men there. "You shouldn't come," I told Brida. "Stay with Rorik." Rorik was younger than us and, after getting soaked in the ditch, he had started shivering and feeling sick and I had made him stay behind.

Brida ignored me. She had equipped herself with a spear and looked excited, though nothing was happening yet. Ragnar was staring over the wall, and more men were assembling at the gate, but Ragnar did not open it to cross the bridge. He did glance back to see how many men he had. "Shields!" he shouted, for in their haste some men had come with nothing but swords or axes, and those men now ran to fetch their shields. I had no shield, but nor was I supposed to be there and Ragnar did not see me.

What he saw was the end of a slaughter as the West Saxon horsemen chopped into the last of the foragers. A few of the enemy were put down by our arrows, but neither the Danes nor the English had many bowmen. I like bowmen. They can kill at a great distance and, even if their arrows do not kill, they make an enemy nervous. Advancing into arrows is a blind business, for you must keep your head beneath the rim of the shield, but shooting a bow is a great skill. It looks easy, and every child has a bow and some arrows, but a man's bow, a bow capable of killing a stag at a hundred paces, is a huge thing, carved from yew and needing immense strength to haul, and the arrows fly wild unless a man has practiced constantly, and so we never had more than a handful of archers. I never mastered the bow. With a spear, an ax, or a sword I was lethal, but with a bow I was like most men, useless.

I sometimes wonder why we did not stay behind our wall. It was virtually finished, and to reach it the enemy must cross the ditch or file over the four bridges, and they would have been forced to do that under a hail of arrows, spears, and throwing axes. They would surely have failed, but then they might have besieged us behind that wall and so Ragnar decided to attack them. Not just Ragnar. While Ragnar was gathering men at the northern gate, Halfdan had been doing the same at the southern end, and when both believed they had enough men, and while the enemy infantry was still some two hundred paces away, Ragnar ordered the gate opened and led his men through.

The West Saxon army, under its great dragon banner, was advancing toward the central bridges, evidently thinking that the slaughter there was a foretaste of more slaughter to come. They had no ladders, so how they thought they would cross the newly made wall I do not know, but sometimes in battle a kind of madness descends and men do things without reason. The men of Wessex had no reason to concentrate on the center of our wall, especially as they could not hope to cross it, but they did, and now our men swarmed from the two flanking gates to attack them from north and south.

"Shield wall!" Ragnar roared. "Shield wall!"

You can hear a shield wall being made. The best shields are made of lime, or else of willow, and the wood knocks together as men overlap the shields. Left side of the shield in front of your neighbor's right side, that way the enemy, most of whom are right-handed, must try to thrust through two layers of wood.

"Make it tight!" Ragnar called. He was in the center of the shield wall, in front of his ragged eagle-wing standard, and he was one of the few men with an expensive helmet, which would mark him to the enemy as a chieftain, a man to be killed. Ragnar still used my father's helmet, the beautiful one made by Ealdwulf with the faceplate and the inlay of silver. He also wore a mail shirt, again one of the few men to possess such a treasure. Most men were armored in leather.

The enemy was turning outward to meet us, making their own shield wall, and I saw a group of horsemen galloping up their center behind the dragon banner. I thought I saw Beocca's red hair among them and that made me certain Alfred was there, probably among a gaggle of black-robed priests who were doubtless praying for our deaths.

The West Saxon shield wall was longer than ours. It was not only longer, but thicker, because while our wall was backed by three ranks of men, theirs had five or six. Good sense would have dictated that we either stay where we were and let them attack us, or that we retreat back across the bridge and ditch, but more Danes were coming to thicken Ragnar's ranks and Ragnar himself was in no mood to be sensible. "Just kill them!" he screamed. "Just kill them! Kill them!" And he led the line forward and, without any pause, the Danes gave a great war shout and surged with him. Usually the shield walls spend hours staring at each other, calling out insults, threatening, and working up the courage to that most awful of moments when wood meets wood and blade meets blade, but Ragnar's blood was fired and he did not care. He just charged.

That attack made no sense, but Ragnar was furious. He had been offended by Æthelwulf's victory, and insulted by the way their horsemen had cut down our foragers, and all he wanted to do was hack into the Wessex ranks, and somehow his passion spread through his men so that they howled as they ran forward. There is something terrible about men eager for battle.

A heartbeat before the shields clashed our rearmost men threw their spears. Some had three or four spears that they hurled one after the other, launching them over the heads of our front ranks. There were spears coming back, and I plucked one from the turf and hurled it back as hard as I could.

I was in the rearmost rank, pushed back there by men who told me to get out of their way, but I advanced with them and Brida, grinning with mischief, came with me. I told her to go back to the town, but she just stuck her tongue out at me and then I heard the hammering crash, the wooden thunder, of shields meeting shields. That was followed by the sound of spears striking limewood, the ringing of blade on blade, but I saw nothing of it because I was not then tall enough, but the shock of the shield walls made the men in front of me reel back, then they were pushing forward again, trying to force their own front rank through the West Saxon shields. The right-hand side of our wall was bending back where the enemy outflanked us, but our reinforcements were hurrying to that place, and the West Saxons lacked the courage to charge home. Those West Saxons had been at the rear of their advancing army, and the rear is always where the timid men congregate. The real fight was to my front and the noise there was of blows, iron shield boss on shield wood, blades on shields, men's feet shuffling, the clangor of weapons, and few voices except those wailing in pain or in a sudden scream. Brida dropped onto all fours and wriggled between the legs of the men in front of her, and I saw she was lancing her spear forward to give the blow that comes beneath the shield's rim. She lunged into a man's ankle, he stumbled, an ax fell, and there was a gap in the enemy line.

Our line bulged forward, and I followed, using Serpent-Breath as a spear, jabbing at men's boots, then Ragnar gave a mighty roar, a shout to stir the gods in the great sky halls of Asgard, and the shout asked for one more great effort. Swords chopped, axes swung, and I could sense the enemy retreating from the fury of the Northmen.

Good lord deliver us.

Blood on the grass now, so much blood that the ground was slick, and there were bodies that had to be stepped over as our shield wall thrust forward, leaving Brida and me behind, and I saw her hands were red because blood had seeped down the long ash shaft of her spear. She licked the blood and gave me a sly smile. Halfdan's men were fighting on the enemy's farther side now, their battle noise suddenly louder than ours because the West Saxons were retreating from Ragnar's attack, but one man, tall and well built, resisted us. He had a mail coat belted with a red leather sword belt and a helmet even more glorious that Ragnar's, for the Englishman's helmet had a silver boar modeled on its crown, and I thought for a moment it could be King Æthelred himself, but this man was too tall, and Ragnar shouted at his men to stand aside and he swung his sword at the boar-helmeted enemy who parried with his shield, lunged with his sword, and Ragnar took the blow on his own shield and rammed it forward to crash against the man who stepped back, tripped on a corpse, and Ragnar swung his sword overhand, as if he was killing an ox, and the blade chopped down onto the mail coat as a rush of enemy came to save their lord.

A charge of Danes met them, shield on shield, and Ragnar was roaring his victory and stabbing down into the fallen man, and suddenly there were no more Wessex men resisting us, unless they were dead or wounded, and their army was running, their king and their prince both spurring away on horseback surrounded by priests, and we jeered and cursed them, told them they were women, that they fought like girls, that they were cowards.

And then we rested, catching breath on a field of blood, our own corpses among the enemy dead, and Ragnar saw me then, and saw Brida, and laughed. "What are you two doing here?"

For answer Brida held up her bloodied spear and Ragnar glanced at Serpent-Breath and saw her reddened tip. "Fools," he said, but fondly, and then one of our men brought a West Saxon prisoner and made him inspect the lord whom

Ragnar had killed. "Who is he?" Ragnar demanded.

I translated for him.

The man made the sign of the cross. "It is the Lord Æthelwulf," he said.

And I said nothing.

"What did he say?" Ragnar asked.

"It is my uncle," I said.

"Ælfric?" Ragnar was astonished. "Ælfric from Northumbria?"

I shook my head. "He is my mother's brother," I explained, "Æthelwulf of Mercia." I did not know that he was my mother's brother, perhaps there was another Æthelwulf in Mercia, but I felt certain all the same that this was Æthelwulf, my kin, and the man who had won the victory over the earls Sidroc. Ragnar, the previous day's defeat revenged, whooped for joy while I stared into the dead man's face. I had never known him, so why was I sad? He had a long face with a fair beard and a trimmed mustache. A good-looking man, I thought, and he was family, and that seemed strange for I knew no family except Ragnar, Ravn, Rorik, and Brida.

Ragnar had his men strip Æthelwulf of his armor and take his precious helmet, and then, because the ealdorman had fought so bravely, Ragnar left the corpse its other clothes and put a sword into its hand so that the gods could take the Mercian's soul to the great hall where brave warriors feast with Odin.

And perhaps the Valkyries did take his soul, because the next morning, when we went out to bury the dead, Ealdorman Æthelwulf's body was gone.

I heard later, much later, that he was indeed my uncle. I also heard that some of his own men had crept back to the field that night and somehow found their lord's body and taken it to his own country for a Christian burial.

And perhaps that is true, too. Or perhaps Æthelwulf is in Odin's corpse hall.

But we had seen the West Saxons off. And we were still hungry. So it was time to fetch the enemy's food.

Why did I fight for the Danes? All lives have questions, and that one still haunts me, though in truth there was no mystery. To my young mind the alternative was to be sitting in some monastery learning to read, and give a boy a choice like that and he would fight for the devil rather than scratch on a tile or make marks on a clay tablet. And there was Ragnar, whom I loved, and who sent his three ships across the Temes to find hay and oats stored in Mercian villages and he found just enough so that by the time the army marched westward our horses were in reasonable condition.

We were marching on Æbbanduna, another frontier town on the Temes between Wessex and Mercia, and, according to our prisoner, a place where the West Saxons had amassed their supplies. Take Æbbanduna and Æthelred's army would be short of food, Wessex would fall, England would vanish, and Odin would triumph.

There was the small matter of defeating the West Saxon army first, but we marched just four days after routing them in front of the walls of Readingum, so we were blissfully confident that they were doomed. Rorik stayed behind, for he was sick again, and the many hostages, like the Mercian twins Ceolberht and Ceolnoth, also stayed in Readingum, guarded there by the small garrison we left to watch over the precious ships.

The rest of us marched or rode. I was among the older of the boys who accompanied the army; our job in battle was to carry the spare shields that could be pushed forward through the ranks in battle. Shields got chopped to pieces in fighting. I have often seen warriors fighting with a sword or ax in one hand, and nothing but the iron shield boss hung with scraps of wood in the other. Brida also came with us, mounted behind Ravn on his horse, and for a time I walked with them, listening as Ravn rehearsed the opening lines of a poem called "The Fall of the West Saxons." He had got as far as listing our heroes, and describing how they readied themselves for battle, when one of those heroes, the gloomy Earl Guthrum, rode alongside us. "You look well," he greeted Ravn in a tone that suggested it was a condition unlikely to last.

"I cannot look at all," Ravn said. He liked puns.

Guthrum, swathed in a black cloak, looked down at the river. We were advancing along a low range of hills and, even in the winter sunlight, the river valley looked lush. "Who will be king of Wessex?" he asked.

"Halfdan?" Ravn suggested mischievously.

"Big kingdom," Guthrum said gloomily. "Could do with an older man." He looked at me sourly. "Who's that?"

"You forget I am blind," Ravn said, "so who is who? Or are you asking me which older man you think should be made king? Me, perhaps?"

"No, no! The boy leading your horse. Who is he?"

"That is the earl Uhtred," Ravn said grandly, "who understands that poets are of such importance that their horses must be led by mere earls."

"Uhtred? A Saxon?"

"Are you a Saxon, Uhtred?"

"I'm a Dane," I said.

"And a Dane," Ravn went on, "who wet his sword at Readingum. Wet it, Guthrum, with Saxon blood." That was a barbed comment, for Guthrum's black-clothed men had not fought outside the walls.

"And who's the girl behind you?"

"Brida," Ravn said, "who will one day be a skald and a sorceress."

Guthrum did not know what to say to that. He glowered at his horse's mane for a few strides, then returned to his original subject. "Does Ragnar want to be king?"

"Ragnar wants to kill people," Ravn said. "My son's ambitions are very few, merely to hear jokes, solve riddles, get drunk, give rings, lie belly to belly with women, eat well, and go to Odin."

"Wessex needs a strong man," Guthrum said obscurely, "a man who understands how to govern."

"Sounds like a husband," Ravn said.

"We take their strongholds," Guthrum said, "but we leave half their land untouched! Even Northumbria is only half garrisoned. Mercia has sent men to Wessex, and they're supposed to be on our side. We win, Ravn, but we don't finish the job."

"And how do we do that?" Ravn asked.

"More men, more ships, more deaths."

"Deaths?"

"Kill them all!" Guthrum said with a sudden vehemence. "Every last one! Not a Saxon alive."

"Even the women?" Ravn asked.

"We could leave some young ones," Guthrum said grudgingly, then scowled at me. "What are you looking at, boy?"

"Your bone, lord," I said nodding at the gold-tipped bone hanging in his hair.

He touched the bone. "It's one of my mother's ribs," he said. "She was a good woman, a wonderful woman, and she goes with me wherever I go. You could do worse, Ravn, than make a song for my mother. You knew her, didn't you?"

"I did indeed," Ravn said blandly. "I knew her well enough, Guthrum, to worry that I lack the poetic skills to make a song worthy of such an illustrious woman."

The mockery flew straight past Guthrum the Unlucky. "You could try," he said. "You could try, and I would pay much gold for a good song about her."

He was mad, I thought, mad as an owl at midday, and then I forgot him because the army of Wessex was ahead, barring our road and offering battle.

The dragon banner of Wessex was flying on the summit of a long low hill that lay athwart our road. To reach Æbbanduna, which evidently lay a short way beyond the hill and was hidden by it, we would need to attack up the slope and across that ridge of open grassland, but to the north, where the hills fell away to the river Temes, there was a track along the river, which suggested we might skirt the enemy position. To stop us he would need to come down the hill and give battle on level ground.

Halfdan called the Danish leaders together and they talked for a long time, evidently disagreeing about what should be done. Some men wanted to attack uphill and scatter the enemy where they were, but others advised fighting the West Saxons in the flat river meadows, and in the end Earl Guthrum the Unlucky persuaded them to do both. That, of course, meant splitting our army into two, but even so I thought it was a clever idea. Ragnar, Guthrum, and the two earls Sidroc would go down to the lower ground, thus threatening to pass by the enemy-held hill, while Halfdan, with Harald and Bagseg, would stay on the high ground and advance toward the dragon banner on the ridge. That way the enemy might hesitate to attack Ragnar for fear that Halfdan's troops would fall on their rear. Most likely, Ragnar said, the enemy would decide not to fight at all, but instead retreat to Æbbanduna where we could besiege them. "Better to have them penned in a fortress than roaming around," he said cheerfully.

"Better still," Ravn commented drily, "not to divide the army."

"They're only West Saxons," Ragnar said dismissively.

It was already afternoon and, because it was winter, the day was short so there was not much time, though Ragnar thought there was more than enough daylight remaining to finish off Æthelred's troops. Men touched their charms, kissed sword hilts, hefted shields; then we were marching down the hill, going off the chalk grasslands into the river valley. Once there, we were half hidden by the leafless trees, but now and again I could glimpse Halfdan's men advancing along the hillcrests and I could see there were West Saxon troops waiting for them, which suggested that Guthrum's plan was working and that we could march clear around the enemy's northern flank. "What we do then," Ragnar said, "is climb up behind them, and the bastards will be trapped. We'll kill them all!"

"One of them has to stay alive," Ravn said.

"One? Why?"

"To tell the tale, of course. Look for their poet. He'll be handsome. Find him and let him live."

Ragnar laughed. There were, I suppose, about eight hundred of us, slightly fewer than the contingent that had stayed with Halfdan, and the enemy army was probably slightly larger than our two forces combined, but we were all warriors and many of the West Saxon fyrd were farmers forced to war and so we saw nothing but victory.

Then, as our leading troops marched out of an oakwood, we saw the enemy had followed our example and divided their own army into two. One half was waiting on the hill for Halfdan while the other half had come to meet us.

Alfred led our opponents. I knew that because I could see Beocca's red hair and, later on, I glimpsed Alfred's long anxious face in the fighting.

His brother, King Æthelred, had stayed on the heights where, instead of waiting for Halfdan to assault him, he was advancing to make his own attack. The Saxons, it seemed, were avid for battle.

So we gave it to them.

Our forces made shield wedges to attack their shield wall. We called on Odin, we howled our war cries, we charged, and the West Saxon line did not break, it did not buckle, but instead held fast and so the slaughterwork began.

Ravn told me time and again that destiny was everything. Fate rules. The three spinners sit at the foot of the tree of life and they make our lives and we are their playthings, and though we think we make our own choices, all our fates are in the spinners' threads. Destiny is everything, and that day, though I did not know it, my destiny was spun. **Wyrd bið ful āræd,** fate is unstoppable.

What is there to say of the battle that the West Saxons said happened at a place they called Æsc's Hill? I assume Æsc was the thegn who had once owned the land, and his fields received a rich tilth of blood and bone that day. The poets could fill a thousand lines telling what happened, but battle is battle. Men die. In the shield wall it is sweat, terror, cramp, half blows, full blows, screaming, and cruel death.

There were really two battles at Æsc's Hill, the one above and the other below, and the deaths came swiftly. Harald and Bagseg died, Sidroc the Older watched his son die and then was cut down himself, and with him died Earl Osbern and Earl Fraena, and so many other good warriors, and the Christian priests were calling on their God to give the West Saxon swords strength, and that day Odin was sleeping and the Christian God was awake.

We were driven back. On top of the hill and in the valley we were driven back, and it was only the weariness of the enemy that stopped a full slaughter and let our survivors retreat from the fight, leaving their companions behind in their death blood. Toki was one of them. The shipmaster, so full of sword skill, died in the ditch behind which Alfred's shield wall had waited for us. Ragnar, blood all over his face and with enemy's blood matted in his unbound hair, could not believe it. The West Saxons were jeering.

The West Saxons had fought like fiends, like men inspired, like men who know their whole future rested on a winter afternoon's work, and they had beaten us.

Destiny is all. We were defeated and went back to Readingum.

SIX

These days, whenever Englishmen talk of the battle of Æsc's Hill, they speak of God giving the West Saxons the victory because King Æthelred and his brother Alfred were praying when the Danes appeared.

Maybe they are right. I can well believe that Alfred was praying, but it helped that he chose his position well. His shield wall was just beyond a deep, winter-flooded ditch and the Danes had to fight their way up from that mud-bottomed trough and they died as they came, and men who would rather have been farmers than warriors beat off an assault of sword Danes, and Alfred led the farmers, encouraged them, told them they could win, and put his faith in God. I think the ditch was the reason that he won, but he would doubtless have said that God dug the ditch.

Halfdan lost as well. He was attacking uphill, climbing a smooth gentle slope, but it was late in the day and the sun was in his men's eyes, or so they said afterward, and King Æthelred, like Alfred, encouraged his men so well that they launched a howling downhill attack that bit deep into Halfdan's ranks that became discouraged when they saw the lower army retreating from Alfred's stubborn defense. There were no angels with fiery swords present, despite what the priests now say. At least I saw none. There was a waterlogged ditch, there was a battle, the Danes lost, and destiny changed.

I did not know the Danes could lose, but at fourteen years old I learned that lesson, and for the first time I heard Saxon cheers and jeers, and something hidden in my soul stirred.

And we went back to Readingum.

There was plenty more fighting as winter turned to spring and spring to summer. New Danes came with the new year, and our ranks were thus restored, and we won all our subsequent encounters with the West Saxons, twice fighting them at Basengas in Hamptonscir, then at Mereton, which was in Wiltunscir and thus deep inside their territory, and again in Wiltunscir at Wiltun, and each time we won, which meant we held the battlefield at day's end, but at none of those clashes did we destroy the enemy. Instead we wore each other out, fought each other to a bloody standstill, and as summer caressed the land we were no nearer conquering Wessex than we had been at Yule.

But we did manage to kill King Æthelred. That happened at Wiltun where the king received a deep ax wound to his left shoulder and, though he was hurried from the field, and though priests and monks prayed over his sickbed, and though cunning men treated him with herbs and leeches, he died after a few days.

And he left an heir, an ætheling, Æthelwold. He was Prince Æthelwold, eldest son of Æthelred, but he was not old enough to be his own master for, like me, he was only fourteen, yet even so some men proclaimed his right to be named the King of Wessex, but Alfred had far more powerful friends and he deployed the legend of the pope having invested him as the future king. The legend must have worked its magic for, sure enough, at the meeting of the Wessex witan, which was the assembly of nobles, bishops, and powerful men, Alfred was acclaimed as the new king. Perhaps the witan had no choice. Wessex, after all, was desperately fighting off Halfdan's forces and it would have been a bad time to make a boy into a king. Wessex needed a leader and so the witan chose Alfred, and Æthelwold and his younger brother were whisked off to an abbey where they were told to get on with their lessons. "Alfred should have murdered the little bastards," Ragnar told me cheerfully, and he was probably right.

So Alfred, the youngest of six brothers, was now the King of Wessex. The year was 871. I did not know it then, but Alfred's wife had just given birth to a daughter he named Æthelflaed. Æthelflaed was fourteen years younger than me and even if I had known of her birth I would have dismissed it as unimportant. But destiny is all. The spinners work and we do their will whether we will it or not.

Alfred's first act as king, other than to bury his brother and put his nephews away in a monastery and have himself crowned and go to church a hundred times and weary God's ears with unceasing prayers, was to send messengers to Halfdan proposing a conference. He wanted peace, it seemed, and as it was midsummer and we were no nearer to victory than we had been at midwinter, Halfdan agreed to the meeting, and so, with his army's leaders and a bodyguard of picked men, he went to Baðum.

I went too, with Ragnar, Ravn, and Brida. Rorik, still sick, stayed in Readingum and I was sorry he did not see Baðum for, though it was only a small town, it was almost as marvelous as Lundene. There was a bath in the town's center, not a small tub, but an enormous building with pillars and a crumbling roof above a great stone hollow that was filled with hot water. The water came from the underworld and Ragnar was certain that it was heated by the forges of the dwarves. The bath, of course, had been built by the Romans, as had all the other extraordinary buildings in Baðum's valley. Not many men wanted to get into the bath because they feared water even though they loved their ships, but Brida and I went in and I discovered she could swim like a fish. I clung to the edge and marveled at the strange experience of having hot water all over my naked skin.

Beocca found us there. The center of Baðum was covered by a truce, which meant no man could carry weapons there, and West Saxons and Danes mixed amicably enough in the streets so there was nothing to stop Beocca searching for me. He came to the bath with two other priests, both gloomy-looking men with running noses, and they watched as Beocca leaned down to me. "I saw you come in here," he said. Then he noticed Brida who was swimming underwater, her long black hair streaming. She reared up and he could not miss her small breasts and he recoiled as though she were the devil's handmaid. "She's a girl, Uhtred!"

"I know," I said.

"Naked!"

"God is good," I said.

He stepped forward to slap me, but I pushed myself away from the edge of the bath and he nearly fell in. The other two priests were staring at Brida. God knows why. They probably had wives, but priests, I have found, get very excited about women. So do warriors, but we do not shake like aspens just because a girl shows us her tits. Beocca tried to ignore her, though that was difficult because Brida swam up behind me and put her arms around my waist. "You must slip away," Beocca whispered to me.

"Slip away?"

"From the pagans! Come to our quarters. We'll hide you."

"Who is he?" Brida asked me. She spoke in Danish.

"He was a priest I knew at home," I said.

"Ugly, isn't he?" she said.

"You have to come," Beocca hissed at me. "We need you!"

"You need me?"

He leaned even closer. "There's unrest in Northumbria, Uhtred. You must have heard what happened." He paused to make the sign of the cross. "All those monks and nuns slaughtered! They were murdered! A terrible thing, Uhtred, but God will not be mocked. There is to be a rising in Northumbria and Alfred will encourage it. If we can say that Uhtred of Bebbanburg is on our side it will help!"

I doubted it would help at all. I was fourteen and hardly old enough to inspire men into making suicidal attacks on Danish strongholds. "She's not a Dane," I told Beocca, who I did not think would have said these things if he believed Brida could understand them. "She's from East Anglia."

He stared at her. "East Anglia?"

I nodded, then let mischief have its way. "She's the niece of King Edmund," I lied, and Brida giggled and ran a hand down my body to try and make me laugh.

Beocca made the sign of the cross again. "Poor

man! A martyr! Poor girl." Then he frowned. "But . . ." he began, then stopped, quite incapable of understanding why the dreaded Danes allowed two of their prisoners to frolic naked in a bath of hot water. Then he closed his squinty eyes because he saw where Brida's hand had come to rest. "We must get you both out of here," he said urgently, "to a place where you can learn God's ways."

"I should like that," I said and Brida squeezed so hard that I almost cried out in pain.

"Our quarters are to the south of here," Beocca said, "across the river and on top of the hill. Go there, Uhtred, and we shall take you away. Both of you."

Of course I did no such thing. I told Ragnar who laughed at my invention that Brida was King Edmund's niece, and shrugged at the news that there would be an uprising in Northumbria. "There are always rumors of revolts," he said, "and they all end the same way."

"He was very certain," I said.

"All it means is that they've sent monks to stir up trouble. I doubt it will amount to much. Anyway, once we've settled Alfred we can go back. Go home, eh?"

But settling with Alfred was not as easy as

Halfdan or Ragnar had supposed. It was true that Alfred was the supplicant and that he wanted peace because the Danish forces had been raiding deep into Wessex, but he was not ready to collapse as Burghred had yielded in Mercia. When Halfdan proposed that Alfred stay king, but that the Danes occupy the chief West Saxon forts, Alfred threatened to walk out and continue the war. "You insult me," he said calmly. "If you wish to take the fortresses, then come and take them."

"We will," Halfdan threatened and Alfred merely shrugged as if to say the Danes were welcome to try, but Halfdan knew, as all the Danes knew, that their campaign had failed. It was true that we had scoured large swaths of Wessex, we had taken much treasure, slaughtered or captured livestock, burned mills and homes and churches, but the price had been high. Many of our best men were dead or else so badly wounded that they would be forced to live off their lords' charity for the rest of their days. We had also failed to take a single West Saxon fortress, which meant that when winter came we would be forced to withdraw to the safety of Lundene or Mercia.

Yet if the Danes were exhausted by the campaign, so were the West Saxons. They had also lost many of their best men, they had lost trea-sure, and Alfred was worried that the Britons, the ancient enemy who had been defeated by his an-cestors, might flood out of their fastnesses in Wales and Cornwalum. Yet Alfred would not suc-cumb to his fears, he would not meekly give in to Halfdan's demands, though he knew he must meet some of them, and so the bargaining went on for a week and I was surprised by Alfred's stubbornness.

He was not an impressive man to look at. There was something spindly about him, and his long face had a weak cast, but that was a decep-tion. He never smiled as he faced Halfdan, he rarely took those clever brown eyes off his en-emy's face, he pressed his point tediously, and he was always calm, never raising his voice even when the Danes were screaming at him. "What we want," he explained again and again, "is peace. You need it, and it is my duty to give it to my country. So you will leave my country." His priests, Beocca among them, wrote down every word, filling precious sheets of parchment with endless lines of script. They must have used every drop of ink in Wessex to record that meeting and I doubt anyone ever read the whole record.

Not that the meetings went on all day. Alfred

insisted they could not start until he had attended church, and he broke at midday for more prayer, and he finished before sundown so that he could return to the church. How that man prayed! But his patient bargaining was just as remorseless, and in the end Halfdan agreed to evacuate Wessex, but only on payment of six thousand pieces of silver and, to make sure it was paid, he insisted that his forces must remain in Readingum where Alfred was required to deliver three wagons of fodder daily and five wagons of rye grain. When the silver was paid, Halfdan promised, the ships would slide back down the Temes and Wessex would be free of pagans. Alfred argued against allowing the Danes to stay in Readingum, insisting that they withdraw east of Lundene, but in the end, desperate for peace, he accepted that they could remain in the town and so, with solemn oaths on both sides, the peace was made.

I was not there when the conference ended, nor was Brida. We had been there most days, serving as Ravn's eyes in the big Roman hall where the talking went on, but when we got bored, or rather when Ravn was tired of our boredom, we would go to the bath and swim. I loved that water.

We were swimming on the day before the talking finished. There were just the two of us in the great echoing chamber. I liked to stand where the water gushed in from a hole in a stone, letting it cascade over my long hair, and I was standing there, eyes closed, when I heard Brida squeal. I opened my eyes and just then a pair of strong hands gripped my shoulders. My skin was slippery and I twisted away, but a man in a leather coat jumped into the bath, told me to be quiet, and seized me again. Two other men were wading across the pool, using long staves to shepherd Brida to the water's edge. "What are you . . ." I began to ask, using Danish.

"Quiet, boy," one of the men answered. He was a West Saxon and there were a dozen of them, and when they had pulled our wet naked bodies out of the water they wrapped us in big, stinking cloaks, scooped up our clothes, and hurried us away. I shouted for help and was rewarded by a thump on my head that might have stunned an ox.

We were pushed over the saddles of two horses and then we traveled for some time with men mounted behind us, and the cloaks were only taken off at the top of the big hill that overlooks Baðum from the south. And there, beaming at

us, was Beocca. "You are rescued, lord," he said
to me, "praise Almighty God, you are rescued! As
are you, my lady," he added to Brida.

I could only stare at him. Rescued? Kid-
napped, more like. Brida looked at me, and I at
her, and she gave the smallest shake of her head
as if to suggest we should keep silent, at least I
took it to mean that, and did so. Then Beocca
told us to get dressed.

I had slipped my hammer amulet and my arm
rings into my belt pouch when I undressed and I
left them there as Beocca hurried us into a
nearby church, little more than a wood and straw
shack that was no bigger than a peasant's pigsty,
and there he gave thanks to God for our deliver-
ance. Afterward he took us to a nearby hall where
we were introduced to Ælswith, Alfred's wife,
who was attended by a dozen women, three of
them nuns, and guarded by a score of heavily
armed men.

Ælswith was a small woman with mouse-
brown hair, small eyes, a small mouth, and a very
determined chin. She was wearing a blue dress
that had angels embroidered in silver thread
about its skirt and about the hem of its wide
sleeves, and she wore a heavy crucifix of gold. A

baby was in a wooden cradle beside her and later, much later, I realized that the baby must have been Æthelflaed, so that was the very first time I ever saw her, though I thought nothing of it at the time. Ælswith welcomed me, speaking in the distinctive tones of a Mercian, and after she had enquired about my parentage, she told me we had to be related because her father was Æthelred who had been an ealdorman in Mercia, and he was first cousin to the late lamented Æthelwulf whose body I had seen outside Readingum. "And now you," she turned to Brida, "Father Beocca tells me you are niece to the holy King Edmund?"

Brida just nodded.

"But who are your parents?" Ælswith demanded, frowning. "Edmund had no brothers, and his two sisters are nuns."

"Hild," Brida said. I knew that had been the name of her aunt, whom Brida had hated.

"Hild?" Ælswith was puzzled, more than puzzled, suspicious. "Neither of good King Edmund's sisters are called Hild."

"I'm not his niece," Brida confessed in a small voice.

"Ah." Ælswith leaned back in her chair, her

sharp face showing the look of satisfaction some people assume when they have caught a liar telling an untruth.

"But I was taught to call him uncle," Brida went on, surprising me, for I thought she had found herself in an impossible quandary and was confessing the lie, but instead, I realized, she was embroidering it. "My mother was called Hild and she had no husband but she insisted I call King Edmund uncle," she spoke in a small, frightened voice, "and he liked that."

"He liked it?" Ælswith snapped. "Why?"

"Because," Brida said, and then blushed, and how she made herself blush I do not know, but she lowered her eyes, reddened, and looked as if she were about to burst into tears.

"Ah," Ælswith said again, catching on to the girl's meaning and blushing herself. "So he was your . . ." She did not finish, not wanting to accuse the dead and holy King Edmund of having fathered a bastard on some woman called Hild.

"Yes," Brida said, and actually started crying. I stared up at the hall's smoke-blackened rafters and tried not to laugh. "He was ever so kind to me," Brida sobbed, "and the nasty Danes killed him!"

Ælswith plainly believed Brida. Folk usually

do believe the worst in other folk, and the saintly King Edmund was now revealed as a secret womanizer, though that did not stop him eventually becoming a saint, but it did condemn Brida because Ælswith now proposed that she be sent to some nunnery in southern Wessex. Brida might have royal blood, but it was plainly tainted by sin, so Ælswith wanted her locked away for life. "Yes," Brida agreed meekly, and I had to pretend I was choking in the smoke. Then Ælswith presented us both with crucifixes. She had two ready, both of silver, but she whispered to one of the nuns and a small wooden one was substituted for one of the silver crucifixes and that one was presented to Brida while I received a silver one which I obediently hung about my neck. I kissed mine, which impressed Ælswith, and Brida hurriedly imitated me, but nothing she could do now would impress Alfred's wife. Brida was a self-condemned bastard.

Alfred returned from Baðum after nightfall and I had to accompany him to church where the prayers and praises went on forever. Four monks chanted, their droning voices half sending me to sleep, and afterward, for it did eventually end, I was invited to join Alfred for a meal. Beocca impressed on me that this was an honor, that not many folk were asked to eat with the king, but I had eaten with Danish chieftains who never seemed to mind who shared their table so long as they did not spit in the gruel, so I was not flattered. I was hungry, though. I could have eaten a whole roasted ox and I was impatient as we ceremonially washed our hands in basins of water held by the servants and then as we stood by our stools and chairs as Alfred and Ælswith were conducted to the table. A bishop allowed the food to cool as he said an interminable prayer asking God to bless what we were about to eat, and then at last we sat, but what a disappointment that supper was! No pork, no beef, no mutton, not a thing a man might want to eat, but only curds, leeks, soft eggs, bread, diluted ale, and barley boiled into a gelid broth as palatable as frogspawn. Alfred kept saying how good it was, but in the end he did confess that he was afflicted with terrible pains in his belly and that this pap-like diet kept the agony at bay.

"The king is a martyr to meat," Beocca explained to me. He was one of the three priests at the high table, another of whom was a bishop who had no teeth and mashed his bread into the broth with a candlestick, and there were also two ealdormen and, of course, Ælswith who did much of the talking. She was opposing the notion of allowing the Danes to stay in Readingum, but in the end Alfred said he had no choice and that it was a small concession to make for peace, and that ended the discussion. Ælswith did rejoice that her husband had negotiated the release of all the young hostages held by Halfdan's army, which Alfred had insisted on for he feared those young ones would be led away from the true church. He looked at me as he spoke about that, but I took little notice, being far more interested in one of the servants who was a young girl, perhaps four or five years older than me, who was startlingly pretty with a mass of black-ringleted hair and I wondered if she was the girl who Alfred kept close so he could thank God for giving him the strength to resist temptation. Later, much later, I discovered she was the same girl. Her name was Merewenna and I thanked God, in time, for not resisting temptation with her, but that lies far ahead in my tale, and for now I was at Alfred's disposal or, rather, at Ælswith's.

"Uhtred must learn to read," she said. What business it was of hers I did not know, but no one disputed her statement.

"Amen," Beocca said.

"The monks at Winburnan can teach him," she suggested.

"A very good idea, my lady," Beocca said, and the toothless bishop nodded and dribbled his approval.

"Abbot Hewald is a very diligent teacher," Ælswith said. In truth Abbot Hewald was one of those bastards who would rather whip the young than teach them, but doubtless that was what Ælswith meant.

"I rather think," Alfred put in, "that young Uhtred's ambition is to be a warrior."

"In time, if God wills it, he will be," Ælswith said, "but what use is a soldier who cannot read God's word?"

"Amen," Beocca said.

"No use at all," Alfred agreed. I thought teaching a soldier to read was about as much use as teaching a dog to dance, but said nothing, though Alfred sensed my skepticism. "Why is it good for a soldier to read, Uhtred?" he demanded of me.

"It is good for everyone to read," I said dutifully, earning a smile from Beocca.

"A soldier who reads," Alfred said patiently, "is a soldier who can read orders, a soldier who will know what his king wants. Suppose you are in Northumbria, Uhtred, and I am in Wessex. How else will you know my will?"

That was breathtaking, though I was too young to realize it at the time. If I was in Northumbria and he was in Wessex, then I was none of his damned business, but of course Alfred was already thinking ahead, far ahead, to a time when there would be one English kingdom and one English king. I just gaped at him and he smiled at me. "So Winburnan it is, young man," he said, "and the sooner you are there, the better."

"The sooner?" Ælswith knew nothing of this suggested haste and was sharply suspicious.

"The Danes, my dear," Alfred explained, "will look for both children. If they discover they are here they may well demand their return."

"But all hostages are to be freed," Ælswith objected. "You said so yourself."

"Was Uhtred a hostage?" Alfred asked softly, staring at me. "Or was he in danger of becoming a Dane?" He left the questions hanging, and I did not try to answer them. "We must make you into a true Englishman," Alfred said, "so you must go south in the morning. You and the girl."

"The girl doesn't matter," Ælswith said dismissively. Brida had been sent to eat with the kitchen slaves.

"If the Danes discover she's Edmund's bastard," one of the ealdormen observed, "they'll use her to destroy his reputation."

"She never told them that," I piped up, "because she thought they might mock him."

"There's some good in her then," Ælswith said grudgingly. She helped herself to one of the soft-boiled eggs. "But what will you do," she demanded of her husband, "if the Danes accuse you of rescuing the children?"

"I shall lie, of course," Alfred said. Ælswith blinked at him, but the bishop mumbled that the lie would be for God and so forgivable.

I had no intention of going to Winburnan. That was not because I was suddenly avid to be a Dane, but it had everything to do with Serpent-Breath. I loved that sword, and I had left it with Ragnar's servants, and I wanted her back before my life took whatever path the spinners required of me and, to be sure, I had no wish to give up life with Ragnar for the scant joys of a monastery and a teacher. Brida, I knew, wished to go back to the Danes, and it was Alfred's sensible insistence that we be removed from Baðum as soon as possible that gave us our opportunity.

We were sent away the next morning, before dawn, going south into a hilly country and escorted by a dozen warriors who resented the job of taking two children deep into the heartland of Wessex. I was given a horse, Brida was provided with a mule, and a young priest called Willibald was officially put in charge of delivering Brida to a nunnery and me to Abbot Hewald. Father Willibald was a nice man with an easy smile and a kind manner. He could imitate bird calls and made us laugh by inventing a conversation between a quarrelsome fieldfare with its chack-chack call and a soaring skylark, then he made us guess what birds he was imitating, and that entertainment, mixed in with some harmless riddles, took us to a settlement high above a soft-flowing river in the heavily wooded countryside. The soldiers insisted on stopping there because they said the horses needed a rest. "They really need ale," Willibald told us, and shrugged as if it was understandable.

It was a warm day. The horses were hobbled outside the hall, the soldiers got their ale, bread, and cheese, then sat in a circle and threw dice and grumbled, leaving us to Willibald's supervision, but the young priest stretched out on a half-collapsed haystack and fell asleep in the sunlight.

I looked at Brida, she looked at me, and it was as simple as that. We crept along the side of the hall, circled an enormous dung heap, dodged through some pigs that rooted in a field, wriggled through a hedge, and then we were in woodland where we both started to laugh. "My mother insisted I call him uncle," Brida said in her small voice, "and the nasty Danes killed him," and we both thought that was the funniest thing we had ever heard, and then we came to our senses and hurried northward.

It was a long time before the soldiers searched for us, and later they brought hunting dogs from the hall where they had purchased ale, but by then we had waded up a stream, changed direction again, found higher ground, and hidden ourselves. They did not find us, though all afternoon we could hear the hounds baying in the valley. They must have been searching the riverbank, thinking we had gone there, but we were safe and alone and high.

They searched for two days, never coming close, and on the third day we saw Alfred's royal cavalcade riding south on the road under the hill. The meeting at Baðum was over, and that meant the Danes were retreating to Readingum and neither of us had any idea how to reach Readingum, but we knew we had traveled west to reach Baðum, so that was a start, and we knew we had to find the river Temes, and our only two problems were food and the need to avoid being caught.

That was a good time. We stole milk from the udders of cows and goats. We had no weapons, but we fashioned cudgels from fallen branches and used them to threaten some poor old man who was patiently digging a ditch and had a small sack with bread and pease pudding for his meal, and we stole that, and we caught fish with our hands, a trick that Brida taught me, and we lived in the woods. I wore my hammer amulet again. Brida had thrown away her wooden crucifix, but I kept the silver one for it was valuable.

After a few days we began traveling by night. We were both frightened at first, for the night is when the sceadugengan stir from their hiding places, but we became good at traversing the darkness. We skirted farms, following the stars, and we learned how to move without noise, how to be shadows. One night something large and growling came close and we heard it shifting, pawing the ground, and we both beat at the leaf mold with our cudgels and yelped and the thing went away. A boar? Perhaps. Or perhaps one of the shapeless, nameless sceadugengan that curdle dreams.

We had to cross a range of high, bare hills where we managed to steal a lamb before the shepherd's dogs even knew we were there. We lit a fire in the woods north of the hills and cooked the meat, and the next night we found the river. We did not know what river, but it was wide, it flowed beneath deep trees, and nearby was a settlement where we saw a small round boat made of bent willow sticks covered with goatskin. That night we stole the boat and let it carry us downstream, past settlements, under bridges, ever going east.

We did not know it, but the river was the Temes, and so we came safe to Readingum.

Rorik had died. He had been sick for so long, but there were times when he had seemed to recover, but whatever illness carried him away had done so swiftly and Brida and I reached Readingum on the day that his body was burned. Ragnar, in tears, stood by the pyre and watched as the flames consumed his son. A sword, a bridle, a hammer amulet, and a model ship had been placed on the fire, and after it was done the melted metal was placed with the ashes in a great pot that Ragnar buried close to the Temes. "You are my second son now," he told me that night, and then remembered Brida, "and you are my daughter." He embraced us both, then got drunk. The next morning he wanted to ride out and kill West Saxons, but Ravn and Halfdan restrained him.

The truce was holding. Brida and I had only been gone a little over three weeks and already the first silver was coming to Readingum, along with fodder and food. Alfred, it seemed, was a man of his word and Ragnar was a man of grief. "How will I tell Sigrid?" he wanted to know.

"It is bad for a man to have only one son," Ravn told me, "almost as bad as having none. I had three, but only Ragnar lives. Now only his eldest lives." Ragnar the Younger was still in Ireland.

"He can have another son," Brida said.

"Not from Sigrid," Ravn said. "But he could take a second wife, I suppose. It is sometimes done."

Ragnar had given me back Serpent-Breath, and another arm ring. He gave a ring to Brida too, and he took some consolation from the story of our escape. We had to tell it to Halfdan and to Guthrum the Unlucky, who stared at us dark-eyed as we described the meal with Alfred, and Alfred's plans to educate me, and even grief-stricken Ragnar laughed when Brida retold the story of how she had claimed to be King Edmund's bastard.

"This Queen Ælswith," Halfdan wanted to know, "what is she like?"

"No queen," I said. "The West Saxons won't have queens." Beocca had told me that. "She is merely the king's wife."

"She is a weasel pretending to be a thrush," Brida said.

"Is she pretty?" Guthrum asked.

"A pinched face," Brida said, "and piggy eyes and a pursed mouth."

"He'll get no joy there then," Halfdan said. "Why did he marry her?"

"Because she's from Mercia," Ravn said, "and Alfred would have Mercia on his side."

"Mercia belongs to us," Halfdan growled.

"But Alfred would take it back," Ravn said, "and what we should do is send ships with rich gifts for the Britons. If they attack from Wales and Cornwalum then he must divide his army."

That was an unfortunate thing to say, for Halfdan still smarted from the memory of dividing his own army at Æsc's Hill, and he just scowled into his ale. So far as I know he never did send gifts to the Britons, and it would have been a good idea if he had, but he was distracted by his failure to take Wessex, and there were rumors of unrest in both Northumbria and Mercia. The Danes had captured so much of England so quickly that they had never really subdued their conquest, nor did they hold all the fortresses in the conquered land and so revolts flared like heathland fires. They were easily put down, but untended they would spread and become dangerous. It was time, Halfdan said, to stamp on the fires and to cow the conquered English into terrified submission. Once that was done, once Northumbria, Mercia, and East Anglia were quiet, the attack on Wessex could be resumed.

The last of Alfred's silver came and the Danish army released the young hostages, including the Mercian twins, and the rest of us went back to Lundene. Ragnar dug up the pot with his younger son's ashes and carried it downstream on **Wind-Viper.** "I shall take it home," he told me, "and bury him with his own people."

We could not travel north that year. It was autumn when we reached Lundene and so we had to wait through the winter, and it was not till spring that Ragnar's three ships left the Temes and sailed north. I was fifteen then, and growing fast so that I was suddenly a head taller than most men, and Ragnar made me take the steering oar. He taught me to guide a ship, how to anticipate the buffet of wind or wave, and how to heave on the steering oar before the ship veered. I learned the subtle touch, though at first the ship swayed drunkenly as I put too much pressure on the oar, but in time I came to feel the ship's will in the long oar's shaft and learned to love the quiver in the ash as the sleek hull gained her full speed.

"I shall make you my second son," Ragnar told me on that voyage.

I did not know what to say.

"I shall always favor my eldest," he went on, meaning Ragnar the Younger, "but you shall still be as a son to me."

"I would like that," I said awkwardly. I gazed at the distant shore that was flecked by the little dun sails of the fishing boats that were fleeing from our ships. "I am honored," I said.

"Uhtred Ragnarson," he said, trying it out, and he must have liked the sound of it for he smiled, but then he thought of Rorik again and the tears came to his eyes and he just stared eastward into the empty sea.

That night we slept in the mouth of the Humber.

And two days later came back to Eoferwic.

The king's palace had been repaired. It had new shutters on its high windows and the roof was freshly thatched with golden rye straw. The palace's old Roman walls had been scrubbed so that the lichen was gone from the joints between the stones. Guards stood at the outer gate and, when Ragnar demanded entry, they curtly told him to wait and I thought he would draw his sword, but before his anger could erupt Kjartan appeared. "My lord Ragnar," he said sourly.

"Since when does a Dane wait at this gate?" Ragnar demanded.

"Since I ordered it," Kjartan retorted, and there was insolence in his voice. He, like the palace, looked prosperous. He wore a cloak of black bear fur, had tall boots, a chain mail tunic, a red leather sword belt, and almost as many arm rings as Ragnar. "No one enters here without my permission," Kjartan went on, "but of course you are welcome, Earl Ragnar." He stepped aside to let Ragnar, myself, and three of Ragnar's men into the big hall where, five years before, my uncle had tried to buy me from Ivar. "I see you still have your English pet," Kjartan said, looking at me.

"Go on seeing while you have eyes," Ragnar said carelessly. "Is the king here?"

"He only grants audience to those people who arrange to see him," Kjartan said.

Ragnar sighed and turned on his erstwhile shipmaster. "You itch me like a louse," he said, "and if it pleases you, Kjartan, we shall lay the hazel rods and meet man to man. And if that does not please you, then fetch the king because I would speak with him."

Kjartan bridled, but decided he did not want to face Ragnar's sword in a fighting space marked by hazel branches, and so, with an ill grace, he went into the palace's back rooms. He made us wait long enough, but eventually King Egbert appeared, and with him were six guards who included one-eyed Sven who now looked as wealthy as his father. Big too, almost as tall as I was, with a broad chest and hugely muscled arms.

Egbert looked nervous but did his best to appear regal. Ragnar bowed to him, then said there were tales of unrest in Northumbria and that Halfdan had sent him north to quell any such disturbances. "There is no unrest," Egbert said, but in such a frightened voice that I thought he would piss his breeches.

"There were disturbances in the inland hills," Kjartan said dismissively, "but they ended." He patted his sword to show what had ended them.

Ragnar persevered, but learned nothing more. A few men had evidently risen against the Danes, there had been ambushes on the road leading to the west coast, the perpetrators had been hunted down and killed, and that was all Kjartan would say. "Northumbria is safe," he finished, "so you can return to Halfdan, my lord, and keep on trying to defeat Wessex."

Ragnar ignored that last barb. "I shall go to my home," he said, "bury my son, and live in peace."

Sven was fingering his sword hilt and looking at me sourly with his one eye, but while the enmity between us, and between Ragnar and Kjartan, was obvious, no one made trouble and we left. The ships were hauled onto shore, the silver fetched from Readingum was shared out among the crews, and we went home carrying Rorik's ashes.

Sigrid wailed at the news. She tore her dress and tangled her hair and screamed, the other women joined her, and a procession carried Rorik's ashes to the top of the nearest hill where

the pot was buried. Afterward Ragnar stayed
there, looking across the hills and watching the
white clouds sail across the western sky.

We stayed home all the rest of that year. There
were crops to grow, hay to cut, a harvest to reap
and to grind. We made cheese and butter. Merchants and travelers brought news, but none
from Wessex where, it seemed, Alfred still ruled
and had his peace, and so that kingdom remained, the last one of England. Ragnar sometimes spoke of returning there, carrying his
sword to gain more riches, but the fight seemed
to have gone from him that summer. He sent a
message to Ireland, asking that his eldest son
come home, but such messages were not reliable
and Ragnar the Younger did not come that year.
Ragnar also thought of Thyra, his daughter. "He
says it's time I married," she said to me one day
as we churned butter.

"You?" I laughed.

"I'm nearly thirteen!" she said defiantly.

"So you are. Who'll marry you?"

She shrugged. "Mother likes Anwend." Anwend was one of Ragnar's warriors, a young man
not much older than me, strong and cheerful, but
Ragnar had an idea she should marry one of
Ubba's sons, but that would mean she would go

away and Sigrid hated that thought and Ragnar slowly came around to Sigrid's way of thinking. I liked Anwend and thought he would make a good husband for Thyra who was growing ever more beautiful. She had long golden hair, wide set eyes, a straight nose, unscarred skin, and a laugh that was like a ripple of sunshine. "Mother says I must have many sons," she said.

"I hope you do."

"I'd like a daughter, too," she said, straining with the churn because the butter was solidifying and the work getting harder. "Mother says Brida should marry as well."

"Brida might have different ideas," I said.

"She wants to marry you," Thyra said.

I laughed at that. I thought of Brida as a friend, my closest friend, and just because we slept with each other, or we did when Sigrid was not watching, did not make me want to marry her. I did not want to marry at all. I thought only of swords and shields and battles, and Brida thought of herbs.

She was like a cat. She came and went secretly, and she learned all that Sigrid could teach her about herbs and their uses. Bindweed as a purgative, toadflax for ulcers, marsh marigold to keep elves away from the milk pails, chickweed for coughs, cornflower for fevers, and she learned other spells she would not tell me, women's spells, and said that if you stayed silent in the night, unmoving, scarce breathing, the spirits would come, and Ravn taught her how to dream with the gods, which meant drinking ale in which pounded red-cap mushrooms had been steeped, and she was often ill for she drank it too strong, but she would not stop, and she made her first songs then, songs about birds and about beasts, and Ravn said she was a true skald. Some nights, when we watched the charcoal burn, she would recite to me, her voice soft and rhythmic. She had a dog now that followed her everywhere. She had found him in Lundene on our homeward journey and he was black and white, as clever as Brida herself, and she called him Nihtgenga, which means night-walker, or goblin. He would sit with us by the charcoal pyre and I swear he listened to her songs. Brida made pipes from straw and played melancholy tunes and Nihtgenga would watch her with big sad eyes until the music over-came him and then he would raise his muzzle and howl, and we would both laugh and Niht-genga would be offended and Brida would have to pet him back to happiness.

We forgot the war until, when the summer was

at its height and a pall of heat lay over the hills, we had an unexpected visitor. Earl Guthrum the Unlucky came to our remote valley. He came with twenty horsemen, all dressed in black, and he bowed respectfully to Sigrid who chided him for not sending warning. "I would have made a feast," she said.

"I brought food," Guthrum said, pointing to some pack horses. "I did not want to empty your stores."

He had come from distant Lundene, wanting to talk with Ragnar and Ravn, and Ragnar invited me to sit with them because, he said, I knew more than most men about Wessex, and Wessex was what Guthrum wished to talk about, though my contribution was small. I described Alfred, described his piety, and warned Guthrum that though the West Saxon king was not an impressive man to look at, he was undeniably clever. Guthrum shrugged at that. "Cleverness is overrated," he said gloomily. "Clever doesn't win battles."

"Stupidity loses them," Ravn put in, "like dividing the army when we fought outside Æbbanduna."

Guthrum scowled, but decided not to pick a fight with Ravn, and instead asked Ragnar's advice on how to defeat the West Saxons, and demanded Ragnar's assurance that, come the new year, Ragnar would bring his men to Lundene and join the next assault. "If it is next year," Guthrum said gloomily. He scratched at the back of his neck, jiggling his mother's gold-tipped bone that still hung from his hair. "We may not have sufficient men."

"Then we will attack the year after," Ragnar said.

"Or the one after that," Guthrum said, then frowned. "But how do we finish the pious bastard?"

"Split his forces," Ragnar said, "because otherwise we'll always be outnumbered."

"Always? Outnumbered?" Guthrum looked dubious at that assertion.

"When we fought here," Ragnar said, "some Northumbrians decided not to fight us and they took refuge in Mercia. When we fought in Mercia and East Anglia the same thing happened, and men fled from us to find sanctuary in Wessex. But when we fight in Wessex they have nowhere to go. No place is safe for them. So they must fight, all of them. Fight in Wessex and the enemy is cornered."

"And a cornered enemy," Ravn put in, "is dangerous."

"Split them," Guthrum said pensively, ignoring Ravn again.

"Ships on the south coast," Ragnar suggested, "an army on the Temes, and British warriors coming from Brycheiniog, Glywysing, and Gwent." Those were the southern Welsh kingdoms where the Britons lurked beyond Mercia's western border. "Three attacks," Ragnar went on, "and Alfred will have to deal with them all and he won't be able to do it."

"And you will be there?" Guthrum asked.

"You have my word," Ragnar said, and then the conversation turned to what Guthrum had seen on his journey, and admittedly he was a pessimistic man and prone to see the worst in everything, but he despaired of England. There was trouble in Mercia, he said, and the East Anglians were restless, and now there was talk that King Egbert in Eoferwic was encouraging revolt.

"Egbert!" Ragnar was surprised at the news. "He couldn't encourage a piss out of a drunk man!"

"It's what I'm told," Guthrum said. "May not be true. Fellow called Kjartan told me."

"Then it's almost certainly not true."

"Not true at all," Ravn agreed.

"He seemed a good man to me," Guthrum said, obviously unaware of Ragnar's history with Kjartan, and Ragnar did not enlighten him, and probably forgot the conversation once Guthrum had traveled on.

Yet Guthrum had been right. Plotting was going on in Eoferwic, though I doubt it was Egbert who did it. Kjartan did it, and he started by spreading rumors that King Egbert was secretly organizing a rebellion, and the rumors became so loud and the king's reputation so poisoned that one night Egbert, fearing for his life, managed to evade his Danish guards and flee south with a dozen companions. He took shelter with King Burghred of Mercia who, though his country was occupied by Danes, had been allowed to keep his own household guard that was sufficient to protect his new guest. Ricsig of Dunholm, the man who had handed the captured monks to Ragnar, was declared the new king of Northumbria, and he rewarded Kjartan by allowing him to ravage any place that might have harbored rebels in league with Egbert. There had been no rebellion, of course, but Kjartan had invented one, and he savaged the few remaining monasteries and nunneries in Northumbria, thus becoming even wealthier, and he stayed as Ricsig's chief warrior and tax collector.

All this passed us by. We brought in the harvest, feasted, and it was announced that at Yule there would be a wedding between Thyra and Anwend. Ragnar asked Ealdwulf the smith to make Anwend a sword as fine as Serpent-Breath, and Ealdwulf said he would and, at the same time, make me a short sword of the kind Toki had recommended for fighting in the shield wall, and he made me help him beat out the twisted rods. All that autumn we worked until Ealdwulf had made Anwend's sword and I had helped make my own saxe. I called her Wasp-Sting because she was short and I could not wait to try her out on an enemy, which Ealdwulf said was foolishness. "Enemies come soon enough in a man's life," he told me. "You don't need to seek them out."

I made my first shield in the early winter, cutting the limewood, forging the great boss with its handle that was held through a hole in the wood, painting it black, and rimming it with an iron strip. It was much too heavy, that shield, and later I learned how to make them lighter, but as the autumn came I carried shield, sword, and saxe everywhere, accustoming myself to their weight, practicing the strokes and parries, dreaming. I half feared and half longed for my first shield wall, for no man was a warrior until he had fought in the shield wall, and no man was a real warrior until he had fought in the front rank of the shield wall, and that was death's kingdom, the place of horror, but like a fool I aspired to it.

And we readied ourselves for war. Ragnar had promised his support to Guthrum and so Brida and I made more charcoal and Ealdwulf hammered out spear points and ax heads and spades, while Sigrid found joy in the preparations for Thyra's wedding. There was a betrothal ceremony at the beginning of winter when Anwend, dressed in his best clothes that were neatly darned, came to our hall with six of his friends and he shyly proposed himself to Ragnar as Thyra's husband. Everyone knew he was going to be her husband, but the formalities were important, and Thyra sat between her mother and father as Anwend promised Ragnar that he would love, cherish, and protect Thyra, and then proposed a bride-price of twenty pieces of silver, which was much too high, but which, I suppose, meant he really loved Thyra.

"Make it ten, Anwend," Ragnar said, generous as ever, "and spend the rest on a new coat."

"Twenty is good," Sigrid said firmly, for the bride-price, though given to Ragnar, would become Thyra's property once she was married.

"Then have Thyra give you a new coat," Ragnar said, taking the money, and then he embraced Anwend and there was a feast and Ragnar was happier that night than he had been since Rorik's death. Thyra watched the dancing, sometimes blushing as she met Anwend's eyes. Anwend's six friends, all warriors of Ragnar, would come back with him for the wedding and they would be the men who would watch Anwend take Thyra to his bed and only when they reported that she was a proper woman would the marriage be deemed to have taken place.

But those ceremonies would have to wait until Yule. Thyra would be wedded then, we would have our feast, the winter would be endured, we would go to war. In other words, we thought the world would go on as it ever did.

And at the foot of Yggdrasil, the tree of life, the three spinners mocked us.

I spent many Christmasses at the West Saxon court. Christmas is Yule with religion, and the West Saxons managed to spoil the midwinter feast with chanting monks, droning priests, and savagely long sermons. Yule is supposed to be a celebration and a consolation, a moment of warm brightness in the heart of winter, a time to eat because you know that the lean times are coming when food will be scarce and ice locks the land, and a time to be happy and get drunk and behave irresponsibly and wake up the next morning wondering if you will ever feel well again, but the West Saxons handed the feast to the priests who made it as joyous as a funeral. I have never really understood why people think religion has a place in the midwinter feast, though of course the Danes remembered their gods at that time, and sacrificed to them, but they also believed Odin, Thor, and the other gods were all feasting in Asgard and had no wish to spoil the feasts in Midgard, our world. That seems sensible, but I have learned that most Christians are fearfully suspicious of enjoyment and Yule offered far too much of that for their taste. Some folk in Wessex knew how to celebrate it, and I always did my best, but if Alfred was anywhere close then you could be sure that we were required to fast, pray, and repent through the whole twelve days of Christmas.

Which is all by way of saying that the Yule feast where Thyra would be married was to be the greatest in Danish memory. We worked hard as it approached. We kept more animals alive than usual, and slaughtered them just before the feast so that their meat would not need to be salted, and we dug great pits where the pigs and cows would be cooked on huge gridirons that Ealdwulf made. He grumbled about it, saying that forging cooking implements took him away from his real work, but he secretly enjoyed it because he loved his food. As well as pork and beef we planned to have herring, salmon, mutton, pike, freshly baked bread, cheese, ale, mead, and, best of all, the puddings that were made by stuffing sheep intestines with blood, offal, oats, horseradish, wild garlic, and juniper berries. I loved those puddings, and still do, all crisp on the outside, but bursting with warm blood when you bite into them. I remember Alfred grimacing with distaste as I ate one and as the bloody juices ran into my beard, but then he was sucking on a boiled leek at the time.

We planned sports and games. The lake in the heart of the valley had frozen and I was fascinated by the way the Danes strapped bones to their feet and glided on the ice, a pastime that lasted until the ice broke and a young man drowned, but Ragnar reckoned the lake would be hard frozen again after Yule and I was determined to learn the skill of ice-gliding. For the moment, though, Brida and I were still making charcoal for Ealdwulf who had decided to make Ragnar a sword, the finest he had ever made, and we were charged with turning two wagonloads of alder-wood into the best possible fuel.

We planned to break the pile the day before the feast, but it was bigger than any we had made before and it was still not cool enough, and if you break a pile before it is ready then the fire will flare up with terrible force and burn all the half-made charcoal into ash, and so we made certain every vent was properly sealed and reckoned we would have time to break it on Yule morning before the celebrations began. Most of Ragnar's men and their families were already at the hall, sleeping wherever they could find shelter and ready for the first meal of the day and for the games that would take place in the meadow before the marriage ceremony, but Brida and I spent that last night up at the pile for fear that some animal would scratch through the turf and so start a draft that would revive the burn. I had Serpent-Breath and Wasp-Sting, for I would go nowhere without them, and Brida had Niht-genga, for she would go nowhere without him, and we were both swathed in furs because the night was cold. When a pile was burning you could rest on the turf and feel the heat, but not that night because the fire was almost gone.

"If you go very still," Brida said after dark, "you can feel the spirits."

I think I fell asleep instead, but sometime toward dawn I awoke and found Brida was also asleep. I sat up carefully, so as not to wake her, and I stared into the dark and I went very still and listened for the sceadugengan. Goblins and elves and sprites and specters and dwarves, all those things come to Midgard at night and prowl among the trees, and when we guarded the charcoal piles both Brida and I put out food for them so they would leave us in peace. So I woke, I listened, and I heard the small sounds of a wood at night, the things moving, the claws in the dead leaves, the wind's soft sighs.

And then I heard the voices.

I woke Brida and we were both still. Nihtgenga growled softly until Brida whispered that he should be quiet.

Men were moving in the dark, and some were coming to the charcoal pile and we slipped away into the blackness under the trees. We could both move like shadows and Nihtgenga would make no sound without Brida's permission. We had gone uphill because the voices were downhill, and we crouched in utter darkness and heard men moving around the charcoal pile, and then there was the crack of flint and iron and a small flame sprung up. Whoever it was searched for the folk they reckoned would be watching the charcoal, but they did not find us, and after a while they moved downhill and we followed.

Dawn was just leeching the eastern sky with a wolf-gray edge. There was frost on the leaves and a small wind. "We should get to Ragnar," I whispered.

"We can't," Brida said, and she was right, for there were scores of men in the trees and they were between us and the hall, and we were much too far away to shout a warning to Ragnar, and so we tried to go around the strangers, hurrying along the hill's ridge so we could drop down to the forge where Ealdwulf slept, but before we had gone halfway the fires burst into life.

That dawn is seared on my memory, burnt there by the flames of a hall-burning. There was nothing we could do except watch. Kjartan and Sven had come to our valley with over a hundred men and now they attacked Ragnar by setting fire to the thatch of his hall. I could see Kjartan and his son, standing amid the flaming torches that lit the space in front of the door, and as folk came from the hall they were struck by spears or arrows so that a pile of bodies grew in the firelight, which became ever brighter as the thatch flared and finally burst into a tumultuous blaze that outshone the light of the gray dawn. We could hear people and animals screaming inside. Some men burst from the hall with weapons in hand, but they were cut down by the soldiers who surrounded the hall, men at every door or window, men who killed the fugitives, though not all of them. The younger women were pushed aside under guard, and Thyra was given to Sven who struck her hard on the head and left her huddled at his feet as he helped kill her family.

I did not see Ravn, Ragnar, or Sigrid die, though die they did, and I suspect they were burned in the hall when the roof collapsed in a roaring gout of flame, smoke, and wild sparks. Ealdwulf also died and I was in tears. I wanted to draw Serpent-Breath and rush into those men around the flames, but Brida held me down, and then she whispered to me that Kjartan and Sven would surely search the nearby woods for any survivors, and she persuaded me to pull back into the lightening trees. Dawn was a sullen iron band across the sky and the sun cloud-hidden in shame as we stumbled uphill to find shelter among some fallen rocks deep in the high wood.

All that day the smoke rose from Ragnar's hall, and the next night there was a glow above the tangled black branches of the trees, and the next morning there were still wisps of smoke coming from the valley where we had been happy. We crept closer, both of us hungry, to see Kjartan and his men raking through the embers.

They pulled out lumps and twists of melted iron, a mail coat fused into a crumpled horror, silver welded into chunks, and they took whatever they found that could be sold or used again. At times they appeared frustrated, as if they had not found enough treasure, though they took enough. A wagon carried Ealdwulf's tools and anvil down the valley. Thyra had a rope put around her neck, was placed on a horse and led away by one-eyed Sven. Kjartan pissed on a heap of glowing cinders, then laughed as one of his men said something. By afternoon they were gone.

I was sixteen and no longer a child.

And Ragnar, my lord, who had made me his son, was dead.

The bodies were still in the ashes, though it was impossible to tell who was who, or even to tell men from women for the heat had shrunk the dead so they all looked like children and the children like babies. Those who had died outside the hall were recognizable and I found Ealdwulf there, and Anwend, both stripped naked. I looked for Ragnar, but could not identify him. I wondered why he had not burst from the hall, sword in hand, and decided he knew he was going to die and did not want to give his enemy the satisfaction of seeing it.

We found food in one of the storage pits that Kjartan's men had missed as they searched the hall. We had to shift hot charred pieces of timber to uncover the pit, and the bread, cheese, and meat had all been soured by smoke and ash, but we ate. Neither of us spoke. At dusk some English folk came cautiously to the hall and stared at the destruction. They were wary of me, thinking of me as a Dane, and they dropped to their knees as I approached. They were the lucky ones, for Kjartan had slaughtered every Northumbrian in Synningthwait, down to the last baby, and had loudly blamed them for the hall-burning. Men must have known it was his doing, but his savagery at Synningthwait confused things and, in time, many folk came to believe that the English had attacked Ragnar and Kjartan had taken revenge for their attack. But these English had escaped his swords. "You will come back in the morning," I told them, "and bury the dead."

"Yes, lord."

"You will be rewarded," I promised them, thinking I would have to surrender one of my precious arm rings.

"Yes, lord," one of them repeated, and then I asked them if they knew why this had happened and they looked nervous, but finally one said he had been told that Earl Ragnar was planning a revolt against Ricsig. One of the Englishmen who served Kjartan had told him that when he went down to their hovels to find ale. He had also told them to hide themselves before Kjartan slaughtered the valley's inhabitants.

"You know who I am?" I asked the man.

"The Lord Uhtred, lord."

"Tell no man I'm alive," I said and he just stared at me. Kjartan, I decided, must think that I was dead, that I was one of the shrunken charred bodies in the hall, and while Kjartan did not care about me, Sven did, and I did not want him hunting me. "And return in the morning," I went on, "and you will have silver."

There is a thing called the blood feud. All societies have them, even the West Saxons have them, despite their vaunted piety. Kill a member of my family and I shall kill one of yours, and so it goes on, generation after generation or until one family is all dead, and Kjartan had just wished a blood feud on himself. I did not know how, I did not know where, I could not know when, but I would revenge Ragnar. I swore it that night.

And I became rich that night. Brida waited until the English folk were gone and then she led me to the burned remnants of Ealdwulf's forge and she showed me the vast piece of scorched elm, a section of a tree's trunk, that had held Ealdwulf's anvil. "We must move that," she said.

It took both of us to tip over that monstrous piece of elm, and beneath it was nothing but earth, but Brida told me to dig there and, for want of other tools, I used Wasp-Sting and had only gone down a handbreadth when I struck metal. Gold. Real gold. Coins and small lumps.

The coins were strange, incised with a writing I had never seen before, neither Danish runes nor English letters, but something weird that I later learned came from the people far away who live in the desert and worship a god called Allah who I think must be a god of fire because **al,** in our English tongue, means burning. There are so many gods, but those folk who worshipped Allah made good coin and that night we unearthed forty-eight of them, and as much again in loose gold, and Brida told me she had watched Ragnar and Ealdwulf bury the hoard one night. There was gold, silver pennies, and four pieces of jet, and doubtless this was the treasure Kjartan had expected to find, for he knew Ragnar was wealthy, but Ragnar had hidden it well. All men hide a reserve of wealth for the day when disaster comes. I have buried hoards in my time, and even forgot where one was and perhaps, years from now, some lucky man will find it. That hoard, Ragnar's hoard, belonged to his eldest son, but Ragnar, it was strange to think he was just Ragnar now, no longer Ragnar the Younger, was far away in Ireland and I doubted he was even alive, for Kjartan would surely have sent men to kill him. But alive or dead he was not here and so we took the hoard.

"What do we do?" Brida asked that night. We were back in the woods.

I already knew what we would do; perhaps I had always known. I am an Englishman of England, but I had been a Dane while Ragnar was alive for Ragnar loved me and cared for me and called me his son, but Ragnar was dead and I had no other friends among the Danes. I had no friends among the English, for that matter, except for Brida, of course, and unless I counted Beocca who was certainly fond of me in a complicated way, but the English were my folk and I think I had known that ever since the moment at Æsc's Hill where for the first time I saw Englishmen beat Danes. I had felt pride then. Destiny is all, and the spinners touched me at Æsc's Hill, and now, at last, I would respond to their touch.

"We go south," I said.

"To a nunnery?" Brida asked, thinking of Ælswith and her bitter ambitions.

"No." I had no wish to join Alfred and learn to read and bruise my knees with praying. "I have relatives in Mercia," I said. I had never met them, knew nothing of them, but they were family and family has its obligations, and the Danish hold on Mercia was looser than elsewhere and perhaps I could find a home and I would not be a burden because I carried gold.

I had said I knew what I would do, but that is not wholly true. The truth is that I was in a well of misery, tempted to despair, and with tears ever close to my eyes. I wanted life to go on as before, to have Ragnar as my father, to feast and to laugh. But destiny grips us and, the next morning, in a soft winter rain, we buried the dead, paid silver coins, and then walked southward. We were a boy on the edge of being a grown man, a girl, and a dog, and we were going to nowhere.

PART TWO

The Last Kingdom

SEVEN

I settled in southern Mercia. I found another uncle, this one called Ealdorman Æthelred, son of
Æthelred, brother of Æthelwulf, father of
Æthelred, and brother to another Æthelred who
had been the father of Ælswith who was married
to Alfred, and Ealdorman Æthelred, with his
confusing family, grudgingly acknowledged me
as a nephew, though the welcome became slightly
warmer when I presented him with two gold
coins and swore on a crucifix that it was all the
money I possessed. He assumed Brida was my
lover, in which he was right, and thereafter he ignored her.

The journey south was wearisome, as all winter journeys are. For a time we sheltered at an
upland homestead near Meslach and the folk
there took us for outlaws. We arrived at their

hovel in an evening of sleet and wind, both of us half frozen, and we paid for food and shelter with a few links from the chain of the silver crucifix Ælswith had given me, and in the night the two eldest sons came to collect the rest of our silver, but Brida and I were awake, half expecting such an attempt, and I had Serpent-Breath and Brida had Wasp-Sting and we threatened to geld both boys. The family was friendly after that, or at least scared into docility, believing me when I told them that Brida was a sorceress. They were pagans, some of the many English heretics left in the high hills, and they had no idea that the Danes were swarming over England. They lived far from any village, grunted prayers to Thor and Odin, and sheltered us for six weeks. We worked for our keep by chopping wood, helping their ewes give birth, and then standing guard over the sheep pens to keep the wolves at bay.

In early spring we moved on. We avoided Hreapandune, for that was where Burghred kept his court, the same court to which the hapless Egbert of Northumbria had fled, and there were many Danes settled around the town. I did not fear Danes, I could talk to them in their own tongue, knew their jests, and even liked them, but if word got back to Eoferwic that Uhtred of Bebbanburg still lived then I feared Kjartan would put a reward on my head. So I asked at every settlement about Ealdorman Æthelwulf who had died fighting the Danes at Readingum, and I learned he had lived at a place called Deoraby, but that the Danes had taken his lands, and his younger brother had gone to Cirrenceastre, which lay in the far southern parts of Mercia, very close to the West Saxon border, and that was good because the Danes were thickest in Mercia's north, and so we went to Cirrenceastre and found it was another Roman town, well walled with stone and timber, and that Æthelwulf's brother, Æthelred, was now ealdorman and lord of the place.

We arrived when he sat in court and we waited in his hall among the petitioners and oath-takers. We watched as two men were flogged and a third branded on the face and sent into outlawry for cattle-thieving, and then a steward brought us forward, thinking we had come to seek redress for a grievance, and the steward told us to bow, and I refused and the man tried to make me bend at the waist and I struck him in the face, and that got Æthelred's attention. He was a tall man, well over forty years old, almost hairless except for a huge beard, and as gloomy as Guthrum. When I struck the steward he beckoned to his guards who were lolling at the hall's edges. "Who are you?" he growled at me.

"I am the ealdorman Uhtred," I said, and the title stilled the guards and made the steward back nervously away. "I am the son of Uhtred of Bebbanburg," I went on, "and of Æthelgifu, his wife. I am your nephew."

He stared at me. I must have looked a wreck for I was travel stained and long haired and ragged, but I had two swords and monstrous pride. "You are Æthelgifu's boy?" he asked.

"Your sister's son," I said, and even then I was not certain this was the right family, but it was, and Ealdorman Æthelred made the sign of the cross in memory of his younger sister, whom he hardly remembered, and waved the guards back to the hall's sides and asked me what I wanted.

"Shelter," I said, and he nodded grudgingly. I told him I had been a prisoner of the Danes ever since my father's death, and he accepted that willingly enough, but in truth he was not very interested in me; indeed my arrival was a nuisance for we were two more mouths to feed, but family imposes obligation, and Ealdorman Æthelred met his. He also tried to have me killed.

His lands, which stretched to the river Sæfern in the west, were being raided by Britons from Wales. The Welsh were old enemies, the ones who had tried to stop our ancestors from taking England; indeed their name for England is Lloegyr, which means the Lost Lands, and they were forever raiding or thinking of raiding or singing songs about raiding, and they had a great hero called Arthur who was supposed to be sleeping in his grave and one day he was going to rise up and lead the Welsh to a great victory over the English and so take back the Lost Lands, though so far that has not happened.

About a month after I arrived Æthelred heard that a Welsh warband had crossed the Sæfern and was taking cattle from his lands near Fromtun and he rode to clear them out. He went southward with fifty men, but ordered the chief of his household troops, a warrior called Tatwine, to block their retreat near the ancient Roman town of Gleawecestre. He gave Tatwine a force of twenty men that included me. "You're a big lad," Æthelred said to me before he left. "Have you ever fought in a shield wall?"

I hesitated, wanting to lie, but decided that poking a sword between men's legs at Readingum was not the same thing. "No, lord," I said.

"Time you learned. That sword must be good for something. Where did you get it?"

"It was my father's, lord," I lied, for I did not want to explain that I had not been a prisoner of the Danes, nor that the sword had been a gift, for Æthelred would have expected me to give it to him. "It is the only thing of my father's I have," I added pathetically, and he grunted, waved me away, and told Tatwine to put me in the shield wall if it came to a fight.

I know that because Tatwine told me so when everything was over. Tatwine was a huge man, as tall as me, with a chest like a blacksmith's and thick arms on which he made marks with ink and a needle. The marks were just blotches, but he boasted that each one was a man he had killed in battle, and I once tried to count them, but gave up at thirty-eight. His sleeves hid the rest. He was not happy to have me in his band of warriors, and even less happy when Brida insisted on accompanying me, but I told him she had sworn an oath to my father never to leave my side and that she was a cunning woman who knew spells that would confuse the enemy, and he believed both lies and probably thought that once I was dead his men could have their joy of Brida while he took Serpent-Breath back to Æthelred.

The Welsh had crossed the Sæfern high up, then turned south into the lush water meadows where cattle grew fat. They liked to come in fast and go out fast, before the Mercians could gather forces, but Æthelred had heard of their coming in good time and, as he rode south, Tatwine led us north to the bridge across the Sæfern, which was the quickest route home to Wales.

The raiders came straight into that trap. We arrived at the bridge at dusk, slept in a field, were awake before dawn, and, just as the sun rose, saw the Welshmen and their stolen cattle coming toward us. They made an effort to ride farther north, but their horses were tired, ours were fresh, and they realized there was no escape and so they returned to the bridge. We did the same and, dismounted, formed the shield wall. The Welsh made their wall. There were twenty-eight of them, all savage-looking men with shaggy hair and long beards and tattered coats, but their weapons looked well cared for and their shields were stout.

Tatwine spoke some of their language and he told them that if they surrendered now they would be treated mercifully by his lord. Their only response was to howl at us, and one of them turned around, lowered his breeches, and showed us his dirty backside, which passed as a Welsh insult.

Nothing happened then. They were in their shield wall on the road, and our shield wall blocked the bridge, and they shouted insults and Tatwine forbade our men to shout back, and once or twice it seemed as if the Welsh were going to run to their horses and try to escape by galloping northward, but every time they hinted at such a move, Tatwine ordered the servants to bring up our horses, and the Welsh understood that we would pursue and overtake them and so they went back to the shield wall and jeered at us for not assaulting them. Tatwine was not such a fool. The Welshmen outnumbered us, which meant that they could overlap us, but by staying on the bridge our flanks were protected by its Roman parapets and he wanted them to come at us there. He placed me in the center of the line, and then stood behind me. I understood later that he was ready to step into my place when I fell. I had an old shield with a loose handle loaned to me by my uncle.

Tatwine again tried to persuade them to surrender, promising that only half of them would be put to death, but as the other half would all lose a hand and an eye, it was not a tempting offer. Still they waited, and might have waited until nightfall had not some local people come along and one of them had a bow and some arrows, and he began shooting at the Welsh who, by now, had been drinking steadily through the morning. Tatwine had given us all some ale, but not much.

I was nervous. More than nervous, I was terrified. I had no armor, while the rest of Tatwine's men were in mail or good leather. Tatwine had a helmet, I had hair. I expected to die, but I remembered my lessons and slung Serpent-Breath on my back, strapping her sword belt around my throat. A sword is much quicker to draw over the shoulder, and I expected to begin the fight with Wasp-Sting. My throat was dry, a muscle in my right leg quivered, my belly felt sour, but entwined with that fear was excitement. This was what life had led to, a shield wall, and if I survived this then I would be a warrior.

The arrows flew one after the other, mostly thumping into shields, but one lucky shaft slid past a shield and sank into a man's chest and he fell back, and suddenly the Welsh leader lost patience and gave a great scream. And they charged.

It was a small shield wall, not a great battle. A

cattle skirmish, not a clash of armies, but it was my first shield wall, and I instinctively rattled my shield against my neighbors' shields, to make sure they touched, and I lowered Wasp-Sting, meaning to bring her up under the rim, and I crouched slightly to receive the charge, and the Welsh were howling like madmen, a noise meant to scare us, but I was too intent on doing what I had been taught to be distracted by the howls.

"Now!" Tatwine shouted and we all lunged our shields forward and there was a blow on mine like Ealdwulf's hammer thumping the anvil, and I was aware of an ax swinging overhead to split my skull and I ducked, raising the shield, and stabbed Wasp-Sting up into the man's groin. She went smooth and true, just as Toki had taught me, and that groin stroke is a wicked blow, one of the killer strikes, and the man screamed a terrible scream, just like a woman in childbirth, and the short sword was stuck in his body, blood pouring down her hilt and the ax tumbled down my back as I straightened. I drew Serpent-Breath across my left shoulder and swung at the man attacking my right-hand neighbor. It was a good stroke, straight into the skull, and I ripped her back, letting Ealdwulf's edge do its work, and the man with Wasp-Sting in his crotch was under my feet so I stamped on his face. I was shouting now, shouting in Danish, shouting their deaths, and it was all suddenly easy, and I stepped over my first victim to finish off the second, and that meant I had broken our shield wall, which did not matter because Tatwine was there to guard the space. I was in the Welsh space now, but with two dead men beside me, and a third man turned on me, sword coming in a great scything stroke that I met with the shield boss and, as he tried to cover his body with his own shield, I lunged Serpent-Breath into his throat, ripped her out, swung her all the way around, and she clanged against a shield behind me, and I turned, all savagery and anger now, and I charged a fourth man, throwing him down with my weight, and he began to shout for mercy and received none.

The joy of it. The sword joy. I was dancing with joy, joy seething in me, the battle joy that Ragnar had so often spoken of, the warrior joy. If a man has not known it, then he is no man. It was no battle, that, no proper slaughter, just a thief-killing, but it was my first fight and the gods had moved in me, had given my arm speed and my shield strength, and when it was done, and when I danced in the blood of the dead, I knew I was good. Knew I was more than good. I could have conquered the world at that moment and my only regret was that Ragnar had not seen me, but then I thought he might be watching from Valhalla and I raised Serpent-Breath to the clouds and shouted his name. I have seen other young men come from their first fights with that same joy, and I have buried them after their next battle. The young are fools and I was young. But I was good.

The cattle thieves were finished. Twelve were dead or so badly wounded as to be near death and the others had fled. We caught them easily enough and, one by one, we killed them, and afterward I went back to the man whose shield had kissed mine when the walls clashed and I had to put my right foot into his bloody crotch to drag Wasp-Sting free of his clinging flesh, and at that moment all I wanted was more enemies to kill.

"Where did you learn to fight, boy?" Tatwine asked me.

I turned on him as though he was an enemy, pride flaring in my face and Wasp-Sting twitching as if she was hungry for blood. "I am an ealdorman of Northumbria," I told him.

He paused, wary of me, then nodded. "Yes, lord," he said, then reached forward and felt the muscles of my right arm. "Where did you learn to fight?" he asked, leaving off the insulting "boy."

"I watched the Danes."

"Watched," he said tonelessly. He looked into my eyes, then grinned and embraced me. "God love me," he said, "but you're a savage one. Your first shield wall?"

"My first," I admitted.

"But not your last, I dare say, not your last."

He was right about that.

I have sounded immodest, but I have told the truth. These days I employ poets to sing my praises, but only because that is what a lord is supposed to do, though I often wonder why a man should get paid for mere words. These word-stringers make nothing, grow nothing, kill no enemies, catch no fish, and raise no cattle. They just take silver in exchange for words, which are free anyway. It is a clever trick, but in truth they are about as much use as priests.

I did fight well, that is no lie, but I had spent my growing years dreaming of little else, and I was young, and the young are reckless in battle, and I was strong and quick, and the enemy were tired. We left their severed heads on the bridge parapets as a greeting for other Britons coming to visit their lost lands. Then we rode south to meet Æthelred who was doubtless disappointed to find me alive and still hungry, but he accepted Tatwine's verdict that I could be useful as a fighter.

Not that there would be much battle, except against outlaws and cattle thieves. Æthelred would have liked to fight the Danes because he fretted under their rule, but he feared their revenge and so took care not to offend them. That was easy enough for Danish rule was light in our part of Mercia, but every few weeks some Danes would come to Cirrenceastre and demand cattle or food or silver and he had little choice but to pay. In truth he did not look north to the impotent King Burghred as his lord, but south to Wessex, and had I possessed any intelligence in those days I would have understood that Alfred was extending his influence over those southern parts of Mercia. The influence was not obvious, no West Saxon soldiers patrolled the country, but Alfred's messengers were forever riding and talking to the chief men, persuading them to bring their warriors south if the Danes attacked Wessex again.

I should have been wary of those West Saxon envoys, but I was too caught up in the intrigues of Æthelred's household to pay them any notice. The ealdorman did not like me much, but his eldest son, also called Æthelred, detested me. He was a year younger than I, but very conscious of his dignity and a great hater of the Danes. He was also a great hater of Brida, mainly because he tried to hump her and got a knee in the groin for his trouble, and after that she was put to work in Ealdorman Æthelred's kitchens and she warned me, the very first day, not to touch the gruel. I did not, but the rest of the table all suffered from liquid bowels for the next two days thanks to the elderberries and iris root she had added to the pot. The younger Æthelred and I were forever quarreling, though he was more careful after I beat him with my fists the day I found him whipping Brida's dog.

I was a nuisance to my uncle. I was too young, too big, too loud, too proud, too undisciplined, but I was also a family member and a lord, and so Ealdorman Æthelred endured me and was happy to let me chase Welsh raiders with Tatwine. We almost always failed to catch them.

I came back from one such pursuit late at night and let a servant rub down the horse while I went to find food and instead, of all people, discovered Father Willibald in the hall where he was sitting close to the embers of the fire. I did not recognize him at first, nor did he know me when I walked in all sweaty with a leather coat, long boots, a shield, and two swords. I just saw a figure by the fire. "Anything to eat there?" I asked, hoping I would not have to light a tallow candle and grope through the servants sleeping in the kitchen.

"Uhtred," he said, and I turned and peered through the gloom. Then he whistled like a blackbird and I recognized him. "Is that Brida with you?" the young priest asked.

She was also in leather, with a Welsh sword strapped to her waist. Nihtgenga ran to Willibald, whom he had never met, and allowed himself to be stroked. Tatwine and the other warriors all tramped in, but Willibald ignored them. "I hope you're well, Uhtred."

"I'm well, father," I said, "and you?"

"I'm very well," he said.

He smiled, obviously wanting me to ask why he had come to Æthelred's hall, but I pretended to be uninterested. "You didn't get into trouble for losing us?" I asked him instead.

"The Lady Ælswith was very angry," he admitted, "but Alfred seemed not to mind. He did chide Father Beocca, though."

"Beocca? Why?"

"Because Beocca had persuaded him you wanted to escape the Danes, and Beocca was wrong. Still, no harm done." He smiled. "And now Alfred has sent me to find you."

I squatted close to him. It was late summer, but the night was surprisingly chilly so I threw another log onto the fire so that sparks flew up and a puff of smoke drifted into the high beams. "Alfred sent you," I said flatly. "He still wants to teach me to read?"

"He wants to see you, lord."

I looked at him suspiciously. I called myself a lord, and so I was by birthright, but I was well imbued with the Danish idea that lordship was earned, not given, and I had not earned it yet. Still, Willibald was showing respect. "Why does he want to see me?" I asked.

"He would talk with you," Willibald said, "and when the talk is done you are free to come back here or, indeed, go anywhere else you wish."

Brida brought me some hard bread and cheese. I ate, thinking. "What does he want to talk to me about?" I asked Willibald. "God?"

The priest sighed. "Alfred has been king for two years, Uhtred, and in those years he has had only two things on his mind. God and the Danes, but I think he knows you cannot help him with the first." I smiled. Æthelred's hounds had woken as Tatwine and his men settled on the high platforms where they would sleep. One of the hounds came to me, hoping for food, and I stroked his rough fur and I thought how Ragnar had loved his hounds. Ragnar was in Valhalla now, feasting and roaring and fighting and whoring and drinking, and I hoped there were hounds in the Northmen's heaven, and boars the size of oxen, and spears sharp as razors. "There is only one condition attached to your journey," Willibald went on, "and that is that Brida is not to come."

"Brida's not to come, eh?" I repeated.

"The Lady Ælswith insists on it," Willibald said.

"Insists?"

"She has a son now," Willibald said. "God be praised, a fine boy called Edward."

"If I was Alfred," I said, "I'd keep her busy, too."

Willibald smiled. "So will you come?"

I touched Brida, who had settled beside me. "We'll come," I promised him, and Willibald shook his head at my obstinacy, but did not try to persuade me to leave Brida behind. Why did I go?

Because I was bored. Because my cousin Æthelred disliked me. Because Willibald's words had suggested that Alfred did not want me to become a scholar, but a warrior. I went because fate determines our lives.

We left in the morning. It was a late summer's day, a soft rain falling on trees heavy with leaf. At first we rode through Æthelred's fields, thick with rye and barley and loud with the rattling noise of corncrakes, but after a few miles we were in the wasteland that was the frontier region between Wessex and Mercia. There had been a time when these fields were fertile, when the villages were full and sheep roamed the higher hills, but the Danes had ravaged the area in the summer after their defeat at Æsc's Hill, and few men had come back to settle the land. Alfred, I knew, wanted folk to come here to plant crops and rear cattle, but the Danes had threatened to kill any man who used the land for they knew as well as Alfred that such men would look to Wessex for protection, that they would become West Saxons and increase the strength of Wessex, and Wessex, as far as the Danes were concerned, existed only because they had yet to take it.

Yet that land was not entirely deserted. A few folk still lived in the villages, and the woods were full of outlaws. We saw none, and that was good for we still had a fair amount of Ragnar's hoard that Brida carried. Each coin was now wrapped in a scrap of rag so that the frayed leather bag did not clink as she moved.

By day's end we were well south of that region and into Wessex and the fields were lush again and the villages full. No wonder the Danes yearned for this land.

Alfred was at Wintanceaster, which was the West Saxon capital and a fine town in a rich countryside. The Romans had made Wintanceaster, of course, and Alfred's palace was mostly Roman, though his father had added a great hall with beautifully carved beams, and Alfred was building a church that was even bigger than the hall, making its walls from stone that were covered with a spiderweb of timber scaffolding when I arrived. There was a market beside the new building and I remember thinking how odd it was to see so many folk without a single Dane among them. The Danes looked like us, but when Danes walked through a market in northern England the crowds parted, men bowed, and there was a hint of fear. None here. Women haggled over apples and bread and cheese and fish, and the only language I heard was the raw accents of Wessex.

Brida and I were given quarters in the Roman part of the palace. No one tried to part us this time. We had a small room, lime-washed, with a straw mattress, and Willibald said we should wait there, and we did until we got bored with waiting, after which we explored the palace, finding it full of priests and monks. They looked at us strangely, for both of us wore arm rings cut with Danish runes. I was a fool in those days, a clumsy fool, and did not have the courtesy to take the arm rings off. True, some English wore them, especially the warriors, but not in Alfred's palace. There were plenty of warriors in his household, many of them the great ealdormen who were Alfred's courtiers, led his retainers, and were rewarded by land, but such men were far outnumbered by priests, and only a handful of men, the trusted bodyguard of the king's household, were permitted to carry weapons in the palace. In truth it was more like a monastery than a king's court. In one room there were a dozen monks copying books, their pens scratching busily, and there were three chapels, one of them beside a courtyard that was full of flowers.

It was beautiful, that courtyard, buzzing with bees and thick with fragrance. Nihtgenga was just pissing on one of the flowering bushes when a voice spoke behind us. "The Romans made the courtyard."

I turned and saw Alfred. I went on one knee, as a man should when he sees a king, and he waved me up. He was wearing woolen breeches, long boots, and a simple linen shirt, and he had no escort, neither guard nor priest. His right sleeve was ink stained. "You are welcome, Uhtred," he said.

"Thank you, lord," I said, wondering where his entourage was. I had never seen him without a slew of priests within fawning distance, but he was quite alone that day.

"And Brida," he said, "is that your dog?"

"He is," she said defiantly.

"He looks a fine beast. Come." He ushered us through a door into what was evidently his own private chamber. It had a tall desk at which he could stand and write. The desk had four candle-holders, though as it was daylight the candles were not lit. A small table held a bowl of water so he could wash the ink off his hands. There was a couch covered in sheepskins, a stool on which were piled six books and a sheaf of parchments, and a low altar on which was an ivory crucifix and two jeweled reliquaries. The remains of a meal were on the window ledge. He moved the plates, bent to kiss the altar, then sat on the ledge and began sharpening some quills for writing. "It is kind of you to come," he said mildly. "I was going to talk with you after supper tonight, but I saw you in the garden, so thought we could talk now." He smiled and I, lout that I was, scowled. Brida squatted by the door with Nihtgenga close to her.

"Ealdorman Æthelred tells me you are a considerable warrior, Uhtred," Alfred said.

"I've been lucky, lord."

"Luck is good, or so my own warriors tell me. I have not yet worked out a theology of luck, and perhaps I never will. Can there be luck if God disposes?" He frowned at me for a few heartbeats, evidently thinking about the apparent contradiction, but then dismissed the problem as an amusement for another day. "So I suppose I was wrong to try to encourage you to the priesthood?"

"There's nothing wrong with encouragement, lord," I said, "but I had no wish to be a priest."

"So you ran away from me. Why?"

I think he expected me to be embarrassed and

to evade his question, but I told him the truth. "I went back to fetch my sword," I told him. I wished I had Serpent-Breath at that moment, because I hated being without her, but the palace doorkeeper had insisted I give up all my weapons, even the small knife I used for eating.

He nodded seriously, as if that was a good reason. "It's a special sword?"

"The best in the world, lord."

He smiled at that, recognizing a boy's misplaced enthusiasm. "So you went back to Earl Ragnar?"

I nodded this time, but said nothing.

"Who did not hold you prisoner, Uhtred," he said sternly. "Indeed he never did, did he? He treated you like a son."

"I loved him," I blurted out.

He stared at me and I became uncomfortable under his gaze. He had very light eyes that gave you the sense of being judged. "Yet in Eoferwic," Alfred went on mildly, "they are saying you killed him."

Now it was my time to stare at him. I was angry, confused, astonished, and surprised, so confused that I did not know what to say. But why was I so surprised? What else would Kjartan claim? Except, I thought, Kjartan must have thought me dead, or I hoped he thought me dead.

"They lie," Brida said flatly.

"Do they?" Alfred asked me, still in a mild voice.

"They lie," I said angrily.

"I never doubted it," he said. He put down his quills and knife and leaned over to the heap of stiff parchments that rested on his pile of books and sifted through them until he found the one he was looking for. He read for a few moments. "Kjartan? Is that how it is pronounced?"

"Kjartan," I corrected him, making the **j** sound like a **y.**

"Earl Kjartan now," Alfred said, "and reckoned to be a great lord. Owner of four ships."

"That's all written down?" I asked.

"Whatever I discover of my enemies is written down," Alfred said, "which is why you are here. To tell me more. Did you know Ivar the Boneless is dead?"

My hand instinctively went to Thor's hammer, which I wore under my jerkin. "No. Dead?" It astonished me. Such was my awe of Ivar that I suppose I had thought he would live forever, but Alfred spoke the truth. Ivar the Boneless was dead.

"He was killed fighting against the Irish," Alfred said, "and Ragnar's son has returned to Northumbria with his men. Will he fight Kjartan?"

"If he knows Kjartan killed his father," I said, "he'll disembowel him."

"Earl Kjartan has sworn an oath of innocence in the matter," Alfred said.

"Then he lies."

"He's a Dane," Alfred said, "and the truth is not in them." He gave me a sharp look, doubtless for the many lies I had fed him over the years. He stood then and paced the small room. He had said that I was there to tell him about the Danes, but in the next few moments he was the one who did the telling. King Burghred of Mercia, he said, was tired of his Danish overlords and had decided to flee to Rome.

"Rome?"

"I was taken there twice as a child," he said, "and I remember the city as a very untidy place"—that was said very sternly—"but a man feels close to God there, so it is a good place to pray. Burghred is a weak man, but he did his small best to alleviate Danish rule, and once he is gone then we can expect the Danes to fill his land. They will be on our frontier. They will be in

Cirrenceastre." He looked at me. "Kjartan knows you're alive."

"He does?"

"Of course he does. The Danes have spies, just as we do." And Alfred's spies, I realized, had to be efficient for he knew so much. "Does Kjartan care about your life?" he went on. "If you tell the truth about Ragnar's death, Uhtred, then he does care because you can contradict his lies and if Ragnar learns that truth from you then Kjartan will certainly fear for his life. It is in Kjartan's interest, therefore, to kill you. I tell you this only so that you may consider whether you wish to return to Cirrenceastre where the Danes have," he paused, "influence. You will be safer in Wessex, but how long will Wessex last?" He evidently did not expect an answer, but kept pacing. "Ubba has sent men to Mercia, which suggests he will follow. Have you met Ubba?"

"Many times."

"Tell me of him."

I told him what I knew, told him that Ubba was a great warrior, though very superstitious, and that intrigued Alfred who wanted to know all about Storri the sorcerer and about the rune-sticks, and I told him how Ubba never picked battles for the joy of fighting, but only when the

runes said he could win, but that once he fought
he did so with a terrible savagery. Alfred wrote it
all down, then asked if I had met Halfdan, the
youngest brother, and I said I had, but very
briefly.

"Halfdan speaks of avenging Ivar," Alfred said,
"so it's possible he will not come back to Wessex.
Not soon, anyway. But even with Halfdan in Ireland there will be plenty of pagans left to attack
us." He explained how he had anticipated an attack this year, but the Danes had been disorga-
nized and he did not expect that to last. "They
will come next year," he said, "and we think
Ubba will lead them."

"Or Guthrum," I said.

"I had not forgotten him. He is in East Anglia
now." He glanced reproachfully at Brida, remembering her tales of Edmund. Brida, quite unwor-
ried, just watched him with half-closed eyes. He
looked back to me. "What do you know of
Guthrum?"

Again I talked and again he wrote. He was intrigued about the bone in Guthrum's hair, and
shuddered when I repeated Guthrum's insistence
that every Englishman be killed. "A harder job
than he thinks," Alfred said drily. He laid the pen
down and began pacing again. "There are differ-

ent kinds of men," he said, "and some are to be
more feared than others. I feared Ivar the Boneless, for he was cold and thought carefully. Ubba?
I don't know, but I suspect he is dangerous. Halfdan? A brave fool, but with no thoughts in his
head. Guthrum? He is the least to be feared."

"The least?" I sounded dubious. Guthrum
might be called the Unlucky, but he was a considerable chieftain and led a large force of warriors.

"He thinks with his heart, Uhtred," Alfred
said, "not his head. You can change a man's
heart, but not his head." I remember staring at
Alfred then, thinking that he spouted foolishness
like a horse pissing, but he was right. Or almost
right because he tried to change me, but never
succeeded.

A bee drifted through the door, Nihtgenga
snapped impotently at it, and the bee droned out
again. "But Guthrum will attack us?" Alfred
asked.

"He wants to split you," I said. "One army by
land, another by sea, and the Britons from
Wales."

Alfred looked at me gravely. "How do you
know that?"

So I told him about Guthrum's visit to Ragnar

and the long conversation that I had witnessed, and Alfred's pen scratched, little flecks of ink spattering from the quill at rough spots on the parchment. "What this suggests," he spoke as he wrote, "is that Ubba will come from Mercia by land and Guthrum by sea from East Anglia." He was wrong about that, but it seemed likely at the time. "How many ships can Guthrum bring?"

I had no idea. "Seventy?" I suggested. "A hundred?"

"Far more than that," Alfred said severely, "and I cannot build even twenty ships to oppose them. Have you sailed, Uhtred?"

"Many times."

"With the Danes?" He asked pedantically.

"With the Danes," I confirmed.

"What I would like you to do," he said, but at that moment a bell tolled somewhere in the palace and he immediately broke off from what he was saying. "Prayers," he said, putting down his quill. "You will come." It was not a question, but a command.

"I have things to do," I said, waited a heartbeat, "lord."

He blinked at me in surprise for he was not used to men opposing his wishes, especially when it came to saying prayers, but I kept a stubborn face and he did not force the issue. There was the slap of sandaled feet on the paved path outside his chamber and he dismissed us as he hurried to join the monks going to their service. A moment later the drone of a chant began, and Brida and I abandoned the palace, going into the town where we discovered a tavern that sold decent ale. I had been offered none by Alfred. The folk there were suspicious of us, partly because of the arm rings with their Danish runes, and partly because of our strange accents, mine from the north and Brida's from the east, but a sliver of our silver was weighed and trusted, and the wary atmosphere subsided when Father Beocca came in, saw us, and raised his inky hands in welcome. "I have been searching high and low for you," he said. "Alfred wanted you."

"He wanted to pray," I said.

"He would have you eat with him."

I drank some ale. "If I live to be a hundred, father," I began.

"I pray you live longer than that," Beocca said. "I pray you live as long as Methuselah."

I wondered who that was. "If I live to be a hundred," I said again, "I hope never to eat with Alfred again."

He shook his head sadly, but agreed to sit with

us and take a pot of ale. He reached over and pulled at the leather thong half hidden by my jerkin and so revealed the hammer. He tutted. "You lied to me, Uhtred," he said sadly. "When you ran away from Father Willibald we made enquiries. You were never a prisoner! You were treated as a son!"

"I was," I agreed.

"But why did you not come to us then? Why did you stay with the Danes?"

I smiled. "What would I have learned here?" I asked. He began to answer, but I stilled him. "You would have made me a scholar, father," I said, "and the Danes made me a warrior. And you will need warriors when they come back."

Beocca understood that, but he was still sad. He looked at Brida. "And you, young lady, I hope you did not lie?"

"I always tell the truth, father," she said in a small voice, "always."

"That is good," he said, then reached over again to hide my amulet. "Are you a Christian, Uhtred?" he asked.

"You baptized me yourself, father," I said evasively.

"We will not defeat the Danes unless we hold

the faith," he said earnestly, then smiled, "but will you do what Alfred wants?"

"I don't know what he wants. He ran off to wear out his knees before he could tell me."

"He wants you to serve on one of the ships he's building," he said. I just gaped at him. "We're building ships, Uhtred," Beocca went on enthusiastically, "ships to fight the Danes, but our sailors are not fighters. They're, well, sailors! And they're fishermen, of course, and traders, but we need men who can teach them what the Danes do. Their ships raid our shore incessantly. Two ships come? Three ships? Sometimes more. They land, burn, kill, take slaves, and vanish. But with ships we can fight them." He punched his withered left hand with his right and winced with the pain. "That's what Alfred wants."

I glanced at Brida who gave a small shrug as if to say that she thought Beocca was telling the truth.

I thought of the two Æthelreds, younger and older, and their dislike of me. I remembered the joy of a ship on the seas, of the wind tearing at the rigging, of the oars bending and flashing back the sun, of the songs of the rowers, of the heart-beat of the steering oar, of the seethe of the long green water against the hull. "Of course I'll do it," I said.

"Praise God," Beocca said. And why not?

I met Æthelflaed before I left Wintanceaster. She was three or four years old, I suppose, and full of words. She had bright gold hair. She was playing in the garden outside Alfred's study and I remember she had a rag doll and Alfred played with her and Ælswith worried he was making her too excited. I remember her laugh. She never lost that laugh. Alfred was good with her for he loved his children. Most of the time he was solemn, pious, and very self-disciplined, but with small children he became playful and I almost liked him as he teased Æthelflaed by hiding her rag doll behind his back. I also remember how Æthelflaed ran over to Nihtgenga and fondled him and Ælswith called her back. "Dirty dog," she told her daughter, "you'll get fleas or worse. Come here!" She gave Brida a very sour look and muttered, "Scrætte!" That means prostitute and Brida pretended not to have heard, as did Alfred. Ælswith ignored me, but I did not mind because Alfred had summoned a palace slave who laid a helmet and a mail coat on the grass. "For you, Uhtred," Alfred said.

The helmet was bright iron, dented on the crown by the blow of a weapon, polished with sand and vinegar, and with a faceplate in which two eyeholes stared like the pits of a skull. The mail was good, though it had been pierced by a spear or sword where the owner's heart had been, but it had been expertly repaired by a good smith and it was worth many pieces of silver. "They were both taken from a Dane at Æsc's Hill," Alfred told me. Ælswith watched disapprovingly.

"Lord," I said, and went on one knee and kissed his hand.

"A year's service," he said, "is all I ask of you."

"You have it, lord," I said, and sealed that promise with another kiss on his ink-stained knuckles.

I was dazzled. The two pieces of armor were rare and valuable, and I had done nothing to deserve such generosity, unless to behave boorishly is to deserve favors. And Alfred had been generous, though a lord should be generous. That is what a lord is, a giver of rings, and a lord who does not distribute wealth is a lord who will lose the allegiance of his men, yet even so I had not earned the gifts, though I was grateful for them. I was dazzled by them and for a moment I thought Alfred a great and good and admirable man.

I should have thought a moment longer. He was generous, of course, but Alfred, unlike his wife, was never grudging with gifts, but why give such valuable armor to a half-fledged youth? Because I was useful to him. Not very useful, but still of use. Alfred sometimes played chess, a game for which I have small patience, but in chess there are pieces of great value and pieces of little worth, and I was one of those. The pieces of great value were the lords of Mercia who, if he could bind them to him, would help Wessex fight the Danes, but he was already looking beyond Mercia into East Anglia and Northumbria and he had no Northumbrian lords in exile except me, and he foresaw a time when he would need a Northumbrian to persuade the northern folk to accept a southern king. If I had been really valuable, if I could have brought him the allegiance of folk nearer his frontier, then he would have given me a noble West Saxon wife, for a woman of high birth is the greatest gift a lord can bestow, but a helmet and a coat of mail were sufficient for the distant idea of Northumbria. I doubt he thought I could deliver that country to him, but he did see that one day I might be useful in its delivery and so he bound me to him with gifts and made the bonds acceptable with flattery. "None of my men has fought on shipboard," he told me, "so they must learn. You might be young, Uhtred, but you have experience which means you know more than they do. So go and teach them."

Me? Know more than his men? I had sailed in **Wind-Viper,** that was all, but I had never fought from a ship, though I was not going to tell Alfred that. Instead I accepted his gifts and went south to the coast, and thus he had tucked away a pawn that might one day be useful. To Alfred, of course, the most valuable pieces on the board were his bishops who were supposed to pray the Danes out of England, and no bishop ever went unfed in Wessex, but I could not complain for I had a coat of mail, a helmet of iron, and looked like a warrior. Alfred loaned us horses for our journey and he sent Father Willibald with us, not as a guardian this time, but because he insisted that his new ships' crews must have a priest to look after their spiritual needs. Poor Willibald. He used to get sick as a dog every time a ripple touched a ship, but he never abandoned his responsibilities, especially toward me. If prayers could make a man into a Christian then I would be a saint ten times over by now.

Destiny is all. And now, looking back, I see the pattern of my life's journey. It began in Bebbanburg and took me south, ever southward, until I reached the farthest coast of England and could go no farther and still hear my own language. That was my childhood's journey. As a man I have gone the other way, ever northward, carrying sword and spear and ax to clear the path back to where I began. Destiny. The spinners favor me, or at least they have spared me, and for a time they made me a sailor.

I took my mail coat and helmet in the year 874, the same year that King Burghred fled to Rome, and Alfred expected Guthrum to come in the following spring, but he did not, nor in the summer, and so Wessex was spared an invasion in 875. Guthrum should have come, but he was a cautious man, ever expecting the worst, and he spent a full eighteen months raising the greatest army of Danes that had ever been seen in England. It dwarfed the Great Army that had marched to Readingum, and it was an army that should have finished Wessex and granted Guthrum's dream of slaughtering the last Englishman in England. Guthrum's host did come in time and when that time came the three spinners cut England's threads one by one until she dangled by a wisp, but that story must wait and I mention it now only to explain why we were given time to prepare ourselves.

And I was given to **Heahengel.** So help me, that was the ship's name. It means Archangel. She was not mine, of course. She had a shipmaster called Werferth who had commanded a tubby boat that had traded across the sea before he was persuaded to steer **Heahengel,** and her warriors were led by a grim old beast called Leofric. And me? I was the turd in the butter churn.

I was not needed. All Alfred's flattering words about me teaching his sailors how to fight were just that, mere words. But he had persuaded me to join his fleet, and I had promised him a year, and here I was in Hamtun, which was a fine port at the head of a long arm of the sea. Alfred had ordered twelve ships made, and their maker was a shipwright who had been an oarsman on a Danish boat before escaping in Frankia and making his way back to England. There was not much about ship fighting that he did not know, and nothing I could teach anyone, but ship fighting is a very simple affair. A ship is a scrap of land afloat. So a ship fight is a land fight at sea. Bang your boat alongside the enemy, make a shield wall, and kill the other crew. But our shipwright, who was a cunning man, had worked out that a larger ship gave its crew an advantage because it could hold more men and its sides, being higher, would serve as a wall, and so he had built twelve big ships, which at first looked odd to me for they had no beast heads at their prows or sterns, though they did all have crucifixes nailed to their masts. The whole fleet was commanded by Ealdorman Hacca, who was brother to the ealdorman of Hamptonscir, and the only thing he said when I arrived was to advise me to wrap my mail coat in an oiled sack so it would not rust. After that he gave me to Leofric.

"Show me your hands," Leofric ordered. I did and he sneered. "You'll have blisters soon, earsling."

That was his favorite word, **earsling**. It means "arseling." That was me, though sometimes he called me Endwerc, which means a pain in the arse, and he made me an oarsman, one of the sixteen on the bæcbord, which is the left-hand side of the ship as you look forward. The other side is the steorbord, for it is on that side that the steering oar is rigged. We had sixty warriors aboard, thirty-two rowed at a time unless the sail could be hoisted, and we had Werferth at the steering oar and Leofric snarling up and down telling us to pull harder.

All autumn and winter we rowed up and down Hamtun's wide channel and beyond in the Solente, which is the sea south of the island called Wiht, and we fought the tide and wind, hammering **Heahengel** through short, cold waves until we had become a crew and could make her leap across the sea. To my surprise, I found that **Heahengel** was a fast ship. I had thought that, being so much bigger, she would be slower than the Danish ships, but she was fast, very fast, and Leofric was turning her into a lethal weapon.

He did not like me and though he called me earsling and Endwerc I did not face him down because I would have died. He was a short, wide man, muscled like an ox, with a scarred face, a quick temper, and a sword so battered that its blade was slim as a knife. Not that he cared, for his preferred weapon was the ax. He knew I was an ealdorman, but did not care, nor did he care that I had once served on a Danish boat. "The only thing the Danes can teach us, earsling," he told me, "is how to die."

He did not like me, but I liked him. At night, when we filled one of Hamtun's taverns, I would sit near him to listen to his few words, which were usually scornful, even about our own ships. "Twelve," he snarled, "and how many can the Danes bring?"

No one answered.

"Two hundred?" he suggested. "And we have twelve?"

Brida beguiled him one night into talking about his fights, all of them ashore, and he talked of Æsc's Hill, how the Danish shield wall had been broken by a man with an ax, and it was obviously Leofric himself who had done that, and he told how the man had held the ax halfway up its shaft because that made it quicker to recover from the blow, though it diminished the force of the weapon, and how the man had used his shield to hold off the enemy on his left, killed the one in front, then the one to the right, and then had slipped his hand down the ax handle to start swinging it in terrible, flashing strokes that carved through the Danish lines. He saw me listening and gave me his usual sneer. "Been in a shield wall, earsling?"

I held up one finger.

"He broke the enemy shield wall," Brida said. She and I lived in the tavern stables and Leofric liked Brida though he refused to allow her on board **Heahengel** because he reckoned a woman brought ill luck to a ship. "He broke the wall," Brida said. "I saw it."

He gazed at me, not sure whether to believe her. I said nothing. "Who were you fighting," he asked after a pause, "nuns?"

"Welshmen," Brida said.

"Oh, Welshmen! Hell, they die easy," he said, which was not true, but it let him keep his scorn of me, and the next day, when we had a practice fight with wooden staves instead of real weapons, he made sure he opposed me and he beat me to the ground as if I was a yapping dog, opening a cut on my skull and leaving me dazed. "I'm not a Welshman, earsling," he said. I liked Leofric a lot.

The year turned. I became eighteen years old. The great Danish army did not come, but their ships did. The Danes were being Vikings again, and their dragon ships came in ones and twos to harry the West Saxon coast, to raid and to rape and to burn and to kill, but this year Alfred had his own ships ready.

So we went to sea.

EIGHT

We spent the spring, summer, and autumn of the year 875 rowing up and down Wessex's south coast. We were divided into four flotillas, and Leofric commanded **Heahengel, Ceruphin,** and **Cristenlic,** which meant Archangel, Cherubim, and Christian. Alfred had chosen the names. Hacca, who led the whole fleet, sailed in the **Evangelista,** which soon acquired the reputation of being an unlucky ship, though her real ill fortune was to have Hacca on board. He was a nice enough man, generous with his silver, but he hated ships, hated the sea, and wanted nothing more than to be a warrior on dry land, which meant that **Evangelista** was always on Hamtun's hard undergoing repairs.

But not the **Heahengel.** I tugged that oar till my body ached and my hands were hard as oak, but the rowing put muscle on me, so much muscle. I was big now, big, tall, and strong, and cocky and belligerent as well. I wanted nothing more than to try **Heahengel** against some Danish ship, yet our first encounter was a disaster. We were off the coast of Suth Seaxa, a marvelous coast of rearing white cliffs, and **Ceruphin** and **Cristenlic** had gone far out to sea while we slid inshore hoping to attract a Viking ship that would pursue us into an ambush sprung by the other two craft. The trap worked, only the Viking was better than us. He was smaller, much smaller, and we pursued him against the falling tide, gaining on him with every dip of our oars, but then he saw **Ceruphin** and **Cristenlic** slamming in from the south, their oar blades flashing back the sunlight and their bow waves seething white, and the Danish shipmaster turned his craft as if she had been mounted on a spindle and, with the strong tide now helping him, dashed back at us.

"Turn into him!" Leofric roared at Werferth who was at the steering oar, but instead Werferth turned away, not wanting to bring on a collision, and I saw the oars of the Danish ship slide into their holes as she neared us and then she ran down our steorbord flank, snapping our oars one by one, the impact throwing the oar shafts back into our rowers with enough force to break some men's ribs, and then the Danish archers—they had four or five aboard—began loosing their arrows. One went into Werferth's neck and there was blood pouring down the steering deck and Leofric was bellowing in impotent rage as the Dane, oars slid out again, sped safely away down the fast ebbing tide. They jeered as we wallowed in the waves.

"Have you steered a boat, earsling?" Leofric asked me, pulling the dying Werferth aside.

"Yes."

"Then steer this one." We limped home with only half our proper oars, and we learned two lessons. One was to carry spare oars and the second was to carry archers, except that Ealdorman Freola, who commanded the fyrd of Hamptonscir, said he could spare no bowmen, that he had too few as it was, and that the ships had already consumed too many of his other warriors, and besides, he said, we should not need archers. Hacca, his brother, told us not to make a fuss. "Just throw spears," he advised Leofric.

"I want archers," Leofric insisted.

"There are none!" Hacca said, spreading his hands.

Father Willibald wanted to write a letter to Alfred. "He will listen to me," he said.

"So you write to him," Leofric said sourly, "and what happens then?"

"He will send archers, of course!" Father Willibald said brightly.

"The letter," Leofric said, "goes to his damn clerks, who are all priests, and they put it in a pile, and the pile gets read slowly, and when Alfred finally sees it he asks for advice, and two damned bishops have their say, and Alfred writes back wanting to know more, and by then it's Candlemas and we're all dead with Danish arrows in our backs." He glared at Willibald and I began to like Leofric even more. He saw me grinning. "What's so funny, Endwerc?" he demanded.

"I can get you archers," I said.

"How?"

With one piece of Ragnar's gold, which we displayed in Hamtun's marketplace and said that the gold coin, with its weird writing, would go to the best archer to win a competition that would be held one week hence. That coin was worth more than most men could earn in a year and Leofric was curious how I had come by it, but I refused to tell him. Instead I set up targets and word spread through the countryside that rich gold was to be had with cheap arrows, and over forty men arrived to test their skill and we simply marched the best twelve on board **Heahengel** and another ten each to **Ceruphin** and **Cristenlic,** then took them to sea. Our twelve protested, of course, but Leofric snarled at them and they all suddenly decided they wanted nothing better than to sail the Wessex coast with him. "For something that dribbled out of a goat's backside," Leofric told me, "you're not completely useless."

"There'll be trouble when we get back," I warned him.

"Of course there'll be trouble," he agreed, "trouble from the shire reeve, from the ealdorman, from the bishop, and from the whole damned lot of them." He laughed suddenly, a very rare occurrence. "So let's kill some Danes first."

We did. And by chance it was the same ship that had shamed us, and she tried the same trick again, but this time I turned **Heahengel** into her and our bows smashed into her quarter and our twelve archers were loosing shafts into her crew. **Heahengel** had ridden up over the other ship, half sinking her and pinning her down, and Leofric led a charge over the prow, and there was blood thickening the water in the Viking bilge. Two of our men managed to tie the ships together, which meant I could leave the steering oar and, without bothering to put on either helmet or mail coat, I jumped aboard with Serpent-Breath and joined the fight. There were shields clashing in the wide midships, spears jabbing, swords and axes swinging, arrows flighting overhead, men screaming, men dying, the rage of battle, the joy of blade song, and it was all over before **Ceruphin** or **Cristenlic** could join us.

How I did love it. To be young, to be strong, to have a good sword, and to survive. The Danish crew had been forty-six strong and all but one died, and he only lived because Leofric bellowed that we must take a prisoner. Three of our men died, and six were foully wounded and they probably all died once we got them ashore, but we bailed out the Viking ship and went back to Hamtun with her in tow, and in her blood-drenched belly we found a chest of silver that she had stolen from a monastery on Wiht. Leofric presented a generous amount to the bowmen, so that when we went ashore and were confronted by the reeve, who demanded that we give up the archers, only two of them wanted to go. The rest could see their way to becoming wealthy, and so they stayed.

The prisoner was called Hroi. His lord, whom we had killed in the battle, had been called Thurkil and he served Guthrum, who was in East Anglia where he now called himself king of that country. "Does he still wear the bone in his hair?" I asked.

"Yes, lord," Hroi said. He did not call me lord because I was an ealdorman, for he did not know that. He called me lord because he did not want me to kill him when the questioning was done.

Hroi did not think Guthrum would attack this year. "He waits for Halfdan," he told me.

"And Halfdan's where?"

"In Ireland, lord."

"Avenging Ivar?"

"Yes, lord."

"You know Kjartan?"

"I know three men so called, lord."

"Kjartan of Northumbria," I said, "father of Sven."

"Earl Kjartan, you mean?"

"He calls himself an earl now?" I asked.

"Yes, lord, and he is still in Northumbria."

"And Ragnar? Son of Ragnar the Fearless?"

"Earl Ragnar is with Guthrum, lord, in East Anglia. He has four boats."

We chained Hroi and sent him under guard to Wintanceaster for Alfred liked to talk with Danish prisoners. I do not know what happened to him. He was probably hanged or beheaded, for Alfred did not extend Christian mercy to pagan pirates.

And I thought of Ragnar the Younger, Earl Ragnar now, and wondered if I would meet his boats on the Wessex coast, and wondered too whether Hroi had lied and that Guthrum would invade that summer. I thought he would, for there was much fighting across the island of Britain. The Danes of Mercia had attacked the Britons in north Wales, I never did discover why, and other Danish bands raided across the West Saxon frontier, and I suspected those raids were meant to discover West Saxon weaknesses before Guthrum launched his great army, but no army came and, as the summer reached its height, Alfred felt safe enough to leave his forces in North Wessex to visit the fleet.

His arrival coincided with news that seven Danish ships had been seen off Heilincigae, an island that lay in shallow waters not far to Hamtun's east, and the news was confirmed when we saw smoke rising from a pillaged settlement. Only half our ships were in Hamtun, the others were at sea, and one of the six in port, the **Evangelista,** was on the hard having her bottom scraped. Hacca was nowhere near Hamtun, gone to his brother's house probably, and he would doubtless be annoyed that he had missed the king's visit, but Alfred had given us no warning of his arrival, probably because he wanted to see us as we really were, rather than as we would have been had we known he was coming. As soon as he heard about the Danes off Heilincigae he ordered us all to sea and boarded **Heahengel** along with two of his guards and three priests, one of whom was Beocca who came to stand beside the steering oar.

"You've got bigger, Uhtred," he said to me, almost reproachfully. I was a good head taller than him now, and much broader in the chest.

"If you rowed, father," I said, "you'd get bigger."

He giggled. "I can't imagine myself rowing," he said, then pointed at my steering oar. "Is that difficult to manage?" he asked.

I let him take it and suggested he turn the boat slightly to the steorbord and his crossed eyes widened in astonishment as he tried to push the oar and the water fought against him. "It needs strength," I said, taking the oar back.

"You're happy, aren't you?" He made it sound like an accusation.

"I am, yes."

"You weren't meant to be," he said.

"No?"

"Alfred thought this experience would humble you."

I stared at the king who was up in the bows with Leofric, and I remembered the king's honeyed words about me having something to teach these crews, and I realized he had known I had nothing to contribute, yet he had still given me the helmet and armor. That, I assumed, was so I would give him a year of my life in which he hoped Leofric would knock the arrogance out of my bumptious youthfulness. "Didn't work, did it?" I said, grinning.

"He said you must be broken like a horse."

"But I'm not a horse, father. I'm a lord of Northumbria. What did he think? That after a year I'd be a meek Christian ready to do his bidding?"

"Is that such a bad thing?"

"It's a bad thing," I said. "He needs proper men to fight the Danes, not praying lickspittles."

Beocca sighed, then made the sign of the cross because poor Father Willibald was feeding the gulls with his vomit. "It's time you were married, Uhtred," Beocca said sternly.

I looked at him in astonishment. "Married! Why do you say that?"

"You're old enough," Beocca said.

"So are you," I retorted, "and you're not married, so why should I be?"

"I live in hope," Beocca said. Poor man, he had a squint, a palsied hand, and a face like a sick weasel, which really did not make him a great favorite with women. "But there is a young woman in Defnascir you should look at," he told me enthusiastically, "a very well born young lady! A charming creature, and . . ." He paused, evidently having run out of the girl's qualities, or else because he could not invent any new ones. "Her father was the shire reeve, rest his soul. A lovely girl. Mildrith, she's called." He smiled at me expectantly.

"A reeve's daughter," I said flatly. "The king's reeve? The shire reeve?"

"Her father was reeve of southern Defnascir," Beocca said, sliding the man down the social ladder, "but he left Mildrith property. A fair piece of land near Exanceaster."

"A reeve's daughter," I repeated, "not an ealdorman's daughter?"

"She's sixteen, I believe," Beocca said, gazing at the shingled beach sliding away to our east.

"Sixteen," I said scathingly, "and unmarried, which suggests she has a face like a bag of maggots."

"That is hardly relevant," he said crossly.

"You don't have to sleep with her," I said, "and no doubt she's pious?"

"She is a devoted Christian, I'm happy to say."

"You've seen her?" I asked.

"No," he admitted, "but Alfred has talked of her."

"This is Alfred's idea?"

"He likes to see his men settled, to have their roots in the land."

"I'm not his man, Father. I'm Uhtred of Bebbanburg, and the lords of Bebbanburg don't marry pious maggot-faced bitches of low birth."

"You should meet her," he persisted, frowning at me. "Marriage is a wonderful thing, Uhtred, ordained by God for our happiness."

"How would you know?"

"It is," he insisted weakly.

"I'm already happy," I said. "I hump Brida and I kill Danes. Find another man for Mildrith.

Why don't you marry her? Good God, Father, you must be near thirty! If you don't marry soon you'll go to your grave a virgin. Are you a virgin?"

He blushed, but did not answer because Leofric came back to the steering deck with a black scowl. He never looked happy, but he appeared grimmer than ever at that moment and I had an idea that he had been arguing with Alfred, an argument he had plainly lost. Alfred himself followed, a serene look of indifference on his long face. Two of his priests trailed him, carrying parchment, ink, and quills, and I realized notes were being taken. "What would you say, Uhtred, was the most crucial equipment for a ship?" Alfred asked me. One of the priests dipped his quill in the ink in readiness for my answer, then staggered as the ship hit a wave. God knows what his writing looked like that day. "The sail?" Alfred prompted me. "Spears? Archers? Shields? Oars?"

"Buckets," I said.

"Buckets?" He looked at me with disapproval, suspecting I was mocking him.

"Buckets to bail the ship, lord," I said, nodding down into **Heahengel**'s belly where four men scooped out seawater and chucked it over the side, though a good deal landed on the rowers. "What we need, lord, is a better way of caulking ships."

"Write that down," Alfred instructed the priests, then stood on tiptoe to look across the intervening low land into the sea lake where the enemy ships had been sighted.

"They'll be long gone," Leofric growled.

"I pray not," Alfred said.

"The Danes don't wait for us," Leofric said. He was in a terrible mood, so terrible that he was willing to snarl at his king. "They aren't fools," he went on. "They land, they raid, and they go. They'll have sailed on the ebb." The tide had just turned and was flooding against us now, though I never did quite understand the tides in the long waters from the sea to Hamtun for there were twice as many high tides there as anywhere else. Hamtun's tides had a mind of their own, or else were confused by the channels.

"The pagans were there at dawn," Alfred said.

"And they'll be miles away by now," Leofric said. He spoke to Alfred as if he was another crewman, using no respect, but Alfred was always patient with such insolence. He knew Leofric's worth.

But Leofric was wrong that day about the

enemy. The Viking ships were not gone, but still off Heilincigae, all seven of them, having been trapped there by the falling tide. They were waiting for the rising water to float them free, but we arrived first, coming into the sea lake through the narrow entrance that leads from the northern bank of the Solente. Once through the entrance a ship is in a world of marshes, sandbanks, islands, and fish traps, not unlike the waters of the Gewæsc. We had a man aboard who had grown up on those waters, and he guided us, but the Danes had lacked any such expertise and they had been misled by a line of withies, stuck into the sand at low tide to mark a channel, which had been deliberately moved to entice them onto a mudbank on which they were now firmly stuck.

Which was splendid. We had them trapped like foxes in a one-hole earth and all we had to do was anchor in the sea-lake entrance, hope our anchors held against the strong currents, wait for them to float off, and then slaughter them, but Alfred was in a hurry. He wanted to get back to his land forces and insisted we return him to Hamtun before nightfall, and so, against Leofric's advice, we were ordered to an immediate attack.

That, too, was splendid, except that we could

not approach the mudbank directly for the channel was narrow and it would mean going in single file and the lead ship would face seven Danish ships on its own, and so we had to row a long way to approach them from the south, which meant that they could escape to the sea lake's entrance if the tide floated them off, which it might very well do, and Leofric muttered into his beard that we were going about the battle all wrong. He was furious with Alfred.

Alfred, meanwhile, was fascinated by the enemy ships, that he had never seen so clearly before. "Are the beasts representations of their gods?" he asked me, referring to the finely carved prows and sterns that flaunted their monsters, dragons, and serpents.

"No, lord, just beasts," I said. I was beside him, having relinquished the steering oar to the man who knew these waters, and I told the king how the carved heads could be lifted off their posts so that they did not terrify the spirits of the land.

"Write that down," he ordered a priest. "And the wind vanes at the mastheads?" he asked me, looking at the nearer one that was painted with an eagle. "Are they designed to frighten the spirits?"

I did not answer. Instead I was staring at the seven ships across the slick hump of the mudbank and I recognized one. **Wind-Viper.** The light-colored strake in the bow was clear enough, but even so I would have recognized her. **Wind-Viper,** lovely **Wind-Viper,** ship of dreams, here at Heilincigae.

"Uhtred?" Alfred prompted me.

"They're just wind vanes, lord," I said. And if **Wind-Viper** was here, was Ragnar here too? Or had Kjartan taken the ship and leased it to a shipmaster?

"It seems a deal of trouble," Alfred said pettishly, "to decorate a ship."

"Men love their ships," I said, "and fight for them. You honor what you fight for, lord. We should decorate our ships." I spoke harshly, thinking we would love our ships more if they had beasts on their prows and had proper names like **Blood-Spiller, Sea-Wolf,** or **Widow-Maker.** Instead the **Heahengel** led the **Ceruphin** and **Cristenlic** through the tangled waters, and behind us were the **Apostol** and the **Eftwyrd,** which meant Judgment Day and was probably the best named of our fleet because she sent more than one Dane to the sea's embrace.

The Danes were digging, trying to deepen the

treacherous channel and so float their ships, but as we came nearer they realized they would never complete such a huge task and went back to their stranded boats to fetch armor, helmets, shields, and weapons. I pulled on my coat of mail, its leather lining stinking of old sweat, and I pulled on the helmet, then strapped Serpent-Breath on my back and Wasp-Sting to my waist. This was not going to be a sea fight, but a land battle, shield wall against shield wall, a maul in the mud, and the Danes had the advantage because they could mass where we must land and they could meet us as we came off the ships, and I did not like it. I could see Leofric hated it, but Alfred was calm enough as he pulled on his helmet. "God is with us," he said.

"He needs to be," Leofric muttered, then raised his voice to shout at the steersman. "Hold her there!" It was tricky to keep **Heahengel** still in the swirling current, but we backed oars and she slewed around as Leofric peered at the shore. I assumed he was waiting for the other ships to catch up so that we could all land together, but he had seen a spit of muddy sand projecting from the shore and had worked out that if we beached **Heahengel** there then our first men off the prow would not have to face a shield wall composed of seven Viking crews. The spit was narrow, only wide enough for three or four men to stand abreast, and a fight there would be between equal numbers. "It's a good enough place to die, earsling," he told me, and led me forward. Alfred hurried behind us. "Wait," Leofric snapped at the king so savagely that Alfred actually obeyed. "Put her on the spit!" Leofric yelled back to the steersman, "Now!"

Ragnar was there. I could see the eagle wing on its pole, and then I saw him, looking so like his father that for a moment I thought I was a boy again.

"Ready, earsling?" Leofric said. He had assembled his half dozen best warriors, all of us in the prow, while behind us the bowmen readied to launch their arrows at the Danes who were hurrying toward the narrow stretch of muddy sand. Then we lurched forward as **Heahengel**'s bow scraped aground. "Now!" Leofric shouted, and we jumped overboard into water that came up to our knees, and then we instinctively touched shields, made the wall, and I was gripping Wasp-Sting as the first Danes ran at us.

"Kill them!" Leofric shouted, and I thrust the shield forward and there was the great clash of iron boss on limewood, and an ax whirled overhead, but a man behind me caught it on his shield and I was stabbing under my shield, bringing the short sword up, but she rammed into a Danish shield. I wrenched her free, stabbed again, and felt a pain in my ankle as a blade sliced through water and boot. Blood swirled in the sea, but I was still standing, and I heaved forward, smelling the Danes, gulls screaming overhead, and more of the Danes were coming, but more of our men were joining us, some up to their waists in the tide, and the front of the battle was a shoving match now because no one had room to swing a weapon. It was a grunting, cursing shield battle, and Leofric, beside me, gave a shout and we heaved up and they stepped back a half pace and our arrows slashed over our helmets and I slammed Wasp-Sting forward, felt her break through leather or mail, twisted her in flesh, pulled her back, pushed with the shield, kept my head down under the rim, pushed again, stabbed again, brute force, stout shield, and good steel, nothing else. A man was drowning, blood streaming in the ripples from his twitching body, and I suppose we were shouting, but I never remember much about that. You remember the pushing, the smell, the snarling bearded faces, the anger, and then **Cristenlic** rammed her bows into the flank of the Danish line, crumpling men into the water, drowning and crushing them, and her crew jumped into the small waves with spears, swords, and axes. A third boat arrived, more men landed, and I heard Alfred behind me, shouting at us to break their line, to kill them. I was ramming Wasp-Sting down at a man's ankles, jabbing again and again, pushing with the shield, and then he stumbled and our line surged forward and he tried to stab up into my groin, but Leofric slammed his ax head down, turning the man's face into a mask of blood and broken teeth. "Push!" Leofric yelled, and we heaved at the enemy, and suddenly they were breaking away and running.

We had not beaten them. They were not running from our swords and spears, but rather because the rising tide was floating their ships and they ran to rescue them, and we stumbled after them, or rather I stumbled because my right ankle was bleeding and hurting, and we still did not have enough men ashore to overwhelm their crews and they were hurling themselves on board their ships, but one crew, brave men all, stayed on the sand to hold us back.

"Are you wounded, earsling?" Leofric asked me.

"It's nothing."

"Stay back," he ordered me. He was forming **Heahengel**'s men into a new shield wall, a wall to thump into that one brave crew, and Alfred was there now, mail armor shining bright, and the Danes must have known he was a great lord, but they did not abandon their ships for the honor of killing him. I think that if Alfred had brought the dragon banner and fought beneath it, so that the Danes could recognize him as the king, they would have stayed and fought us and might very well have killed or captured Alfred, but the Danes were always wary of taking too many casualties and they hated losing their beloved ships, and so they just wanted to be away from that place. To which end they were willing to pay the price of the one ship to save the others, and that one ship was not **Wind-Viper.** I could see her being pushed into the channel, could see her creeping away backward, see her oars striking against sand rather than water, and I splashed through the small waves, skirting our shield wall and leaving the fight to my right as I bellowed at the ship. "Ragnar! Ragnar!"

Arrows were flicking past me. One struck my shield and another glanced off my helmet with a

click. That reminded me that he would not recognize me with the helmet on and so I dropped
Wasp-Sting and bared my head. "Ragnar!"

The arrows stopped. The shield walls were
crashing, men were dying, most of the Danes
were escaping, and Earl Ragnar stared at me
across the widening gap and I could not tell from
his face what he was thinking, but he had
stopped his handful of bowmen from shooting at
me, and then he cupped his hands to his mouth.
"Here!" he shouted at me. "Tomorrow's dusk!"
Then his oars bit water, the **Wind-Viper** turned
like a dancer, the blades dragged the sea, and she
was gone.

I retrieved Wasp-Sting and went to join the
fight, but it was over. Our crews had massacred
that one Danish crew, all except a handful of men
who had been spared on Alfred's orders. The rest
were a bloody pile on the tide line and we
stripped them of their armor and weapons, took
off their clothes, and left their white bodies to the
gulls. Their ship, an old and leaking vessel, was
towed back to Hamtun.

Alfred was pleased. In truth he had let six
ships escape, but it had still been a victory and
news of it would encourage his troops fighting in

the north. One of his priests questioned the prisoners, noting their answers on parchment. Alfred asked some questions of his own, which the priest translated, and when he had learned all that he could he came back to where I was steering and looked at the blood staining the deck by my right foot. "You fight well, Uhtred."

"We fought badly, lord," I said, and that was true. Their shield wall had held, and if they had not retreated to rescue their ships they might even have beaten us back into the sea. I had not done well. There are days when the sword and shield seem clumsy, when the enemy seems quicker, and this had been one such day. I was angry with myself.

"You were talking to one of them," Alfred said accusingly. "I saw you. You were talking to one of the pagans."

"I was telling him, lord," I said, "that his mother was a whore, his father a turd of hell, and that his children are pieces of weasel shit."

He flinched at that. He was no coward, Alfred, and he knew the anger of battle, but he never liked the insults that men shouted. I think he would have liked war to be decorous. He looked behind **Heahengel** where the dying sun's light was rippling our long wake red. "The year you promised to give me will soon be finished," he said.

"True, lord."

"I pray you will stay with us."

"When Guthrum comes, lord," I said, "he will come with a fleet to darken the sea and our twelve ships will be crushed." I thought perhaps that was what Leofric had been arguing about, about the futility of trying to stem a seaborne invasion with twelve ill-named ships. "If I stay," I asked, "what use will I be if the fleet dares not put to sea?"

"What you say is true," Alfred said, suggesting that his argument with Leofric had been about something else, "but the crews can fight ashore. Leofric tells me you are as good a warrior as any he has seen."

"Then he has never seen himself, lord."

"Come to me when your time is up," he said, "and I will find a place for you."

"Yes, lord," I said, but in a tone that only acknowledged that I understood what he wanted, not that I would obey him.

"But you should know one thing, Uhtred." His voice was stern. "If any man commands my troops, that man must know how to read and write."

I almost laughed at that. "So he can read the Psalms, lord?" I asked sarcastically.

"So he can read my orders," Alfred said coldly, "and send me news."

"Yes, lord," I said again.

They had lit beacons in Hamtun's waters so we could find our way home, and the night wind stirred the liquid reflections of moon and stars as we slid to our anchorage. There were lights ashore, and fires, and ale, and food and laughter, and best of all the promise of meeting Ragnar the next day.

Ragnar took a huge risk, of course, in going back to Heilincigae, though perhaps he reckoned, truthfully as it turned out, that our ships would need a day to recover from the fight. There were injured men to tend, weapons to sharpen, and so none of our fleet put to sea that day.

Brida and I rode horses to Hamanfunta, a village that lived off trapping eels, fishing, and making salt, and a sliver of a coin found stabling for our horses and a fisherman willing to take us out to Heilincigae where no one now lived, for the

Danes had slaughtered them all. The fisherman would not wait for us, too frightened of the coming night and the ghosts that would be moaning and screeching on the island, but he promised to return in the morning.

Brida, Nihtgenga, and I wandered that low place, going past the previous day's Danish dead who had already been pecked ragged by the gulls, past burned-out huts where folk had made a poor living from the sea and the marsh before the Vikings came and then, as the sun sank, we carried charred timbers to the shore and I used flint and steel to make a fire. The flames flared up in the dusk and Brida touched my arm to show me **Wind-Viper,** dark against the darkening sky, coming through the sea lake's entrance. The last of the daylight touched the sea red and caught the gilding on **Wind-Viper**'s beast head.

I watched her, thinking of all the fear that such a sight brought on England. Wherever there was a creek, a harbor, or a river mouth, men feared to see the Danish ships. They feared those beasts at the prow, feared the men behind the beasts, and prayed to be spared the Northmen's fury. I loved the sight. Loved **Wind-Viper.** Her oars rose and fell, I could hear the shafts creaking in their leather-lined holes, and I could see mailed men at her prow, and then the bows scrunched on the sand and the long oars went still.

Ragnar put the ladder against the prow. All Danish ships have a short ladder to let them climb down to a beach, and he came down the rungs slowly and alone. He was in full mail coat, helmeted, with a sword at his side, and once ashore he paced to the small flames of our fire like a warrior come for vengeance. He stopped a spear's length away and then stared at me through the black eyeholes of his helmet. "Did you kill my father?" he asked harshly.

"On my life," I said, "on Thor," I pulled out the hammer amulet and clutched it, "on my soul," I went on, "I did not."

He pulled off his helmet, stepped forward, and we embraced. "I knew you did not," he said.

"Kjartan did it," I said, "and we watched him." We told him the whole story, how we had been in the high woods watching the charcoal cool, and how we had been cut off from the hall, and how it had been fired, and how the folk had been slaughtered.

"If I could have killed one of them," I said, "I would, and I would have died doing it, but Ravn always said there should be at least one survivor to tell the tale."

"What did Kjartan say?" Brida asked.

Ragnar was sitting now, and two of his men had brought bread and dried herrings and cheese and ale. "Kjartan said," Ragnar spoke softly, "that the English rose against the hall, encouraged by Uhtred, and that he revenged himself on the killers."

"And you believed him?" I asked.

"No," he admitted. "Too many men said he did it, but he is Earl Kjartan now. He leads three times more men than I do."

"And Thyra?" I asked. "What does she say?"

"Thyra?" He stared at me, puzzled.

"Thyra lived," I told him. "She was taken away by Sven."

He just stared at me. He had not known that his sister lived and I saw the anger come on his face, and then he raised his eyes to the stars and he howled like a wolf.

"It is true," Brida said softly. "Your sister lived."

Ragnar drew his sword and laid it on the sand and touched the blade with his right hand. "If it is the last thing I do," he swore, "I shall kill Kjartan, kill his son, and all his followers. All of them!"

"I would help," I said. He looked at me

through the flames. "I loved your father," I said, "and he treated me like a son."

"I will welcome your help, Uhtred," Ragnar said formally. He wiped the sand from the blade and slid it back into its fleece-lined scabbard. "You will sail with us now?"

I was tempted. I was even surprised at how strongly I was tempted. I wanted to go with Ragnar, I wanted the life I had lived with his father. But fate rules us. I was sworn to Alfred for a few more weeks, and I had fought alongside Leofric for all these months, and fighting next to a man in the shield wall makes a bond as tight as love. "I cannot come," I said, and wished I could have said the opposite.

"I can," Brida said, and somehow I was not surprised by that. She had not liked being left ashore in Hamtun as we sailed to fight. She felt trammeled and useless, unwanted, and I think she yearned after the Danish ways. She hated Wessex. She hated its priests, hated their disapproval, and hated their denial of all that was joy.

"You are a witness of my father's death," Ragnar said to her, still formal.

"I am."

"Then I would welcome you," he said, and looked at me again.

I shook my head. "I am sworn to Alfred for the moment. By winter I shall be free of the oath."

"Then come to us in the winter," Ragnar said, "and we shall go to Dunholm."

"Dunholm?"

"It is Kjartan's fortress now. Ricsig lets him live there."

I thought of Dunholm's stronghold on its soaring crag, wrapped by its river, protected by its sheer rock and its high walls and strong garrison. "What if Kjartan marches on Wessex?" I asked.

Ragnar shook his head. "He will not, because he does not go where I go, so I must go to him."

"He fears you then?"

Ragnar smiled, and if Kjartan had seen that smile he would have shivered. "He fears me," Ragnar said. "I hear he sent men to kill me in Ireland, but their boat was driven ashore and the skraelings killed the crew. So he lives in fear. He denies my father's death, but he still fears me."

"There is one last thing," I said, and nodded at Brida who brought out the leather bag with its gold, jet, and silver. "It was your father's," I said, "and Kjartan never found it, and we did, and we have spent some of it, but what remains is yours."

I pushed the bag toward him and made myself instantly poor.

Ragnar pushed it back without a thought, making me rich again. "My father loved you, too," he said, "and I am wealthy enough."

We ate, we drank, we slept, and in the dawn, when a light mist shimmered over the reed beds, the **Wind-Viper** went. The last thing Ragnar said to me was a question. "Thyra lives?"

"She survived," I said, "so I think she must still live."

We embraced, he went, and I was alone.

I wept for Brida. I felt hurt. I was too young to know how to take abandonment. During the night I had tried to persuade her to stay, but she had a will as strong as Ealdwulf's iron, and she had gone with Ragnar into the dawn mist and left me weeping. I hated the three spinners at that moment, for they wove cruel jests into their vulnerable threads, and then the fisherman came to fetch me and I went back home.

Autumn gales tore at the coast and Alfred's fleet was laid up for the winter, dragged ashore by horses and oxen, and Leofric and I rode to Wintanceaster, only to discover that Alfred was at his estate at Cippanhamm. We were permitted into the Wintanceaster palace by the doorkeeper, who either recognized me or was terrified of Leofric, and we slept there, but the place was still haunted by monks, despite Alfred's absence, and so we spent the day in a nearby tavern. "So what will you do, earsling?" Leofric asked me. "Renew your oath to Alfred?"

"Don't know."

"Don't know," he repeated sarcastically. "Lost your decision with your girl?"

"I could go back to the Danes," I said.

"That would give me a chance to kill you," he said happily.

"Or stay with Alfred."

"Why not do that?"

"Because I don't like him," I said.

"You don't have to like him. He's your king."

"He's not my king," I said. "I'm a Northumbrian."

"So you are, earsling, a Northumbrian ealdorman, eh?"

I nodded, demanded more ale, tore a piece of bread in two, and pushed one piece toward Leofric. "What I should do," I said, "is go back to Northumbria. There is a man I have to kill."

"A feud?"

I nodded again.

"There is one thing I know about blood feuds," Leofric said, "which is that they last a lifetime. You will have years to make your killing, but only if you live."

"I'll live," I said lightly.

"Not if the Danes take Wessex, you won't. Or maybe you will live, earsling, but you'll live under their rule, under their law, and under their swords. If you want to be a free man, then stay here and fight for Wessex."

"For Alfred?"

Leofric leaned back, stretched, belched, and took a long drink. "I don't like him either," he admitted, "and I didn't like his brothers when they were kings here, and I didn't like his father when he was king, but Alfred's different."

"Different?"

He tapped his scarred forehead. "The bastard thinks, earsling, which is more than you or I ever do. He knows what has to be done, and don't underestimate him. He can be ruthless."

"He's a king," I said. "He should be ruthless."

"Ruthless, generous, pious, boring, that's Alfred," Leofric spoke gloomily. "When he was a child his father gave him toy warriors. You know, carved out of wood? Just little things. He used to line them up and there wasn't one out of place, not one, and not even a speck of dust on any of them!" He seemed to find that appalling, for he scowled. "Then when he was fifteen or so he went wild for a time. Humped every slave girl in the palace, and I've no doubt he lined them up, too, and made sure they didn't have any dust before he rammed them."

"He had a bastard, too, I hear," I said.

"Osferth," Leofric said, surprising me with his knowledge, "hidden away in Winburnan. Poor little bastard must be six, seven years old now? You're not supposed to know he exists."

"Nor are you."

"It was my sister he whelped him on," Leofric said, then saw my surprise. "I'm not the only good-looking one in my family, earsling." He poured more ale. "Eadgyth was a palace servant and Alfred claimed to love her." He sneered, then shrugged. "But he looks after her now. Gives her money, sends priests to preach to her. His wife knows all about the poor little bastard, but won't let Alfred go near him."

"I hate Ælswith," I said.

"A bitch from hell," he agreed happily.

"And I like the Danes," I said.

"You do? So why do you kill them?"

"I like them," I said, ignoring his question, "because they're not frightened of life."

"They're not Christians, you mean."

"They're not Christians," I agreed. "Are you?"

Leofric thought for a few heartbeats. "I suppose so," he said grudgingly, "but you're not, are you?" I shook my head, showed him Thor's hammer, and he laughed. "So what will you do, earsling," he asked me, "if you go back to the pagans? Other than follow your blood feud?"

That was a good question and I thought about it as much as the ale allowed me. "I'd serve a man called Ragnar," I said, "as I served his father."

"So why did you leave his father?"

"Because he was killed."

Leofric frowned. "So you can stay there so long as your Danish lord lives, is that right? And without a lord you're nothing?"

"I'm nothing," I admitted. "But I want to be in Northumbria to take back my father's fortress."

"Ragnar will do that for you?"

"He might do it. His father would have done it, I think."

"And if you get back your fortress," he asked, "will you be lord of it? Lord of your own land? Or will the Danes rule you?"

"The Danes will rule."

"So you settle to be a slave, eh? Yes, lord, no, lord, let me hold your prick while you piss all over me, lord?"

"And what happens if I stay here?" I asked sourly.

"You'll lead men," he said.

I laughed at that. "Alfred has lords enough to serve him."

Leofric shook his head. "He doesn't. He has some good warlords, true, but he needs more. I told him, that day on the boat when he let the bastards escape, I told him to send me ashore and give me men. He refused." He beat the table with a massive fist. "I told him I'm a proper warrior, but still the bastard refused me!"

So that, I thought, was what the argument had been about. "Why did he refuse you?" I asked.

"Because I can't read," Leofric snarled, "and I'm not learning now! I tried once, and it makes no damn sense to me. And I'm not a lord, am I? Not even a thegn. I'm just a slave's son who happens to know how to kill the king's enemies, but that's not good enough for Alfred. He says I can assist"—he said that word as if it soured his tongue—"one of his ealdormen, but I can't lead

men because I can't read, and I can't learn
to read."

"I can," I said, or the drink said.

"You take a long time to understand things,
earsling," Leofric said with a grin. "You're a
damned lord, and you can read, can't you?"

"No, not really. A bit. Short words."

"But you can learn?"

I thought about it. "I can learn."

"And we have twelve ships' crews," he said,
"looking for employment, so we give them to Alfred and we say that Lord Earsling is their leader
and he gives you a book and you read out the
pretty words, then you and I take the bastards to
war and do some proper damage to your beloved
Danes."

I did not say yes, nor did I say no, because I
was not sure what I wanted. What worried me
was that I found myself agreeing with whatever
the last person suggested I did; when I had been
with Ragnar I had wanted to follow him, and
now I was seduced by Leofric's vision of the future. I had no certainty, so instead of saying yes
or no I went back to the palace and I found
Merewenna, and discovered she was indeed the
maid who had caused Alfred's tears on the night

that I had eavesdropped on him in the Mercian camp outside Snotengaham, and I did know what I wanted to do with her, and I did not cry afterward.

And next day, at Leofric's urging, we rode to Cippanhamm.

NINE

I suppose, if you are reading this, that you have learned your letters, which probably means that some damned monk or priest rapped your knuckles, cuffed you around the head, or worse. Not that they did that to me, of course, for I was no longer a child, but I endured their sniggers as I struggled with letters. It was mostly Beocca who taught me, complaining all the while that I was taking him from his real work, which was the making of a life of Swithun, who had been Bishop of Winchester when Alfred was a child, and Beocca was writing the bishop's life. Another priest was translating the book into Latin, Beocca's mastery of that tongue not being good enough for the task, and the pages were being sent to Rome in hopes that Swithun would be named a saint. Alfred took a great interest in the book, forever coming to Beocca's room and asking whether he knew that Swithun had once preached the gospel to a trout or chanted a psalm to a seagull, and Beocca would write the stories in a state of great excitement, and then, when Alfred was gone, reluctantly return to whatever text he was forcing me to decipher. "Read it aloud," he would say, then protest wildly. "No, no, no! Forliðan is to suffer shipwreck! This is a life of Saint Paul, Uhtred, and the apostle suffered shipwreck! Not the word you read at all!"

I looked at it again. "It's not forlegnis?"

"Of course it's not!" he said, going red with indignation. "That word means . . ." He paused, realizing that he was not teaching me English, but how to read it.

"Prostitute," I said, "I know what it means. I even know what they charge. There's a redhead in Chad's tavern who . . ."

"Forliðan," he interrupted me, "the word is forliðan. Read on."

Those weeks were strange. I was a warrior now, a man, yet in Beocca's room it seemed I was a child again as I struggled with the black letters crawling across the cracked parchments. I learned from the lives of the saints, and in the end Beocca could not resist letting me read some of his own growing life of Swithun. He waited for my praise, but instead I shuddered. "Couldn't we find something more interesting?" I asked him.

"More interesting?" Beocca's good eye stared at me reproachfully.

"Something about war," I suggested, "about the Danes. About shields and spears and swords."

He grimaced. "I dread to think of such writings! There are some poems." He grimaced again and evidently decided against telling me about the belligerent poems. "But this," he tapped the parchment, "this will give you inspiration."

"Inspiration! How Swithun mended some broken eggs?"

"It was a saintly act," Beocca chided me. "The woman was old and poor, the eggs were all she had to sell, and she tripped and broke them. She faced starvation! The saint made the eggs whole again and, God be praised, she sold them."

"But why didn't Swithun just give her money," I demanded, "or take her back to his house and give her a proper meal?"

"It is a miracle," Beocca insisted, "a demonstration of God's power!"

"I'd like to see a miracle," I said, remembering King Edmund's death.

"That is a weakness in you," Beocca said

sternly. "You must have faith. Miracles make belief easy, which is why you should never pray for one. Much better to find God through faith than through miracles."

"Then why have miracles?"

"Oh, read on, Uhtred," the poor man said tiredly, "for God's sake, read on."

I read on. But life in Cippanhamm was not all reading. Alfred hunted at least twice a week, though it was not hunting as I had known it in the north. He never pursued boar, preferring to shoot at stags with a bow. The prey was driven to him by beaters, and if a stag did not appear swiftly he would get bored and go back to his books. In truth I think he only went hunting because it was expected of a king, not because he enjoyed it, but he did endure it. I loved it, of course. I killed wolves, stags, foxes, and boars, and it was on one of those boar hunts that I met Æthelwold.

Æthelwold was Alfred's oldest nephew, the boy who should have succeeded his father, King Æthelred, though he was no longer a boy for he was only a month or so younger than me, and in many ways he was like me, except that he had been sheltered by his father and by Alfred and so had never killed a man or even fought in a battle.

He was tall, well built, strong, and as wild as an unbroken colt. He had long dark hair, his family's narrow face, and strong eyes that caught the attention of serving girls. All girls, really. He hunted with me and with Leofric, drank with us, whored with us when he could escape the priests who were his guardians, and constantly complained about his uncle, though those complaints were only spoken to me, never to Leofric whom Æthelwold feared. "He stole the crown," Æthelwold said of Alfred.

"The witan thought you were too young," I pointed out.

"I'm not young now, am I?" he asked indignantly. "So Alfred should step aside."

I toasted that idea with a pot of ale, but said nothing.

"They won't even let me fight!" Æthelwold said bitterly. "He says I ought to become a priest. The stupid bastard." He drank some ale before giving me a serious look. "Talk to him, Uhtred."

"What am I to say? That you don't want to be a priest?"

"He knows that. No, tell him I'll fight with you and Leofric."

I thought about that for a short while, then shook my head. "It won't do any good."

"Why not?"

"Because," I said, "he fears you making a name for yourself."

Æthelwold frowned at me. "A name?" he asked, puzzled.

"If you become a famous warrior," I said, knowing I was right, "men will follow you. You're already a prince, which is dangerous enough, but Alfred won't want you to become a famous warrior prince, will he?"

"The pious bastard," Æthelwold said. He pushed his long black hair off his face and gazed moodily at Eanflæd, the redhead who was given a room in the tavern and brought it a deal of business. "God, she's pretty," he said. "He was caught humping a nun once."

"Alfred was? A nun?"

"That's what I was told. And he was always after girls. Couldn't keep his breeches buttoned! Now the priests have got hold of him. What I ought to do," he went on gloomily, "is slit the bastard's gizzard."

"Say that to anyone but me," I said, "and you'll be hanged."

"I could run off and join the Danes," he suggested.

"You could," I said, "and they'd welcome you."

"Then use me?" he asked, showing that he was not entirely a fool.

I nodded. "You'll be like Egbert or Burghred, or that new man in Mercia."

"Ceolwulf."

"King at their pleasure," I said. Ceolwulf, a Mercian ealdorman, had been named king of his country now that Burghred was on his knees in Rome, but Ceolwulf was no more a real king than Burghred had been. He issued coins, of course, and he administered justice, but everyone knew there were Danes in his council chamber and he dared do nothing that would earn their wrath. "So is that what you want?" I asked. "To run off to the Danes and be useful to them?"

He shook his head. "No." He traced a pattern on the table with spilled ale. "Better to do nothing," he suggested.

"Nothing?"

"If I do nothing," he said earnestly, "then the bastard might die. He's always ill! He can't live long, can he? And his son is just a baby. So if he dies I'll be king! Oh, sweet Jesus!" This blasphemy was uttered because two priests had entered the tavern, both of them in Æthelwold's entourage, though they were more like jailers than courtiers and they had come to find him and take him off to his bed.

Beocca did not approve of my friendship with Æthelwold. "He's a foolish creature," he warned me.

"So am I, or so you tell me."

"Then you don't need your foolishness encouraged, do you? Now let us read about how the holy Swithun built the town's East Gate."

By the Feast of the Epiphany I could read as well as a clever twelve-year-old, or so Beocca said, and that was good enough for Alfred who did not, after all, require me to read theological texts, but only to decipher his orders, should he ever decide to give me any, and that, of course, was the heart of the matter. Leofric and I wanted to command troops, to which end I had endured Beocca's teaching and had come to appreciate the holy Swithun's skill with trout, sea-gulls, and broken eggs, but the granting of those troops depended on the king, and in truth there were not many troops to command.

The West Saxon army was in two parts. The first and smaller part was composed of the king's own men, his retainers who guarded him and his family. They did nothing else because they were professional warriors, but they were not many and neither Leofric nor I wanted anything to do with them because joining the household guard would mean staying in close proximity to Alfred, which, in turn, would mean going to church.

The second part of the army, and by far the largest, was the fyrd, and that, in turn, was divided among the shires. Each shire, under its ealdorman and reeve, was responsible for raising the fyrd that was supposedly composed of every able-bodied man within the shire boundary. That could raise a vast number of men. Hamptonscir, for example, could easily put three thousand men under arms, and there were nine shires in Wessex capable of summoning similar numbers. Yet, apart from the troops who served the ealdormen, the fyrd was mostly composed of farmers. Some had a shield of sorts, spears and axes were plentiful enough, but swords and armor were in short supply, and worse, the fyrd was always reluctant to march beyond its shire borders, and even more reluctant to serve when there was work to be done on the farm. At Æsc's Hill, the one battle the West Saxons had won against the Danes, it had been the household troops who had gained the victory. Divided between Alfred and his brother, they had spearheaded the fighting while the fyrd, as it usually did, looked menacing, but only became engaged when the real soldiers had already won the fight. The fyrd, in brief, was about as much use as a hole in a boat's bottom, but that was where Leofric could expect to find men.

Except there were those ships' crews getting drunk in Hamtun's winter taverns and those were the men Leofric wanted, and to get them he had to persuade Alfred to relieve Hacca of their command, and luckily for us Hacca himself came to Cippanhamm and pleaded to be released from the fleet. He prayed daily, he told Alfred, never to see the ocean again. "I get seasick, lord."

Alfred was always sympathetic to men who suffered sickness because he was so often ill himself, and he must have known that Hacca was an inadequate commander of ships, but Alfred's problem was how to replace him. To which end he summoned four bishops, two abbots, and a priest to advise him, and I learned from Beocca that they were all praying about the new appointment. "Do something!" Leofric snarled at me.

"What the devil am I supposed to do?"

"You have friends who are priests! Talk to

them. Talk to Alfred, earsling." He rarely called me that anymore, only when he was angry.

"He doesn't like me," I said. "If I ask him to put us in charge of the fleet, he'll give it to anyone but us. He'll give it to a bishop, probably."

"Hell!" Leofric said.

In the end it was Eanflæd who saved us. The redhead was a merry soul and had a particular fondness for Leofric, and she heard us arguing and sat down, slapped her hands on the table to silence us, and then asked what we were fighting about. Then she sneezed because she had a cold.

"I want this useless earsling," Leofric jerked his thumb at me, "to be named commander of the fleet, only he's too young, too ugly, too horrible, and too pagan, and Alfred's listening to a pack of bishops who'll end up naming some wizened old fart who doesn't know his prow from his prick."

"Which bishops?" Eanflæd wanted to know.

"Scireburnan, Wintanceaster, Winburnan, and Exanceaster," I said.

She smiled, sneezed again, and two days later I was summoned to Alfred's presence. It turned out that the Bishop of Exanceaster was partial to redheads.

Alfred greeted me in his hall, a fine building with beams, rafters, and a central stone hearth. His guards watched us from the doorway where a group of petitioners waited to see the king, and a huddle of priests prayed at the hall's other end, but the two of us were alone by the hearth where Alfred paced up and down as he talked. He said he was thinking of appointing me to command the fleet. Just thinking, he stressed. God, he went on, was guiding his choice, but now he must talk with me to see whether God's advice chimed with his own intuition. He put great store by intuition. He once lectured me about a man's inner eye and how it could lead us to a higher wisdom, and I dare say he was right, but appointing a fleet commander did not need mystical wisdom, it needed finding a raw fighter willing to kill some Danes. "Tell me," he went on, "has learning to read bolstered your faith?"

"Yes, lord," I said with feigned eagerness.

"It has?" He sounded dubious.

"The life of Saint Swithun," I said, waving a hand as if to suggest it had overwhelmed me, "and the stories of Chad!" I fell silent as if I could not think of praise sufficient for that tedious man.

"The blessed Chad!" Alfred said happily. "You

know men and cattle were cured by the dust of his corpse?"

"A miracle, lord," I said.

"It is good to hear you say as much, Uhtred," Alfred said, "and I rejoice in your faith."

"It gives me great happiness, lord," I replied with a straight face.

"Because it is only with faith in God that we shall prevail against the Danes."

"Indeed, lord," I said with as much enthusiasm as I could muster, wondering why he did not just name me commander of the fleet and be done with it.

But he was in a discursive mood. "I remember when I first met you," he said, "and I was struck by your childlike faith. It was an inspiration to me, Uhtred."

"I am glad of it, lord."

"And then"—he turned and frowned at me— "I detected a lessening of faith in you."

"God tries us, lord," I said.

"He does! He does!" He winced suddenly. He was always a sick man. He had collapsed in pain at his wedding, though that might have been the horror of realizing what he was marrying, but in truth he was prone to bouts of sudden griping agony. That, he had told me, was better than his first illness, which had been an affliction of ficus, which is a real endwerc, so painful and bloody that at times he had been unable to sit, and sometimes that ficus came back, but most of the time he suffered from the pains in his belly. "God does try us," he went on, "and I think God was testing you. I would like to think you have survived the trial."

"I believe I have, lord," I said gravely, wishing he would just end this ridiculous conversation.

"But I still hesitate to name you," he admitted. "You are young! It is true you have proved your diligence by learning to read and that you are nobly born, but you are more likely to be found in a tavern than in a church. Is that not true?"

That silenced me, at least for a heartbeat or two, but then I remembered something Beocca had said to me during his interminable lessons and, without thinking, without even really knowing what they meant, I said the words aloud. "The son of man is come eating and drinking," I said, "and . . ."

" 'You say, look, a greedy man and a drinker!' " Alfred finished the words for me. "You are right, Uhtred, right to chide me. Glory to God! Christ was accused of spending his time in taverns, and I forgot it. It is in the Scriptures!"

The gods help me, I thought. The man was drunk on God, but he was no fool, for now he turned on me like a snake. "And I hear you spend time with my nephew. They say you distract him from his lessons."

I put my hand on my heart. "I will swear an oath, lord," I said, "that I have done nothing except dissuade him from rashness." And that was true, or true enough. I had never encouraged Æthelwold in his wilder flights of fancy that involved cutting Alfred's throat or running away to join the Danes. I did encourage him to ale, whores, and blasphemy, but I did not count those things as rash. "My oath on it, lord," I said.

The word **oath** was powerful. All our laws depend on oaths. Life, loyalty, and allegiance depend on oaths, and my use of the word persuaded him. "I thank you," he said earnestly, "and I should tell you, Uhtred, that to my surprise the Bishop of Exanceaster had a dream in which a messenger of God appeared to him and said that you should be made commander of the fleet."

"A messenger of God?" I asked.

"An angel, Uhtred."

"Praise God," I said gravely, thinking how Eanflæd would enjoy discovering that she was now an angel.

"Yet," Alfred said, and winced again as pain flared in his arse or belly. "Yet," he said again, and I knew something unexpected was coming. "I worry," he went on, "that you are of Northumbria, and that your commitment to Wessex is not of the heart."

"I am here, lord," I said.

"But for how long?"

"Till the Danes are gone, lord."

He ignored that. "I need men bound to me by God," he said, "by God, by love, by duty, by passion, and by land." He paused, looking at me, and I knew the sting was in that last word.

"I have land in Northumbria," I said, thinking of Bebbanburg.

"West Saxon land," he said, "land that you will own, land that you will defend, land that you will fight for."

"A blessed thought," I said, my heart sinking at what I suspected was coming.

Only it did not come immediately. Instead he abruptly changed the subject and talked, very sensibly, about the Danish threat. The fleet, he said, had succeeded in reducing the Viking raids, but he expected the new year to bring a Danish fleet, and one much too large for our twelve ships to oppose. "I dare not lose the fleet," he said, "so I doubt we should fight their ships. I'm expecting a land army of pagans to come down the Temes and for their fleet to assault our south coast. I can hold one, but not the other, so the fleet commander's job will be to follow their ships and harry them. Distract them. Keep them looking one way while I destroy their land army."

I said I thought that was a good idea, which it probably was, though I wondered how twelve ships were supposed to distract a whole fleet, but that was a problem that would have to wait until the enemy fleet arrived. Alfred then returned to the matter of the land and that, of course, was the deciding factor that would give me or deny me the fleet. "I would tie you to me, Uhtred," he said earnestly.

"I shall give you an oath, lord," I said.

"You will indeed," he responded tartly, "but I still want you to be of Wessex."

"A high honor, lord," I said. What else could I say?

"You must belong to Wessex," he said, then smiled as though he did me a favor. "There is an orphan in Defnascir," he went on, and here it came, "a girl, who I would see married."

I said nothing. What is the point of protesting when the executioner's sword is in midswing?

"Her name is Mildrith," he went on, "and she is dear to me. A pious girl, modest, and faithful. Her father was reeve to Ealdorman Odda, and she will bring land to her husband, good land, and I would have a good man hold that good land."

I offered a smile that I hoped was not too sickly. "He would be a fortunate man, lord," I said, "to marry a girl who is dear to you."

"So go to her," he commanded me, "and marry her"—the sword struck—"and then I shall name you commander of the fleet."

"Yes, lord," I said.

Leofric, of course, laughed like a demented jackdaw. "He's no fool, is he?" he said when he had recovered. "He's making you into a West Saxon. So what do you know about this miltewærc?" Miltewærc was a pain in the spleen.

"Mildrith," I said, "and she's pious."

"Of course she's pious. He wouldn't want you to marry her if she was a leg-spreader."

"She's an orphan," I said, "and aged about sixteen or seventeen."

"Christ! That old? She must be an ugly sow! But poor thing, she must be wearing out her knees praying to be spared a rutting from an earsling like you. But that's her fate! So let's get you married. Then we can kill some Danes."

It was winter. We had spent the Christmas feast at Cippanhamm, and that was no Yule, and now we rode south through frost and rain and wind. Father Willibald accompanied us, for he was still priest to the fleet, and my plan was to reach Defnascir, do what was grimly necessary, and then ride straight to Hamtun to make certain the winter work on the twelve boats was being done properly. It is in winter that ships are caulked, scraped, cleaned, and made tight for the spring, and the thought of ships made me dream of the Danes, and of Brida, and I wondered where she was, what she did, and whether we would meet again. And I thought of Ragnar. Had he found Thyra? Did Kjartan live? Theirs was another world now, and I knew I drifted away from it and was being entangled in the threads of Alfred's tidy life. He was trying to make me into a West Saxon, and he was half succeeding. I was sworn now to fight for Wessex and it seemed I must marry into it, but I still clung to that ancient dream of retaking Bebbanburg.

I loved Bebbanburg and I almost loved Defnascir as much. When the world was made by
Thor from the carcass of Ymir he did well when
he fashioned Defnascir and its shire next door,
Thornsæta. Both were beautiful lands of soft hills
and quick streams, of rich fields and thick soil, of
high heaths and good harbors. A man could live
well in either shire, and I could have been happy
in Defnascir had I not loved Bebbanburg more.
We rode down the valley of the river Uisc,
through well-tended fields of red earth, past
plump villages and high halls until we came to
Exanceaster, which was the shire's chief town. It
had been made by the Romans who had built a
fortress on a hill above the Uisc and surrounded
it with a wall of flint, stone, and brick, and the
wall was still there and guards challenged us as
we reached the northern gate.

"We come to see Ealdorman Odda," Willibald
said.

"On whose business?"

"The king's," Willibald said proudly, flourish-
ing a letter that bore Alfred's seal, though I doubt
the guards would have recognized it, but they
seemed properly impressed and let us through
into a town of decaying Roman buildings amid

which a timber church reared tall next to Ealdorman Odda's hall.

The ealdorman made us wait, but at last he came with his son and a dozen retainers, and one of his priests read the king's letter aloud. It was Alfred's pleasure that Mildrith should be married to his loyal servant, the ealdorman Uhtred, and Odda was commanded to arrange the ceremony with as little delay as possible. Odda was not pleased at the news. He was an elderly man, at least forty years old, with gray hair and a face made grotesque by bulbous wens. His son, Odda the Younger, was even less pleased, for he scowled at the news. "It isn't seemly, Father," he complained.

"It is the king's wish."

"But . . ."

"It is the king's wish!"

Odda the Younger fell silent. He was about my age, nineteen, good-looking, black haired, and elegant in a black tunic that was as clean as a woman's dress and edged with gold thread. A golden crucifix hung at his neck. He gave me a grim look, and I must have appeared travel stained and ragged to him, and after inspecting me and finding me about as appealing as a wet mongrel, he turned on his heel and stalked from the hall.

"Tomorrow morning," Odda announced unhappily, "the bishop can marry you. But you must pay the bride-price first."

"The bride-price?" I asked. Alfred had mentioned no such thing, though of course it was customary.

"Thirty-three shillings," Odda said flatly, and with the hint of a smirk.

Thirty-three shillings was a fortune. A hoard. The price of a good war horse or a ship. It took me aback and I heard Leofric give a gasp behind me. "Is that what Alfred says?" I demanded.

"It is what I say," Odda said, "for Mildrith is my goddaughter."

No wonder he smirked. The price was huge and he doubted I could pay it, and if I could not pay it then the girl was not mine and, though Odda did not know it, the fleet would not be mine either. Nor, of course, was the price merely thirty-three shillings, or three hundred and ninety-six silver pence, it was double that, for it was also customary for a husband to give his new wife an equivalent sum after the marriage was consummated. That second gift was none of Odda's business and I doubted very much

whether I would want to pay it, just as Ealdorman Odda was now certain, from my hesitation,
that I would not be paying him the bride-price
without which there could be no marriage
contract.

"I can meet the lady?" I asked.

"You may meet her at the ceremony tomorrow
morning," Odda said firmly, "but only if you pay
the bride-price. Otherwise, no."

He looked disappointed as I opened my pouch
and gave him one gold coin and thirty-six silver
pennies. He looked even more disappointed
when he saw that was not all the coin I possessed,
but he was trapped now. "You may meet her," he
told me, "in the cathedral tomorrow."

"Why not now?" I asked.

"Because she is at her prayers," the ealdorman
said, and with that he dismissed us.

Leofric and I found a place to sleep in a tavern
close to the cathedral, which was the bishop's
church, and that night I got drunk as a spring
hare. I picked a fight with someone, I have no
idea who, and only remember that Leofric, who
was not quite as drunk as me, pulled us apart and
flattened my opponent, and after that I went into
the stable yard and threw up all the ale I had just
drunk. I drank some more, slept badly, woke to

hear rain seething on the stable roof, and then vomited again.

"Why don't we just ride to Mercia?" I suggested to Leofric. The king had lent us horses and I did not mind stealing them.

"What do we do there?"

"Find men?" I suggested. "Fight?"

"Don't be daft, earsling," Leofric said. "We want the fleet. And if you don't marry the ugly sow, I don't get to command it."

"I command it," I said.

"But only if you marry," Leofric said, "and then you'll command the fleet and I'll command you."

Father Willibald arrived then. He had slept in the monastery next door to the tavern and had come to make sure I was ready, and looked alarmed at my ragged condition. "What's that mark on your face?" he asked.

"Bastard hit me last night," I said, "I was drunk. So was he, but I was more drunk. Take my advice, father. Never get into a fight when you're badly drunk."

I drank more ale for breakfast. Willibald insisted I wear my best tunic, which was not saying much for it was stained, crumpled, and torn. I would have preferred to wear my coat of mail, but Willibald said that was inappropriate for a church, and I suppose he was right, and I let him brush me down and try to dab the worst stains out of the wool. I tied my hair with a leather lace, strapped on Serpent-Breath and Wasp-Sting, which again Willibald said I should not wear in a holy place, but I insisted on keeping the weapons, and then, a doomed man, I went to the cathedral with Willibald and Leofric.

It was raining as if the heavens were being drained of all their water. Rain bounced in the streets, flowed in streams down the gutters, and leaked through the cathedral's thatch. A brisk cold wind was coming from the east and it found every crack in the cathedral's wooden walls so that the candles on the altars flickered and some blew out. It was a small church, not much bigger than Ragnar's burned hall, and it must have been built on a Roman foundation for the floor was made of flagstones that were now being puddled by rainwater. The bishop was already there, two other priests fussed with the guttering candles on the high altar, and then Ealdorman Odda arrived with my bride.

Who took one look at me and burst into tears.

⋆   ⋆   ⋆

What was I expecting? A woman who looked like a sow, I suppose, a woman with a pox-scarred face and a sour expression and haunches like an ox. No one expects to love a wife, not if they marry for land or position, and I was marrying for land and she was marrying because she had no choice, and there really is no point in making too much of a fuss about it, because that is the way the world works. My job was to take her land, work it, make money, and Mildrith's duty was to give me sons and make sure there was food and ale on my table. Such is the holy sacrament of marriage.

I did not want to marry her. By rights, as an ealdorman of Northumbria, I could expect to marry a daughter of the nobility, a daughter who would bring much more land than twelve hilly hides in Defnascir. I might have expected to marry a daughter who could increase Bebbanburg's holdings and power, but that was plainly not going to happen, so I was marrying a girl of ignoble birth who would now be known as Lady Mildrith and she might have shown some gratitude for that, but instead she cried and even tried to pull away from Ealdorman Odda.

He probably sympathized with her, but the

bride-price had been paid, and so she was brought to the altar and the bishop, who had come back from Cippanhamm with a streaming cold, duly made us man and wife. "And may the blessing of God the Father," he said, "God the son, and God the Holy Ghost be on your union." He was about to say **amen,** but instead sneezed mightily.

"Amen," Willibald said. No one else spoke.

So Mildrith was mine.

Odda the Younger watched as we left the church and he probably thought I did not see him, but I did, and I marked him down. I knew why he was watching.

For the truth of it, which surprised me, was that Mildrith was desirable. That word does not do her justice, but it is so very hard to remember a face from long ago. Sometimes, in a dream, I see her, and she is real then, but when I am awake and try to summon her face I cannot do it. I remember she had clear, pale skin, that her lower lip jutted out too much, that her eyes were very blue and her hair the same gold as mine. She was tall, which she disliked, thinking it made her unwomanly, and had a nervous expression, as though she constantly feared disaster, and that can be very attractive in a woman and I confess I found her attractive. That did surprise me, indeed it astonished me, for such a woman should have long been married. She was almost seventeen years old, and by that age most women have already given birth to three or four children or else been killed in the attempt, but as we rode to her holdings that lay to the west of the river Uisc's mouth, I heard some of her tale. She was being drawn in a cart by two oxen that Willibald had insisted garlanding with flowers. Leofric, Willibald, and I rode alongside the cart, and Willibald asked her questions and she answered him readily enough for he was a priest and a kind man.

Her father, she said, had left her land and debts, and the debts were greater than the value of the land. Leofric sniggered when he heard the word **debts.** I said nothing, but just stared doggedly ahead.

The trouble, Mildrith said, had begun when her father had granted a tenth of his holdings as ælmesæcer, which is land devoted to the church. The church does not own it, but has the right to all that the land yields, whether in crops or cattle, and her father had made the grant, Mildrith explained, because all his children except her had died and he wanted to find favor with God. I suspected he had wanted to find favor with Alfred, for in Wessex an ambitious man was well advised to look after the church if he wanted the king to look after him.

But then the Danes had raided, cattle had been slaughtered, a harvest failed, and the church took her father to law for failing to provide the land's promised yield. Wessex, I discovered, was very devoted to the law, and all the men of law are priests, every last one of them, which means that the law is the church, and when Mildrith's father died the law had decreed that he owed the church a huge sum, quite beyond his ability to pay, and Alfred, who had the power to lift the debt, refused to do so. What this meant was that any man who married Mildrith married the debt, and no man had been willing to take that burden until a Northumbrian fool wandered into the trap like a drunk staggering downhill.

Leofric was laughing. Willibald looked worried.

"So what is the debt?" I asked.

"Two thousand shillings, lord," Mildrith said in a very small voice.

Leofric almost choked laughing and I could have cheerfully killed him on the spot.

"And it increases yearly?" Willibald asked shrewdly.

"Yes," Mildrith said, refusing to meet my eyes. A more sensible man would have explored Mildrith's circumstances before the marriage contract was made, but I had just seen marriage as a route to the fleet. So now I had the fleet, I had the debt, and I had the girl, and I also had a new enemy, Odda the Younger, who had plainly wanted Mildrith for himself, though his father, wisely, had refused to saddle his family with the crippling debt, nor, I suspected, did he want his son to marry beneath him.

There is a hierarchy among men. Beocca liked to tell me it reflected the hierarchy of heaven, and perhaps it does, but I know nothing of that, but I do know how men are ranked. At the top is the king, and beneath him are his sons, and then come the ealdormen who are the chief nobles of the land and without land a man cannot be noble, though I was, because I have never abandoned my claim to Bebbanburg. The king and his ealdormen are the power of a kingdom, the men who hold great lands and raise the armies, and beneath them are the lesser nobles, usually called reeves, and they are responsible for law in a lord's land, though a man can cease to be a reeve if he displeases his lord. The reeves are drawn from the ranks of thegns, who are wealthy men who can lead followers to war, but who lack the wide holdings of noblemen like Odda or my father. Beneath the thegns are the ceorls, who are all free men, but if a ceorl loses his livelihood then he could well become a slave, which is the bottom of the dung heap. Slaves can be, and often are, freed, though unless a slave's lord gives him land or money he will soon be a slave again. Mildrith's father had been a thegn, and Odda had made him a reeve, responsible for keeping the peace in a wide swath of southern Defnascir, but he had also been a thegn of insufficient land, whose foolishness had diminished the little he possessed, and so he had left Mildrith impoverished, which made her unsuitable as a wife for an ealdorman's son, though she was reckoned good enough for an exiled lord from Northumbria. In truth she was just another pawn on Alfred's chessboard and he had only given her to me so that I became responsible for paying the church a vast sum.

He was a spider, I thought sourly, a priestly black spider spinning sticky webs, and I thought I had been so clever when I talked to him in the hall at Cippanhamm. In truth I could have prayed openly to Thor before pissing on the relics of Alfred's altar and he would still have given me the fleet because he knew the fleet would have little to do in the coming war, and he had only wanted to trap me for his future ambitions in the north of England. So now I was trapped, and the bastard Ealdorman Odda had carefully let me walk into the trap.

The thought of Defnascir's ealdorman prompted a question from me. "What bride-price did Odda give you?" I asked Mildrith.

"Fifteen shillings, lord."

"Fifteen shillings?" I asked, shocked.

"Yes, lord."

"The cheap bastard," I said.

"Cut the rest out of him," Leofric snarled. A pair of very blue eyes looked at him, then at me, then vanished under the cloak again.

Her twelve hides of land, that were now mine, lay in the hills above the river Uisc's sea reach, in a place called Oxton, which simply means a farm where oxen are kept. It was a shieling, as the Danes would say, a farmstead, and the house had a thatch so overgrown with moss and grass that it looked like an earth mound. There was no hall, and a nobleman needs a hall in which to feed his followers, but it did have a cattle shed and a pig shed and land enough to support sixteen slaves and five families of tenants, all of whom were summoned to greet me, as well as half a dozen household servants, most of whom were also slaves, and they welcomed Mildrith fondly for, since her father's death, she had been living in the household of Ealdorman Odda's wife while the farmstead was managed by a man called Oswald who looked about as trustworthy as a stoat.

That night we made a meal of peas, leeks, stale bread, and sour ale, and that was my first marriage feast in my own house, which was also a house under threat of debt. The next morning it had stopped raining and I breakfasted on more stale bread and sour ale, and then walked with Mildrith to a hilltop from where I could stare down at the wide sea reach that lay across the land like the flattened gray blade of an ax. "Where do these folk go," I asked, meaning her slaves and tenants, "when the Danes come?"

"Into the hills, lord."

"My name is Uhtred."

"Into the hills, Uhtred."

"You won't go into the hills," I said firmly.

"I won't?" Her eyes widened in alarm.

"You will come with me to Hamtun," I said, "and we shall have a house there so long as I command the fleet."

She nodded, plainly nervous, and then I took her hand, opened it, and poured in thirty-three shillings, so many coins that they spilled onto her lap. "Yours, wife," I said.

And so she was. My wife. And that same day we left, going eastward, man and wife.

The story hurries now. It quickens like a stream coming to a fall in the hills and, like a cascade foaming down jumbled rocks, it gets angry and violent, confused even. For it was in that year, 876, that the Danes made their greatest effort yet to rid England of its last kingdom, and the onslaught was huge, savage, and sudden.

Guthrum the Unlucky led the assault. He had been living in Grantaceaster, calling himself King of East Anglia, and Alfred, I think, assumed he would have good warning if Guthrum's army left that place, but the West Saxon spies failed and the warnings did not come, and the Danish army was all mounted on horses, and Alfred's troops were in the wrong place and Guthrum led his men south across the Temes and clear across all Wessex to capture a great fortress on the south coast. That fortress was called Werham and it lay not very far west of Hamtun, though between us and it lay a vast stretch of inland sea called the Poole. Guthrum's army assaulted Werham, captured it, raped the nuns in Werham's nunnery, and did it all before Alfred could react. Once inside the fortress Guthrum was protected by two rivers, one to the north of the town and the other to the south. To the east was the wide placid Poole and a massive wall and ditch guarded the only approach from the west.

There was nothing the fleet could do. As soon as we heard that the Danes were in Werham, we readied ourselves for sea, but no sooner had we reached the open water than we saw their fleet and that ended our ambitions.

I have never seen so many ships. Guthrum had marched across Wessex with close to a thousand horsemen, but now the rest of his army came by sea and their ships darkened the water. There were hundreds of boats. Men later said three hundred and fifty, though I think there were fewer, but certainly there were more than two hundred. Ship after ship, dragon prow after serpent head, oars churning the dark sea white, a fleet going to battle, and all we could do was slink back into Hamtun and pray that the Danes did not sail up Hamtun Water to slaughter us.

They did not. The fleet sailed on to join Guthrum in Werham, so now a huge Danish army was lodged in southern Wessex, and I remembered Ragnar's advice to Guthrum. Split their forces, Ragnar had said, and that surely meant another Danish army lay somewhere to the north, just waiting to attack, and when Alfred went to meet that second army, Guthrum would erupt from behind Werham's walls to attack him in the rear.

"It's the end of England," Leofric said darkly. He was not much given to gloom, but that day he was downcast. Mildrith and I had taken a house in Hamtun, one close to the water, and he ate with us most nights we were in the town. We were still taking the ships out, now in a flotilla of twelve, always in hope of catching some Danish ships unawares, but their raiders only sallied out of the Poole in large numbers, never fewer than thirty ships, and I dared not lose Alfred's navy in a suicidal attack on such large forces. In the height of the summer a Danish force came to Hamtun's water, rowing almost to our anchorage, and we lashed our ships together, donned armor, sharpened weapons, and waited for their attack. But they were no more minded for battle than we were. To reach us they would have to negotiate a mud-bordered channel and they could only put two ships abreast in that place and so they were content to jeer at us from the open water and then leave.

Guthrum waited in Werham and what he waited for, we later learned, was for Halfdan to lead a mixed force of Northmen and Britons out of Wales. Halfdan had been in Ireland, avenging Ivar's death, and now he was supposed to bring his fleet and army to Wales, assemble a great army there, and lead it across the Sæfern Sea and attack Wessex. But, according to Beocca, God intervened. God or the three spinners. Fate is everything, for news came that Halfdan had died in Ireland, and of the three brothers only Ubba now lived, though he was still in the far wild north. Halfdan had been killed by the Irish, slaughtered along with scores of his men in a vicious battle, and so the Irish saved Wessex that year.

We knew none of that in Hamtun. We made our impotent forays and waited for news of the second blow that must fall on Wessex, and still it did not come, and then, as the first autumn gales fretted the coast, a messenger came from Alfred, whose army was camped to the west of Werham, demanding that I go to the king. The messenger was Beocca and I was surprisingly pleased to see him, though annoyed that he gave me the command verbally. "Why did I learn to read," I demanded of him, "if you don't bring written orders?"

"You learned to read, Uhtred," he said happily, "to improve your mind, of course." Then he saw Mildrith and his mouth began to open and close like a landed fish. "Is this?" he began, and was struck dumb as a stick.

"The Lady Mildrith," I said.

"Dear lady," Beocca said, then gulped for air and twitched like a puppy wanting a pat. "I have known Uhtred," he managed to say to her, "since he was a little child! Since he was just a little child."

"He's a big one now," Mildrith said, which Beocca thought was a wonderful jest for he giggled immoderately.

"Why," I managed to stem his mirth, "am I going to Alfred?"

"Because Halfdan is dead, God be praised, and no army will come from the north, God be praised, and so Guthrum seeks terms! The discussions have already started, and God be praised for that, too." He beamed at me as though he was responsible for this rush of good news, and perhaps he was because he went on to say that Halfdan's death was the result of prayers. "So many prayers, Uhtred. You see the power of prayer?"

"God be praised indeed," Mildrith answered

instead of me. She was indeed very pious, but no one is perfect. She was also pregnant, but Beocca did not notice and I did not tell him.

I left Mildrith in Hamtun, and rode with Beocca to the West Saxon army. A dozen of the king's household troops served as our escort, for the route took us close to the northern shore of the Poole and Danish boats had been raiding that shore before the truce talks opened. "What does Alfred want of me?" I asked Beocca constantly, insisting, despite his denials, that he must have some idea, but he claimed ignorance and in the end I stopped asking.

We arrived outside Werham on a chilly autumn evening. Alfred was at his prayers in a tent that was serving as his royal chapel and Ealdorman Odda and his son waited outside and the ealdorman gave me a guarded nod while his son ignored me. Beocca went into the tent to join the prayers while I squatted, drew Serpent-Breath, and sharpened her with the whetstone I carried in my pouch.

"Expecting to fight?" Ealdorman Odda asked me sourly.

I looked at his son. "Maybe," I said, then looked back to the father. "You owe my wife money," I said, "eighteen shillings." He reddened, said nothing, though the son put a hand to his sword hilt and that made me smile and stand, Serpent-Breath's naked blade already in my grip. Ealdorman Odda pulled his son angrily away. "Eighteen shillings!" I called after them, then squatted again and ran the stone down the sword's long edge.

Women. Men fight for them, and that was another lesson to learn. As a child I thought men struggled for land or for mastery, but they fight for women just as much. Mildrith and I were un-expectedly content together, but it was clear that Odda the Younger hated me because I had mar-ried her, and I wondered if he would dare do any-thing about that hatred. Beocca once told me the tale of a prince from a faraway land who stole a king's daughter and the king led his army to the prince's land and thousands of great warriors died in the struggle to get her back. Thousands! And all for a woman. Indeed the argument that began this tale, the rivalry between King Osbert of Northumbria and Ælla, the man who wanted to be king, all began because Ælla stole Osbert's wife. I have heard some women complain that they have no power and that men control the world, and so they do, but women still have the power to drive men to battle and to the grave beyond.

I was thinking of these things as Alfred came from the tent. He had the look of beatific pleasure he usually wore when he had just said his prayers, but he was also walking stiffly, which probably meant the ficus was troubling him again, and he looked distinctly uncomfortable when we sat down to supper that night. The meal was an unspeakable gruel I would hesitate to serve to pigs, but there was bread and cheese enough so I did not starve. I did note that Alfred was distant with me, hardly acknowledging my presence, and I put that down to the fleet's failure to achieve any real victory during that summer, yet he had still summoned me and I wondered why if all he intended to do was ignore me.

Yet, the next morning he summoned me after prayers and we walked up and down outside the royal tent where the dragon banner flew in the autumn sun. "The fleet," Alfred said, frowning, "can it prevent the Danes leaving the Poole?"

"No, lord."

"No?" That was said sharply. "Why not?"

"Because, lord," I said, "we have twelve ships

and they have over two hundred. We could kill a few of them, but in the end they'll overwhelm us and you won't have any fleet left and they'll still have more than two hundred ships."

I think Alfred knew that, but he still did not like my answer. He grimaced, then walked in silence for a few more paces. "I am glad you married," he said abruptly.

"To a debt," I said sharply.

He did not like my tone, but allowed it. "The debt, Uhtred," he said reprovingly, "is to the church, so you must welcome it. Besides, you're young, you have time to pay. The Lord, remember, loves a cheerful giver." That was one of his favorite sayings and if I heard it once I heard it a thousand times. He turned on his heel, then looked back. "I shall expect your presence at the negotiations," he said, but did not explain why, nor wait for any response, but just walked on.

He and Guthrum were talking. A canopy had been raised between Alfred's camp and Werham's western wall, and it was beneath that shelter that a truce was being hammered out. Alfred would have liked to assault Werham, but the approach was narrow, the wall was high and in very good repair, and the Danes were numerous. It would have been a very risky fight, and one that the

Danes could expect to win, and so Alfred had abandoned the idea. As for the Danes, they were trapped. They had been relying on Halfdan coming to attack Alfred in the rear, but Halfdan was dead in Ireland, and Guthrum's men were too many to be carried away on their ships, big as their fleet was, and if they tried to break out by land they would be forced to fight Alfred on the narrow strip of land between the two rivers, and that would cause a great slaughter. I remembered Ravn telling me how the Danes feared to lose too many men for they could not replace them quickly. Guthrum could stay where he was, of course, but then Alfred would besiege him and Alfred had already ordered that every barn, granary, and storehouse within raiding distance of the Poole was to be emptied. The Danes would starve in the coming winter.

Which meant that both sides wanted peace, and Alfred and Guthrum had been discussing terms, and I arrived just as they were finishing the discussions. It was already too late in the year for the Danish fleet to risk a long journey around Wessex's southern coast, and so Alfred had agreed that Guthrum could remain in Werham through the winter. He also agreed to supply them with food on condition that they made no raids, and he agreed to give them silver because he knew the Danes always wanted silver, and in return they promised that they would stay peaceably in Werham and leave peaceably in the spring when their fleet would go back to East Anglia and the rest of their army would march north through Wessex, guarded by our men, until they reached Mercia.

No one, on either side, believed the promises, so they had to be secured, and for that each side demanded hostages, and the hostages had to be of rank, or else their lives would be security for nothing. A dozen Danish earls, none of whom I knew, were to be delivered to Alfred, and an equivalent number of English nobles given to Guthrum.

Which was why I had been summoned. Which was why Alfred had been so distant with me, for he knew all along that I was to be one of the hostages. My use to him had lessened that year, because of the fleet's impotence, but my rank still had bargaining power, and so I was among the chosen. I was Ealdorman Uhtred, and only useful because I was a noble, and I saw Odda the Younger smiling broadly as my name was accepted by the Danes.

Guthrum and Alfred then swore oaths. Alfred

insisted that the Danish leader make his oath with one hand on the relics that Alfred always carried in his baggage. There was a feather from the dove that Noah had released from the ark, a glove that had belonged to Saint Cedd, and, most sacred of all, a toe ring that had belonged to Mary Magdalene. The holy ring, Alfred called it, and a bemused Guthrum put his hand on the scrap of gold and swore he would keep his promises, then insisted that Alfred put a hand on the bone he hung in his hair and he made the King of Wessex swear on a dead Danish mother that the West Saxons would keep the treaty. Only when those oaths were made, sanctified by the gold of a saint and the bone of a mother, were the hostages exchanged, and as I walked across the space between the two sides Guthrum must have recognized me for he gave me a long, contemplative look, and then we were escorted, with ceremony, to Werham.

Where Earl Ragnar, son of Ragnar, welcomed me.

There was joy in that meeting. Ragnar and I embraced like brothers, and I thought of him as a brother, and he thumped my back, poured ale, and gave me news. Kjartan and Sven still lived and were still in Dunholm. Ragnar had confronted them in a formal meeting where both sides were forbidden to carry weapons, and Kjartan had sworn that he was innocent of the hall-burning and declared he knew nothing of Thyra. "The bastard lied," Ragnar told me, "and I know he lied. And he knows he will die."

"But not yet?"

"How can I take Dunholm?"

Brida was there, sharing Ragnar's bed, and she greeted me warmly, though not as hotly as Nihtgenga who leaped all over me and washed my face with his tongue. Brida was amused that I was going to be a father. "But it will be good for you," she said.

"Good for me? Why?"

"Because you'll be a proper man."

I thought I was that already, yet there was still one thing lacking, one thing I had never confessed to anyone, not to Mildrith, not to Leofric, and not now to Ragnar or Brida. I had fought the Danes, I had seen ships burn and watched men drown, but I had never fought in a great shield wall. I had fought in small ones, I had fought ship's crew against ship's crew, but I had never stood on a wide battlefield and watched the enemy's banners hide the sun, and known the fear that comes when hundreds or thousands of men are coming to the slaughter. I had been at Eoferwic and at Æsc's Hill and I had seen the shield walls clash, but I had not been in the front rank. I had been in fights, but they had all been small and small fights end quickly. I had never endured the long bloodletting, the terrible fights when thirst and weariness weaken a man and the enemy, no matter how many you kill, keeps on coming. Only when I had done that, I thought, could I call myself a proper man.

I missed Mildrith, and that surprised me. I also missed Leofric, though there was huge pleasure in Ragnar's company, and the life of a hostage was not hard. We lived in Werham, received enough food, and watched the gray of winter shorten the days. One of the hostages was a cousin of Alfred's, a priest called Wælla, who fretted and sometimes wept, but the rest of us were content enough. Hacca, who had once commanded Alfred's fleet, was among the hostages, and he was the only one I knew well, but I spent my time with Ragnar and his men who accepted me as one of them and even tried to make me a Dane again. "I have a wife," I told them.

"So bring her!" Ragnar said. "We never have enough women."

But I was English now. I did not hate the Danes, indeed I preferred their company to the company of the other hostages, but I was English. That journey was done. Alfred had not changed my allegiance, but Leofric and Mildrith had, or else the three spinners had become bored with teasing me, though Bebbanburg still haunted me and I did not know how, if I was to keep my loyalty to Alfred, I would ever see that lovely place again.

Ragnar accepted my choice. "But if there's peace," he said, "will you help me fight Kjartan?"

"If?" I repeated the word.

He shrugged. "Guthrum still wants Wessex. We all do."

"If there's peace," I promised, "I will come north."

Yet I doubted there would be peace. In the spring Guthrum would leave Wessex, the hostages would be freed, and then what? The Danish army still existed and Ubba yet lived, so the onslaught on Wessex must begin again, and Guthrum must have been thinking the same for he talked with all the hostages in an effort to discover Alfred's strength. "It is a great strength," I told him. "You may kill his army and another will spring up." It was all nonsense, of course, but what else did he expect me to say?

I doubt I convinced Guthrum, but Wælla, the priest who was Alfred's cousin, put the fear of God into him. Guthrum spent hours talking with Wælla, and I often interpreted for him, and Guthrum was not asking about troops or ships, but about God. Who was the Christian God? What did he offer? He was fascinated by the tale of the crucifixion and I think, had we been given time enough, Wælla could even have persuaded Guthrum to convert. Wælla certainly thought so himself for he enjoined me to pray for such a conversion. "It's close, Uhtred," he told me excitedly, "and once he has been baptized then there will be peace!"

Such are the dreams of priests. My dreams were of Mildrith and the child she carried. Ragnar dreamed of revenge. And Guthrum?

Despite his fascination with Christianity, Guthrum dreamed of just one thing.

He dreamed of war.

PART THREE

The Shield Wall

TEN

Alfred's army withdrew from Werham. Some West Saxons stayed to watch Guthrum, but very few, for armies are expensive to maintain and, once gathered, they always seem to fall sick, so Alfred took advantage of the truce to send the men of the fyrds back to their farms while he and his household troops went to Scireburnan, which lay a half day's march north of Werham and, happily for Alfred, was home to a bishop and a monastery. Beocca told me that Alfred spent that winter reading the ancient law codes from Kent, Mercia, and Wessex, and doubtless he was readying himself to compile his own laws, which he eventually did. I am certain he was happy that winter, criticizing his ancestors' rules and dreaming of the perfect society where the church told us what not to do and the king punished us for doing it.

Huppa, Ealdorman of Thornsæta, commanded the few men who were left facing Werham's ramparts, while Odda the Younger led a troop of horsemen who patrolled the shores of the Poole, but the two bands made only a small force and they could do little except keep an eye on the Danes, and why should they do more? There was a truce, Guthrum had sworn on the holy ring, and Wessex was at peace.

The Yule feast was a thin affair in Werham, though the Danes did their best and at least there was plenty of ale so men got drunk, but my chief memory of that Yule is of Guthrum crying. The tears poured down his face as a harpist played a sad tune and a skald recited a poem about Guthrum's mother. Her beauty, the skald said, was rivaled only by the stars, while her kindness was such that flowers sprang up in winter to pay her homage. "She was a rancid bitch," Ragnar whispered to me, "and ugly as a bucket of shit."

"You knew her?"

"Ravn knew her. He always said she had a voice that could cut down a tree."

Guthrum was living up to his name "the Unlucky." He had come so close to destroying Wessex and it had only been Halfdan's death that had cheated him of the prize, and that was not

Guthrum's fault, yet there was a simmering resentment among the trapped army. Men muttered that nothing could ever prosper under Guthrum's leadership, and perhaps that distrust had made him gloomier than ever, or perhaps it was hunger.

For the Danes were hungry. Alfred kept his word and sent food, but there was never quite enough, and I did not understand why the Danes did not eat their horses that were left to graze on the winter marshes between the fortress and the Poole. Those horses grew desperately thin, their pathetic grazing supplemented by what little hay the Danes had discovered in the town, and when that was gone they pulled the thatch from some of Werham's houses, and that poor diet kept the horses alive until the first glimmerings of spring. I welcomed those new signs of the turning year: the song of a missel thrush, the dog violets showing in sheltered spots, the lambs' tails on the hazel trees, and the first frogs croaking in the marsh. Spring was coming, and when the land was green Guthrum would leave and we hostages would be freed.

We received little news other than what the Danes told us, but sometimes a message was delivered to one or other of the hostages, usually nailed to a willow tree outside the gate, and one such message was addressed to me. For the first time, I was grateful that Beocca had taught me to read for Father Willibald had written and told me I had a son. Mildrith had given birth before Yule and the boy was healthy and she was also healthy and the boy was called Uhtred. I wept when I read that. I had not expected to feel so much, but I did, and Ragnar asked why I was crying and I told him and he produced a barrel of ale and we gave ourselves a feast, or as much of a feast as we could make, and he gave me a tiny silver arm ring as a gift for the boy. I had a son. Uhtred.

The next day I helped Ragnar relaunch **Wind-Viper,** which had been dragged ashore so her timbers could be caulked, and we stowed her bilges with the stones that served as ballast and rigged her mast and afterward killed a hare that we had trapped in the fields where the horses tried to graze, and Ragnar poured the hare's blood on the **Wind-Viper**'s stem and called on Thor to send her fair winds and for Odin to send her great victories. We ate the hare that night and drank the last of the ale, and the next morning a dragon boat arrived, coming from the sea, and I was amazed that Alfred had not ordered our fleet to patrol the waters off the Poole's mouth, but none of our boats was there, and so that single Danish ship came upriver and brought a message for Guthrum.

Ragnar was vague about the ship. It came from East Anglia, he said, which turned out to be untrue, and merely brought news of that kingdom, which was equally untrue. It had come from the west, around Cornwalum, from the lands of the Welsh, but I only learned that later and, at the time, I did not care, because Ragnar also told me that we should be leaving soon, very soon, and I only had thoughts for the son I had not seen. Uhtred Uhtredson.

That night Guthrum gave the hostages a feast, a good feast, too, with food and ale that had been brought on the newly arrived dragon ship, and Guthrum praised us for being good guests and he gave each of us an arm ring, and promised we would all be free soon. "When?" I asked.

"Soon!" His long face glistened in the firelight as he raised a horn of ale to me. "Soon! Now drink!"

We all drank, and after the feast we hostages went to the nunnery's hall where Guthrum insisted we slept. In the daytime we were free to roam wherever we wanted inside the Danish lines, and free to carry weapons if we chose, but at night he wanted all the hostages in one place so that his black-cloaked guards could keep an eye on us, and it was those guards who came for us in the night's dark heart. They carried flaming torches and they kicked us awake, ordering us outside, and one of them kicked Serpent-Breath away when I reached for her. "Get outside," he snarled, and when I reached for the sword again a spear stave cracked across my skull and two more spears jabbed my arse, and I had no choice but to stumble out the door into a gusting wind that was bringing a cold, spitting rain, and the wind tore at the flaming torches that lit the street where at least a hundred Danes waited, all armed, and I could see they had saddled and bridled their thin horses and my first thought was that these were the men who would escort us back to the West Saxon lines.

Then Guthrum, cloaked in black, pushed through the helmeted men. No words were spoken. Guthrum, grim faced, the white bone in his hair, just nodded, and his black-cloaked men drew their swords and poor Wælla, Alfred's cousin, was the first hostage to die. Guthrum winced slightly at the priest's death, for I think he had liked Wælla, but by then I was turning, ready to fight the men behind me even though I had no weapon and knew that fight could only end with my death. A sword was already coming for me, held by a Dane in a leather jerkin that was studded with metal rivets, and he was grinning as he ran the blade toward my unprotected belly and he was still grinning as the throwing ax buried its blade between his eyes. I remember the thump of that blade striking home, the spurt of blood in the flamelight, the noise as the man fell onto the flint and shingle street, and all the while the frantic protests from the other hostages as they were murdered, but I lived. Ragnar had hurled the ax and now stood beside me, sword drawn. He was in his war gear, in polished chain mail, in high boots and a helmet that he had decorated with a pair of eagle wings, and in the raw light of the wind-fretted fires he looked like a god come down to Midgard.

"They must all die," Guthrum insisted. The other hostages were dead or dying, their hands bloodied from their hopeless attempts to ward off the blades, and a dozen war Danes, swords red, now edged toward me to finish the job.

"Kill this one," Ragnar shouted, "and you must kill me first." His men came out of the crowd to stand beside their lord. They were out-numbered by at least five to one, but they were Danes and they showed no fear.

Guthrum stared at Ragnar. Hacca was still not dead and he twitched in his agony and Guthrum, irritated that the man lived, drew his sword and rammed it into Hacca's throat. Guthrum's men were stripping the arm rings from the dead, rings that had been gifts from their master just hours before. "They all must die," Guthrum said when Hacca was still. "Alfred will kill our hostages now, so it must be man for man."

"Uhtred is my brother," Ragnar said, "and you are welcome to kill him, lord, but you must first kill me."

Guthrum stepped back. "This is no time for Dane to fight Dane," he said grudgingly, and sheathed his sword to show that I could live. I stepped across the street to find the man who had stolen Serpent-Breath, Wasp-Sting, and my armor, and he gave them to me without protest.

Guthrum's men were mounting their horses. "What's happening?" I asked Ragnar.

"What do you think?" he asked truculently.

"I think you're breaking the truce."

"We did not come this far," he said, "to march

away like beaten dogs." He watched as I buckled Serpent-Breath's belt. "Come with us," he said.

"Come with you where?"

"To take Wessex, of course."

I do not deny that there was a tug on my heart strings, a temptation to join the wild Danes in their romp across Wessex, but the tug was easily resisted. "I have a wife," I told him, "and a child."

He grimaced. "Alfred has trapped you, Uhtred."

"No," I said, "the spinners did that." Urðr, Verðandi, and Skuld, the three women who spin our threads at the foot of Yggdrasil, had decided my fate. Destiny is all. "I shall go to my woman," I said.

"But not yet," Ragnar said with a half smile, and he took me to the river where a small boat carried us to where the newly launched **Wind-Viper** was anchored. A half crew was already aboard, as was Brida, who gave me a breakfast of bread and ale. At first light, when there was just enough gray in the sky to reveal the glistening mud of the river's banks, Ragnar ordered the anchor raised and we drifted downstream on current and tide, gliding past the dark shapes of other Danish ships until we came to a reach wide enough to turn **Wind-Viper** and there the oars were fitted, men tugged, and she swiveled gracefully, both oar banks began to pull, and she shot out into the Poole where most of the Danish fleet rode at anchor. We did not go far, just to the barren shore of a big island that sits in the center of the Poole, a place of squirrels, seabirds, and foxes. Ragnar let the ship glide toward the shore and, when her prow touched the beach, he embraced me. "You are free," he said.

"Thank you," I said fervently, remembering those bloodied corpses by Werham's nunnery.

He held on to my shoulders. "You and I," he said, "are tied as brothers. Don't forget that. Now go."

I splashed through the shallows as the **Wind-Viper,** a ghostly gray in the dawn, backed away. Brida called a farewell, I heard the oars bite, and the ship was gone.

That island was a forbidding place. Fishermen and fowlers had lived there once, and an anchorite, a monk who lives by himself, had occupied a hollow tree in the island's center, but the coming of the Danes had driven them all away and the remnants of the fishermen's houses were nothing but charred timbers on blackened ground. I had the island to myself, and it was from its shore that I watched the vast Danish fleet row toward the Poole's entrance, though they stopped there rather than go to sea because the wind, already brisk, had freshened even more and now it was a half gale blowing from the south and the breakers were shattering wild and white above the spit of sand that protected their new anchorage. The Danish fleet had moved there, I surmised, because to stay in the river would have exposed their crews to the West Saxon bowmen who would be among the troops reoccupying Werham.

Guthrum had led his horsemen out of Werham, that much was obvious, and all the Danes who had remained in the town were now crammed onto the ships where they waited for the weather to calm so they could sail away, but to where, I had no idea.

All day that south wind blew, getting harder and bringing a slashing rain, and I became bored of watching the Danish fleet fret at its anchors and so I explored the island's shore and found the remnants of a small boat half hidden in a thicket and I hauled the wreck down to the water and discovered it floated well enough, and the wind would take me away from the Danes and so I waited for the tide to turn and then, half swamped in the broken craft, I floated free. I used a piece of wood as a crude paddle, but the wind was howling now and it drove me wet and cold across that wide water until, as night fell, I came to the Poole's northern shore and there I became one of the sceadugengan again, picking my way through reeds and marshes until I found higher ground where bushes gave me shelter for a broken sleep. In the morning I walked eastward, still buffeted by wind and rain, and so came to Hamtun that evening.

Where I found that Mildrith and my son were gone.

Taken by Odda the Younger.

Father Willibald told me the tale. Odda had come that morning, while Leofric was down at the shore securing the boats against the bruising wind, and Odda had said that the Danes had broken out, that they would have killed their hostages, that they might come to Hamtun at any moment, and that Mildrith should flee. "She did not want to go, lord," Willibald said, and I could hear the timidity in his voice. My anger was frightening him. "They had horses, lord," he said, as if that explained it.

"You didn't send for Leofric?"

"They wouldn't let me, lord." He paused.

"But we were scared, lord. The Danes had broken the truce and we thought you were dead."

Leofric had set off in pursuit, but by the time he learned Mildrith was gone Odda had at least a half morning's start and Leofric did not even know where he would have gone. "West," I said, "back to Defnascir."

"And the Danes?" Leofric asked. "Where are they going?"

"Back to Mercia?" I guessed.

Leofric shrugged. "Across Wessex? With Alfred waiting? And you say they went on horseback? How fit were the horses?"

"They weren't fit. They were half starved."

"Then they haven't gone to Mercia," he said firmly.

"Perhaps they've gone to meet Ubba," Willibald suggested.

"Ubba!" I had not heard that name in a long time.

"There were stories, lord," Willibald said nervously, "that he was among the Britons in Wales. That he had a fleet on the Sæfern."

That made sense. Ubba was replacing his dead brother, Halfdan, and evidently leading another force of Danes against Wessex, but where? If he crossed the Sæfern's wide sea then he would be in Defnascir, or perhaps he was marching around the river, heading into Alfred's heartland from the north, but for the moment I did not care. I only wanted to find my wife and child. There was pride in that desire, of course, but more than pride. Mildrith and I were suited to each other, I had missed her, I wanted to see my child. That ceremony in the rain-dripping cathedral had worked its magic and I wanted her back and I wanted to punish Odda the Younger for taking her away. "Defnascir," I said again, "that's where the bastard's gone. And that's where we go to-morrow." Odda, I was certain, would head for the safety of home. Not that he feared my revenge, for he surely assumed I was dead, but he would be worried about the Danes, and I was worried that they might have found him on his westward flight.

"You and me?" Leofric asked.

I shook my head. "We take **Heahengel** and a full fighting crew."

Leofric looked skeptical. "In this weather?"

"The wind's dropping," I said, and it was, though it still tugged at the thatch and rattled the shutters, but it was calmer the next morning, but not by much for Hamtun's water was still flecked white as the small waves ran angrily ashore, suggesting that the seas beyond the Solente would be huge and furious. But there were breaks in the clouds, the wind had gone into the east, and I was in no mood to wait. Two of the crew, both seamen all their lives, tried to dissuade me from the voyage. They had seen this weather before, they said, and the storm would come back, but I refused to believe them and they, to their credit, came willingly, as did Father Willibald, which was brave of him for he hated the sea and was facing rougher water than any he had seen before.

We rowed up Hamtun's water, hoisted the sail in the Solente, brought the oars inboard, and ran before that east wind as though the serpent Corpse-Ripper was at our stern. **Heahengel** hammered through the short seas, threw the white water high, and raced, and that was while we were still in sheltered waters. Then we passed the white stacks at Wiht's end, the rocks that are called the Nædles, and the first tumultuous seas hit us and the **Heahengel** bent to them. Yet still we flew, and the wind was dropping and the sun shone through rents in the dark clouds to glitter on the churning sea, and Leofric suddenly roared a warning and pointed ahead.

He was pointing to the Danish fleet. Like me they believed the weather was improving, and they must have been in a hurry to join Guthrum, for the whole fleet was coming out of the Poole and was now sailing south to round the rocky headland, which meant, like us, they were going west. Which could mean they were going to Defnascir or perhaps planning to sail clear about Cornwalum to join Ubba in Wales.

"You want to tangle with them?" Leofric asked me grimly.

I heaved on the steering oar, driving us south. "We'll go outside them," I said, meaning we would head out to sea and I doubted any of their ships would bother with us. They were in a hurry to get wherever they were going and with luck, I thought, **Heahengel** would outrun them for she was a fast ship and they were still well short of the headland.

We flew downwind and there was joy in it, the joy of steering a boat through angry seas, though I doubt there was much joy for the men who had to bail **Heahengel,** chucking the water over the side, and it was one of those men who looked astern and called a sudden warning to me. I turned to see a black squall seething across the broken seas. It was an angry patch of darkness and rain, coming fast, so fast that Willibald, who had been clutching the ship's side as he vomited overboard, fell to his knees, made the sign of the cross, and began to pray. "Get the sail down!" I shouted at Leofric, and he staggered forward, but too late, much too late, for the squall struck.

One moment the sun had shone, then we were abruptly thrust into the devil's playground as the squall hit us like a shield wall. The ship shuddered, water and wind and gloom smashing us in sudden turmoil, and **Heahengel** swung to the blow, going broadside to the sea and nothing I could do would hold her straight, and I saw Leofric stagger across the deck as the steorbord side went under water. "Bail!" I shouted desperately. "Bail!" And then, with a noise like thunder, the great sail split into tatters that whipped off the yard, and the ship came slowly upright, but she was low in the water, and I was using all my strength to keep her coming around, creeping around, reversing our course so that I could put her bows into that turmoil of sea and wind, and the men were praying, making the sign of the cross, bailing water, and the remnants of the sail and the broken lines were mad things, ragged demons, and the sudden gale was howling like the furies in the rigging and I thought how futile it would be to die at sea so soon after Ragnar had saved my life.

Somehow we got six oars into the water and then, with two men to an oar, we pulled into that seething chaos. Twelve men pulled six oars, three men tried to cut the rigging's wreckage away, and the others threw water over the side. No orders were given, for no voice could be heard above that shrieking wind that was flensing the skin from the sea and whipping it in white spindrift. Huge swells rolled, but they were no danger for the **Heahengel** rode them, but their broken tops threatened to swamp us, and then I saw the mast sway, its shrouds parting, and I shouted uselessly, for no one could hear me, and the great spruce spar broke and fell. It fell across the ship's side and the water flowed in again, but Leofric and a dozen men somehow managed to heave the mast overboard and it banged down our flank, then jerked because it was still held to the ship by a tangle of seal-hide ropes. I saw Leofric pluck an ax from the swamped bilge and start to slash at that tangle of lines, but I screamed at him with all my breath to put the ax down.

Because the mast, tied to us and floating behind us, seemed to steady the ship. It held **Heahengel** into the waves and wind, and let the great seas go rolling beneath us, and we could catch our breath at last. Men looked at each other as if amazed to find themselves alive, and I could even let go of the steering oar because the mast, with the big yard and the remnants of its sail still attached, was holding us steady. I found my body aching. I was soaked through, must have been cold, but did not notice.

Leofric came to stand beside me. **Heahengel**'s prow was facing eastward, but we were traveling westward, driven backward by the tide and wind, and I turned to make certain we had sea room, and then touched Leofric's shoulder and pointed toward the shore.

Where we saw a fleet dying.

The Danes had been sailing south, following the shore from the Poole's entrance to the rearing headland, and that meant they were on a lee shore, and in that sudden resurgence of the storm they stood no chance. Ship after ship was being driven ashore. A few had made it past the headland, and another handful were trying to row clear of the cliffs, but most were doomed. We could not see their deaths, but I could imagine them. The crash of hulls against rocks, the churning water breaking through the planks, the pounding of sea and wind and timber on drowning men, dragon prows splintering and the halls of the sea god filling with the souls of warriors and, though they were the enemy, I doubt any of us felt anything but pity. The sea gives a cold and lonely death.

Ragnar and Brida. I just gazed, but could not distinguish one ship from another through the rain and broken sea. We did watch one ship, which seemed to have escaped, suddenly sink. One moment she was on a wave, spray flying from her hull, oars pulling her free, and next she was just gone. She vanished. Other ships were banging one another, oars tangling and splintering. Some tried to turn and run back to the Poole and many of those were driven ashore, some on the sands and some on the cliffs. A few ships, pitifully few, beat their way clear, men hauling on the oars in a frenzy, but all the Danish ships were overloaded, carrying men whose horses had died, carrying an army we knew not where, and that army now died.

We were south of the headland now, being driven fast to the west, and a Danish ship, smaller than ours, came close and the steersman looked across and gave a grim smile as if to acknowledge there was only one enemy now, the sea. The Dane drifted ahead of us, not slowed by trailing wreckage as we were. The rain hissed down, a malevolent rain, stinging on the wind, and the sea was full of planks, broken spars, dragon prows, long oars, shields, and corpses. I saw a dog swimming frantically, eyes white, and for a moment I thought it was Nihtgenga, then saw this dog had black ears while Nihtgenga had white. The clouds were the color of iron, ragged and low, and the water was being shredded into streams of white and green-black, and the **Heahengel** reared to each sea, crashed down into the troughs, and shook like a live thing with every blow, but she lived. She was well built, she kept us alive, and all the while we watched the Danish ships die and Father Willibald prayed.

Oddly his sickness had passed. He looked pale, and doubtless felt wretched, but as the storm pummeled us his vomiting ended and he even came to stand beside me, steadying himself by holding on to the steering oar. "Who is the Danish god of the sea?" he asked me over the wind's noise.

"Njorð!" I shouted back.

He grinned. "You pray to him and I'll pray to God."

I laughed. "If Alfred knew you'd said that you'd never become a bishop!"

"I won't become a bishop unless we survive this! So pray!"

I did pray, and slowly, reluctantly, the storm eased. Low clouds raced over the angry water, but the wind died and we could cut away the wreckage of mast and yard and unship the oars and turn **Heahengel** to the west and row through the flotsam of a shattered war fleet. A score of Danish ships were in front of us, and there were others behind us, but I guessed that at least half their fleet had sunk, perhaps more, and I felt an immense fear for Ragnar and Brida. We caught up with the smaller Danish ships and I steered close to as many as I could and shouted across the broken seas. "Did you see **Wind-Viper?**"

"No," they called back. No, came the answer, again and again. They knew we were an enemy ship, but did not care for there was no enemy out in that water except the water itself, and so we rowed on, a mastless ship, and left the Danes behind us, and as night fell, and as a streak of sunlight leaked like seeping blood into a rift of the western clouds, I steered **Heahengel** into the crooked reach of the river Uisc, and once we were behind the headland the sea calmed and we rowed, suddenly safe, past the long spit of sand and turned into the river and I could look up into the darkening hills to where Oxton stood, and I saw no light there.

We beached **Heahengel** and staggered ashore and some men knelt and kissed the ground while others made the sign of the cross. There was a small harbor in the wide river reach and some houses by the harbor and we filled them, demanded that fires were lit and food brought, and then, in the darkness, I went back outside and saw the sparks of light flickering upriver. I realized they were torches being burned on the remaining Danish boats that had somehow found their way into the Uisc and now rowed inland, going north toward Exanceaster, and I knew that was where Guthrum must have ridden and that the Danes were there, and the fleet's survivors would thicken his army and Odda the Younger, if he lived, might well have tried to go there, too.

With Mildrith and my son. I touched Thor's hammer and prayed they were alive.

And then, as the dark boats passed upstream, I slept.

In the morning we pulled **Heahengel** into the small harbor where she could rest on the mud when the tide fell. We were forty-eight men, tired but alive. The sky was ribbed with clouds, high and gray-pink, scudding before the storm's dying wind.

We walked to Oxton through woods full of bluebells. Did I expect to find Mildrith there? I think I did, but of course she was not. There was only Oswald the steward and the slaves and none of them knew what was happening.

Leofric insisted on a day to dry clothes, sharpen weapons, and fill bellies, but I was in no mood to rest so I took two men, Cenwulf and Ida, and walked north toward Exanceaster, which lay on the far side of the Uisc. The river settlements were empty for the folk had heard of the Danes coming and had fled into the hills, and so we walked the higher paths and asked them what happened, but they knew nothing except that there were dragon ships in the river, and we could see those for ourselves. There was a storm-battered fleet drawn up on the riverbank beneath Exanceaster's stone walls. There were more ships than I had suspected, suggesting that a good part of Guthrum's fleet had survived by staying in the Poole when the storm struck, and a few of those ships were still arriving, their crews rowing up the narrow river. We counted hulls and reckoned there were close to ninety boats, which meant that almost half of Guthrum's fleet had survived, and I tried to distinguish **Wind-Viper**'s hull among the others, but we were too far away.

Guthrum the Unlucky. How well he deserved that name, though in time he came close to earning a better, but for now he had been unfortunate indeed. He had broken out of Werham, had doubtless hoped to resupply his army in Exanceaster and then strike north, but the gods of sea and wind had struck him down and he was left with a crippled army. Yet it was still a strong army and, for the moment, safe behind Exanceaster's Roman walls.

I wanted to cross the river, but there were too many Danes by their ships, so we walked farther north and saw armed men on the road that led west from Exanceaster, a road that crossed the bridge beneath the city and led over the moors toward Cornwalum, and I stared a long time at those men, fearing they might be Danes, but they were staring east, suggesting that they watched the Danes and I guessed they were English and so we went down from the woods, shields slung on our backs to show we meant no harm.

There were eighteen men, led by a thegn named Withgil who had been the commander of Exanceaster's garrison and who had lost most of his men when Guthrum attacked. He was reluctant to tell the story, but it was plain that he had expected no trouble and had posted only a few guards on the eastern gate, and when they had seen the approaching horsemen the guards had thought they were English and so the Danes had been able to capture the gate and then pierce the town. Withgil claimed to have made a fight at the fort in the town's center, but it was obvious from his men's embarrassment that it had been a pathetic resistance, if it amounted to any resistance at all, and the probable truth was that Withgil had simply run away.

"Was Odda there?" I asked.

"Ealdorman Odda?" Withgil asked. "Of course not."

"Where was he?"

Withgil frowned at me as if I had just come from the moon. "In the north, of course."

"The north of Defnascir?"

"He marched a week ago. He led the fyrd."

"Against Ubba?"

"That's what the king ordered," Withgil said.

"So where's Ubba?" I demanded.

It seemed that Ubba had brought his ships across the wide Sæfern sea and had landed far to the west in Defnascir. He had traveled before the storm struck, which suggested his army was intact, and Odda had been ordered north to block Ubba's advance into the rest of Wessex, and if Odda had marched a week ago then surely Odda the Younger would know that and would have ridden to join his father. Which suggested that Mildrith was there, wherever there was. I asked Withgil if he had seen Odda the Younger, but he said he had neither seen nor heard of him since Christmas.

"How many men does Ubba have?" I asked.

"Many," Withgil said, which was not helpful, but all he knew.

"Lord." Cenwulf touched my arm and pointed east and I saw horsemen appearing on the low fields that stretched from the river toward the hill on which Exanceaster is built. A lot of horsemen, and behind them came a standard bearer and, though we were too far away to see the badge on the flag, the green and white proclaimed that it was the West Saxon banner. So Alfred had come here? It seemed likely, but I was in no mind to cross the river and find out. I was only interested in searching for Mildrith.

War is fought in mystery. The truth can take days to travel, and ahead of truth flies rumor, and it is ever hard to know what is really happening, and the art of it is to pluck the clean bone of fact from the rotting flesh of fear and lies.

So what did I know? That Guthrum had broken the truce and had taken Exanceaster, and that Ubba was in the north of Defnascir. Which suggested that the Danes were trying to do what they had failed to do the previous year, split the West Saxon forces, and while Alfred faced one army the other would ravage the land or, perhaps, descend on Alfred's rear, and to prevent that the fyrd of Defnascir had been ordered to block Ubba. Had that battle been fought? Was Odda alive? Was his son alive? Were Mildrith and my son alive? In any clash between Ubba and Odda I would have reckoned on Ubba. He was a great warrior, a man of legend among the Danes, and Odda was a fussy, worried, graying, and aging man.

"We go north," I told Leofric when we were back at Oxton. I had no wish to see Alfred. He would be besieging Guthrum, and if I walked into his camp he would doubtless order me to join the troops ringing the city and I would sit there, wait, and worry. Better to go north and find Ubba.

So the next morning, under a spring sun, the **Heahengel**'s crew marched north.

★ ★ ★

The war was between the Danes and Wessex. My war was with Odda the Younger, and I knew I was driven by pride. The preachers tell us that pride is a great sin, but the preachers are wrong. Pride makes a man, it drives him, it is the shield wall around his reputation and the Danes understood that. Men die, they said, but reputation does not die.

What do we look for in a lord? Strength, generosity, hardness, and success, and why should a man not be proud of those things? Show me a humble warrior and I will see a corpse. Alfred preached humility, he even pretended to it, loving to appear in church with bare feet and prostrating himself before the altar, but he never possessed true humility. He was proud, and men feared him because of it, and men should fear a lord. They should fear his displeasure and fear that his generosity will cease. Reputation makes fear, and pride protects reputation, and I marched north because my pride was endangered. My woman and child had been taken from me, and I would take them back, and if they had been harmed then I would take my revenge and the stink of that man's blood would make other men fear me. Wessex could fall for all I cared, my reputation was more important and so we marched, skirting Exanceaster, following a twisting cattle track into the hills until we reached Twyfyrde, a small place crammed with refugees from Exanceaster, and none of them had seen or heard news of Odda the Younger, nor had they heard of any battle to the north, though a priest claimed that lightning had struck thrice in the previous night, which he swore was a sign that God had struck down the pagans.

From Twyfyrde we took paths that edged the great moor, walking through country that was deep-wooded, hilly, and lovely. We would have made better time if we had possessed horses, but we had none, and the few we saw were old and sick and there were never enough for all our men, so we walked, sleeping that night in a deep combe bright with blossom and sifted with bluebells, and a nightingale sang us to sleep and the dawn chorus woke us and we walked on beneath the white mayflower, and that afternoon we came to the hills above the northern shore and we met folk who had fled the coastal lands, bringing with them their families and livestock, and their presence told us we must soon see the Danes.

I did not know it but the three spinners were making my fate. They were thickening the threads, twisting them tighter, making me into what I am, but staring down from that high hill I only felt a flicker of fear, for there was Ubba's fleet, rowing east, keeping pace with the horsemen and infantry who marched along the shore.

The folk who had fled their homes told us that the Danes had come from the Welsh lands across the wide Sæfern sea, and that they had landed at a place called Beardastopol, which lies far in Defnascir's west, and there they had collected horses and supplies, but then their attack eastward into the West Saxon heartland had been delayed by the great storm that had wrecked Guthrum's fleet. Ubba's ships had stayed in Beardastopol's harbor until the storm passed and then, inexplicably, they had still waited even when the weather improved and I guessed that Ubba, who would do nothing without the consent of the gods, had cast the runesticks, found them unfavorable, and so waited until the auguries were better. Now the runes must have been good for Ubba's army was on the move. I counted thirty-six ships, which suggested an army of at least twelve or thirteen hundred men.

"Where are they going?" One of my men asked.

"East," I grunted. What else could I say? East

into Wessex. East into the rich heartland of England's last kingdom. East to Wintanceaster or to any of the other plump towns where the churches, monasteries, and nunneries were brimming with treasure, east to where the plunder waited, east to where there was food and more horses, east to invite more Danes to come south across Mercia's frontier, and Alfred would be forced to turn around and face them, and then Guthrum's army would come from Exanceaster and the army of Wessex would be caught between two hosts of Danes, except that the fyrd of Defnascir was somewhere on this coast and it was their duty to stop Ubba's men.

We walked east, passing from Defnascir into Sumorsæte, and shadowing the Danes by staying on the higher ground, and that night I watched as Ubba's ships came inshore and the fires were lit in the Danish camp, and we lit our own fires deep in a wood and were marching again before dawn and thus got ahead of our enemies and by midday we could see the first West Saxon forces. They were horsemen, presumably sent to scout the enemy, and they were now retreating from the Danish threat, and we walked until the hills dropped away to where a river flowed into the Sæfern sea, and it was there that we discovered that Ealdorman Odda had decided to make his stand, in a fort built by the old people on a hill near the river.

The river was called the Pedredan and close to its mouth was a small place called Cantucton, and near Cantucton was the ancient earth-walled fort that the locals said was named Cynuit. It was old, that fort; Father Willibald said it was older than the Romans, that it had been old when the world was young, and the fort had been made by throwing up earth walls on a hilltop and digging a ditch outside the walls. Time had worked on those walls, wearing them down and making the ditch shallower, and grass had overgrown the ramparts, and on one side the wall had been plowed almost to nothing, plowed until it was a mere shadow on the turf, but it was a fortress and the place where Ealdorman Odda had taken his forces and where he would die if he could not defeat Ubba, whose ships were already showing in the river's mouth.

I did not go straight to the fort, but stopped in the shelter of some trees and dressed for war. I became Ealdorman Uhtred in his battle glory. The slaves at Oxton had polished my mail coat with sand and I pulled it on, and over it I buckled a leather sword belt for Serpent-Breath and

Wasp-Sting. I pulled on tall boots, put on the shining helmet, and picked up my iron-bossed shield and, when all the straps were tight and the buckles firm, I felt like a god dressed for war, dressed to kill. My men buckled their own straps, laced their boots, tested their weapons' edges, and even Father Willibald cut himself a stave, a great piece of ash that could break a man's skull. "You won't need to fight, father," I told him.

"We all have to fight now, lord," he said. He took a step back and looked me up and down, and a small smile came to his face. "You've grown up," he said.

"It's what we do, father," I said.

"I remember when I first saw you. A child. Now I fear you."

"Let's hope the enemy does," I said, not quite sure what enemy I meant, whether Odda or Ubba, and I wished I had Bebbanburg's standard, the snarling wolf's head, but I had my swords and my shield and I led my men out of the wood and across the fields to where the fyrd of Defnascir would make its stand.

The Danes were a mile or so to our left, spilling from the coast road and hurrying to surround the hill called Cynuit, though they would be too late to bar our path. To my right were more Danes, ship Danes, bringing their dragon-headed boats up the Pedredan.

"They outnumber us," Willibald said.

"They do," I agreed. There were swans on the river, corncrakes in the uncut hay, and crimson orchids in the meadows. This was the time of year when men should be haymaking or shearing their sheep. **I need not be here,** I thought to myself. **I need not go to this hilltop where the Danes will come to kill us.** I looked at my men and wondered if they thought the same, but when they caught my eye they only grinned, or nodded, and I suddenly realized that they trusted me. I was leading them and they were not questioning me, though Leofric understood the danger. He caught up with me.

"There's only one way off that hilltop," he said softly.

"I know."

"And if we can't fight our way out," he said, "then we'll stay there. Buried."

"I know," I said again, and I thought of the spinners and knew they were tightening the threads, and I looked up Cynuit's slope and saw there were some women at the very top, women being sheltered by their men, and I thought Mildrith might be among them, and that was why I climbed the hill: because I did not know where else to seek her.

But the spinners were sending me to that old earth fort for another reason. I had yet to stand in the big shield wall, in the line of warriors, in the heave and horror of a proper battle where to kill once is merely to invite another enemy to come. The hill of Cynuit was the road to full manhood and I climbed it because I had no choice; the spinners sent me.

Then a roar sounded to our right, down in the Pedredan's valley, and I saw a banner being raised beside a beached ship. It was the banner of the raven. Ubba's banner. Ubba, last and strongest and most frightening of the sons of Lothbrok, had brought his blades to Cynuit. "You see that boat?" I said to Willibald, pointing to where the banner flew. "Ten years ago," I said, "I cleaned that ship. I scoured it, scrubbed it, cleaned it." Danes were taking their shields from the shield strake and the sun glinted on their myriad spear blades. "I was ten years old," I told Willibald.

"The same boat?" he asked.

"Maybe. Maybe not." Perhaps it was a new

ship. It did not matter, really. All that mattered was that it had brought Ubba.

To Cynuit.

The men of Defnascir had made a line where the old fort's wall had eroded away. Some, a few, had spades and were trying to remake the earth barrier, but they would not be given time to finish, not if Ubba assaulted the hill, and I pushed through them, using my shield to thrust men out of my way and ignoring all those who questioned who we were, and so we made our way to the hill's summit where Odda's banner of a black stag flew.

I pulled off my helmet as I neared him. I tossed the helmet to Father Willibald, then drew Serpent-Breath for I had seen Odda the Younger standing beside his father, and he was staring at me as though I were a ghost, and to him I must have appeared just that. "Where is she?" I shouted, and I pointed Serpent-Breath at him. "Where is she?"

Odda's retainers drew swords or leveled spears, and Leofric drew his battle-thinned blade, Dane-Killer.

"No!" Father Willibald shouted and he ran forward, his staff raised in one hand and my helmet in the other. "No!" He tried to head me off, but I pushed him aside, only to find three of Odda's priests barring my way. That was one thing about Wessex, there were always priests. They appeared like mice out of a burning thatch, but I thrust the priests aside and confronted Odda the Younger. "Where is she?" I demanded.

Odda the Younger was in mail, mail so brightly polished that it hurt the eye. He had a helmet inlaid with silver, boots to which iron plates were strapped, and a blue cloak held about his neck by a great brooch of gold and amber.

"Where is she?" I asked a fourth time, and this time Serpent-Breath was a hand's length from his throat.

"Your wife is at Cridianton," Ealdorman Odda answered. His son was too scared to open his mouth.

I had no idea where Cridianton was. "And my son?" I stared into Odda the Younger's frightened eyes. "Where is my son?"

"They are both with my wife at Cridianton," Ealdorman Odda answered, "and they are safe."

"You swear to that?" I asked.

"Swear?" The ealdorman was angry now, his ugly, bulbous face red. "You dare ask me to swear?" He drew his own sword. "We can cut you down like a dog," he said and his men's swords twitched.

I swept my own sword around till it pointed down to the river. "You know whose banner that is?" I asked, raising my voice so that a good portion of the men on Cynuit's hill could hear me. "That is the raven banner of Ubba Lothbrokson. I have watched Ubba Lothbrokson kill. I have seen him trample men into the sea, cut their bellies open, take off their heads, wade in their blood, and make his sword screech with their death song, and you would kill me who is ready to fight him alongside you? Then do it." I spread my arms, baring my body to the ealdorman's sword. "Do it," I spat at him, "but first swear my wife and child are safe."

He paused a long time, then lowered his blade. "They are safe," he said, "I swear it."

"And that thing," I pointed Serpent-Breath at his son, "did not touch her?"

The ealdorman looked at his son who shook his head. "I swear I did not," Odda the Younger said, finding his voice. "I only wanted her to be safe. We thought you were dead and I wanted her to be safe. That is all, I swear it."

I sheathed Serpent-Breath. "You owe my wife eighteen shillings," I said to the ealdorman, then turned away.

I had come to Cynuit. I had no need to be on that hilltop. But I was there. Because destiny is everything.

ELEVEN

Ealdorman Odda did not want to kill Danes. He wanted to stay where he was and let Ubba's forces besiege him. That, he reckoned, would be enough. "Keep their army here," he said heavily, "and Alfred can march to attack them."

"Alfred," I pointed out, "is besieging Exanceaster."

"He will leave men there to watch Guthrum," Odda said loftily, "and march here." He did not like talking to me, but I was an ealdorman and he could not bar me from his council of war that was attended by his son, the priests, and a dozen thegns, all of whom were becoming irritated by my comments. I insisted Alfred would not come to our relief, and Ealdorman Odda was refusing to move from the hilltop because he was sure Alfred would come. His thegns, all of them big men with heavy coats of mail and grim, weather-hardened faces, agreed with him. One muttered that the women had to be protected.

"There shouldn't be any women here," I said.

"But they are here," the man said flatly. At least a hundred women had followed their men and were now on the hilltop where there was no shelter for them or their children.

"And even if Alfred comes," I asked, "how long will it take?"

"Two days?" Odda suggested. "Three?"

"And what will we drink while he's coming?" I asked. "Bird piss?"

They all just stared at me, hating me, but I was right for there was no spring on Cynuit. The nearest water was the river, and between us and the river were Danes, and Odda understood well enough that we would be assailed by thirst, but he still insisted we stay. Perhaps his priests were praying for a miracle.

The Danes were just as cautious. They outnumbered us, but not by many, and we held the high ground, which meant they would have to fight up Cynuit's steep slope, and so Ubba chose to surround the hill rather than assault it. The Danes hated losing men, and I remembered Ubba's caution at the Gewæsc where he had hesitated to attack Edmund's forces up the two paths from the marsh, and perhaps that caution was reinforced by Storri, his sorcerer, if Storri still lived. Whatever the reason, instead of forming his men into the shield wall to assault the ancient fort, Ubba posted them in a ring about Cynuit and then, with five of his shipmasters, climbed the hill. He carried no sword or shield, which showed he wanted to talk.

Ealdorman Odda, his son, two thegns, and three priests went to meet Ubba and, because I was an ealdorman, I followed them. Odda gave me a malevolent look, but again he was unable to deny me, and so we met halfway down the slope where Ubba offered no greeting and did not even waste time on the usual ritual insults, but pointed out that we were trapped and that our wisest course was to surrender. "You will give up your weapons," he said. "I shall take hostages, and you will all live."

One of Odda's priests translated the demands to the ealdorman. I watched Ubba. He looked older than I remembered, with gray hairs among the black tangle of his beard, but he was still a frightening man: huge chested, confident, and harsh.

Ealdorman Odda was plainly frightened.

Ubba, after all, was a renowned Danish chieftain, a man who had ranged across long seas to give great slaughter, and now Odda was forced to confront him. He did his best to sound defiant, retorting that he would stay where he was and put his faith in the one true god.

"Then I shall kill you," Ubba answered.

"You may try," Odda said.

It was a feeble response and Ubba spat in scorn. He was about to turn away, but then I spoke and needed no interpreter. "Guthrum's fleet is gone," I said. "Njord reached from the deep, Ubba Lothbrokson, and he snatched Guthrum's fleet down to the seabed. All those brave men are gone to Ran and Ægir." Ran was Njord's wife and Ægir the giant who guarded the souls of drowned men. I brought out my hammer charm and held it up. "I speak the truth, Lord Ubba," I said. "I watched that fleet die and I saw its men go under the waves."

He stared at me with his flat, hard eyes and the violence in his heart was like the heat of a forge. I could feel it, but I could also sense his fear, not of us, but of the gods. He was a man who did nothing without a sign from the gods, and that was why I had talked of the gods when I spoke about the fleet's drowning. "I know you," he growled, pointing at me with two fingers to avert the evil of my words.

"And I know you, Ubba Lothbrokson," I said, and I let go of the charm and held up three fingers. "Ivar dead," I folded one finger down, "Halfdan dead," the second finger, "and only you are left. What did the runes say? That by the new moon there will be no Lothbrok brother left in Midgard?"

I had touched a nerve, as I intended to, for Ubba instinctively felt for his own hammer charm. Odda's priest was translating, his voice a low murmur, and the ealdorman was staring at me with wide astonished eyes.

"Is that why you want us to surrender?" I asked Ubba. "Because the runesticks tell you we cannot be killed in battle?"

"I shall kill you," Ubba said. "I shall cut you from your crotch to your gullet. I shall spill you like offal."

I made myself smile, though that was hard when Ubba was making threats. "You may try, Ubba Lothbrokson," I said, "but you will fail. And I know. I cast the runes, Ubba. I cast the runes under last night's moon, and I know."

He hated it, for he believed my lie. He wanted to be defiant, but for a moment he could only stare at me in fear because his own runesticks, I guessed, had told him what I was telling him, that any attack on Cynuit would end in failure. "You're Ragnar's boy," he said, placing me at last.

"And Ragnar the Fearless speaks to me," I said. "He calls from the corpse hall. He wants vengeance, Ubba, vengeance on the Danes, for Ragnar was killed treacherously by his own folk. I'm his messenger now, a thing from the corpse hall, and I have come for you."

"I didn't kill him!" Ubba snarled.

"Why should Ragnar care?" I asked. "He just wants vengeance and to him one Danish life is as good as another, so cast your runes again and then offer us your sword. You are doomed, Ubba."

"And you're a piece of weasel shit," he said and said no more, but just turned and hurried away.

Ealdorman Odda was still staring at me. "You know him?" he asked.

"I've known Ubba since I was ten years old," I said, watching the Danish chieftain walk away. I was thinking that if I had a choice, that if I could follow my warrior's heart, I would rather fight alongside Ubba than against him, but the spinners had decreed otherwise. "Since I was ten," I went on, "and the one thing I know about Ubba is that he fears the gods. He's terrified now. You can attack him and his heart will let him down because he thinks he will lose."

"Alfred will come," Odda said.

"Alfred watches Guthrum," I said. I was not certain of that, of course. For all I knew Alfred could be watching us now from the hills, but I doubted he would leave Guthrum free to plunder Wessex. "He watches Guthrum," I said, "because Guthrum's army is twice as large as Ubba's. Even with his fleet half drowned Guthrum has more men, and why would Alfred let them loose from Exanceaster? Alfred won't come," I finished, "and we shall all die of thirst before Ubba attacks us."

"We have water," his son said sulkily, "and ale." He had been watching me resentfully, awed that I had spoken so familiarly with Ubba.

"You have ale and water for a day," I said scornfully and saw from the ealdorman's expression that I was right.

Odda turned and stared south down the Pedredan's valley. He was hoping to see Alfred's troops, yearning for a glimpse of sunlight on spear heads, but of course there was nothing there except the trees stirring in the wind.

Odda the Younger sensed his father's uncertainty. "We can wait for two days," he urged.

"Death will be no better after two days," Odda said heavily. I admired him then. He had been hoping not to fight, hoping that his king would rescue him, but in his heart he knew I was right and knew that these Danes were his responsibility and that the men of Defnascir held England in their hands and must preserve it. "Dawn," he said, not looking at me. "We shall attack at dawn."

We slept in war gear. Or rather men tried to sleep when they were wearing leather or mail, with sword belts buckled, helmets, and weapons close, and we lit no fires for Odda did not want the enemy to see that we were readied for battle, but the enemy had fires, and our sentries could watch down the slopes and use the enemy's light to look for infiltrators. None came. There was a waning moon sliding in and out of ragged clouds. The Danish fires ringed us, heaviest to the south by Cantucton where Guthrum camped. More fires burned to the east, beside the Danish ships, the flames reflecting off the gilded beast heads and painted dragon prows. Between us and the river was a meadow at the far side of which the Danes watched the hill, and beyond them was a wide stretch of marsh and at the marsh's far side was a strip of firmer land beside the river where some hovels offered the Danish ship-guards shelter. The hovels had belonged to fishermen, long fled, and fires were lit between them. A handful of Danes paced the bank beside those fires, walking beneath the carved prows, and I stood on the ramparts and gazed at those long, graceful ships and prayed that **Wind-Viper** still lived.

I could not sleep. I was thinking of shields and Danes and swords and fear. I was thinking of my child that I had never seen and of Ragnar the Fearless, wondering if he watched me from Valhalla. I was worrying that I would fail the next day when, at last, I came to the life gate of a shield wall, and I was not the only one denied sleep for, at the heart of the night, a man climbed the grassy rampart to stand beside me and I saw it was Ealdorman Odda. "How do you know Ubba?" he asked.

"I was captured by the Danes," I said, "and

was raised by them. The Danes taught me to fight." I touched one of my arm rings. "Ubba gave me this one."

"You fought for him?" Odda asked, not accusingly, but with curiosity.

"I fought to survive," I said evasively.

He looked back to the moon-touched river. "When it comes to a fight," he said, "the Danes are no fools. They will be expecting an attack at dawn." I said nothing, wondering whether Odda's fears were changing his mind. "And they outnumber us," he went on.

I still said nothing. Fear works on a man, and there is no fear like the prospect of confronting a shield wall. I was filled with fear that night, for I had never fought man to man in the clash of armies. I had been at Æsc's Hill, and at the other battles of that far-off summer, but I had not fought in the shield wall. Tomorrow, I thought, tomorrow, and like Odda I wanted to see Alfred's army rescue us, but I knew there would be no rescue. "They outnumber us," Odda said again, "and some of my men have nothing but reaping hooks as weapons."

"A reaping hook can kill," I said, though it was a stupid thing to say. I would not want to face a

Dane if I carried nothing but a reaping hook. "How many have proper weapons?" I asked.

"Half?" he guessed.

"Then those men are our front ranks," I said, "and the rest pick up weapons from the enemy dead." I had no idea what I was speaking of, but only knew I must sound confident. Fear might work on a man, but confidence fights against fear.

Odda paused again, gazing at the dark ships below. "Your wife and son are well," he said after a while.

"Good."

"My son merely rescued her."

"And prayed I was dead," I said.

He shrugged. "Mildrith lived with us after her father's death and my son became fond of her. He meant no harm and he gave none." He held a hand out to me and I saw, in the small moonlight, that he offered me a leather purse. "The rest of the bride-price," he said.

"Keep it, lord," I said, "and give it to me after the battle, and if I die, give it to Mildrith."

An owl went overhead, pale and fast, and I wondered what augury that was. Far off to the east, up the coast, far beyond the Pedredan, a tiny fire flickered and that, too, was an augury, but I could not read it.

"My men are good men," Odda said, "but if they are outflanked?" Fear was still haunting him. "It would be better," he went on, "if Ubba were to attack us."

"It would be better," I agreed, "but Ubba will do nothing unless the runesticks tell him to do it."

Fate is all. Ubba knew that, which is why he read the signs from the gods, and I knew the owl had been a sign, and it had flown over our heads, across the Danish ships, and gone toward that distant fire burning along the Sæfern's shore, and I suddenly remembered King Edmund's four boats coming to the East Anglian beach and the fire arrows thumping into the beached Danish ships and I realized I could read the auguries after all. "If your men are outflanked," I said, "they will die. But if the Danes are outflanked, they will die. So we must outflank them."

"How?" Odda asked bitterly. All he could see was slaughter in the dawn—an attack, a fight, and a defeat—but I had seen the owl. The owl had flown from the ships to the fire, and that was the sign. Burn the ships. "How do we outflank them?" Odda asked.

And still I remained silent, wondering if I

should tell him. If I followed the augury it would mean splitting our forces, and that was the mistake the Danes had made at Æsc's Hill, and so I hesitated, but Odda had not come to me because he suddenly liked me, but because I had been defiant with Ubba. I alone on Cynuit was confident of victory, or seemed to be, and that, despite my age, made me the leader on this hill. Ealdorman Odda, old enough to be my father, wanted my support. He wanted me to tell him what to do, me who had never been in a great shield wall, but I was young and I was arrogant and the auguries had told me what must be done, and so I told Odda.

"Have you ever seen the sceadugengan?" I asked him.

His response was to make the sign of the cross.

"When I was a child," I said, "I dreamed of the sceadugengan. I went out at night to find them and I learned the ways of the night so I could join them."

"What has that to do with the dawn?" he asked.

"Give me fifty men," I said, "and they will join my men and at dawn they will attack there." I pointed toward the ships. "We'll start by burning their ships."

Odda looked down the hill at the nearer fires, which marked where the enemy sentries were posted in the meadow to our east. "They'll know you're coming," he said, "and be ready for you." He meant that a hundred men could not cross Cynuit's skyline, go downhill, break through the sentries, and cross the marsh in silence. He was right. Before we had gone ten paces the sentries would have seen us and the alarm would be sounded and Ubba's army, which was surely as ready for battle as our own, would stream from its southern encampment to confront my men in the meadow before they reached the marsh.

"But when the Danes see their ships burning," I said, "they will go to the river's bank, not to the meadow. And the riverbank is hemmed by marsh. They can't outflank us there." They could, of course, but the marsh would give them uncertain footing so it would not be so dangerous as being outflanked in the meadow.

"But you will never reach the riverbank," he said, disappointed in my idea.

"A shadow-walker can reach it," I said.

He looked at me and said nothing.

"I can reach it," I said, "and when the first ship burns every Dane will run to the bank, and that's when the hundred men make their charge. The Danes will be running to save their ships, and that will give the hundred men time to cross the marsh. They go as fast as they can, they join me, we burn more ships, and the Danes will be trying to kill us." I pointed to the riverbank, showing where the Danes would go from their camp along the strip of firm ground to where the ships were beached. "And when the Danes are all on that bank," I went on, "between the river and the marsh, you lead the fyrd to take them in the rear."

He brooded, watching the ships. If we attacked at all then the obvious place was down the southern slope, straight into the heart of Ubba's forces, and that would be a battle of shield wall against shield wall, our nine hundred men against his twelve hundred, and at the beginning we would have the advantage for many of Ubba's men were posted around the hill and it would take time for those men to hurry back and join the Danish ranks, and in that time we would drive deep into their camp, but their numbers would grow and we might well be stopped, outflanked, and then would come the hard slaughter. And in that hard slaughter they would have the advantage of numbers and they would wrap around our ranks and our rearmost men, those with sickles instead of weapons, would begin to die.

But if I went down the hill and began to burn the boats, then the Danes would race down the riverbank to stop me, and that would put them on the narrow strip of riverside land, and if the hundred men under Leofric joined me, then we might hold them long enough for Odda to reach their rear and then it would be the Danes who would die, trapped between Odda, my men, the marsh, and the river. They would be trapped like the Northumbrian army had been trapped at Eoferwic.

But at Æsc's Hill disaster had come to the side that first split its forces.

"It could work," Odda said tentatively.

"Give me fifty men," I urged him, "young ones."

"Young?"

"They have to run down the hill," I said. "They have to go fast. They have to reach the ships before the Danes, and they must do it in the dawn." I spoke with a confidence I did not feel and I paused for his agreement, but he said nothing. "Win this, lord," I said, and I did not call him "lord" because he outranked me, but because he was older than me, "then you will have saved Wessex. Alfred will reward you."

He thought for a while and maybe it was the thought of a reward that persuaded him, for he nodded. "I will give you fifty men," he said.

Ravn had given me much advice and all of it was good, but now, in the night wind, I remembered just one thing he had said to me on the night we first met, something I had never forgotten.

Never, he had said, never fight Ubba.

The fifty men were led by the shire reeve, Edor, a man who looked as hard as Leofric and, like Leofric, had fought in the big shield walls. He carried a cutoff boar spear as his favorite weapon, though a sword was strapped to his side. The spear, he said, had the weight and strength to punch through mail and could even break through a shield.

Edor, like Leofric, had simply accepted my idea. It never occurred to me that they might not accept it, yet looking back I am astonished that the battle of Cynuit was fought according to the idea of a twenty-year-old who had never stood in a slaughter wall. Yet I was tall, I was a lord, I had grown up among warriors, and I had the arrogant confidence of a man born to battle. I am Uhtred, son of Uhtred, son of another Uhtred, and we had not held Bebbanburg and its lands by whimpering at altars. We are warriors.

Edor's men and mine assembled behind Cynuit's eastern rampart where they would wait until the first ship burned in the dawn. Leofric was on the right with the **Heahengel**'s crew, and I wanted him there because that was where the blow would fall when Ubba led his men to attack us at the river's edge. Edor and the men of Defnascir were on the left and their chief job, apart from killing whomever they first met on the riverbank, was to snatch up flaming timbers from the Danish fires and hurl them into more ships. "We're not trying to burn all the ships," I said. "Just get four or five ablaze. That'll bring the Danes like a swarm of bees."

"Stinging bees," a voice said from the dark.

"You're frightened?" I asked scornfully. "They're frightened! Their auguries are bad, they think they're going to lose, and the last thing they want is to face men of Defnascir in a gray dawn. We'll make them scream like women, we'll kill them, and we'll send them to their Danish hell." That was the extent of my battle speech. I should have talked more, but I was nervous because I had to go down the hill first, first and alone. I had to live my childhood dream of shadow-walking, and Leofric and Edor would not lead the hundred men down to the river until they saw the Danes go to rescue their ships, and if I could not touch fire to the ships then there would be no attack and Odda's fears would come back and the Danes would win and Wessex would die and there would be no more England. "So rest now," I finished lamely. "It will be three or four hours till dawn."

I went back to the rampart and Father Willibald joined me there, holding out his crucifix that had been carved from an ox's thigh bone. "You want God's blessing?" he asked me.

"What I want, father," I said, "is your cloak." He had a fine woolen cloak, hooded and dyed a dark brown. He gave it to me and I tied the cords around my neck, hiding the sheen of my mail coat. "And in the dawn, father," I said, "I want you to stay up here. The riverbank will be no place for priests."

"If men die there," he said, "then it is my place."

"You want to go to heaven in the morning?"

"No."

"Then stay here." I spoke more savagely than

I intended, but that was nervousness, and then it was time to go for, though the night was still dark and the dawn a long way off, I needed time to slink through the Danish lines. Leofric saw me off, walking with me to the northern flank of Cynuit, which was in moon-cast shadow. It was also the least guarded side of the hill, for the northern slope led to nothing except marshes and the Sæfern sea. I gave Leofric my shield. "I don't need it," I said. "It will just make me clumsy."

He touched my arm. "You're a cocky bastard, earsling, aren't you?"

"Is that a fault?"

"No, lord," he said, and that last word was high praise. "God go with you," he added, "whichever god it is."

I touched Thor's hammer, then tucked it under my mail. "Bring the men fast when you see the Danes go to the ships," I said.

"We'll come fast," he promised me, "if the marsh lets us."

I had seen Danes cross the marsh in the daylight and had noted that it was soft ground, but not rank bogland. "You can cross it fast," I said, then pulled the cloak's hood over my helmet. "Time to go," I said.

Leofric said nothing and I dropped down from

the rampart into the shallow ditch. So now I would become what I had always wanted to be, a shadow-walker. Childhood's dream had become life and death, and touching Serpent-Breath's hilt for luck, I crossed the ditch's lip. I went at a crouch, and halfway down the hill I dropped to my belly and slithered like a serpent, black against the grass, inching my way toward a space between two dying fires.

The Danes were sleeping, or close to sleep. I could see them sitting by the dying fires, and once I was out of the hill's shadow there was enough moonlight to reveal me and there was no cover for the meadow had been cropped by sheep, but I moved like a ghost, a belly-crawling ghost, inching my way, making no noise, a shadow on the grass, and all they had to do was look, or walk between the fires, but they heard nothing, suspected nothing, and so saw nothing. It took an age, but I slipped through them, never going closer to an enemy than twenty paces, and once past them I was in the marsh and there the tussocks offered shadow and I could move faster, wriggling through slime and shallow water, and the only scare came when I startled a bird from its nest and it leapt into the air with a cry of alarm and a swift whirr of wings. I sensed the

Danes staring toward the marsh, but I was motionless, black, and unmoving in the broken shadow, and after a while there was only silence. I waited, water seeping through my mail, and I prayed to Hoder, blind son of Odin and god of the night. Look after me, I prayed, and I wished I had made a sacrifice to Hoder, but I had not, and I thought that Ealdwulf would be looking down at me and I vowed to make him proud. I was doing what he had always wanted me to do, carrying Serpent-Breath against the Danes.

I worked my way eastward, behind the sentries, going to where the ships were beached. No gray showed in the eastern sky. I still went slowly, staying on my belly, going slowly enough for the fears to work on me. I was aware of a muscle quivering in my right thigh, of a thirst that could not be quenched, of a sourness in the bowels. I kept touching Serpent-Breath's hilt, remembering the charms that Ealdwulf and Brida had worked on the blade. Never, Ravn had said, never fight Ubba.

The east was still dark. I crept on, close to the sea now so I could gaze up the wide Sæfern and see nothing except the shimmer of the sinking moon on the rippled water that looked like a sheet of hammered silver. The tide was flooding, the muddy shore narrowing as the sea rose. There would be salmon in the Pedredan, I thought, salmon swimming with the tide, going back to the sea, and I touched the sword hilt for I was close to the strip of firm land where the hovels stood and the ship guards waited. My thigh shivered. I felt sick.

But blind Hoder was watching over me. The ship guards were no more alert than their comrades at the hill's foot, and why should they be? They were farther from Odda's forces, and they expected no trouble; indeed they were there only because the Danes never left their ships unguarded, and these ship guards had mostly gone into the fishermen's hovels to sleep, leaving just a handful of men sitting by the small fires. Those men were motionless, probably half asleep, though one was pacing up and down beneath the high prows of the beached ships.

I stood.

I had shadow-walked, but now I was on Danish ground, behind their sentries, and I undid the cloak's cords, took it off, and wiped the mud from my mail, and then walked openly toward the ships, my boots squelching in the last yards of marshland, and then I just stood by the northernmost boat, threw my helmet down in the shadow of the ship, and waited for the one Dane who was on his feet to discover me.

And what would he see? A man in mail, a lord, a shipmaster, a Dane, and I leaned on the ship's prow and stared up at the stars. My heart thumped, my thigh quivered, and I thought that if I died this morning at least I would be with Ragnar again. I would be with him in Valhalla's hall of the dead, except some men believed that those who did not die in battle went instead to Niflheim, that dreadful cold hell of the Norsemen where the corpse goddess Hel stalks through the mists and the serpent Corpse-Ripper slithers across the frost to gnaw the dead, but surely, I thought, a man who died in a hall-burning would go to Valhalla, not to gray Niflheim. Surely Ragnar was with Odin, and then I heard the Dane's footsteps and I glanced at him with a smile. "A chilly morning," I said.

"It is." He was an older man with a grizzled beard and he was plainly puzzled by my sudden appearance, but he was not suspicious.

"All quiet," I said, jerking my head to the north to suggest I had been visiting the sentries on the Sæfern's side of the hill.

"They're frightened of us," he said.

"So they should be." I faked a huge yawn, then

pushed myself away from the ship and walked a couple of paces north as though I was stretching tired limbs, then pretended to notice my helmet at the water's edge. "What's that?"

He took the bait, going into the ship's shadow to bend over the helmet, and I drew my knife, stepped close to him, and drove the blade up into his throat. I did not slit his throat, but stabbed it, plunging the blade straight in and twisting it and at the same time I pushed him forward, driving his face into the water and I held him there so that if he did not bleed to death he would drown, and it took a long time, longer than I expected, but men are hard to kill. He struggled for a time and I thought the noise he made might bring the men from the nearest fire, but that fire was forty or fifty paces down the beach and the small waves of the river were loud enough to cover the Dane's death throes, and so I killed him and no one knew of it, none but the gods saw it, and when his soul was gone I pulled the knife from his throat, retrieved my helmet, and went back to the ship's prow.

And waited there until dawn lightened the eastern horizon. Waited till there was a rim of gray at the edge of England.

And it was time.

★   ★   ★

I strolled toward the nearest fire. Two men sat there. "Kill one," I sang softly, "and two then three, kill four and five, and then some more." It was a Danish rowing chant, one that I had heard so often on the **Wind-Viper.** "You'll be relieved soon," I greeted them cheerfully.

They just stared at me. They did not know who I was, but just like the man I had killed, they were not suspicious even though I spoke their tongue with an English twist. There were plenty of English in the Danish armies.

"A quiet night," I said, and leaned down and took the unburned end of a piece of flaming wood from the fire. "Egil left a knife on his ship," I explained, and Egil was a common enough name among the Danes to arouse no suspicion, and they just watched as I walked north, presuming I needed the flame to light my way onto the ships. I passed the hovels, nodded to three men resting beside another fire, and kept walking until I had reached the center of the line of beached ships. There, whistling softly as though I did not have a care in the world, I climbed the short ladder left leaning on the ship's prow and jumped down into the hull and made my way between the rowers' benches. I had half expected to find men asleep in the ships, but the boat was deserted except for the scrabble of rats' feet in the bilge.

I crouched in the ship's belly where I thrust the burning wood beneath the stacked oars, but I doubted it would be sufficient to set those oars aflame and so I used my knife to shave kindling off a rower's bench. When I had enough scraps of wood, I piled them over the flame and saw the fire spring up. I cut more, then hacked at the oar shafts to give the flames purchase, and no one shouted at me from the bank. Anyone watching must have thought I merely searched the bilge and the flames were still not high enough to cause alarm, but they were spreading and I knew I had very little time and so I sheathed the knife and slid over the boat's side. I lowered myself into the Pedredan, careless what the water would do to my mail and weapons, and once in the river I waded northward from ship's stern to ship's stern, until at last I had cleared the last boat and had come to where the gray-bearded corpse was thumping softly in the river's small waves, and there I waited.

And waited. The fire, I thought, must have gone out. I was cold.

And still I waited. The gray on the world's rim

lightened, and then, suddenly, there was an angry shout and I moved out of the shadow and saw the Danes running toward the flames that were bright and high on the ship I had fired, and so I went to their abandoned fire and took another burning brand and hurled that into a second ship, and the Danes were scrambling onto the burning boat that was sixty paces away and none saw me. Then a horn sounded, sounded again and again, sounding the alarm, and I knew Ubba's men would be coming from their camp at Cantucton, and I carried a last piece of fiery wood to the ships, burning my hand as I thrust it under a pile of oars. Then I waded back into the river to hide beneath the shadowed belly of a boat.

The horn still sounded. Men were scrambling from the fishermen's hovels, going to save their fleet, and more men were running from their camp to the south, and so Ubba's Danes fell into our trap. They saw their ships burning and went to save them. They streamed from the camp in disorder, many without weapons, intent only on quenching the flames that flickered up the rigging and threw lurid shadows on the bank. I was hidden, but knew Leofric would be coming, and now it was all timing. Timing and the blessing of the spinners, the blessing of the gods, and the Danes were using their shields to scoop water into the first burning ship, but then another shout sounded and I knew they had seen Leofric, and he had surely burst past the first line of sentries, slaughtering them as he went, and was now in the marsh. I waded out of the shadow, out from beneath the ship's overhanging hull, and saw Leofric's men coming, saw thirty or forty Danes running north to meet his charge, but then those Danes saw the new fires in the northernmost ships and they were assailed by panic because there was fire behind them and warriors in front of them, and most of the other Danes were still a hundred paces away and I knew that so far the gods were fighting for us.

I waded from the water. Leofric's men were coming from the marsh and the first swords and spears clashed, but Leofric had the advantage of numbers and **Heahengel**'s crew overran the handful of Danes, chopping them with ax and sword, and one crewman turned fast, panic in his face when he saw me coming, and I shouted my name, stooped to pick up a Danish shield, and Edor's men were behind us and I called to them to feed the ship fires while the men of **Heahengel** formed a shield wall across the strip of firm land. Then we walked forward. Walked toward Ubba's army that was only just realizing that they were being attacked.

We marched forward. A woman scrambled from a hovel, screamed when she saw us, and fled up the bank toward the Danes where a man was roaring at men to form a shield wall. "Edor!" I shouted, knowing we would need his men now, and he brought them to thicken our line so that we made a solid shield wall across the strip of firm land, and we were a hundred strong and in front of us was the whole Danish army, though it was an army in panicked disorder, and I glanced up at Cynuit and saw no sign of Odda's men. They would come, I thought, they would surely come, and then Leofric bellowed that we were to touch shields, and the limewood rattled on limewood and I sheathed Serpent-Breath and drew Wasp-Sting.

Shield wall. It is an awful place, my father had said, and he had fought in seven shield walls and was killed in the last one. Never fight Ubba, Ravn had said.

Behind us the northernmost ships burned and in front of us a rush of maddened Danes came for revenge and that was their undoing, for they did not form a proper shield wall, but came at us like mad dogs, intent only on killing us, sure they could beat us for they were Danes and we were West Saxons, and we braced and I watched a scar-faced man, spittle flying from his mouth as he screamed, charge at me and it was then that the battle calm came. Suddenly there was no more sourness in my bowels, no dry mouth, no shaking muscles, but only the magical battle calm. I was happy.

I was tired, too. I had not slept. I was soaking wet. I was cold, yet suddenly I felt invincible. It is a wondrous thing, that battle calm. The nerves go, the fear wings off into the void, and all is clear as precious crystal and the enemy has no chance because he is so slow, and I swept the shield left, taking the scar-faced man's spear thrust, lunged Wasp-Sting forward, and the Dane ran onto her point. I felt the impact run up my arm as her tip punctured his belly muscles, and I was already twisting her, ripping her up and free, sawing through leather, skin, muscle, and guts, and his blood was warm on my cold hand, and he screamed, ale breath in my face, and I punched him down with the shield's heavy boss, stamped on his groin, killed him with Wasp-Sting's tip in his throat, and a second man was on my right, beating at my neighbor's shield with an ax, and he was easy to kill, point into the throat, and then we were going forward. A woman, hair unbound, came at me with a spear and I kicked her brutally hard, then smashed her face with the shield's iron rim so that she fell screaming into a dying fire and her unbound hair flared up bright as burning kindling, and **Heahengel**'s crew was with me, and Leofric was bellowing at them to kill and to kill fast. This was our chance to slaughter Danes who had made a foolish attack on us, who had not formed a proper shield wall, and it was ax work and sword work, butchers' work with good iron, and already there were thirty or more Danish dead and seven ships were burning, their flames spreading with astonishing speed.

"Shield wall!" I heard the cry from the Danes. The world was light now, the sun just beneath the horizon. The northernmost ships had become a furnace. A dragon's head reared in the smoke, its gold eyes bright. Gulls screamed above the beach. A dog chased along the ships, yelping. A mast fell, spewing sparks high into the silver air, and then I saw the Danes make their shield wall, saw them organize themselves for our deaths, and saw the raven banner, the triangle of cloth that proclaimed that Ubba was here and coming to give us slaughter.

"Shield wall!" I shouted, and that was the first time I ever gave that order. "Shield wall!" We had grown ragged, but now it was time to be tight. To be shield to shield. There were hundreds of Danes in front of us and they came to overwhelm us, and I banged Wasp-Sting against the metal rim of my shield. "They're coming to die!" I shouted. "They're coming to bleed! They're coming to our blades!"

My men cheered. We had started a hundred strong but had lost half a dozen men in the early fighting. The remaining men cheered even though five or six times their number came to kill them, and Leofric began the battle chant of Hegga, an English rower's chant, rhythmic and harsh, telling of a battle fought by our ancestors against the men who had held Britain before we came, and now we fought for our land again, and behind me a lone voice uttered a prayer and I turned to see Father Willibald holding a spear. I laughed at his disobedience.

Laughter in battle. That was what Ragnar had taught me, to take joy from the fight. Joy in the morning, for the sun was touching the east now, filling the sky with light, driving darkness beyond the world's western rim, and I hammered Wasp-Sting against my shield, making a noise to drown the shouts of the Danes, and I knew we would be hard hit and that we must hold until Odda came, but I was relying on Leofric to be the bastion on our right flank where the Danes were sure to try to lap around us by going through the marsh. Our left was safe, for that was by the ships, and the right was where we would be broken if we could not hold.

"Shields!" I bellowed, and we touched shields again for the Danes were coming and I knew they would not hesitate in their attack. We were too few to frighten them, they would not need to work up courage for this battle, they would just come.

And come they did. A thick line of men, shield to shield, new morning light touching ax heads and spear heads and swords.

The spears and throwing axes came first, but in the front rank we crouched behind shields and the second rank held their shields above ours and the missiles thumped home, banging hard, but doing no injury, and then I heard the wild war shout of the Danes, felt a last flutter of fear, and then they were there.

The thunder of shield hitting shield, my shield knocked back against my chest, shouts of rage, a spear between my ankles, Wasp-Sting lunging forward and blocked by a shield, a scream to my left, an ax flailing overhead. I ducked, lunged again, hit shield again, pushed back with my own shield, twisted the saxe free, stamped on the spear, stabbed Wasp-Sting over my shield into a bearded face and he twisted away, blood filling his mouth from his torn cheek. I took a half pace forward, stabbed again, and a sword glanced off my helmet and thumped my shoulder. A man pulled me hard backward because I was ahead of our line and the Danes were shouting, pushing, stabbing, and the first shield wall to break would be the shield wall to die. I knew Leofric was hard-pressed on the right, but I had no time to look or help because the man with the torn cheek was thrashing at my shield with a short ax, trying to splinter it. I lowered the shield suddenly, spoiling his stroke, and slashed Wasp-Sting at his face a second time. She grated on skull bone, drew blood, and I hammered his shield with my own. He staggered back, but was pushed forward by the men behind him. This time Wasp-Sting took his throat and he was bubbling blood and air from a slit gullet. He fell to his knees, and the man behind him slammed a spear forward that broke through my shield, but stuck there, and the Danes were still heaving, but their own dying man obstructed them and the spearman tripped on him. The man to my right chopped his shield edge onto his head and I kicked him in the face, then slashed Wasp-Sting down. A Dane pulled the spear from my shield, stabbed with it, and was cut down by the man on my left. More Danes came and we were stepping back, bending back, because there were Danes in the marshland who were turning our right flank, but Leofric brought the men steadily around till our backs were to the burning ships. I could feel the heat of their burning and I thought we must die here. We would die with swords in our hands and flames at our backs and I hacked frantically at a red-bearded Dane, trying to shatter his shield. Ida, the man to my right, was on the ground, guts spilling through torn leather, and a Dane came at me from that side and I flicked Wasp-Sting at his face, ducked, took his ax blow on my breaking shield, shouted at the men behind to fill the gap, and stabbed Wasp-Sting at the axman's feet, slicing into an ankle. A spear took him in the side of the head and I gave a great shout and heaved at the oncoming Danes, but there was no space to fight, no space to see, just a grunting mass of men hacking and stabbing and dying and bleeding, and then Odda came.

The ealdorman had waited till the Danes were crowded on the riverbank, waited till they were pushing one another in their eagerness to reach and to kill us, and then he launched his men across Cynuit's brow and they came like thunder with swords and axes and sickles and spears. The Danes saw them and there were shouts of warning and almost immediately I felt the pressure lessen to my front as the rearward Danes turned to meet the new threat. I rammed Wasp-Sting out to pierce a man's shoulder, and she went deep in, grating against bone, but the man twisted away, snatching the blade out of my hand, so I drew Serpent-Breath and shouted at my men to kill the bastards. This was our day, I shouted, and Odin was giving us victory.

Forward now. Forward to battle slaughter. Beware the man who loves battle. Ravn had told me that only one man in three or perhaps one man in four is a real warrior and the rest are reluctant fighters, but I was to learn that only one man in twenty is a lover of battle. Such men were the most dangerous, the most skillful, the ones who reaped the souls, and the ones to fear. I was such a one, and that day, beside the river where the blood flowed into the rising tide, and beside the burning boats, I let Serpent-Breath sing her song of death. I remember little except a rage, an exultation, a massacre. This was the moment the skalds celebrate, the heart of the battle that leads to victory, and the courage had gone from those Danes in a heartbeat. They had thought they were winning, thought they had trapped us by the burning ships, and thought to send our miserable souls to the afterworld, and instead the fyrd of Defnascir came on them like a storm.

"Forward!" I shouted.

"Wessex!" Leofric bellowed. "Wessex!" He was hacking with his ax, chopping men to the ground, leading the **Heahengel**'s crew away from the fiery ships.

The Danes were going backward, trying to escape us, and we could choose our victims; Serpent-Breath was lethal that day. Hammer a shield forward, strike a man off balance, thrust the blade forward, push him down, stab into the throat, find the next man. I pushed a Dane into the smoldering remnants of a campfire, killed him while he screamed, and some Danes were now fleeing to their unburned ships, pushing them into the flooding tide, but Ubba was still fighting. Ubba was shouting at his men to form a new shield wall, to protect the boats, and such was Ubba's hard will, such his searing anger, that the new shield wall held. We hit it hard, hammered it with sword and ax and spear, but again there was no space, just the heaving, grunting, breath-stinking struggle, only this time it was the Danes who stepped back, pace by pace, as Odda's men joined mine to wrap around the Danes and hammer them with iron.

But Ubba was holding. Holding his rearguard firm, holding them under the raven banner. In every moment that he held us off another ship was pushed away from the river's bank. All he wanted to achieve now was to save men and ships, to let a part of his army escape, to let them get away from this press of shield and blade. Six Danish ships were already rowing out to the Sæfern sea, and more were filling with men. I screamed at my troops to break through, to kill them, but there was no space to kill, only blood-slicked ground and blades stabbing under shields, and men heaving at the opposing wall, and the wounded crawling away from the back of our line.

And then, with a roar of fury, Ubba hacked into our line with his great war ax. I remembered how he had done that in the fight beside the Gewæsc, how he had seemed to disappear into the ranks of the enemy only to kill them, and his huge blade was whirling again, making space, and our line went back and the Danes followed Ubba who seemed determined to win this battle on his own and to make a name that would never be forgotten among the annals of the Northmen. The battle madness was on him, the runesticks were forgotten, and Ubba Lothbrokson was making his legend. Another man went down, crushed by the ax, and Ubba bellowed defiance, the Danes stepped forward behind him, and now Ubba threatened to pierce our line clean through. I shoved backward, going through my men, and went to where Ubba fought. There I shouted his name, called him the son of a goat, a turd of men, and he turned, eyes wild, and saw me.

"You bastard whelp," he snarled, and the men in front of me ducked aside as he came forward, mail coat drenched in blood, a part of his shield missing, his helmet dented and his ax blade red.

"Yesterday," I said, "I saw a raven fall."

"You bastard liar," he said, and the ax came around and I caught it on the shield and it was like being struck by a charging bull. He wrenched the ax free and a great sliver of wood was torn away to let the new daylight through the broken shield.

"A raven," I said, "fell from a clear sky."

"You whore's pup," he said and the ax came again, and again the shield took it and I staggered back, the rent in the shield widening.

"It called your name as it fell," I said.

"English filth," he shouted and swung a third time, but this time I stepped back and flicked Serpent-Breath out in an attempt to cut off his ax hand, but he was fast, snake fast, and he pulled back just in time.

"Ravn told me I would kill you," I said. "He foretold it. In a dream by Odin's pit, among the blood, he saw the raven banner fall."

"Liar!" he screamed and came at me, trying to throw me down with weight and brute force. I met him, shield boss to shield boss, and I held him, swinging Serpent-Breath at his head. But the blow glanced off his helmet and I leaped back a heartbeat before the ax swung where my legs had been, lunged forward, and took him clean on the chest with Serpent-Breath's point. But I did not have any force in the blow and his mail took the lunge and stopped it, and he swung the ax up, trying to gut me from crotch to chest, but my ragged shield stopped his blow, and we both stepped back.

"Three brothers," I said, "and you alone of

them live. Give my regards to Ivar and to Half-dan. Say that Uhtred Ragnarson sent you to join them."

"Bastard," he said, and he stepped forward, swinging the ax in a massive sideways blow that was intended to crush my chest, but the battle calm had come on me, and the fear had flown and the joy was there and I rammed the shield sideways to take his ax strike, felt the heavy blade plunge into what was left of the wood, and I let go of the shield's handle so that the half-broken tangle of metal and wood dangled from his blade, and then I struck at him. Once, twice, both of them huge blows using both hands on Serpent-Breath's hilt and using all the strength I had taken from the long days at **Heahengel**'s oar. I drove him back, cracked his shield, and he lifted his ax, my shield still cumbering it, and then slipped. He had stepped on the spilled guts of a corpse, and his left foot slid sideways. While he was unbalanced, I stabbed Serpent-Breath forward and the blade pierced the mail above the hollow of his elbow and his ax arm dropped, all strength stolen from it. Serpent-Breath flicked back to slash across his mouth, and I was shouting. There was blood in his beard and he knew then, knew he would die, knew he would see his brothers in the corpse hall. He did not give up. He saw death coming and fought it by trying to hammer me with his shield again, but I was too quick, too exultant, and the next stroke was in his neck and he staggered, blood pouring onto his shoulder, more blood trickling between the links of his chain mail, and he looked at me as he tried to stay upright.

"Wait for me in Valhalla, lord," I said.

He dropped to his knees, still staring at me. He tried to speak, but nothing came and I gave him the killing stroke.

"Now finish them!" Ealdorman Odda shouted, and the men who had been watching the duel screamed in triumph and rushed at the enemy and there was panic now as the Danes tried to reach their boats. Some were throwing down weapons and the cleverest were lying flat, pretending to be dead, and men with sickles were killing men with swords. The women from Cynuit's summit were in the Danish camp now, killing and plundering.

I knelt by Ubba and closed his nerveless right fist about the handle of his war ax. "Go to Valhalla, lord," I said. He was not dead yet, but he was dying for my last stroke had pierced deep into his neck, and then he gave a great shudder and there was a croaking noise in his throat and I kept on holding his hand tight to the ax as he died.

A dozen more boats escaped, all crowded with Danes, but the rest of Ubba's fleet was ours, and while a handful of the enemy fled into the woods where they were hunted down, the remaining Danes were either dead or prisoners, and the Raven banner fell into Odda's hands, and we had the victory that day, and Willibald, spear point reddened, was dancing with delight.

We took horses, gold, silver, prisoners, women, ships, weapons, and mail. I had fought in the shield wall.

Ealdorman Odda had been wounded, struck on the head by an ax that had pierced his helmet and driven into his skull. He lived, but his eyes were white, his skin pale, his breath shallow, and his head matted with blood. Priests prayed over him in one of the small village houses and I saw him there, but he could not see me, could not speak, perhaps could not hear, but I shoved two of the priests aside, knelt by his bed, and thanked him for taking the fight to the Danes. His son, unwounded, his armor apparently unscratched in the battle, watched me from the darkness of the room's far corner.

I straightened from his father's low bed. My back ached and my arms were burning with weariness. "I am going to Cridianton," I told young Odda.

He shrugged as if he did not care where I went. I ducked under the low door where Leofric waited for me. "Don't go to Cridianton," he told me.

"My wife is there," I said. "My child is there."

"Alfred is at Exanceaster," he said.

"So?"

"So the man who takes news of this battle to Exanceaster gets the credit for it," he said.

"Then you go," I said.

The Danish prisoners wanted to bury Ubba, but Odda the Younger had ordered the body to be dismembered and its pieces given to the beasts and birds. That had not been done yet, though the great battle-ax that I had put in Ubba's dying hand was gone, and I regretted that, for I had wanted it, but I wanted Ubba treated decently as well and so I let the prisoners dig their grave. Odda the Younger did not confront me, but let the Danes bury their leader and make a mound over his corpse and thus send Ubba to his brothers in the corpse hall.

And when it was done I rode south with a

score of my men, all of us mounted on horses we had taken from the Danes.

I went to my family.

These days, so long after that battle at Cynuit, I employ a harpist. He is an old Welshman, blind, but very skillful, and he often sings tales of his ancestors. He likes to sing of Arthur and Guinevere, of how Arthur slaughtered the English, but he takes care not to let me hear those songs, instead praising me and my battles with outrageous flattery by singing the words of my poets who describe me as Uhtred Strong-Sword or Uhtred Death-Giver or Uhtred the Beneficent. I sometimes see the old blind man smiling to himself as his hands pluck the strings and I have more sympathy with his skepticism than I do with the poets who are a pack of sniveling sycophants.

But in the year 877 I employed no poets and had no harpist. I was a young man who had come dazed and dazzled from the shield wall, and who stank of blood as I rode south. Yet, for some reason, as we threaded the hills and woods of Defnascir, I thought of a harp.

Every lord has a harp in the hall. As a child, before I went to Ragnar, I would sometimes sit by the harp in Bebbanburg's hall and I was in-

trigued by how the strings would play themselves. Pluck one string and the others would
shiver to give off a tiny music. "Wasting your
time, boy?" my father had snarled as I crouched
by the harp one day, and I suppose I had been
wasting it, but on that spring day in 877 I remembered my childhood's harp and how its
strings would quiver if just one was touched. It
was not music, of course, just noise, and scarcely
audible noise at that, but after the battle in Pedredan's valley it seemed to me that my life was
made of strings and if I touched one then the
others, though separate, would make their sound.
I thought of Ragnar the Younger and wondered if
he lived, and whether his father's killer, Kjartan,
still lived, and how he would die if he did, and
thinking of Ragnar made me remember Brida,
and her memory slid on to an image of Mildrith,
and that brought to mind Alfred and his bitter
wife, Ælswith, and all those separate people were
a part of my life, strings strung on the frame of
Uhtred, and though they were separate they affected one another and together they would
make the music of my life.

Daft thoughts, I told myself. Life is just life.
We live, we die, we go to the corpse hall. There is
no music, just chance. Fate is relentless.

"What are you thinking?" Leofric asked me. We were riding through a valley that was pink with flowers.

"I thought you were going to Exanceaster," I said.

"I am, but I'm going to Cridianton first, then taking you on to Exanceaster. So what are you thinking? You look gloomy as a priest."

"I'm thinking about a harp."

"A harp!" He laughed. "Your head's full of rubbish."

"Touch a harp," I said, "and it just makes noise, but play it and it makes music."

"Sweet Christ!" He looked at me with a worried expression. "You're as bad as Alfred. You think too much."

He was right. Alfred was obsessed by order, obsessed by the task of marshaling life's chaos into something that could be controlled. He would do it by the church and by the law, which are much the same thing, but I wanted to see a pattern in the strands of life. In the end I found one, and it had nothing to do with any god, but with people. With the people we love. My harpist is right to smile when he chants that I am Uhtred the Gift-Giver or Uhtred the Avenger or Uhtred the Widow-Maker, for he is old and he has learned what I have learned, that I am really Uhtred the Lonely. We are all lonely and all seek a hand to hold in the darkness. It is not the harp, but the hand that plays it.

"It will give you a headache," Leofric said, "thinking too much."

"Earsling," I said to him.

Mildrith was well. She was safe. She had not been raped. She wept when she saw me, and I took her in my arms and wondered that I was so fond of her, and she said she had thought I was dead and told me she had prayed to her god to spare me, and she took me to the room where our son was in his swaddling clothes and, for the first time, I looked at Uhtred, son of Uhtred, and I prayed that one day he would be the lawful and sole owner of lands that are carefully marked by stones and by dykes, by oaks and by ash, by marsh and by sea. I am still the owner of those lands that were purchased with our family's blood, and I will take those lands back from the man who stole them from me and I will give them to my sons. For I am Uhtred, Earl Uhtred, Uhtred of Bebbanburg, and destiny is everything.

HISTORICAL NOTE

Alfred, famously, is the only monarch in English history to be accorded the honor of being called "the Great," and this novel, with the ones that follow, will try to show why he gained that title. I do not want to anticipate those other novels, but broadly, Alfred was responsible for saving Wessex and, ultimately, English society from the Danish assaults, and his son Edward, daughter Æthelflæd, and grandson Æthelstan finished what he began to create, which was, for the first time, a political entity they called Englaland. I intend Uhtred to be involved in the whole story.

But the tale begins with Alfred, who was, indeed, a very pious man and frequently sick. A recent theory suggests that he suffered from Crohn's disease, which causes acute abdominal pains, and from chronic piles, details we can glean from a book written by a man who knew him very well, Bishop Asser, who came into Alfred's life after the events described in this novel. Currently there is a debate whether Bishop Asser did write that life, or whether it was forged a hundred years after Alfred's death, and I am utterly unqualified to judge the arguments of the contending academics, but even if it is a forgery, it contains much that has the smack of truth, suggesting that whoever wrote it knew a great deal about Alfred. The author, to be sure, wanted to present Alfred in a glowing light, as warrior, scholar, and Christian, but he does not shy away from his hero's youthful sins. Alfred, he tells us, "was unable to abstain from carnal desire" until God generously made him sick enough to resist temptation. Whether Alfred did have an illegitimate son, Osferth, is debatable, but it seems very possible.

The biggest challenge Alfred faced was an invasion of England by the Danes. Some readers may be disappointed that those Danes are called Northmen or pagans in the novel, but are rarely described as Vikings. In this I follow the early English writers who suffered from the Danes, and who rarely used the word **Viking,** which, anyway, describes an activity rather than a people or a tribe. To go viking meant to go raiding, and the Danes who fought against England in the ninth century, though undoubtedly raiders, were preeminently invaders and occupiers. Much fanciful imagery has been attached to them, chief of which are the horned helmet, the berserker, and the ghastly execution called the spread-eagle, by which a victim's ribs were splayed apart to expose the lungs and heart. That seems to have been a later invention, as does the existence of the berserker, the crazed naked warrior who attacked in a mad frenzy. Doubtless there were insanely frenzied warriors, but there is no evidence that lunatic nudists made regular appearances on the battlefield. The same is true of the horned helmet for which there is not a scrap of contemporary evidence. Viking warriors were much too sensible to place a pair of protuberances on their helmets so ideally positioned as to enable an enemy to knock the helmet off. It is a pity to abandon the iconic horned helmets, but alas, they did not exist.

The assault on the church by the Danes is well recorded. The invaders were not Christians and saw no reason to spare churches, monasteries, and nunneries from their attacks, especially as those places often contained considerable treasures. Whether the concerted attack on the northern monastic houses happened is debatable. The source is extremely late, a thirteenth-century chronicle written by Roger of Wendover, but what is certain is that many bishoprics and monasteries did disappear during the Danish assault, and that assault was not a great raid, but a deliberate attempt to eradicate English society and replace it with a Danish state.

Ivar the Boneless, Ubba, Halfdan, Guthrum, the various kings, Alfred's nephew Æthelwold, Ealdorman Odda, and the ealdormen whose names begin with Æ (a vanished letter, called the ash) all existed. Alfred should properly be spelled Ælfred, but I preferred the usage by which he is known today. It is not certain how King Edmund of East Anglia died, though he was certainly killed by the Danes and in one ancient version the future saint was indeed riddled with arrows like Saint Sebastian. Ragnar and Uhtred are fictional, though a family with Uhtred's name did hold Bebbanburg (now Bamburgh Castle) later in the Anglo-Saxon period, and as that family are my ancestors, I decided to give them that magical place a little earlier than the records suggest. Most of the major events happened; the assault on York, the siege of Nottingham, the attacks on the four kingdoms, all are recorded in the Anglo-Saxon Chronicle or in Asser's life of King Alfred, which together are the major sources for the period.

I used both those sources and also consulted a host of secondary works. Alfred's life is remarkably well documented for the period, some of that documentation written by Alfred himself, but even so, as Professor James Campbell wrote in an essay on the king, "Arrows of insight have to be winged by the feathers of speculation." I have feathered lavishly, as historical novelists must, yet as much of the novel as possible is based on real events. Guthrum's occupation of Wareham, the exchange of hostages and his breaking of the truce, his murder of the hostages and occupation of Exeter all happened, as did the loss of most of his fleet in a great storm off Durlston Head near Swanage. The one large change I have made was to bring Ubba's death forward by a year, so that, in the next book, Uhtred can be elsewhere, and, persuaded by the arguments in John Peddie's book, **Alfred, Warrior King,** I placed that action at Cannington in Somerset rather than at the more traditional site of Countisbury Head in north Devon.

Alfred was the king who preserved the idea of

England, which his son, daughter, and grandson made explicit. At a time of great danger, when the English kingdoms were perilously near to extinction, he provided a bulwark that allowed the Anglo-Saxon culture to survive. His achievements were greater than that, but his story is far from over, so Uhtred will campaign again.